CLEO F

To My Sister
With Love,
Cleo
9-27-11

THE GOOD FOREIGNER

Outskirts Press, Inc.
Denver, Colorado

This is a work of fiction. The events and characters described herein are imaginary and are not intended to refer to specific places or living persons. The opinions expressed in this manuscript are solely the opinions of the author and do not represent the opinions or thoughts of the publisher. The author has represented and warranted full ownership and/or legal right to publish all the materials in this book.

The Good Foreigner

v2.0

Outskirts Press, Inc.
http://www.outskirtspress.com

ISBN: 978-1-4327-6868-3

PRINTED IN THE UNITED STATES OF AMERICA

History Notes, historical and personal

1947, two years after World War II had ended, China was recovering from years of domination by foreign powers. Struggling to find itself, China became embroiled in a Civil War. For years corruption had kept the rich rich, the poor poor. Mao Tse-Tung and his Communists offered change. Chiang Kai-shek had offered more of what has been. The communist message – equality for all – sounded wonderful. By 1949 the Communists had driven Chiang and his followers to Taiwan and taken over the mainland, renaming the country The People's Republic of China. Mao's style of communism appeared to work, but not for long. Soon no commerce and very little communication existed between East and West. The communist state closed its doors to all but communist countries. Famine followed. Political horrors were perpetrated on the people. They endured the illogic of the Cultural Revolution.

With its vast population, a China willing to trade with the West could prove advantageous for all. Henry Kissinger, Assistant to the President for National Security Affairs, used diplomatic maneuvering to contact the Communist leaders in China. As a consequence, President Nixon, Henry Kissinger, First Lady, Pat Nixon, the Secretary of State and other leaders as well as newsmen, staff and others parted the Bamboo

Curtain and opened China to the world in 1972.

Trade between countries started; China's middle class grew. The PRC's brightest students came to America to study; people from the West visited China in ever increasing numbers. Western ways fascinated Chinese students. In 1989 they called for democratic reform and made their headquarters in Beijing's Tiananmen Square. Eventually they were joined by countless other Chinese. Cracking down, the government attacked, killing many, imprisoning others. Although the Bamboo Curtain stayed open and trade continued, the democracy movement was squelched.

Today most Chinese have embraced the modern world. They want the technology that makes life easier for them. The new rich buy luxuries hitherto unheard of in China. Shanghai is a grand metropolis. But change is still curtailed. Freedom of speech and press don't exist. A misplaced phrase, a wrong word can brand the perpetrator an enemy of the state. In 2010, behind bars, Liu Xiaobo could not receive his Nobel Peace Prize in person, and his wife was prohibited from attending the ceremonies in Oslo, Norway.

In my novel, *The Good Foreinger*, because of its drama, and because I was most familiar with the period preceding and during the time of the Tiananmen Square Massacre, I wrote about the historical period from 1947 to 1989.

My husband, Hank, and I spent a month in China on our own in 1986. Before we went, Hank studied Mandarin, and we both contacted people in the People's Republic and were issued invitations to speak. My lecture, in English, took place at Guangxi Province Teachers' University; Hank spoke at the Institute for Nuclear Medicine in Tianjin. Subsequently, we were entertained in private homes as well as in public places. After we returned to the United States, we hosted Chinese graduate students who came to study at the University of Washington.

In addition, before writing *The Good Foeigner*, I read many books about the history of China, including both Henry Kissinger's and President Nixon's accounts of the historic 1972 meeting, Fox Butterfield's *China, Alive in the Bitter Sea*, Liang Heng & Judith Shapiro's *Son of the Revolution*, Barbara Tuchman's *Notes From China*, and many other books that showed the period covered in my novel. The early meeting between Mao, Zhou, Nixon, and Kissinger I presented very much as the two preeminent Americans reported it in their books. I didn't change their words.

As always in a historic novel, while the history has to be as true as the author can make it, the story is paramount. Wu Gang-jo, Wu Huixia, and Lin Sulin are fictional characters as are Logan Wainwright, Christine Wainwright, Jason, and Matt as well as other minor characters. Names of famous newsmen and political figures are mentioned at times because they were in China during President Nixon's historical trip, but primarily the fictional characters carry the story forward against the very real and dramatic historical happenings.

My thanks go as always to my wonderful husband who shared our Chinese adventure. He was also with me in Egypt before I wrote my novel, *Cleopatra, Immortal Queen*. He took me to Virginia City, Nevada, where my novel *Fitzhugh's Woman* became a reality. He has been unfailing in his support, always applauding my various writing projects.

Also, this is for Jen, my favorite Chinese graduate student.

I hope his life has gone well. He deserves success and happiness. I will always remember him with fondness.

And a big thanks to Gerard Wong who made sure the Chinese language I used was accurate. Gerard spent the first seventeen years of his life in China before becoming an American and earning a PhD in chemistry.

–Cleo Fellers Kocol

Chapter 1

Logan

The People's Republic of China – 1971

In November when cold winds swept down from Beijing's north, Logan appeared at Qinghua University as instructed. A strong chlorine smell assailed him as he entered the pool area and looked around for Mao Tse-Tung. Mist from the hot water almost obscured the Chairman. No one shared the only heated pool in the city, although people leaned against the far walls, and Logan supposed others lingered in the entryway behind him. *Mao's men.*

Steam rising around him, Mao stroked awkwardly, a whale—bleached white—floundering in shallow water, Logan thought, moving slowly toward him, stopping a discreet distance away. Stomach churning, he waited for a sign from the Chairman.

China's number one man swam slowly to the end of the pool, took hold of the side, looked up and said, "Ah, my friend, come, come, don't be timid. The water is good exercise, ridding the body of humors, waking the lazy liver, reviving the sluggish digestive processes. My doctors, who recommend rest, would make an invalid of me. So I swim."

Logan dropped his towel on the pool's edge, stood in his borrowed 1930's wool swimsuit, looking robust and overwhelmingly Caucasian in contrast to Mao, his middle- aged years seeming young in comparison.

While Mao shifted from one side to the other in a vague set of exercises, Logan lowered himself into the pool. The hot water sent great clouds of steam into the frigid air. "I am honored to be here," he said, liking the feel of the water on his tired body, the many years he'd been isolated from the West roiling his mind.

"I prefer a river where one can feel the current, ride with it or fight against it," Mao replied, turning to face Logan. "You are a swimmer?"

"I swam in shallow lakes when I was a child. The ocean was too cold."

"Ah, yes, the Northwest of the United States of America. I remember when you first came to us you had an American name."

"That is true."

"I never learned English. It is such a barbaric language." Mao stretched out on his left side and began to swim in a lazy sidestroke. "Come with me. I don't like to shout, and I haven't completed my laps yet. Your good wife is well?"

"She's fine, thank you." Logan stretched out on his right side and swam facing the Chairman, keeping pace with him.

"If I said I have forgotten your American name, what would you say?"

"I would say it was Logan Wainwright, and the Chairman never forgets anything."

"It is one thing to forget purposefully, and another not to be able to assimilate facts and details and remember them with clarity later. I see no need for remembering your American name." Mao flipped over on his back and floated, only his face, belly, and toes showing above the water. "But you remembered." He flipped over to his belly with a great deal of grunting, and using the breaststroke, reached the side of the pool. Resting his arms on the lip, he looked toward Logan who swam to him. "Do you remember also how to speak the language of the foreign devils?"

Logan wondered what trap he had already fallen into and pushed down the need to defend Americans, defend himself. "I remember." He, too, held on to the side.

"Do you know the language of the rich and powerful as well as the language of the people?" Mao let his legs drift up and at the surface kicked them one at a time.

"It is the same."

Mao shook his head. "That I don't believe. Do you mean a leader talks the same as a street sweeper?" He brought his legs down until his toes rested against the side.

Logan took the same stance. "I would venture to say the president knows more words than a street-sweeper."

"Of course. It is what I said, a different language for workers and leaders. Nixon's polite phrases mask his true meanings. Americans are duplicitous. We must be alert. I understand you can get to the core meaning of English words, that you can translate whole sentences immediately into Chinese. Do you know the subtleties necessary in translation?"

To answer in the affirmative would show a lack of the humbleness thought necessary, but to say he was incapable would also not be acceptable. "I do my modest best." Logan lowered his eyes.

Mao pushed off and began to stroke slowly to the end of the pool where Logan had entered. "Do you also remember American manners, witticisms, jokes, sayings?"

"Yes," Logan said, catching up with the Chairman and answering without pause, adding when Mao's eyebrows went up, "I am probably out of date with some things, but basic manners remain the same."

"You are fast, Logan Wainwright," Mao said when he reached the end of the pool. "But no one in the People's Republic is a better English speaker. The American leader, Richard Nixon, is coming to China. You will be needed." Turning, he added, "You may go. I need to swim alone so I can concentrate on the exercise only and not have to deal with Western thought."

As Logan climbed out of the pool, he heard a tremendous splashing and saw the Chairman slapping the water in a crude approximation of an Australian crawl.

At home, within walls that had once seemed a refuge, Logan found himself longing to share his grand moment. But experience had taught him to weigh each word, each movement. Glad he had said nothing to his family, he watched as Wu Huixia, and his son, Gang-jo, arrived in Huixia's large, black, chauffeur-driven car. The day had been warm, but Logan suppressed a shiver as he watched the car come to a stop in the driveway and Gang-jo jumped out and helped his father alight. The boy, who had learned English from Logan, had studied with him for years, was now a man with an imposing presence. He went to the door and waited.

Both father and son glanced at the house, removed from its neighbors by high walls and intricate planting, trees gracefully pruned. Logan tried not to put thoughts into their minds, but the good and the bad kept coming together in a rush of memories he couldn't escape. Greeting both men politely, he motioned them in, offered the best Blackwood chairs, poured fragrant tea and waited until they had exchanged the proper chit-chat before he said, "To what can I attribute this visit by Wu Huixia and his son?"

Huixia said, "I have spoken with Chairman Mao."

Logan felt a fluttering inside his chest.

Wu Huixia smiled. "He said you have a grasp of the language and American culture that is deep and apparent. That is indeed good. He was impressed by your memory of things American." He set his teacup down, replaced the lid.

Logan tried not to betray his excitement. *To hear, to see Americans again.* Keeping his reactions neutral, his voice calm, he said, "To work with the President of the United States and the Chairman of the People's Republic would be an honor."

Wu Huixia frowned. "The Chairman maintains some skepticism however. He says your memory of things American is too good. And just now I noticed you spoke of the President first, the Chairman last. It is a small thing, but telling. I will say nothing about this slip, but it only carries out what the Chairman, in his ultimate wisdom, noticed. That is why he wants you to teach Gang-jo nuances of English speech and manners so that he can interpret for Mao when the time comes." Wu Huixia walked toward the door and put his hand on the knob. "I leave with the knowledge that my son will study with the best." It was a sop to the past and the days when they had walked in step.

As the outside door closed, with words locked in his throat, Logan paused before turning to Gang-jo, the purr of Huixia's limousine slowly dying. Where his father had recently gone fleshy, Gang-jo's body had the look of an athlete, and he wore a tunic of lighter color than the traditional dark blue most people wore, his western shoes bearing a high shine. All marked him as far from average. "So," Logan said, drawing out the word. He wanted to shout his distrust, the past rising like worms crawling from a sewer. Instead, he raised his brow and said in English, "Did you ask for this position?"

Gang-jo shook his head. "I knew nothing about it until my father told me minutes before we came here." He leaned forward, his face open, his eyes unwavering. "I am older now and see with different eyes. I come with respect and an eagerness to learn."

Logan nodded, disappointment lessening as the thought rushed at him: as Gang-

jo's teacher he might see the Americans, speak to them, and ask questions that had festered unspoken for almost twenty-five years. While the glow of diplomacy reigned, much might be possible. He turned to Gang-jo. "Let's talk about idiomatic expressions first. The slang I grew up with may be out of date, but neither the President nor the Secretary of State is young. They could well use the words I remember. Shall we begin?" Once more the flutter in his chest started as thoughts of the daughter he had left behind bombarded him with images he'd managed for so long to forget.

Chapter 2

Christine

The People's Republic of China
February 21 through Feb. 28,1972

For years Christine Wainwright, living in Washington D.C., growing up in Seattle, had invested everything Chinese with the romance of her own yearnings, and her longing for her father. When he disappeared into China, it became in her mind a land of silken and brocade fabrics, a land of promise. She'd memorized the one letter he'd written directly to her. "My Dearest Daughter, You are a young lady now, and one I most fervently hope to see soon. It bothers me that I couldn't be with you as you were growing up to become the beautiful young woman I'm sure you are. Remember always, no matter what happens, that I love you, will always love you."

Now she was on the way to China, having ingested facts, read biographies and studied photographs until the names of the modern rulers—Mao Tse-Tung, Zhou En-lai, Deng Xiaoping and Wu Huixia—were as familiar as details about the last Empress, history she'd studied growing up. With the Red takeover, the Bamboo Curtain had slammed shut, but with President Nixon she was opening up the Communist State to the world! She admitted to herself that might be a bit dramatic, the truth being diplomatic maneuvering, by National Security Advisor Henry Kissinger, had borne fruit.

As the Presidential plane reached altitude and leveled out,

she loosened her seat belt and opened the State Department briefing materials. Filling in as a translator when Dr. Taylor, her teacher and mentor, had become ill, she'd barely had time to be cleared for takeoff. At twenty-eight and unmarried, she had no one to tell her concerns to. Now, she kept reminding herself she spoke Chinese as well as the State Department interpreters and was every bit as knowledgeable about Chinese history. She smiled, making her blue eyes sparkle, her cheeks glow. But despite her excitement, she had to fight apprehension. She'd never served as an interpreter before. Knowing the language was not the same. Even her knowledge was bound to be outdated. For years she'd thought China resembled the Egypt of the pharaohs, unchanging in its basic tenets, a Confucian society now in Communist dress, a country where her father had disappeared. But was that the reality?

Shifting in her seat, she skimmed the briefing pages again. Couched in official language, China and its people sounded remote. Was her father still there? She'd always assumed he was, but was that wishful thinking?

She'd barely brought her thoughts to the present when President Nixon, head jutting forward characteristically, came through the plane, greeting people, making jokes. She leaned forward, head cocked listening. Several seats away, he stopped to chat, and not wanting to appear to eavesdrop, although she tried her best to hear, she busied herself with her journal. She'd met the First Lady, had talked to Julie, but she'd never officially met the President. She scribbled in her notebook: *dark suit, blue tie, wing-tip shoes. Line between eyes offset by smile.* His familiar voice interrupted her.

"Understand you know Chinese."

Startled, she started to rise and half-in and half-out of her seat dislodged a waterfall of paper. Flushing, she grabbed at it, said, "Yes, Mr. President, I speak Mandarin Chinese."

Smiling and rubbing at the scratchy-looking stubble on his jaw, he said, "Oh, no, no, sit still. Too crowded in here for formality." He retrieved a paper from the aisle. "They say Chinese is a hard language for the Western tongue."

She felt foolish and awed and yet comfortable, for he seemed to understand her embarrassment, patting her hand briefly and smiling as she sank back into her seat, he looming above her. "I've studied the language for a long time, sir." She pondered speaking to him in Chinese, but decided that would only earn her scorn from the State Department interpreters.

"The problem is all those sounds. One word meaning many different things, depending on the tone."

"Yes, sir."

He spoke earnestly. "Dr. Taylor swears by you. And over in Justice, they say you'll do us proud, no smirch on your record. And State swears by you."

"I'll certainly do my best, sir." She smiled.

"You realize if I need you, I want you to follow the example of the Chinese interpreters. Work like they do. I understand they're cracker-jacks. Word for word. Think you can do that?"

How do you tell a president that word for word is impossible? You don't. "Yes, sir. I'm sure I can."

"Good girl. You must give Dr. Taylor my regards, and tell him to lay off those coffin nails. Pulmonary trouble, wasn't it?"

She nodded.

Frowning, going from somber to cheerful, he said, "It's a great time to be living. We're making history, and you, young lady, are part of it. You understand that?"

"Oh, yes, Mr. President." But he had already moved on, stopping here and there for personal comments, laughing and joking as he went through the plane. Christine reclined her chair. The clouds had shifted, allowing a quick glimpse of gray ocean far below. She closed her eyes and drifted to sleep.

Hours later, writing in her journal, stopovers in Hawaii and Guam behind her, the ocean appearing beneath the plane again, she underlined the words, "I can't believe I'm almost there." Throughout the flight, she'd scribbled brief notes to amplify later and slipped easily into and out of sleep. This time a floating sensation hit her stomach, and sleep would come no more. Sitting on the edge of her seat, her forehead pressed against the glass, she waited for her first glimpse of the Chinese mainland. Far ahead the ocean changed color, became lighter and then darkened as silt-laden rivers cut channels to the sea, a strip of earth appearing and stretching as far as she could see. China! Any fears she'd harbored slid away like her fatigue.

Soon the Spirit of '76 was landing in Shanghai. At the field, Chinese Foreign Ministry officials and a Chinese navigator emerged from a line of soldiers and boarded the plane to accompany the U.S. delegation on to Beijing.

In the air again, hushed expectation followed. The China Christine had read about as a child, the China of sedan chairs undoubtedly gone, she girded herself for its Communist face. Was it a clone of the USSR? Would she, perhaps, achieve the impossible, see her father? Some Americans had become friends of the Chinese during the days when Japan had swaggered through China with guns and imperialistic design while Chiang Kai-shek fought the Communists. Hadn't Americans traveled to the Soviet Union during the shakedown before Russia evolved into its present state, achieving a cult following in the United States? The possibilities for her father were vast, not all good.

As thoughts spun top-like through her mind, talk and laughter ceased, and utter quiet descended on the plane. The silence, broken now and then by whispers and exclamations, increased as a great sweep of land showed below. Like silk unwinding from a huge bolt, the land stretched out, shimmering, dull, full of shadows and bright, hard sun, a landscape undulating into the future. Chinese words and phrases hummed in her head, music unlike any other became odes to the many years she'd studied, first with the Changs in Seattle, then at Washington State and Harvard, and finally with Dr. Taylor. Completely awake, even though she'd slept little, she kept her gaze below.

The land, showing agrarian images of a past she'd seen only in history books, composed a vast brown canvas punctuated by clusters of buildings with tiled roofs and walled courtyards. As the plane descended, she identified people, water buffalo, donkeys, and mules. The people stared at the foreign plane overhead, its shadow marching along the land like a giant bird announcing the American presence.

Closer to the Capital, the cold look of winter prevailed Seeing the harsh, treeless, windswept plains, Christine shivered. Joking and laughter had ceased completely, followed by whispered exclamations and comments floating unanswered. She estimated an hour-and-a-half had passed since they'd left

Shanghai before she glimpsed the Oriental rooftops, the walls and the busyness of the buildings of the Imperial City.

She felt as if she'd been struck in the stomach. It was one thing to dream of meeting her father, another to be an interpreter for the President of the most powerful country in the world. Although the State Department's interpreters would preside at official meetings, she had to be ready at a moment's notice if the President or Secretary of State called upon her for an unscheduled meeting. What if the Chinese spoke rapid-fire or with regional accents? State Department staff had told her to expect late hours, strong drink. She'd have to interpret conversations complicated by subtle nuances. She'd have to use words that wouldn't offend. Despite her knowledge, possibilities for failure raced like wild speculation through her mind. She barely managed not to glance at herself in her pocket mirror, knowing she'd see the same confident-appearing, good-looking face. Still, she put a hand to her dark hair, checking to see that it was properly in place.

As the plane taxied to a stop, she stared out the window, hardly hearing the buzz of conversation around her. It was eleven-thirty in the morning. The first time she'd changed her watch's setting, she'd been over California. Now, it was seven-thirty Sunday night in Seattle, and hopefully Aunt Betty would see the arrival on television. Probably the whole world would be watching.

She leaned closer to the window. An honor guard of Chinese revolutionary soldiers stood at attention on the gray asphalt runway. Hatless, standing alone in front of them, she spotted Zhou En-lai, the Chinese Premier, a thin aging man weighed down by a heavy overcoat but still appearing elegant.

Around the landing strip, the red and yellow flag of Chinese Communism flapped in the wind.

She pressed her forehead to the window as the President and the First Lady de-planed, the First Lady's vivid red coat and her half smile glittering in the cold, bright sun.

Zhou En-lai clapped his hands as the President started down the stairs and President Nixon returned the applause before holding out his hand in friendship. Witnessing the momentous event, Christine sighed. China had opened its doors to America and the United States had replied in kind.

As opening statements drifted like smoke into the cold air, and national anthems swelled, she watched, mesmerized. A stiff wind whipped the men's pants and picked at Mrs. Nixon's coat while Christine wiped away a tear. A new world was unfolding, and she was part of it. Gathering impressions, she jotted notes: Nixon and Zhou showed dignified statesmanlike appearances. The other Chinese were wooden, unsmiling, and the Americans smiled too much. *No one knows how to act*, she scrawled in her notebook. She didn't either.

Soon, she, too, was deplaning. The frigid cold blowing words of welcome past her ears, Christine squeezed into a Russian-built automobile with other staffers. Her eyes felt raw, her mind spun; she needed sleep badly. Leading the official party, the Nixons rode with Zhou, and behind them a string of cars zoomed into the city. Whizzing along, she peered ahead, a tingling awareness of the moment zipping through her.

They were making history, making pageantry unseen by the Chinese people, the streets deserted, cross streets closed to traffic. Behind barricades she glimpsed several bicycles and occasional drab-looking military vehicles, but few people.

The gray buildings appeared colder than she felt, her coat, perfect for the American Capital, too light for Beijing. She'd visualized colorful people going about their business, waving greetings, perhaps cheering as President Nixon's car passed. She hadn't anticipated the silence or the cold. Rivers and moats were frozen, the wind frigid, and snow dusted the city like the yellow dust she had read would cling to everything later in the spring.

Briefly, she glimpsed the huge buildings of Tiananmen Square, the aristocratic rooflines of dynastic structures, the tiles, the carvings, and then she was in the Spartan but comfortable room assigned to her.

Overwhelmed by fatigue, she slipped out of her shoes, unfastened her long hair, pinned up in an effort to appear older, and tried to nap. But behind her eyelids scenes from the trip played non-stop. She recalled the White House guard, heard Henry Kissinger's voice growling good-naturedly to his staff, saw Rita de Santis, Mrs. Nixon's hairdresser, checking her supplies. Sleep continuing to elude her, she got up, unpacked toilet articles, hung her clothes in the closet, and studied Mrs. Nixon's agenda, having previously memorized the President's schedule. No meetings had been scheduled for him with Mao Tse-Tung, but several with Zhou En-lai were interspersed with banquets and sightseeing trips for the First Lady. She lay down again. Deliberately conjuring the hum of the plane, she slept.

A persistent knocking woke her. Breathlessly, a messenger informed her that the President wanted her immediately. Richard Nixon and Mao Tse-Tung would meet informally. There would be other interpreters, but she should be on hand as well.

She splashed water on her face, twisted her long hair into a bun and stuck pins in it. There was no time to fix it properly, no time to change her clothes, no time to be afraid. Despite its wrinkles, the pin-striped slack suit she'd worn to Beijing would have to do. Pushing her feet into shoes, she grabbed her briefcase and ran downstairs.

As the President's Chief of Staff briefed her, she was vaguely aware of Americans and Chinese milling around the lobby, of cars lining up in front of the hotel. The Chinese interpreters would translate both Chinese and English, but she should be on hand in case the President wished her to translate, too. She should stand where he could see her, follow the conversation and later write a transcript of what she heard for his private file. If a problem developed, a semantic impasse arose, a difficulty involving American slang or colloquial speech came up, he or someone would signal to her. She should go forward immediately.

She nodded, murmured, "yes," nodded again. Kissinger and Nixon were leaving in limousines with red flags fluttering. She was seated in another, swept into Tiananmen Square and through the Gate of New China, past two sentries and up to Mao's house.

It seemed like a dream.

Following President Nixon, her pulse thumping wildly, Christine entered Mao's study. Overflowing with books and papers, it looked lived in, used daily, slightly rumpled like the man himself, nothing as grand as Dr. Taylor's Georgetown residence. The overstuffed chairs set in a semi-circle looked well used, maybe rump-sprung.

The President and Henry Kissinger were approaching the

Chairman. His flesh settling into its softness like a dumpling, Mao sat in a large upholstered armchair, a woman Christine supposed was a nurse at his side. Books were open on tables; papers were piled near the Chinese leader who looked to Christine like a tired, old panda bear.

She stood against the wall across from the circle of chairs. Although spare, the room was unmistakably oriental with ubiquitous pots of tea, cups with lids, and a flurry of people moving around, placing tables closer to the chairs, backing away to come back and move something else.

As Nixon and Kissinger drew closer, Mao motioned to the young woman near him. She rushed forward, her soft cloth shoes making a swishing sound. Leaning on her arm, Mao rose.

As the two leaders shook hands, Christine smiled, seeing history shaped and molded, set in a pattern the world would follow. Awed, she took a deep breath as the leader of the People's Republic of China took the hand of the President of the United States in both of his.

For a brief time, silence prevailed, broken only by the clearing of throats, the sound of nervous coughs. Christine wet her lips.

Near her someone whispered in Chinese, "Now the foreigners come to him."

And then voices in Chinese and English intruded in a sudden, brisk fashion. Several Chinese lugging photographic equipment burst into the room, pushing by Christine who flattened herself against the wall. As they rushed by, laughter trapped beneath protocol bubbled forth.

"They get pictures for Chinese paper," a little man said

proudly to Christine in English, waving the photographers this way and that. "I will write story."

"You are a reporter?"

"I am official writer." The man bobbed his head, his smile growing until his eyes were lost in his cheekbones.

Christine found her lips moving. "I have heard of an American who possibly works for a Chinese paper. His name is Logan Wainwright. Do you know such a man?"

He shook his head. "My knowledge is very small." He jerked his head, and the cameramen moved their equipment.

Caught up in the bustle as the leaders and photographic crew discussed poses, Christine lost her place and found herself next to a tall, young Chinese man who looked at her with unabashed curiosity. His eyes glinted with excitement and amusement barely concealed as he said in unaccented English, "You are an American interpreter?"

She nodded. A few feet away the President and the Chairman posed. People jockeyed for position. The Chinese man next to her, taller and considerably younger than the other Chinese, didn't move.

"I did not expect a woman." His dark-eyed gaze skipped over her face rapidly. His face had a sculpted quality, fine-hewn with bold, hard lines softened by the light from his eyes, the mellow sound of his voice. "I am Wu Gang-jo, your Chinese counterpart. *Huanying*, welcome to the People's Republic." She was surprised to hear English spoken with an American accent, but everything had happened rapidly. She felt off base, half put together. "I didn't expect a man so young," she said truthfully. "I'm Christine Wainwright."

"My pleasure." He met her eyes directly.

Brown sable, she thought, moving slightly for a cameraman who was adjusting a light meter. "Where did you learn to speak English with an American accent? I expected a British accent, but you..." Her voice trailed off as the room became quieter and flash bulbs went off.

"We will talk later," Wu Gang-jo said.

The wind outside had blown wisps of her hair loose, and she pushed at the strands the pins didn't hold in place. She heard Gang-jo take a quick breath before he moved forward. Within seconds the official meeting began, and he was translating, swiftly and smoothly.

Richard Nixon sat in a chair next to Mao, and Christine observed them as a unit, the angular-faced President, the round-faced Chairman. The two men appeared excited but relaxed, as if they were alone and this was an ordinary meeting. Except for dark circles beneath the President's eyes, he looked rested. Henry Kissinger, looking like a German beer baron, and Zhou En-lai, looking like a well-dressed leader of a Chinatown tong, exchanged small talk through interpreters. Unlike Mao and the others who wore the ubiquitous blue Mao suit, Zhou's suit fit well and hung without a wrinkle. The photographers bustled around, shooting from all angles before moving back. Sips of tea taken, cigarettes lit, smoke wreathing the room, the meeting began.

Christine had expected solemn exchanges, for these weren't game players or minor functionaries. When these men spoke, worlds could tumble, lives could be lost. But jokes and laughter and teasing comments popped back and forth like ping-pong balls.With a gesture Mao indicated everyone taking part in the talk. "Our common old friend,

Generalissimo Chiang Kai-shek doesn't approve of this. He calls us Communist bandits." His smile softened the history behind the words and reminded Christine of the deep schism between the Chinese on the mainland and those on Taiwan.

The President flashed a smile. "Chiang Kai-shek calls the Chairman a bandit, what does the Chairman call Chiang Kai-shek?"

Christine suppressed the laugh she felt tickling her throat as Wu Gang-jo translated Nixon's question. The journalists who'd accompanied the presidential party would love to be in her place! She'd sworn to tell no one what she heard and write nothing except notes to be given to the President.

Mao chuckled, and everyone smiled.

Zhou En-lai said, "Generally speaking, we call the Taiwanese 'Chiang Kai-shek's clique.' In the newspapers, we call him a bandit; he calls us bandits. Anyway, we abuse each other."

Mao gestured toward Kissinger. "That one is clever. He kept his first trip to Beijing secret."

"He doesn't look like a secret agent," Nixon said. "He is the only man in captivity who could go to Paris twelve times and Beijing once and no one knew it...except possibly a couple of pretty girls."

"They didn't know it," Kissinger said, his voice rumbling throughout the room. "I used them as a cover."

"In Paris?" Mao's face registered mock disbelief. Zhou lifted an eyebrow.

For a second Wu Gang-jo's gaze met Christine's. His eyes crinkled, and she noted he was very handsome. It surprised her she'd not noticed before.

"Anyone who uses pretty girls as a cover must be the greatest diplomat of all time." The President crossed his legs, his ankles in dress socks visible beneath sharply pressed pants. He'd changed or someone had pressed the pants he'd worn on arrival, Christine decided.

"So you often make use of your girls?" Mao asked. He waved nicotine-stained fingers and closed his eyes for an instant as if to hide his thoughts.

Wondering if Mao was giving Kissinger a subtle dig, Christine crossed her arms in a protective gesture. After the Communist takeover, conditions for women were supposed to improve. No more female slavery, arranged marriage or prostitution. Women worked alongside men, and on paper had the same status. But had they? She glanced quickly at the President.

He looked relaxed. "His girls, not mine," he replied, gesturing toward Kissinger. "It would get me into great trouble if I used girls as a cover."

"Especially during an election," Zhou said, showing his knowledge of the American political system.

Mao joined in the general laughter and then cleared his throat, as if he would launch into something more important now that the photographers were leaving.

Zhou waved with a delicate but commanding gesture, and the military and civilian Chinese who stood near Christine went out into the hall, too.

For a second Wu Gang-jo's gaze met hers, his brows lifted slightly. As an interpreter, he was very smooth, his English and Chinese impeccable.

She shifted slightly as the President quoted from Chairman

Mao. "I know you are one who sees when an opportunity comes, and then knows that you must seize the hour and seize the day."

The words from Mao's little red book brought a smile to the Chairman's lips. Nodding his head, he pointed toward Kissinger, "Seize the hour, seize the day. Generally speaking, people like me sound like a lot of big cannons."

Zhou laughed. "Especially when we say, the whole world should unite and defeat imperialism, establish socialism. Very big cannons."

"Like me," Nixon said, looking from Zhou to Mao, the barest hint of a challenge behind his smile. "And bandits."

Smiling, but passing his hand over his forehead, Mao indicated Nixon and Kissinger, "You two would be spared. If all of you were overthrown, we wouldn't have any more friends left."

Friends, Christine thought as chuckles and smiles wove through the room and underlined the conversation, which continued in much the same vein. It was diplomacy, it was friendship, it was saber rattling. It was so impressive and astounding she'd hardly noticed the nose-tickling closeness of the room. Too soon, Zhou glanced at his watch and the meeting ended.

Disappointed, Christine noted in amazement that sixty-five minutes had flown by. She waited while Mao shuffled halfway to the door with Richard Nixon, the President looking vigorous, the Chairman old and very ill. "Your book, *Six Crises*, is not a bad book," the Chinese leader said.

Smiling, the President turned to Zhou, and shook his head. "He reads too much." He pointed at Mao.

Zhou returned Nixon's smile. "We all should."

Mao mumbled something about not feeling well lately. "Forgive me if I don't go farther."

Swept along with the crowd, Wu Gang-jo at her side, Christine followed the leaders out.

"So our work is over for the time being," he said.

"It went very fast." She glanced at him. "And I didn't have to do anything."

"No, but you were ready." He smiled. "I'm sure you are very proficient. I want to thank you for your compliment about my English. I speak in an acceptable fashion because I had an excellent teacher. He made me memorize rules of grammar as well as had me speak with an American accent." He directed her through the door ahead of him.

She sucked in the cold, clear air. "Your teacher did a good job. You must congratulate him for me." Waving to Gang-jo, she got in the car that was waiting for her. "Who was your teacher?" she asked as the door was being closed.

He smiled and leaned down to the window she opened. "A man who studied in your country."

She nodded. It had been crazy of her to think it might have been her father.

She settled back and began scribbling notes about the historic meeting. Back in her room she turned on the television. The Chinese news featured a new locomotive. No mention was made, no photographs shown of the Americans.

Arriving at the Great Hall of the People, Christine noticed the lights outlining the roof''s distinctly oriental pattern. Etched against a dark sky, the stone and marble building, erected in ten months, had her shaking her head in wonder. Nine hundred attendees were gathering for the welcoming banquet, although, according to the literature she had studied, the gigantic hall could seat three thousand for dinner at one time. The numbers were astounding. According to statistics, China had the largest population in the world. Awestruck, she followed the President and Mrs. Nixon, Henry Kissinger, and other American leaders, up the grand staircase.

Relieved to find Pat Nixon's conservative frock validating her own choice of a dress with long sleeves and slim, unpretentious lines, Christine relaxed. The only flashy element, in her hastily drawn together wardrobe, were long, dangling silver earrings. Yet, she felt glamorous, in tune with the exotic buildings she'd glimpsed.

At the head of the stairs, smiling Chinese leaders waited. Behind them wooden stands had been set up in rows for a group picture, and in less than five minutes people were arranged according to rank. Christine stood in back between an American man who quipped nervously about "breaking the lens" and a Chinese man who said "Hello" so that it sounded like "halo." But both remained silent as lights flashed and cameras clicked.

Picture taking over, the President, the Secretary of State, and other high-ranking Americans were escorted to their tables. Christine waited with the rest of the American party and their Chinese counterparts, everyone smiling at everyone else. The Chinese murmured greetings in English, the Americans answered with nods, sometimes a word of Chinese.

"So few of them learn our language," a Chinese man of

mature years murmured as the waiting group was led in.

Christine spotted the speaker, his unflinching stare familiar from the briefing papers. "Some of us do, Wu Huixia, *Tongzhi*, comrade." She smiled at his momentary look of surprise.

He rendered a half bow. "You speak Chinese and you know my name. The two things do not come easily to people from the West." Although his face took on polite lines, it did not change appreciably.

I've goofed, Christine thought, her gaze faltering.

But his face softened as he added, "Americans usually say one name or the other, not the two as is our custom, family name first." He extended a hand.

She put hers in it and raising her voice above the din of voices calling and exclaiming now in both Chinese and English, she explained, "Not everyone studies the Chinese language, but everyone here has seen your picture, Wu Huixia." She moved aside to let the crowd flow around her.

Wu Huixia inclined his head slightly, a man deep into middle age, his young self showing through an alert awareness. "It appears I am more well known than I realized although I am merely a humble servant of the government. But, forgive me for being so stupid, I do not recognize your face."

"Christine Wainwright," she said. "Filling in for Dr. Taylor. You could not have recognized my photograph, as it wasn't among your briefing papers." She moved slowly forward.

"Dr. Taylor, of course. You, perhaps, saw my son earlier. He, too, is an interpreter."

"Wu Gang-jo?"

"A single bloom smells sweeter than a bouquet when some

are wilting, some are dead. Once I considered it a misfortune to have one son only. Now I realize, a one child family is right and proper"

"Yes, of course," she said quickly. Undoubtedly he referred to the government one child rule. Did he want to argue the policy with her? As she ruminated, a young woman tapped her on the arm and urged Christine to take her seat. Most everyone else was already seated. It was evident Wu Huixia was important, but not important enough to sit with the President. She hurried to her place at a round table steps away from the stage. Porcelain dinnerware flanked by ivory chopsticks and silver knives and forks gave the settings a regal appearance. A menu, stamped with a red and gold seal, was hand-printed in English.

She looked around the vast hall. President and Mrs. Nixon, Henry Kissinger, Secretary of State William Rogers and their parties sat with Zhou En-lai and other Chinese leaders at head tables at the foot of a stage, but Chairman Mao was not in evidence.

On the platform workmen, trying out the volume, were whispering into the two microphones. U.S. and Chinese flags hung along the wall, and throughout the room, Caucasians and Orientals laughed and joked in studied earnestness. Marching music played. The fragrance of flowers wafted. It was a curious blend of East and West, a pageant of pomp and circumstance, both casual and formal and terribly exciting. She wanted to laugh and dance, the idea of being part of such a historical event bringing color to her cheeks, sparkle to her eyes. She smiled.

"Tonight you get your baptism by fire," John Morgan, the

State Department interpreter sitting at her left said leaning toward her.

Feeling in awe of his expertise and knowledge—he had worked the diplomatic circuit for years—she shook her head. "No, I'm off duty tonight." Unless one of the leaders called an unscheduled meeting later, she could relax. Gossip said Nixon and Kissinger were too tired and the Chinese too polite to suggest a meeting.

Morgan shook his head in denial. Near him, other men from the State Department beamed at her, as if they were smiling at someone who would learn the hard way. "Perhaps," Morgan said.

A frisson of alarm shot up Christine's spine. "I thought," she began but didn't finish as the band boomed the American national anthem. She jumped to her feet.

As the Star Spangled Banner crashed to a close, Wu Gang-jo took the empty seat next to her. "So we meet again," she said.

He answered with amusement lighting his eyes, "This is a table for interpreters."

Morgan and the others smiled.

"I'd say interpreters do all right." She indicated the trays of hors d'oeuvres a waiter was placing on the Lazy Susan, indicating everyone should help themselves. For years, after lessons were concluded, she and Dr. Taylor had ordered from the Famous Chinese Café near his office, chop suey, sweet and sour pork. Chopsticks were not new to her, but the sea cucumbers, slippery and slug-like, slid from her chopsticks and fork alike. Flushing, she gave up.

Gang-jo pointed toward thick, sweet bean puree and delicately spiced shrimp. "I have trouble with sea cucumbers, too. You may like these better. Both seem to please Western palates. May I help you?" Swiftly, he placed small portions of each on her plate and, leaning toward her, asked, "So how do you like China so far?"

Struck by the symmetry of his features, the ease of his movements, and the probability the opening gambits at all tables holding Chinese and Americans was similar, she said, "I've hardly seen China. What I've seen is very interesting."

"Is not 'interesting' a euphemism for boring?"

Surprised, she glanced at him from the corners of her eyes, saw his slightly challenging smile. "Truthfully, I cut my teeth on pictures of old China. Robes embroidered with gold thread, that sort of thing. So far I've seen little color."

"Ah yes, the Western press has written we are drab-looking. It is the price for equality—conformity in dress. Not at all like Americans who are peacocks, I've heard."

"Architectural conformity as well?" Again she gave him a sidewise look, not knowing why she fell into a semi-debate mood.

He shook his head. "Ah, you have me. The old city wall was torn down to make way for some of this modernization, but wait until you see the Forbidden City, the Great Wall. There you will find the China of old." He flashed a warm smile.

She didn't say she'd been prepared for bland food, look-alike people, and think-alike politics, but the preparation had been an intellectual understanding, not a real knowing. All her life she'd been told communism threatened world security. She'd hidden beneath her school desk during air raid drills, heard talk about McCarthyism, fellow travelers, people who believed the communist line. She glanced away. If her father were in China, America would brand him a communist. Was he? More than likely he'd left China long ago. "Actually, I'm favorably impressed by what I've seen." She tasted a dumpling stuffed with minced pork and rice. "This is delicious."

"We aim to please Western palates." As dish followed dish of tasty food, he filled her plate with tidbits, reaching out with his chopsticks and selecting a piece of abalone or a pastry filled with sesame seeds or almond paste, leaning close to place it on her plate. Or would she prefer a slice of watermelon or a hot banana dipped in icy sugar water?

After a while she felt pampered and as close to the China of the past as she could get, Gang-jo as solicitous as a personal tour guide, telling about places she should visit, explaining to her, asking questions, clearly interested in more than the obvious. Morgan was deep into a discussion with the man at his left, and she could hear little of what was said at the other side of the table. It was as if she and Wu Gang-jo were alone.

"You studied our culture a long time?" he asked, his tone polite, his look probing.

"Since I was a girl. I saw ivory and jade artifacts in a museum when I was six and became intrigued by Chinese art."

"No wonder you speak with nostalgia of things like gold embroidery." His voice was soft but chiding.

Looking up, she found him watching her with an amused expression. She glanced away to discover that the President had left his table and was on stage. One of the interpreters from the opposite side of her table was summoned to the other microphone.

"Your turn will come," Morgan said, nudging her

shoulder, his eyes crinkling.

Feeling like the new kid in a school with a group of post-graduates, Christine lifted her eyebrows, but Morgan, who seemed bent on teasing her, shook his head before turning his attention to the stage.

President Nixon's voice, furry with feeling, rose over the clink of china, the soft murmur of voices. "So many deeds cry out to be done and always urgently," he said. "The world rolls on. Time passes. Ten thousand years are too long. Seize the day, seize the hour."

"Your President recites Mao like a Chinese," Wu Gang-jo said in her ear.

"We pride ourselves on knowing pertinent facts regarding any country, any occasion," Christine murmured, feeling slightly pompous but powerful too, the might of America behind her.

Gang-jo's smile increased, and he shook his head as if in disbelieving admiration. "Americans are so direct. Without false modesty. A refreshing thing to hear. In the past we Chinese felt it was not seemly to show pride in accomplishment. We are changing, doing away with old thinking, but it takes time."

"Perhaps we Americans are too direct," Christine said politely. As President Nixon finished his statement with, "This is the hour, this is the day for our two peoples to rise to the heights of greatness which can build a new and a better world," she waited until the applause dimmed, and then she said to Gang-jo, "I don't want to leave you with the wrong impression."

Gang-jo shook his head. "No bad impression has been detected. But perhaps I am a bad detective." He grinned. Then his voice going serious, he added, "You are a good as well as beautiful representative of the American people."

Smiling, aware of the interest in his eyes, she added, "And if I had been Russian?"

He laughed. "I might say the Soviet Union overstayed their visit."

"Might?"

"I try to be diplomatic." His eyes were gleaming at her.

She took a chance, the moment riding on blue sky days, moonlit nights, a world where all were in step, friends forever. "So does a mutual non-friend make us friends?"

"I think, perhaps so." He nodded slowly, his gaze staying with hers a trifle too long, his eyes saying more than his words.

For years she had concentrated on learning – a BA, an MA, a PhD and then post- graduate study with Dr. Taylor. She'd had arranged dates with government officials and two extended liaisons with eligible men that had superficiality written all over them. She'd vacationed in the Caribbean with the first, spent ten months in the second's apartment, but neither understood her fascination with China. With difficulty she looked away from Gang-jo and turned toward Morgan. Everything that had happened so far seemed like a step out of time. Within the confines of protocol, a wide-open area existed, and she could ignore it, or sample it, or savor it as she savored the food that was piling on her plate. Gang-jo's face was classically Oriental but also Caucasian in structure, his eyes big, with dark, rich centers that reminded her of warm, hidden places, special times. She imagined him in movies playing all the Asian parts.

Zhou En-lai had joined the president on the platform and was concluding introductory remarks. Following him, Chinese and American leaders read opening remarks into the microphones, formal toasts were read aloud and interpreted, and glasses filled with *mao tai*. The President and Zhou En-lai lifted their glasses in salute while cameras recorded the momentous occasion that would undoubtedly be played over and over again on American television screens. Applause rocked the room.

"To Chinese-American friendship." Gang-jo lifted his glass and looked directly at her.

She lifted her glass in salute, noticed people throughout the room doing the same, and touched the drink to her lips. It was far from mild.

"*Gan bei*," Gang-jo gestured.

"Empty glass? No, I can't." She shook her head as his smile inched its way through her, exploding in her mind. The President was going from table to table, saluting this and that Chinese official. Everyone seemed to be smiling; everyone seemed to be drinking.

Laughing, Gang-jo shook his head and downed his drink. "Oh, but you must. It's the way it is done. As you say, bottoms up."

Someone said in English, "Down the stuff, for Christ sake. You wanta cause a problem?"

Smiling ruefully, she drank the liquid to the bottom.

Everyone at the table applauded. Morgan said she had the makings of a diplomat.

Within minutes she felt a loosening of the tension that had

held her since she'd left home—the last minute cramming, standing by Dr. Taylor's hospital bed and realizing he could not help her. Now, her face flushed from the alcohol, the sharp edges of the room blurred, everything seemed easier. "To friendship!" she cried.

Following the prepared toasts, President Nixon added a few bold extemporaneous remarks and Zhou was forced to answer. For a moment the two leaders stood alone on the stage. Morgan suggested Christine translate. Before she had time to protest, the others nodded and Gang-jo pulled back her chair, his smile challenging her.

Taking a deep breath, she went to the front, Gang-jo behind her. She climbed the stairs to the platform and looked down on the room. A sea of Chinese faces showed above blue or gray Mao tunics, American faces above three-piece suits or muted American dresses, hundred of faces all turned toward her. Beyond them the vastness of the hall stretched, seemingly unending. From the head table, Mrs. Nixon watched with pride, her smile broader than usual as Christine took the stage.

"There is a Chinese saying," Zhou said, "that one shouldn't break the bridge after crossing it. We have crossed that bridge, and we are now at an enviable place where other Americans and Chinese may cross behind us. May we remember this night with fondness and look to future meetings with unfeigned anticipation."

As Zhou paused, Gang-jo put Zhou's Chinese into English, and her moment of nervousness passed. She knew her job, and did it well when the President spoke, and felt pride in the doing. Still, she was glad he elected to make a few comments only. Her head had started to swim, but it all seemed worth it as the President shook her hand afterward and said she'd done a "crackerjack job." Zhou nodded at her and said in English, "It is indeed an honor to have such a young and beautiful translator on our stage."

Smiling broadly, she returned to her seat flushed with success.

Everyone smiled, and Morgan said she needed to slow down her delivery, but her translation was fine. He confessed he had had no qualms. "Anyone who studied with Dr. Taylor..."

Gang-jo raised his glass and his eyes paid tribute to more than her ability to understand and interpret Chinese correctly. She grinned.

America The Beautiful rang through the hall, the President waved a hand in time with the music, the First Lady mouthed the words, and the Americans sang along. Christine sang in Chinese, knowing Gang-jo watched admiringly; it was not an easy task, the Chinese words not quite fitting the music, she improvising, leaving out words occasionally. The evening was ending, the President and party leaving, Morgan and the others tagging along. She and Gang-jo were the only two left at her table.

"Do you write our language as well as you speak and sing it?" Gang-jo asked, his arm on the back of her chair.

"*Bushi*, no." She turned to face him. "With difficulty."

Gang-jo's smile grew warmer. Rising, he bowed slightly, drew her up beside him. "Tomorrow I will accompany you when you interpret for the First Lady's sight-seeing trip."

He was so close she detected the faint odor of food and

liquor on his breath. *So he knew her schedule* "I thought you were supposed to go with the Premier."

"The schedule was changed. I mentioned your name to someone who knows of such things." His voice went lower. "I wanted to be sure to see you again."

"Your father is in charge of scheduling," she said, not looking away. Gang-jo's eyes were fringed with dark thick lashes. His mouth was wide, his lips ordinary, the bow sensuous.

"Of course." He grinned.

She looked away.

"So," he said, as if the next move was up to her.

Nothing in the State Department briefing had addressed fraternization. She supposed no one had expected it to take place, but as she moved from the table, he fit his stride to hers, and she knew that somewhere, somehow, she and this man would fraternize in a wholly exciting fashion having nothing to do with politics but everything to do with feelings.

Chapter 3

Christine

The People's Republic of China, 1972

A whirlwind of sightseeing and political activity, banquets and small meetings came together in Christine's mind like an ever-changing kaleidoscope. Itineraries listed destinations, daily departure times and estimated times of arrival back at the hotel. But nothing indicated how long they would be at any one location, giving room for flexibility. The First Lady and her party took extra time at the zoo. Christine's duties less than demanding, she was aware of Gang-jo on the periphery, part of the Chinese delegation. Later, at the Summer Palace he walked beside her, his voice washing over her like water rippling over sand, his smile drawing her in.

He explained with charming insouciance about the Dowager Empress who didn't want war. She had used her treasury to build a marble boat instead. Ostensibly he was explaining to the First Lady, but Christine knew he was speaking to her. The day was bright but cold, making the highly carved, brightly colored fanciful buildings stand out like relics of a profligate but elegant time.

"It's very beautiful," Pat Nixon said, her little half smile growing.

Christine glanced by a long pergola with hand-painted designs, eyed marble bridges spanning ravines, red-tiled buildings climbing a hill, all spectacularly reflected in a lake, and shook her head. “A marble boat isn’t very practical is it?” She spoke to the Chinese in the party, but she was sure Gang-jo knew she was addressing him.

“When a billion and more people are involved, practicality is a necessity, of course.” Gang-jo’s voice rang authoritatively.

“But we can still admire the artistry, the beauty,” she added, noticing the First Lady glancing at her watch, ready to go back to the hotel.

“One can always admire beauty.” Gang-jo’s voice made clear he was talking to her, his eyes laughing, his delight in her unmistakable. She couldn’t resist returning his smile. He radiated youth and enthusiasm and couldn’t be many years her senior.

The next day the First Lady joined the President and his Security Advisor for a visit to the Great Wall. Walking the ramparts that had once been used as a highway, Christine lost track of time. As a child she’d imagined being on the wall with her father. Now, the image of her yearning-self rose like a ghost needing to be appeased. The Wall, so vast it was the only human structure visible with a naked eye from the moon, had been built to keep foes out. It hadn’t.

Facing into the wind, she imagined signals flashing from one tower to the next, announcing enemy troop movements. Despite wind whipping her hair, touching her with icy fingers, she climbed to the third tower. Her ears ached, her nose tingled, her toes felt numb, but, plunged into the past, she ignored discomfort. Trying to concentrate on history, recall the Qin, the Zhao, and the Yan who started the wall, the Ming who had finished it, the present kept intruding. Could she trust Gang-jo? His father was an insider, and Gang-jo had probably been in the thick of things for years. But maybe he could tell her something about her father. She stood quietly, the slapping of her scarf the only sound intruding on the silence, like the past blustering in the bright light of day.

Shivering slightly, she glanced below and saw only the everlasting wall. Had everyone gone? She started down on a run, her feet pounding against stone and brick. Beijing was eighty kilometers away. If she missed her ride, it could be reported in the press, become an international incident. Her heart became a lead weight, berating her with each beat. If only she hadn't let time get away from her while she daydreamed.

Rounding a curve, she caught sight of Gang-jo standing in the thin sun below the final steps at Badaling and knew he was waiting for her, his scarf floating like a beacon in the wind, giving him a jaunty air. The cars containing the Nixons, Zhou En-lai and the other officials were swinging out, the others following. Only one car remained.

Gang-jo directed her toward his automobile. As she got in, settled back against the plushy interior and rubbed her numb hands together, the man in the backseat the two in front, greeted her in Chinese. She replied and everyone smiled at everyone.

"Are you warm enough?" Gang-jo asked, quietly, his English a whisper as the car moved ahead.

"I'm fine," she said. If they were alone, would he take her hands in his, rub life back into hers, breathe on them?

"Did our wall live up to its reputation?" he asked as their vehicle hurried after the cars moving out.

Aunt Betty had said she had the Wainwright family features, and all the old pictures showed beauty. Is that what he saw, or was he, too, caught up by the idea, not only of the history being made but of the two diverse cultures coming together? Jammed together in the back seat of the boxy black car, his shoulder tight against hers, a current was running between them, like the throbbing of an electric guitar, and it would not matter what they said in English, for she knew what he meant. Her skin, her eyes, her hair, so different from his had to be an aphrodisiac, a thought she had never entertained before. "It was magnificent."

"Of course. It is one of a kind."

She had trouble not returning his smile, telling herself she needed to assert herself, show him, no matter how this was heading, she was not to be taken for granted, even if she were an America out of her element. As, indeed, she was. She murmured in Chinese, "I had hoped to see the Ming tombs today, also. I've read so much about them."

Looking very serious, Gang-jo said, "If it's important to you, we'll stop on our way back to the city."

Recognizing a surge of feminine power, Christine hid her smile.

Gang-jo gave new directions in a Chinese dialect she didn't understand, and the driver complied. Staring rigidly ahead, the other men's faces tightened. Everything seemed to be moving more rapidly than she could tie her mind around. But the thought fled when the car slowed down for a corridor leading between two rows of enormous carved animals. Spying elephants, camels, and horses, she clapped her hands in delight. This was the China that had grabbed her fascination. "These are fantastic! Absolutely great." Words bubbling from her, she looked right and left, leaned against Gang-jo, as well as the man on the other side of her. "Tell me the significance of the carvings. Why are some of the animals standing, some kneeling?" She couldn't stop smiling to Gang-jo's obvious delight as her questions rose like soap bubbles to be burst only to be followed by more.

"The animals formed an imperial guard of honor the Mings called a spirit road. The kneeling animals were, of course, female." His eyes teased her even though he spoke in a serious fashion.

She grinned. "I would hardly say, of course. You've had women leaders."

"But the dynasties oppressed the people." His eyes danced merrily.

She let hers romp as well. "But dynasties were part of your history. Sedan chairs. Women wielding ivory-handled fans. Students brushing delicate strokes into poetic phrases." She wanted to embrace the words, the sameness of modern China like a deep gouge in the side of a delicate marble carving. Her thoughts intruded on her smile, almost nullifying it when she noticed the man on her left scowling. Did he understand English as well as Chinese? Not impossible for a secretive regime. Had she goofed? The day had a quality reminiscent of a different time, letting her forget for a time she was a visitor in a Communist State.

As if sensing her thoughts, Gang-jo switched to Chinese. "The past is gone. Today *we* make history. An American president comes to us. Soon, the whole world will follow America's example and come to China." His eyes no longer danced.

Christine shook her head. "We say *we* are making history."

He shrugged, gave another command. The driver made a

u-turn and started back to Beijing. No one spoke. Everyone looked out the windows.

Christine observed people peddling bicycles making way for their car, donkey carts giving ground, pedicabs being pulled by skinny men, their muscles long and rippling, the men never glancing their way. At a construction site, men hauled concrete and building materials in buckets, attacked the ground with shovels, forks, and spades. All stared expressionlessly at the chauffeured car.

"Our Revolution brought us to the attention of the world," Gang-jo said in Chinese as if their earlier conversation had not been interrupted. The teasing and baiting quality in the depths of his eyes was gone, the emotional timber of his voice absent. "Other countries can no longer afford to ignore us."

"I believe we made the first overture." She wasn't sure about that, but she felt obligated to take America's side. Anyway, she wasn't going to let him back her into a corner. "We also opened Japan to the world in an earlier era. Actually, since we arrived, we have been very busy." Gesturing, she ticked off facts. "Our television stations beam daily satellite programs about official meetings. Our journalists file stories. Photojournalists take pictures. Historians gather information. People back home are fascinated with your vast untapped resources."

"Ah, yes, the capitalistic view." Once more he was smiling.

The other men in the car nodded. They too smiled.

"You make it sound mercenary, yet there are advantages on both sides." Christine took a deep breath, ready to continue while wondering how much of the exchange was age-old man/woman sparring? Or were his comments made for the benefit of the others in the car? She glanced at him, saw laughter gurgling around the edges of Gang-jo's smile.

"You mentioned the word 'mercenary,' not me." His eyes, meeting hers, were warm.

She should cut off the answering smile that played at the corners of her mouth and point out the cheerless monotony of modern China, but their countries were making history, and they could agree on that, and if her pulse raced faster than usual, couldn't she count it an added benefit?

"Tonight," he said, again speaking English, "before you leave for the theater, I'll send you some articles that will explain what I so poorly touched upon."

"I didn't know the theater was on my agenda." She leaned toward the window as their car honked past a road crew where women pushed wheelbarrows, gathered loose rock, worked with pick and shovel. The air was thick with dust.

"I suggested you should be included." Again that quick, probing look.

If he had set out to impress her, he had. "Aren't you young to have such authority?" A high floating sensation inundating her, she knew her teasing question would please him. The first day Mao had remarked on the "youth" of the American delegation, singling out an American Assistant Secretary of State who was fifty-six. None of the Chinese leaders would see sixty again.

"While I went through war and famine, you had Elvis Presley." He flashed a smile at her. "As for youth, I am two years older than you."

"Then we're both young," she said with finality. Today, behind-the-scenes power plays were creating new alignments and new Chinese leaders. Would Gang-jo be one? As the city approached squat hovels leading up to Soviet-style apartment buildings, Christine said, "What do women wear to the theater in Beijing?"

He looked surprised and busied himself lighting a cigarette. "The same thing that they wear to the zoo: what you Americans call a Mao suit."

Christine suspected he had not exaggerated the dress code at all.

That night a messenger brought her a packet of papers stamped with Gang-jo's seal. Before leaving for the theater, wearing a fresh blouse with her traveling pants and jacket, she stuffed the articles into her airline carry-on bag to read on the way home.

The orchestra members were filing in, musicians tuning their instruments when she slipped into her seat, everyone else already in place. A few rows ahead of her the President and First Lady sat with Chiang Ching, Chairman Mao's wife. Official host for the evening's festivities, Chiang Ching had been an actress, young and pretty when she caught Mao's eye. Now garish makeup aged her. Word was that her talents were limited, but she had reportedly charmed him and for twenty years had wielded influence privately. Now, with Mao's backing, her reform of China's artistic endeavors had taken hold, and she no longer sat back. Morgan had hinted she was trying to reform other things as well as opera, ballet, and theater; her hold on the youth of China firm.

As Christine settled into her seat, the overture clashed,

tinkled and shrieked, like wind whipping down from the stratosphere, water trickling into a slow-moving stream, combining as she'd imagined it would, the oriental sounds unfamiliar and yet known. Thrilled, she applauded with alacrity and watched astounded as gymnasts leaped on stage, seeming to defy gravity. But the ballet following struggled under a load of propaganda, dancers in quasi uniforms brandishing fake guns, shouting communist slogans, singing communist songs. Bored, she looked around, spotted John Morgan and other Americans. Some were sleeping, others fighting it. She smiled and nodded at the newsmen and women she recognized, everyone as amused as she at the ballet's story.

During a quiet moment in the dancing, the lead dancer protesting China's old rule, Chiang Ching's loud, rasping voice rang through the hall, her English accented but clear, "Do the people of America appreciate ballet?"

The President answered, "Some do, some don't," as a girl in toe shoes raced across the stage toward the dancers depicting the troops.

Chiang Ching, in a louder voice demanded of the President, "Why did you not come to China before? We have been here many years. Why do you only now deign to recognize us?"

The President kept his gaze on the stage as if engrossed with the ballet as a chorus of girl dancers, toe shoes thudding, followed the lead dancer, toy guns pointed.

An American flashed a peace sign and said loud enough for all in the first rows to hear, "Hey, people, you're supposed to watch the stage."

Christine spotted Zhou En-lai. Already stories were circulating, one saying Zhou never let meetings be interrupted by phone calls and defended his position by saying, "Human relations must not be displaced by technical capabilities." Another story had Zhou rearranging a newspaper's front page for the next day. Hearing about it, President Nixon supposedly muttered, "I'd like to rearrange a front page now and then!"

Shortly after the cast bowed and left the stage to polite applause from the American guests, the entertainment ended. Christine rose, put on her coat, and plunged into the stream of people leaving the theater, the Americans heading toward the waiting limousines. Buffeted by the crowd, she lost her place amid a sea of Chinese faces. "Excuse me, " she said, trying to push ahead. Suddenly Gang-jo appeared at her side, clearing a path with his elbows and voice. "This way." He took her arm, led her toward an outside door.

"Thank you, I think I was going in the wrong direction." Pushed from behind, she burst through the door. The sudden raw cold nipped at her face, burned her lungs; shivering, she fastened her coat, belted it tightly. She was surrounded by Chinese, no Americans in sight and everyone seemed to be talking at once. Shouting above the chatter, she said, "Wu Gang-jo, please direct me to my car. I seem to have lost it."

He whispered in her ear, "It's over there, but please call me Jo in the American way and I will call you Christine, also in the American way. Okay?"

Startled, she glanced up at him. He definitely was an enigma, not even looking at her now, but pointing past her to where a few cars were idling. She started toward them when, above the ongoing murmur of Chinese, English rose like a metronome, ringing bell-like in the frigid air.

Wu Gang-jo took her arm. "This way. You're riding back

with me." He ushered her toward a Soviet-built vehicle. His smile became a grin. "As you might say, I took advantage of my father's position."

"You sound like a capitalist," she muttered, starting to get in when a voice rang out in unaccented English. She hesitated hearing a male voice repeat, "I want to see them, god damn it. Let go of me!"

Christine hesitated. "What is it? What's going on?" She looked around, but it was hard to know exactly where the sound had come from, and she saw nothing except the Chinese hurrying past her, the Americans leaving, the President's car in the lead.

As she frowned, Gang-jo said quickly, "Some minor disturbance." His hand on her arm pushed gently.

She shook it off. "No, I see someone." Off to the right, at the edge of the pool of light spilling from the building, three men held back a fourth. He was larger than the others, and almost slipped from their grasp, giving Christine a fleeting glimpse of a large man with Caucasian features, but the light was dim, the image indistinct. As she tried to focus, the man cried out again, this time in Chinese. "I've been waiting since October."

"What's that mean, October?" she asked as Gang-jo all but forced her into the car. "Why not let him get closer? He spoke both Chinese and English. I distinctly heard him." She perched on the edge of the seat and looked past Gang-jo who got in beside her. Could it have been her father? The letter from him had been rife with ambiguity. Ridiculous. Her father would never have been in such a position. Would he? "What did that mean about October?"

"It could mean anything. Someone wanting to get too close. Many of our people have never seen an American, not even a photo."

"No." She shook her head. "He didn't look Chinese. And he spoke English."

Gang-jo sighed and sat down beside her, not as close this time. "I speak English, too, and not all of our people are descended from Han Chinese." His face wore a patient expression. "You might say China, like America, is a melting pot. We do not all look alike or speak the same language. We speak with accents or we don't. We're short or we're tall." He shrugged. "You get the point." The driver, leaning on the car horn, scattered people leaving the theater.

Christine shook her head. It wasn't the same. The man had said "God damn it." That was very American. But were the words restricted to America? Forgetting momentarily the briefing paper warnings about argumentative or provocative speech, she blurted, "Ever since I got here, ordinary people have been kept at a remove. Something seems wrong. Everywhere we go, we're isolated." Her voice rose.

"You're here with me and two other Chinese. I certainly wouldn't call that isolation." Gang-jo's smile skidded past her. The man's words whirling through her mind, she blurted, "When we arrived at the Great Wall, six and seven-year-old children were spouting politics. Kids don't talk politics, unless they're rehearsed. John Morgan protested the incident."

Gang-jo met her gaze. "What can I say? Zhou En-lai apologized and criticized those responsible."

"Does that mean China's concerned about people-to-people contact?"

His smile faded. "I did not say that, although I understand the validity of your complaint. If Zhou can apologize, I can, too, although I do not see the necessity." He spread his hands. "I'm sorry."

She looked up in time to catch the driver watching her in the rear-view mirror, the front seat passenger turning his head in her direction, watching her with a stony-faced expression. It was clear they didn't understand English. Or had she also spoken Chinese? Talking with Gang-jo she often forgot she was among Chinese Communists.

For a long while no one said anything. As swooping roof lines showed up in the headlights, reminding her of the China she'd imagined during her childhood—tea steeping in delicate cups, the whisper of silk, the deep, clear depth of jade—she addressed Gang-jo in English, her voice low as she spoke the words that had been racing through her. "My father came to China after World War II. After a few letters no one heard from him after that. I'd like to find him. Can you help?"

"Find your father?"

She nodded. "I was told he came here to work."

"Twenty some years is a long time. I doubt I can do much."

Couldn't *your* father help, she wanted to say, but the man in the front seat made it plain he was watching her, and the driver kept glancing at her in the rear-view mirror, both as if they had either understood or were trying to. Had she betrayed herself with her voice, her passion? Certainly she'd not told the story properly, had made a botch of it.

Silence followed, and a swirl of snowflakes showed in the headlights.

When they were almost at her hotel, Gang-jo asked in

Chinese, his voice full of formality, "Did you enjoy your evening, Miss Wainwright?"

She hesitated a second before answering, wondering if she had imagined the slight jerk of his head toward the front seat, as if warning her to be careful what she said. She forced herself to sound as pleasant and distant as he. "Thank you, it was a most fascinating evening. The acrobats were fantastic and the ballet very interesting." Silently she berated herself for trusting in him.

A muscle in Gang-jo's cheek tightened, and his mouth held the barest suggestion of a smile. "It was our pleasure to entertain you."

As the car stopped at the hotel especially built for foreigners, he got out and said softly in English as she followed, "Tell me the name of your father."

Aware of the two men in the front seat nodding at her, she wanted to blurt out her father's name, but didn't. At the last second, she said so low only Gang-jo could hear, "Logan Wainwright."

"I will see what I can do."

"Thank you." She darted into the lobby.

In her room she fell into an exhausted sleep, the scene outside the theater repeating, the words "god damn it" ringing in her ears, waking her.

The next day her schedule of sightseeing trips with the First Lady continued, and she had time to think of little else. In addition, the President asked her to shop for gifts for the staff. "The First Lady has her own flurry of last minute gift buying." She had barely arrived back at the hotel after another banquet when someone knocked on her door. She opened it cautiously to see a hatless Gang-jo standing in the hall. "May I come in?"

She nodded, stepping back as he entered. "Please take a seat." She indicated the table and chairs near the window.

Instead he made a circuit of the room, running his hands under the surface of tables, examining light fixtures, looking at the baseboards, the molding, behind pictures. Aware of his serious expression, a warning signal flashed in her mind. He was checking for electronic listening devices. She busied herself with the large thermos of hot water, the cups and a bowl of jasmine tea-bags sitting on a tray in the middle of the polished oak table. Pouring water into two cups, she added teabags, put lids in place and said, "This meeting wasn't on my schedule."

A fleeting smile crossed his face as he sat down. "Or mine." He took the teacup she offered, his features wearing a serious cast, lending added importance to his words. "Today Chairman Mao added more security police. Everywhere."

A hollow feeling invaded her belly. "What has that to do with me?"

"It makes it impossible for ordinary citizens to get near Americans."

He wasn't going to be able to help her. She saw it, felt it. Her hands shook as she sat down.

He leaned toward her, held her with the force of his gaze. "I may have good news. I believe the man you saw outside the theater was your father."

The room suddenly went off keel. Her head spun. My god, why hadn't he said so in the first place? She threw out her arm, knocking the table. The lids jiggled against the cups. Steadying herself, she sat facing him, seeing his face, realizing how in proportion each of his features were, and all the while a nerve throbbed at the back of her head, and agonizing pain exploded in her skull. Unable to sit still, she jumped up, walked briskly to the bedside table where she had put schedules, menus, book marks, newspaper articles and other items she'd take home as souvenirs of the trip. She stared at them sightlessly before turning. "You knew all along he was my father."

Gang-jo shook his head. "I surmised it, but I was not at liberty to say anything." He shrugged. "I must be careful."

"But my father is an American citizen."

Gang-jo shook his head. "Your father is a citizen of the People's Republic."

"No, he's American. I should know."

"Your father became a citizen of the People's Republic of China. He has a Chinese name."

She shook her head. "My father wouldn't renounce his American citizenship." She moved toward the door. "I must talk to my people, do something immediately. "

Once again the muscle in Gang-jo's cheek twitched. "No American, not even your President can dictate China's policies, and as a citizen your father has to obey."

She raised her head imperiously. "Does that go for me, too? If I speak up or try to see him, will I be held incommunicado or something?"

He held up a hand. "Please don't misunderstand me. I am not saying I condone or criticize the policy. It is just so. As for you, as a guest in our country, nothing you say or do will be held against you."

"I'm delighted to know that. I'm sure Mao Tse-Tung and

Zhou En-lai will applaud your honesty in explaining this to me. President Nixon will say 'good going' and you will.... I don't know what the hell you'll do." She knew she was not making complete sense, but thoughts were exploding in her head like bombs. Her father a citizen of China! How could that be? And Gang-jo sat there so quietly, as if this was just another in an interesting but not earth-shaking set of problems. She returned to her chair, sat gripping the arms.

He shook his head. "Listen to me, please. It's not easy to say the things I must say." He glanced down and then up, looking at her from under his eyelashes. "I studied English with your father, but I never knew his American name, never asked."

Christine frowned. "I don't understand that at all."

He leaned across the table, lowered his voice again, "Sometimes to ask is dangerous."

She could say nothing.

"Listen, please. Chairman Mao is not well. For a long time he hasn't appeared in public. Before you came no one was sure he would live to see the Americans. The other day when Chairman Mao decided to see the President immediately, you cannot imagine the rush. Mao had gained weight. He needed new clothes, shoes, a haircut. What a scramble. Two hours before the meeting the reception room was a sick room."

"What are you getting at?" Christine asked bluntly, still reeling from what she'd heard about her father.

"The Chairman gives high praise to those of low birth and small pursuits and neglects others who bear the burden of office. Since before the Long March Zhou En-lai has been loyal and hardworking without a single word of congratulation or approval from the Chairman."

"That hardly sounds like one for all and all for one. Good old communism." What in the hell was this all about? She crossed her legs, found her foot beating the air, toe pointed.

"You speak with sarcasm. Your father explained how this art is implemented in English." Gang-jo made a slight gesture as if dismissing her interruption. "As you know, Zhou En-lai is second in command, and the people love him. I tell you this so you will understand when I say Zhou runs the government, but as long as Mao lives, Zhou does everything with the Chairman's approval." He paused. "You understand I am trusting you." His eyes demanded her cooperation.

Heart racing, she nodded.

"For your father, for me, nothing is automatic. I cannot arrange a meeting without much difficulty, but I will try. If all goes right, tomorrow night when you go to dinner, a car will be waiting. Your father will be in it." Gang-jo's eyes, his mouth, his very posture said he was speaking in earnest.

She nodded slowly. Her voice very soft, she asked, "What is he like?"

"What can I say? When I was a child my father arranged the lessons, wanting me to have it easier than he did. Your father is a man I eventually came to respect."

She looked away, noticing again the wrinkle in the carpet near the door, seeing again the firm crease in Gang-jo's pants, remembering the depth of sincerity in his eyes and the "eventually" in his last sentence. "Does he know I'm here?" She darted a glance at him. She needed all the details he could give her. "Did he ever talk about me?"

"Once he said he had a child about my age who was lost to him." He paused and then looked deep into her eyes. "Everyone in China wants you to enjoy your visit, he and I most of all."

For a long moment she returned his look but knew if she didn't glance away soon, he would kiss her, and she didn't want that. They had been skirting the edges of propriety since the beginning. Soon the Bamboo Curtain would open completely and she would see the man whose picture she had memorized, whose letter had wound its way into her heart. She didn't want to complicate that. "Thank you," she murmured. "I appreciate your delicate position and am grateful for your help." Now that the moment was almost here, she felt unable to appreciate it properly. As long as Logan remained nebulous, she could endow him with all the fatherly attributes she had yearned for, but what would this unknown man be like? Fifteen years since his last letter. "Who else knows about this?"

"I am the only one. My father knows nothing."

Again a look developed between them, and she felt it go to her head like the *mao-tai* at the banquets. "Thank you."

"You are most welcome, Christine. Your father taught me American manners, too." He grinned.

She almost laughed, with relief, with abandon, with joy. Yes, she would see her father. Yes, it was what she had always wanted, no matter her fears, and no matter he'd apparently deserted America. He had to have had a reason. She couldn't believe otherwise.

She stood, and suddenly Gang-jo was next to her. She was aware of the length of his legs, the warmth of his eyes, the feel of his hand touching hers briefly.

And then he was gone.

The next day passed in a blur, thoughts of Gang-jo, of her father, blotting out the excitement of international politics. Back in her room, Christine grabbed her purse and was ready to leave for dinner when the summons came. The Chairman of the People's Republic wanted to meet with the President again. Except for the Chinese interpreter, Wu Gang-jo, Christine would be alone with the leaders. She must delay her dinner and come at once.

A sinking feeling raced through her as she hurried outside. What did this mean? Already the sun was dipping into the west, leaving a glow upon the clouds riding the eastern sky. As the President's men handed her into the Red Flag limousine, she glanced at her watch. If the conference lasted any length of time, would her meeting with Logan still be possible?

"We must hurry," the driver said, obviously excited at the last minute chore. "To keep Chairman Mao waiting is like asking a rooster not to crow at dawn." Making a wrong turn, he passed the barrier of roped-off streets and was immediately in the middle of bicycle-clogged traffic. "Out of the way," he shouted and held his hand on the horn. As bicycles veered right and left, he zigzagged down the wide thoroughfare.

Christine stared. People stared back, not smiling or waving, merely staring. She was thrown across the seat as the driver screeched around another turn and passed the entrance to the Forbidden City. Ahead the imperial red columns marked the gate. Two soldiers stood guard, their presence and the column's gold leaf and jade green lacquer trim the only indication they were entering Mao's compound.

She held on as the driver zoomed through parks and past lakes where Marco Polo had strolled and emperors and their concubines had dallied. She glimpsed houses and courtyards and remembered that it was here that Kublai Khan had built his pleasure palaces. When the driver stopped in front of Mao's villa, she felt relieved, yet filled with nervous energy, alert for anything and everything. She jumped out and was waiting when President Nixon alighted from his limousine.

"Ah, Miss Wainwright," he said. "Enjoying your visit?"
"It's quite an adventure." More than he'd ever know.

"Nothing like travel to broaden the mind and perhaps other areas also. I must say these Chinese know how to feed a man." He smiled and ushered her through the outside door ahead of him, dismissing the Secret Service who were flanking him.

She stepped back and let him precede her. Lit by a single lamp, the room where Mao waited, Gang-jo at his side, appeared cozy. Dark shadows hid the clutter and softened the worn upholstery of the overstuffed chairs, took away from the Chinese leader's rumpled appearance and pinpointed his smiling, nodding congeniality.

Mao straightened slightly against the mound of pillows at his back. "Forgive me if I don't get up."

Nixon shook his head. "It's perfectly understandable." He crossed the room, hand outstretched.

As the two men shook hands, and chatted, Gang-jo interpreted smoothly, quickly, for both men. Mao and Nixon talked about the weather, about the city, about history, exchanging absurdities, as the Chinese described the requisite preface to all meetings. Christine slipped off her coat, relinquished it to a servant who hung it on a rack near the door.

Mao waved her to a chair on the other side of the President

who looked remarkably relaxed, leaning back in a deeply upholstered chair.

As she took her seat, Mao said to Nixon, "Is this one of your pretty girls?"

Keeping a noncommittal expression on her face, Christine interpreted the President's words, speaking both to Mao and Gang-jo.

"Not mine," Nixon said, shaking his head so his jowls shook. "I mean, she's my unofficial official interpreter, not a part of my regular office staff." He pointed at Mao. "But the Chairman is clever and tries to trip me up."

Mao chuckled. "I only use the words you used the other day to both praise and bedevil your Mr. Kissinger. But now, we are without in-between men telling us what is best. We meet as true leaders, men who know what is best for our two countries."

"My Congress tells me what is best."

"But do you listen?"

Nixon laughed. "A wise man always listens, but with alternatives in mind."

"Some people don't deserve listening to."

The exchanges were coming so fast, Christine had no time to think. She glanced at Nixon as he said, "So you have it easier than me."

"But I am plagued with illness, forced to plan from outside the arena and use others to see if my plans have been implemented properly. I cannot be everywhere at once."

"No man can. Other men are at times necessary."

"Ah, yes. Your Mr. Kissinger. His name comes up so often, I wonder if he is more than one person. But we in the

People's Republic have many capable people. Today I think of Deng Xiaoping."

Nixon nodded. "Good man. Also Zhou En-lai."

"Zhou does what I say. I second what he does – if I deem it wise. You see what I mean?"

Nixon said, "I think the Chairman talks in riddles, but riddles are to be solved."

Once again Christine was absorbed in the give and take of the leaders, listening intently even as her thoughts skipped to Gang-jo. They were in this together in ways neither leader could surmise.

Mao asked, "You can work with the men I mentioned?"

"I can work with you," Nixon said, a slight, tight smile adding to the gleam in his eyes.

Mao laughed. "So if you can work with the devil, it would be no problem to work with Deng or Zhou."

"At home I, too, am called the devil by some people. Particularly the Democrats." The President leaned back and crossed his legs. His black shoes shone. His ankles looked patrician, slender. "Mr. Deng undoubtedly is very capable, but I have not had the opportunity to talk much with him." Christine repeated his words.

Mao lit a cigarette, coughed, and set it down. "You have picked wisely. Deng is a dagger wrapped in layers of cotton. My blade is often blunt, but always on display. Deng I might send to America."

"China's answer to Henry Kissinger?"

"All of us are China's answer to Chiang Kai-shek." Mao lifted his cigarette between thumb and forefinger and puffed.

While the two heads of state joked about the Generalissimo,

Christine studied Gang-jo. His face was bland, but a crease appeared between his eyes.

Mao said, "We Chinese are capable of dealing with round problems set in square holes. Perhaps Deng will go, perhaps not. I may change my mind. What have you to offer except refrigerators?"

"American technology sent men to the moon, but if you are more interested in refrigerators..." Nixon shrugged delicately. Mao laughed and clapped his hands. "I understand you are a poker player. I play chess, which is infinitely more complex. But you Americans hold high cards. So we will be friends, and I will send my men to America to learn the ways of poker."

As Nixon murmured, "It's a deal." Christine knew future foreign policy had been forged. She felt the tightness in her body slowly dissipate as Mao said it was late.

"I must sleep so I can hear what you are up to tomorrow." He cocked his head at Nixon.

The President chuckled. "Tomorrow I wear my poker face."

Mao puffed on his cigarette. Smoke collected beneath the lamp, wreathed to the ceiling. "Tomorrow will take care of tomorrow. Good night, Mr. President of the United States of America."

"Good night, Chairman of the People's Republic of China." Nixon walked briskly to the door, Christine following in order to hear whatever he said and interpret properly.

Mao called, "Get some rest, Dick Nixon. I intend to be extra sharp tomorrow."

As Christine slipped on her coat and started after the President, Mao detained her. "A moment, Miss Wainwright."

She turned, saw Gang-jo putting papers into a briefcase, heard Nixon's voice speaking to his bodyguards, saw Mao pushing to his feet. The nurse rushed from the back of the room to help him.

He waved her away. "A panda is tougher than the Russian bear or the American eagle. Leave me alone."

She backed a few steps, and muttered a few indistinguishable words.

"*Wah*, you speak like my jailer." Mao balanced himself against the lamp table and addressed Christine. "The other day, before my meeting with your president began, you made certain inquiries about an American."

She frowned, her conversation with the journalist coming back in a rush. It had been before Gang-jo came in, before she had realized the futility of questioning strangers.

Mao continued. "The journalist you spoke to, his father and mother were shot by Chiang Kai-shek and his henchmen. I saw that the orphan boy got schooling. He never forgot."

Hoping her voice sounded normal, she said, "Yes, I asked about an American." It was clear that the Chinese did not act and react in American ways. Carefully, she refrained from looking in Gang-jo's direction.

Mao regarded the glowing tip of his cigarette. "As a country we are old; as a political entity, we are young. But America is young in both respects. Your actions personify this delightful but ultimately dangerous naiveté." He looked at her, his smile enigmatic.

Christine buttoned her coat, relieved that her hand wasn't shaking. Zhou En-lai had sent flowers and visited an American diplomat who got ill. She doubted Mao would ever show such warmth. His eyes seemed to measure her coldly, and she felt compelled to speak. "What is it you want, sir?"

Mao shook his head. "It is not a question of my wanting, but of yours. We believe the most helpless, the most feeble, the most in need are equal to those who have the most power." He moved around the table, this time letting the nurse take his arm. "You, of course, are young, but you are not without considerable power. The power of beauty. For this I can forgive you. I am not without compassion. I am also not without resources. If the man you seek exists, I will find him for you." Again came the enigmatic smile.

Before her courage left her, Christine said the thoughts that were slowly jelling in her mind. She must deny that her words to the journalist were anything but idle. "The Chairman is right. I was impetuous when I spoke to the journalist. After so many years, I used a man who couldn't possibly still be in China to begin a conversation. But I was eager to talk to Chinese people, tell anyone who would listen how much I applaud my President for coming here. For years I've studied Chinese because of my admiration for the Chinese people." Her words were hurried, but apparently Mao bought them or pretended to, for he shrugged and turned aside, gesturing for his nurse, his breath coming quickly.

"So your question was idle chatter, but your decision not to detract from your President's decision is commendable. Now, can I help in any way? I certainly don't want a member of the American delegation leaving without doing everything in my power to make them comfortable, but as we chess players say, it is your move."

"I'm most comfortable, thank you."

"I believe you're keeping your driver waiting." He waved her out. "You, too," he said to Gang-jo. "I have no more need of you tonight." Turning to the nurse, he said. "Earn your keep, and do not bob around so when I would walk." He started out.

Gang-jo said, his voice loud. "We have arranged tours to the countryside for tomorrow, Miss Wainwright. Cars will be outside your hotel for all who wish to go."

Is he trying to tell me something? Christine glanced to where Mao shuffled from the room, his back to her. She left, Gang-jo following.

Wind blew cold like a blast from a snow blower and she noted night had fallen fully during the meeting, the floodlights around the compound making deep shadows. Gang-jo leaning down, spoke softly and rapidly, "I'm sorry. The person you wanted to see became unavailable." He opened the back door to her waiting limousine.

No one waited in the limousine but the white-gloved driver.

What had happened to her father? The conversation with Mao moved through her head as swiftly as wine absorbed by the bloodstream. Should she feel threatened? Nothing remained clear.

"I'll be in touch," Gang-jo said in English and turned away.

As her car, conspicuous in the bright, garish light, left the compound, the awful thought hit her. Her father could have been arrested. Right now the government could be interrogating him, slamming him around a jail cell. The government had certainly made it clear they wanted minimal contact between their people and the Americans. It was not a comforting thought.

On the flight to Hangzhou and during the last days of the trip, Christine felt as if knives were cutting into her intestines. The trip to China had offered dreams and then snatched them away. She had run to catch a train that wasn't there.

Had Gang-jo let her down? How was she to know? Perhaps she'd never see him again, and she'd never know if he said one thing and did another. Still, he'd seemed sincere. Was she growing paranoid?

When the plane landed in the city that Marco Polo had called the most beautiful in the world, she hoped to glimpse Gang-jo or get some clue to what had happened. But the tarmac was empty of all save the usual welcoming committee.

As soon as she registered at her hotel, she went out, needing to walk off the thoughts crowding her head. The meeting with Mao frightened her. Despite her being with the President on this historic trip, was Mao toying with her? Long ago she'd stored in her mind an image of her father. It kept popping up. What would he look like today? Had she really glimpsed him?

Still, Marco Polo was right. West Lake was as pretty as he had claimed. Gardens and mountains rose in the mist like an ethereal Chinese painting. Pagodas and moon gates and dragon ships ringed the marine blue waters. Yet, the beauty was overtaken by frustration. As she strolled the lakeshore in air crisp with winter's sting, a knot grew tighter and tighter in her belly. The oriental-style buildings housing the official party seemed out of a fairy tale, not real. Her rooms had a musty smell, the bathtub had no shower, and the Chinese people she glimpsed in the distance were blue dots on the horizon.

On the inner island she peeked through a series of wooden frames that reduced the sweeping vistas to paintings waiting to be judged. As she looked through the southern frame, the President's men, Haldeman and Ziegler, took turns at the western frame. Later she glimpsed TV anchor Walter Cronkite, laden with photographic equipment, viewing the tranquil scene that the President later likened to a picture postcard.

"Almost everyone was there," Christine wrote in her diary that night. Everyone but her father and Gang-jo.

In Shanghai, the last night in China, again she was seated with the other interpreters at the official banquet and grateful she wasn't called upon to interpret. Her sleep had been fitful, fatigue lifted somewhat by the vast array of food. Cucumber slices floated on oyster broth. Eggs were purportedly from another century. Quail, duck, and prawns came in quantities. White Cloud beer, and Panda cigarettes, orange soda and green tea filled out the menu. She had difficulty paying attention to the program. Then Zhou En-lai, reading the joint American/Sino agreement into six microphones, caught her attention. After the reading, both President Nixon and Henry Kissinger smiled broadly, and the *mao tai* began to flow. As she drank, the pressures of the past week slowly seeped away.

Soon everyone was table-hopping, toasting and hugging acquaintances as if they were old friends. The trip had bound the Americans, who would go their separate ways at home, close to one another. They hugged, laughed and joked. One woman confided she'd forgotten to pack underarm deodorant. "I tried everywhere to get some. They didn't know what

I was talking about. I even pantomimed. I think they thought I was touched in the head."

Christine admitted, "I broke down after that day at the Great Wall and put thermal underwear on under my slacks. I'll never complain about the weather at home again." "I'm glad I don't have to listen to any more revolutionary songs. Until we complained, they piped it into our hotel room!" someone else added.

Infectious laughter spread.

Christine thanked the Chinese at the next table for their great hospitality, but she felt like a hypocrite mouthing the words. The glimpse she'd gotten of communism had frightened and confused her. What had happened to her father and Gang-jo?

"So what are you going to do now that you've had a taste of the high life?" John Morgan asked when she returned to her seat at the interpreters table.

"I'll continue teaching, I suppose. I expect people will want to learn Chinese." The thought seemed foreign, something apart, the recent life all there was. While her mouth formed the words, Gang-jo suddenly appeared across the room, beyond the blue-clad Chinese and the Americans who looked like peacocks and penguins, the women breaking out brightly colored gowns, the men correctly formal for this last night. A tingling began in her scalp, spread to her fingertips.

"That's it?" Morgan said. "No rah, rah, rah enthusiasm?"

"It's too soon to assess it all." *Not once had Gang-jo glanced her way.*

"You could go to work for the State Department," Morgan mumbled as he finished working his way through the last bits of food on his plate. "If you want, I'll put in a word for you. Give it some serious thought. You're a good interpreter. Excuse me." He joined a friend across the room.

A step sounded behind her, and she expected another celebrant ready to hug her, but it was Gang-jo, and he merely slid into Morgan's vacated seat.

Christine said without thought, "I wondered what happened to you. I can't get that last meeting out of my mind." Would he tell her what happened?

"Me, too," he said, his gaze darting away acknowledging the others at the table.

Was that a signal to her that they had to be circumspect? She put down her glass. A giddy feeling seemed to have pervaded the Americans, the journalists already busy filing stories, others wondering if their being along could be parlayed into celebrity. As words rose and fell, everyone offering toasts, she tried to beg off, but it was impossible. She floated on a sea of alcohol laced with feelings too deep to examine.

Gang-jo leaned toward her as the table hopping slowed and people formed little groups around the room. "I understand you are an inveterate reader." Although the sound level in the room had risen, everyone talking, hardly anyone listening, he spoke in an over loud voice. "What American books do you recommend, Miss Wainwright?"

Other Chinese below diplomatic status wore cloth shoes and had utilitarian watches, but Gang-jo wore leather slip-on shoes, and a glittery gold watch circled his right wrist. She answered while thoughts of his difference zipped through her. "I understand *Gone With the Wind* was a favorite book with the Chairman's wife. I've been told she also has a print of the movie."

Pushing chopsticks and silver out of his way, Gang-jo rested his right elbow on the table. "I have not read that book, but I have read other American novelists such as Ernest Hemingway and John Steinbeck."

Speaking swiftly, softly so only he could hear, determination in each syllable, she said, "Tell me about my father."

Gang-jo shifted slightly, his chair angled toward her and away from the others at the table. "He was detained overnight only. I wanted to get word to you, but I had to guide a group of visiting Albanians."

She regarded him critically. In other circumstances would she like this man? She had seen instances of his bravery, his caring, his intelligence and wit, and he held the key to the vacant spot in her heart. She'd loved Aunt Betty who had taken the place of the mother she'd never known, but she'd worshipped the father whose words she'd memorized. Was that why she was tremendously drawn to Gang-jo? Her thoughts warmed her body, brought color to her cheeks. She dropped her menu, and as she bent to pick it up, Gang-jo leaned down, too. "Is he all right?" she whispered.

Handing her the menu, he said very softly, "Yes," and put a piece of paper into her hands. "It is a note from him. He wants your address so he can write to you when possible."

She put the note into her handbag. "It's allowed?"

"There are ways."

Straightening, she fanned herself with the menu, touched burning fingers to the hot flesh of her face, wet her lips with a dry tongue.

In a carrying voice, Gang-jo continued the previous conversation. "I have read your Jack London, of course."

"He had admirers world-wide." She spoke for the benefit of listeners. Yet, his eyes were playing tricks with hers, telling her that his thoughts were not entirely with the words he spoke even as hers were increasingly concerned with the fine arch of his brows, the delicate curve of his lips and the secrets he would tell her. *My father has written to me.* She wanted to shout the words, could hardly wait to read the note. Instead she stuffed it into her evening bag.

"Everyone everywhere names the same authors," she said turning so her words were heard around the table. "Steinbeck and London must be on an accepted list. I have difficulty understanding such unanimity of choice." Pleased that she had mustered an argument even while her heart beat like a vibrating temple bell, she smiled. Thank the Buddha and all the Oriental beings that her father was all right. She cracked open her purse, unfolded the note, held it so she could read the first words: *My dear daughter.*

Gang-jo moved the tiniest bit closer. "I have heard Americans admire the same authors I mentioned."

She wet her lips again. "Americans admire movies and movie stars." She laughed and dropped her hand beneath the edge of the table. "It's something most everyone agrees on." She lowered her voice. "So most Chinese conform?"

"We have dissent and discussion within a policy but unanimity about the policy. The thinking today is that free thought, a mind going in its own direction, leads to bourgeois propaganda." His eyes relayed his admiration for her as if he believed and didn't believe the words he uttered while his voice sounded soft as a feather floating in the breeze.

She lowered her voice again. "Do you believe that?"

Pitching his answer for her ears alone, he took a deep breath and said, "It is wiser to say so."

She lifted an eyebrow and rested her forearm on the table. If he stretched his fingers, they would touch hers.

"Ah, but I speak one thing and think another. Two people can look at one another and know these things." He spoke quietly, but for a second or two his mouth lost its smile as if he spoke words so serious his face had to fall in line.

"I almost didn't think I'd see you again." She leaned toward him, not denying her attraction. Gang-jo was young in body but old in knowledge. She needed to know so much, and he was the only one she could ask. "Please, tell me what will happen to my father."

"He will be reprimanded. Perhaps given some other minor punishment." His eyes met hers directly. "Now, that America has come to us, I think nothing serious will happen."

He appeared sincere, serious, the laughing, teasing element that infused his eyes often, now gone. "Thank you." She felt as if she were on a sea leading in one direction. Although her table was close to the President's, it seemed a mile away. Henry Kissinger's gravelly growl was lost in the general uproar, and the rest of the room blacked out, unimportant. It was as if she and Gang-jo were alone, bobbing on a suddenly tranquil sea. "I hear Zhou En-lai has traveled in the West, particularly France. If you could travel anywhere, would you come to America?"

He nodded. "If it had been possible, I would have come to San Francisco last year, or was it a year or two before when I should have been there?"

"What?" She raised her eyebrows, shrugged.

"I heard your student riots ended in a famous summer."

"Oh! You mean the summer of love," she said without thinking, wishing she could pull the words back, but Gang-jo's eyes were glittering and he was looking at her in a way that was unmistakable. After a moment's hesitation, she said, "Our thoughts seem to be taking the same paths." *But what did she really mean? What did he?*

"I'm thinking of you." His words had a serious ring.

"I, you," she admitted, amazed that she could mouth the words so easily.

A quick smile softened the lines of his face. He nodded slightly, and for a few seconds he looked at her until she turned away, examined the room as if she hadn't seen it before, the vastness, the people, the flags. When she looked back at him, he was properly expressionless, his smile distant as he bade her to have a good trip home, his voice unnaturally loud.

She stared at him, unable to follow the swift change in his demeanor. "Thank you, Mr. Wu," she managed. Was this how it would end?

He started to rise, leaned closer to the table, closer to her, as if it were necessary to get to his feet in one easy motion. "I know where your room is," he said softly. "Wait for me."

Had she heard what she thought she'd heard? Her heart slammed against her ribs. But hadn't they been moving toward this moment from the first? As he went to the next table and stood bidding everyone a safe journey home, she bid good night to the mixed group at her table, left the banquet hall and went to the elevator that sped to her floor. Through large hall windows the increasing bright lights of the city gleamed below. In no time, one of the Chinese diplomats had told her,

Shanghai will challenge the best cities in the world. She had no doubt now. She'd witnessed too much to ever be sanguine about China again.

In her small room she gathered up her American briefing book and stuffed it into the closet, added other American papers, and tried to remain calm. Her legs felt like liquid, her mind billowed and expanded.

After a while, she heard the elevator and opened the door a crack. Gang-jo got off the lift and walked swiftly to where she waited. Smoke curled from a cigarette he held between thumb and forefinger, his watch glittered. He seemed foreign, exotic, forbidden, but somehow familiar. She stepped back so he could enter.

Moving past her, he took hold of the door, shut and locked it before turning to her.

She took a deep breath. If she hadn't slugged down all that *mao tai*, would she be wary, frightened by the cloak and dagger she'd witnessed? But as yearning raced through her, she turned off speculation and smiled up at him.

His answering smile spoke volumes and his words made clear his desires, "I want to see you with your hair down." The words were like a prayer offered to her. He snuffed his cigarette in a glass ashtray and added, "please."

She held up a hand. "First tell me, did my father ask about me?"

"I told him you were very beautiful, very intelligent." He stepped closer to her, his smile like an embrace. "Your hair." His lips warmed her forehead.

Feeling like a woman in an old-time movie, she lifted her arms and took out the pins, loosened the fancy rhinestone barrette and let her hair fall over her shoulders. Once a man from Justice had said she should loosen up, get wild. She had never dated him again.

Gang-jo said, "I read that in a Western novel. I have no experience in these things." He touched her face with his fingertips before running his fingers through her soft tresses. Brushing her cheeks with his lips, he touched her eyelids, tasted her lips.

She felt her legs might buckle beneath her.

"Here, men and women do not even hold hands in public. In China, we get acquainted in the bedroom after we are married." He pulled her closer.

A thought hit her. All Chinese married before they were thirty. "Are you...married?" She pulled away from him.

He said nothing, and she knew he was. "What is she like?"

He shrugged. "She is...nothing like you. She lives in a peasant village. I am assigned to diplomatic affairs. We...have nothing in common." He looked beyond her. "It was a marriage of convenience." His gaze came back to her. "Arranged by my father." Taking a deep breath, he added, "Do you prefer me to go?"

If he left she'd regret it all of her life. "At home people kiss when greeting friends. Hand holding is for lovers," she whispered, putting her hand in his and then touching his arms lightly, feeling the shape of him through that one touch, imagining the rest.

"And do lovers kiss also?"

"Yes."

"Then we are doing what you are used to doing." He kissed her again, the touch light but sweet with promise. He enfolded her, his lips dropping kisses in her hair between words. "To me you are a dream."

"I am very real," she said. "You are the fantasy."

"Again we are in agreement. I was enchanted – is not that the word – from the moment I saw you." Holding her, he moved slowly but resolutely toward the bed, pausing every few feet. "In school we learned that the United States was run by Nazis and the Ku Klux Klan and you, my beautiful American, were either a victim or a victimizer." Sitting on the edge of the bed, he pulled her down next to him. "And now you are here, next to me. A fiction come true. As real as the emotions I feel for you."

His lips found her neck; his hands molded her hips. The room swirled around her, and she lay back, dizzy from the *mao tai* and the thought that this was China and this was treading on dangerous ground, but she had never tasted danger, and she wanted it, craved it now in this man. As his hands worked the buttons of her blouse, she exulted in the moment. Soon she was lying next to him in her lace and satin underwear, and he was laughing a deep throaty laugh.

"I have never seen such decadence," he said touching her bra, running his fingers beneath the band of her satin panties. His eyes gleamed.

"But you like it," she said, enjoying his admiration.

"There are things for the masses, things for others." He freed her breasts from the bra's constraints.

"You sound like a capitalist."

"Never." He grinned and threw off his own clothing and once more reached for her panties. She felt drugged, exhausted, but very alive, eyeing his strong body, admiring it as he admired her. Someday she'd tell her grandchildren about the Chinese Mandarin who had wooed her. But no, this was no Mandarin, this was a Communist and this was 1972, not something from a book.

Afterward, her blood pulsed gently, and her body tingled. They had come together in a way more gratifying, more natural than she had ever known before. His ginseng aroma clung to her; she tasted it in her mouth, recalled his taste, his gentle love terms, the Chinese words seeming so right. She ran her hands over his chest. He lit a cigarette, and she watched, fascinated by the movements of his hands and mouth, so innocent and ordinary at their task, yet sublimely sensual. When his head shifted in her direction, she took a deep breath.

"My home is in a village you would not understand. No forest, no trees, no beauty. My father and I left when I was young. I grew up loyal to Mao, loyal to the Red Guards, loyal to the thought of China. Now, I question all I see, but the questions are in my head."

"Don't say anything that will bring you trouble later," she whispered.

For a time he regarded her through a wreath of smoke as shifting as morning mists. "You are like a willow bud bursting into life." His voice was soft with feeling.

"Are you a poet, too?"

"You make me feel like one. I want to make love to you again. This time will be better. We are no longer strangers."

"I don't agree with your definition, but I agree to your proposal," she said laughter bubbling from some deep well within her. She kissed the hollow spot near his neck. No, she could never tell her grandchildren about this.

Gang-jo's love banished the ocean that separated their countries, made little of the political differences. As faint touches of dawn came in over the waterfront, Christine said, "Besides my father, did you ever know other Americans?" She wanted to trust him, to cry out that love could cross all barriers.

"China has had many American friends. I was named after your General, Vinegar Joe."

"General Stillwell?"

"Yes, only my father didn't know Jo contained an E. We Chinese adopted a pinyin alphabet in 1958 but it wasn't official and still isn't. Most people don't know about it."

"I know. Pinyin, meaning an amalgamation of sounds like our alphabet."

"Ah, but you're not most people." His smile bathed her.

"And is my father an important man?"

"Once. Now, he has much responsibility but little power." He got up, began putting his clothes on slowly, methodically.

Christine sat up, reached for her robe. The floor felt cold to her bare feet. She balanced for a while on one foot and then the other, padded around the bed to his side.

He laughed and pulled her into his arms again. "A little cold won't hurt. Your father was a strong man. In the early years he was with the Liberation Army. And you, my American sweetmeat, are water to a man who thirsts." He kissed her again.

She put her head on his shoulder, not wanting to hear the words that came so easily to his lips. Her father, a stranger, was a Communist. Gang-jo was a Communist.

He hugged her close before stepping away. "I must go."

She still knew the feel of his hands upon her, of the muscles in his chest flattening her breasts, of his hips thrusting hard against her. She felt let down.

His gaze came down to meet hers.

She'd never known there were Chinese his height.

He shook his head. "I am sorry. I am rude rushing off like a peasant with no manners." He looked past the top of her head. "If I stayed until the sun touched all your secret places, it would be known I wasn't in my room. I cannot take that chance."

Reality striking again, she stiffened her spine.

"I want you to know, Christine Wainwright, I will never forget you or this night. But one cannot work a dead water buffalo, or make the willow buds bloom in winter. What has been can never be again. It saddens me." Gently, he lifted a strand of hair from her face, ran his fingers down its length and said. "I have thought and thought how we can be together and always I come up against a locked moon gate. I see myself on one side looking through. The view is limitless, over an ocean, past cities, but I never find you." He moved to the door.

She followed, the trembling inside her beginning again. "We have a saying, where there's a will, there's a way."

"So American." He smiled, and then reverting to Chinese said. "*Zai jin*."

She was leaving for home in hours. Since meeting they had often spoken Chinese, but in her room he had used English only until now. She could not answer his goodbye; the soft click of the door closing sounded like a gunshot. She put her luggage on the bed, packed and tried not to think of him. She had taken part in a wonderful historical moment, and she must put that first.

She bathed, dressed, and waiting for the call saying her car had arrived, she read the note from her father.

My dear daughter,

Fate has ways of working that are not always clear.

I will write to you by way of a friend in Hong Kong.

Until then remember that a father's love goes with you.

Logan Wainwright.

She hoped a dove gray morning promised a luminescent day.

Chapter 4
Logan

The People's Republic of China –1947

House arrest in1972 nearing an end, Logan allowed himself to think about Christine. He had attempted to draw out Gang-jo, but as with everyone in China today, he had been taciturn, having put himself in jeopardy attempting to arrange a meeting. He said only that Christine spoke Chinese well, had shown interest in seeing her father. He had stared at Logan with a closed expression. To ask further would have been futile. Gang-jo needed to protect himself as much as Logan needed to be circumspect. He had lived with the thought of his daughter next to his heart too many years to risk antagonizing the one person who could possibly help him.

He had left Seattle in 1947. Crossing the ocean, he had felt renewed, excited, as if time had turned backwards, and once more anything was possible. Life was opening up, offering new possibilities, and when he returned to America, little Christine would be waiting. She'd given him a reason for living. In some way, he'd always miss Nancy, his first love, his wife. But the mourning that had descended on him was taking its rightful place in the past. As the ship plowed through a roiling sea that made grizzled sailors reel, he watched clear-eyed for signs of land. During the War, his ability to remain calm under stress had brought admiration as well as responsibility. Now, a civilian, change was like a seed within him, ready to grow. He leaned against the railing and squinted into the dawn.

He'd always been quietly envious of people with siblings and extended family. Popular and admired, he had stayed a little apart, sensing a difference others apparently didn't see. During college his aloofness, coupled, he supposed, with his looks and good grades, drew attention. He was courted by fraternities and confided in by professors with leftist leanings. He partied with the first and listened to the others, but the loneliness persisted until he met Nancy. With World War II on the horizon, he'd loved her wholeheartedly. But during four years of marriage, he'd been gone more than he was home, helping make the world free of fascism. An inebriated driver, celebrating the end of the fighting, had careened through a crosswalk, struck and dragged Nancy like a rag doll for two blocks. It had taken almost two years to get over her loss.

When he spotted gulls wheeling overhead, he strained to see more, but nothing except trash washed from a distant beach sloshed against the side of the ship. Would this be just another episode in life or something meaningful? Leaving little Christine had been hard, but she was too young to know, and he'd send for her later or return to her with his yearning for the past gone.

Land finally meeting his gaze, he watched as the ship steamed up the Yangtze River toward Shanghai. Drinking in the rawness of the air, gulping the lingering sea smell, he absorbed the feel of China. Squat thatch-roofed houses and wattle and daub buildings topping the river bluffs shot into view. Women tended cooking fires, hauled water from the river, and men in long gowns did a form of calisthenics, their movements so graceful he felt a moment of awe. Cigarettes in hand, other men hacked and spit while small children casually pulled aside split trousers to relieve themselves. Logan shook his head in amazement. He'd wanted a change of scene, some place totally different, and this was certainly it. Vintage trucks and cars raced full throttle down narrow dirt roads. Great swirls of dust rose behind the vehicles and obscured for a while tall buildings on the horizon, rising ten or fifteen stories.

As the ship glided by wharves and docks lining the river, the buildings of the downtown area came into focus. Modern offices and apartments looked down on piers sheltering an ever-changing population of boats. While his steamer maneuvered into place beside a ferry, he rushed forward, not wanting to miss anything. He'd accepted Freddy's offer. Freddy, who had done duty in Hawaii with him, was starting an English language paper in Shanghai, and Logan would be in on the ground floor.

He smiled genuinely for the first time in weeks. Junks with rainbow-colored sails rode the water beside majestic ocean liners, oily tramp steamers, and foreign warships bristling with guns. Gripping the rail, Logan shook his head in astonishment. By contrast, the waterfront in Seattle, where he'd said goodbye to little Christine and Nancy's sister, Betty, seemed sharp and mechanistic, too modern.

On the pier below, and on adjacent streets, people on foot, on bicycles, in pedicabs and trolleys jammed the walks and alleyways, peered from all manner of conveyances and buildings, their voices mingling in a rapid-fire barrage—melodious, raucous, unending. Shocked by the vast number of people, annoyed because he understood so little of what he heard, Logan stared, and a tingle of renewed energy raced through him. People swarmed the streets like bees buzzing around a hive. At first they seemed alike, different from him, but similar to one another. Then he saw that they were far from homogenous. Elegant passengers sat in isolated splendor in long shiny limousines or entered fancy, modern buildings, while on the street ragged urchins begged and workers started their day.

Even as the noisy scene irritated him with its sense of bedlam—loudspeakers blaring Chinese opera, horns tooting, people shouting—the force of the scene fascinated him, and the vitality intrigued him. Leaning against the railing, he drank it in as if it were water and he was thirsty. Sun, filtered by clouds and haze, softened harsh lines, one scene flowing into another effortlessly, endlessly.

Far back on the dock, he spied Freddy Patterson. In his brown gabardine suit and white shirt, his wide blue and yellow striped tie, he looked out of place among the workers with their tunics, trousers, and soft shoes, or the sprinkling of Chinese businessmen in their dark Western suits.

Freddy's gaze climbed to the ship above, and a smile lifted the lines of his long face. "Hey, Logan! Welcome to Shanghai," he shouted.

Logan wrinkled his nose as the wind shifted, and the odor from a "honey" barge with its load of human excrement drifted by. Watching Freddy's progress through the masses of people, Logan grabbed his suitcases and started down the gangplank. Smoke and steam rose from curbside stalls. Peddlers and hawkers cried their wares, and beggars, their clothes patched and tattered, held out their hands. Greeted by shopkeepers, nodded at by others, women in traditional long sheath gowns darted glances as the tall ungainly foreigner rushed by them all.

Logan waited where bare-chested stevedores were already unloading cargo from the ship. As Freddy flagged down a taxi, he plunged into the swirling mass of people to join his new partner. They talked non-stop until the car came to a stop in front of a tall, shabby building in what had been the Japanese concessions.

"It's not the best area. There was some heavy fighting here before the Japs pulled out. But it's fairly cheap, and here I can work, eat, and play without going outside." Freddy led the way up four flights of stairs.

On the landings, Logan edged past men and women squatted over chess boards or stoves. A thick pall of smoke rose from cigarettes and cooking fires.

"Once this was strictly an office building. There aren't any kitchens," Freddy pointed out. "They use the landings as additional rooms." He rolled his eyes. "Watch your step. You almost annihilated a kid."

"No shit!"

Freddy winked, threw laughter over his shoulder.

Logan grinned. Freddy would be good for him.

"The elevator stopped working after I moved in. I complained to the people in Chiang Kaishek's office, but they just laughed. I'm told the French still control the electric lines, the British run most of the shipping and banking, and we Americans are getting our licks in, too." Freddy unlocked a door and said, "My office."

Magazines, newspapers, books, and typewriters covered three battered desks. A hand-cranked adding machine, mimeograph equipment, purple ink, and other supplies were piled on ersatz shelves in a closet-sized room. Another room contained an old-fashioned printing press. Posters proclaiming the ageless charms of China plastered the walls.

Freddy opened another door. "I live in here."

Logan followed him into three small rooms jammed with overstuffed furniture, lacquered Chinese tables, and inlaid screens. A kitchen of sorts had been jerry-rigged in the smallest room—a sink emptied into a bucket beneath the drain. Curtained shelves held canned food; a glass-fronted cabinet held good china.

"I like a bit of luxury," Freddy said, opening doors to show his suits hanging neatly in a French armoire; his shoes, all shining and in good repair, properly treed. "You can sleep on the couch until you find yourself a flat. This one has modern facilities." He threw open a door to the bathroom. A pull chain dangled above the toilet; the tub came with huge claw feet; the shower had a stationary head. "I have a cook, a houseboy, and a woman to clean. Cheap Chinese labor. Anyway, I like having people around as you'll see."

Entertaining was part of the business process, Freddy explained, leading Logan back to the largest room, a cluttered rectangle that looked almost elegant in lamplight. Scrolls and wall hangings hid most of the cracks in the plaster. A Persian carpet covered three-fourths of the scarred floor.

Logan shook his head in admiration.

"It's not the Ritz, but it serves," Freddy said with a slightly defensive air as Logan grew silent. "They all come here:

Europeans, Americans, Chinese, people wanting a bit of adventure, others out to make a fast buck. I gather them together and then listen. Makes for good copy." Freddy opened faded draperies. The large windows framed a view of the river and beyond that to the lowlands leading to the sea. "When it gets hot I have a breeze, and when it gets cold, I just add another charcoal brazier. Come on, sit down, I'll tell you what I have in mind."

Late one day three months later, when Logan entered Freddy's, a murmur of voices came from Freddy's free-flowing salon. On the threshold Logan hesitated, The New Citizens, the article he'd finally completed, in his hands. It had been difficult. He'd felt done in by the constant need to repeat to get his points across in any Chinese conversation. Even when he made no mistakes with diction, the Chinese didn't understand him. Surprised to find a tall, large American speaking their tongue, they giggled or looked at him with suspicion. Twice Logan had been the center of a babbling, pointing throng of Chinese. Although he'd finally found a flat, gotten his laundry done and hired a cook and cleaning woman, that wasn't the same as conducting interviews and putting out a magazine. He'd relied heavily on a White Russian, a German Jew, and a Chinese man born and educated in the U.S. Logan said as much to Freddy when he gave him the article, his gaze spanning the room. People of all ages, sexes and nationalities filled the couches and chairs, drank tea or gin and tonic, talked all at once, and laughed often.

Freddy perused the pages, frowned and then getting up

said, "My boy, are you sure your translation is correct? You need a tutor, someone to show you the finer points of the language so you don't make a real faux pas."

Ruefully, Logan agreed.

As Freddy crossed the room, speaking to friends, introducing Logan, refilling glasses, a woman rose. She was part of a group of Chinese women clustered at the other end of the room, all of them speaking in quick, animated sentences. She stood out from the others, their standard prettiness made drab by contrast. In the soft light her long, body-hugging dress glowed like rich, full wine, and her luxuriant hair, dressed in braids and bunched at the back of her head, shone like black coral set around the porcelain of her face. Her composure and elegance seemed soothing among the boisterous, always fast-talking crowd. As Freddy turned the pages of Logan's essay, Logan strained to hear her voice among the many voices talking exports and imports, business and politics, music and art. She made her points softly, but swiftly, and he recognized a smattering of French dropped into the flow of Chinese and English.

So much about her reminded him of Nancy. Her skin had that same pale porcelain look of fragility belying the overwhelming strength underneath. Nancy had lived long enough to tell him he'd find someone like her. That he should believe in reincarnation. She had injected a note of levity when he was overcome with grief. They'd both smiled. Now, Logan felt his heart beat accelerate. Over three years since he'd lost Nancy.

Quietly, in a social ballet orchestrated by subtle signals, the woman and Freddy changed places. Aware of her in a gut-wrenching way that had nothing to do with speech or cultural differences, Logan held his breath in anticipation.

"Lin Sulin," she said, announcing her name in the Chinese way.

Following her style, he said, "Wainwright, Logan," and made room for her next to him on the sofa.

"Freddy say you speak Chinese," she said sitting down, amusement in her eyes.

"Poorly." She was like air scrubbed clean by rain.

"You will improve," she said in English. "I speak to you in Chinese and English."

He grinned at her. "English with a British accent."

"Poorly also. But my father, he believe in education for women. I am most fortunate." She crossed her legs delicately.

"That's evident," he said trying not to look her over. Her clothes were expensive, her heels high, her manner assured. "Tell me about your father."

"He teach me to read and to enjoy classic literature. When I apply at the university in Shanghai, much to my astonishment, for I am very poor in many subjects, they accept me."

"They don't take girls?"

"Oh, no. Well brought up girls do not leave home. I was one of first at university. Perhaps, as you would say, a test case. But now, they don't like me so much."

"I can't imagine that." Sandalwood, he thought, identifying the faint scent that rose so beguilingly from her. He let his eyes speak, not flirting like he would have with a girl at home, but letting her know his admiration.

If she noticed, she paid no attention but answered him in all seriousness and in English. "Oh, but it is true. I point out bad things in Chiang Kai-shek's government. They don't like this. I am force to leave university." She giggled and covered her mouth with her hands. "I am bad."

Logan shook his head. He had become fiercely patriotic during the War to defeat Hitler, Tojo. "Wait a minute. Our government backs Chiang Kai-shek. Millions of dollars of American goods and equipment, stuff left over from the Pacific theater, sits in warehouses here."

Sulin shook her head even more emphatically and looked up at him through her eyelashes as she took a cigarette from a silver case.

Surprised, he said, "You smoke. Not many women do."

She smiled. "I do not inhale, only puff like a movie star." She shrugged.

He lit her cigarette and said, "Tell me why you don't like Chiang?" Since the War, he had never heard anyone question the role of the Generalisimo.

She cocked her head as if considering, and then said brightly. "No, I'll tell you instead why I like your American novelists." Her back was straight, not touching the couch.

"You've read American books?"

"Of course. Haven't you read Chinese novels?'

He laughed, seeing the challenge in her eyes, the sense of fun. "No. What have you read in English?"

"I particularly like your Mr. Fitzgerald. I do not understand the decadence of the characters, but I think I understand the impression of the men and the women. Roman- tic, I believe you say." She smiled at him, fixing him with a look similar to the one he had given her earlier.

He was enchanted. "Why won't you explain what you meant about Chiang Kai-shek?"

She stubbed out her cigarette. "It would take much time."

"I have all night."

She shook her head. "I don't, Mr. Wainwright." She held out a slim hand. "To talk with you was very nice, but I must go now." With polite phrases and a wave of the hand, she left.

"Where does she live?" Logan asked when he and Freddy were alone again, snifters of brandy warming in their hands, the lights of the city winking below.

"Lin Sulin? I don't know."

"But surely you know something about her."

Smiling, Freddy nodded. "She's editor of a small magazine, *Shanghai Arts*. It's beautiful and prestigious, but no one can afford it now." He stretched his legs out in front of him. "In case you're still interested in opening up a branch office in Beijing, she's agreed to tutor you in Chinese."

She had known about him, Logan thought, his interest quickening.

The next day he waited for her outside the *Shanghai Arts* office.

When she came out, she said, matter-of-factly. "In there it is—what you say?—hectic? Money is gone. We shut down. No more magazine." Even though she was out of a job, the smile she turned on him was serene, friendly.

Logan said, "I'm sorry. If I could help I would, but…" He shook his head, waited a beat before asking, "Can I take you to tea?"

She raised her eyebrows slightly. "How British. I think Americans drink coffee."

"We do, but I thought you'd prefer tea." If she decided she didn't want him as a pupil, would he grovel, plead with her?

"At least all Chinese drink tea in the movies."

"So you learn from movies, too. I learn about treatment of Indian people in America. I know about your Lone Ranger. He was bad to his friend, Tonto. He never gave him any lines." Her eyes glittered.

He chuckled, his sense of relief vast.

She took his arm, apparently oblivious to the stares from passersby.

Logan led her toward a restaurant down the block. "Aren't you pushing things, taking my arm, even being seen with a big-footed foreigner?"

"Lin Sulin does what she pleases. Once they arrested me for holding a boy's hand. Now, Chiang's people do not know what to do about anything. You Americans prop up—is that not the correct expression— Chiang's corrupt regime, and Chiang does not dare to anger Americans. It is simple, you and I could do practically anything." She tossed her head. Her hair which she wore loose that day, danced around her shoulders...like Nancy's had done.

"Really?" That Chiang was a hero to most Americans seemed irrelevant now.

"No, but almost. But we must hurry if I am to teach you good Chinese, make a refined foreigner out of you."

He tucked her hand closer under his arm, and during a lunch of steamed buns and rice and cup after cup of fragrant tea, he marveled continuously. She seemed unafraid of the future. Yet, she couldn't be more than mid-twenties, young to be so coolly self-possessed while out of a job, but old not to be married. In the Orient arranged marriage abounded. He looked around. The air was thick with the smell of cooking oil and cigarette smoke. "What will you do now that the magazine's dead?"

"I am not sure. My parents are with their ancestors, and my brothers are with Chiang. I am alone."

"Like me. I don't have any family here and very few in the states. We weren't a prolific bunch." He said the words easily, but he felt as if they were weighted with lead, the last time he'd seen Christine still fresh in his mind. Before Sulin could react, he added, "You talk like your brothers don't count." He couldn't talk about his daughter—not yet.

She smiled slightly. "It makes me sad knowing they are with the Generalisimo. Chiang never fought the Japanese, but he attacked the people who did. His own people!" Although she spoke softly, her eyes flashed. Leaning closer to him, she added, "He makes money from the misery of others, and Madame Chiang sleeps on silk sheets while people starve."

Logan poured more tea, and for a moment it was almost as if he were in a college dorm arguing world affairs. "So if you don't back Chiang, whom do you back?"

"There are some who would change the old order. No more number two wives. No more concubines." Her chin lifted defiantly.

"I see. Is it true you were arrested for holding a man's hand?" He stretched out his legs, and inadvertently touched hers.

She pulled hers back. "Speak Chinese, please. This is a lesson."

"If so, you haven't said a word about grammar and structure, and you've mostly spoken English." He sent her a teasing look.

Her back became ruler straight. "These are strange times, Mr. Wainwright. I tell you things in degree of importance."

He grinned. "You're pretty when you're serious." So many

years since he'd felt this lighthearted.

She glared at him. "Do not patronize me, Mr. Wainwright. I am not old order woman."

Considering, he nodded slowly, "I'm not interested in binding women's feet."

"I'm not interested in binding ambitions. Chiang would hold people down." She stared imperiously at Logan.

He stared back, taking the look toward something from which he couldn't retreat, and didn't want to, a longing that went past the man/woman thing developing between them. Her words made him want to look deeper than the surface.

She lowered her eyelids and folded her hands and then, peeking from beneath the fringe of her eyes met his gaze and, seemingly startled, looked down again.

Scarcely breathing, Logan whispered, "Maybe we should get on with the lesson."

"That would be fine." She took rice paper from a leather case, set out brushes and ink and made several interwoven marks on the paper. "This is *fan*."

"Rice."

She raised her eyebrows. "So you read characters, too." She made another few strokes. "And this is *fan*, too. To buy, to sell, as a peddler. All the same syllable. And this is also *fan*, meaning a model, a pattern, and this.... And don't scowl at me. It is necessary to determine how much you really know, or whether you merely parrot words and sounds."

Seeing the effort it took for her to act stern with him, he said, "Of course," and began to laugh. "Truthfully, I memorized a few characters, mostly the one for the men's toilets *Cesuo*."

She ducked her head, hid her mouth and after a short time, she laughed along with him.

After that at the end of each lesson, Sulin seemed as reluctant as he to leave. Lingering to talk, her conversation ranged from music and art to politics and people, and each time Logan found himself in agreement with her, he felt a knot of anxiety some- where deep within him unwind. She smiled often, and once he took her hand, lifting the fingers singly as if they were digits made of a rare material not before handled but seen from afar.

Sulin told him when her parents died she'd been crazy with disappointment when her brothers weren't interested in her thoughts or ideas.

Logan said his father had been a shadow figure, symbolic, loved, but dying when Logan was pre-teen, his mother a mentor and friend until she died when he was in college. There'd been no other family. Then he'd married. It was the first time he mentioned Nancy to anyone. "She is gone, too."

"You loved her very much." Her words were gently spoken.

"I did." As he told the story, Sulin's eyes misted, and her hand fluttered over his and touched fleetingly. He half expected to see a stigmata or something to show that she had touched him.

She conducted the next lesson in her flat. Unlike Freddy's, the two rooms were bare of all but essentials. "I do not want to become attached to objects," she explained. "I am too attracted to pretty things. It is my failing."

"You deserve pretty things, Sulin," he said seriously.

She shook her head. "In the New China all women will be pretty. All people will share. No more beggars. No more party girls. No more Mandarins in big black cars." She put paper and brushes on the scrubbed kitchen table, added cups with lids. A sink without drain-boards, open shelves, a three-burner stove crowded the corner. She took a seat opposite him at the table. "Before we review, I must say, given names are used only between close friends, Logan. *Ni dong bu dong?*"

"Yes, I understand," he answered, the words catching in his throat. As she continued with the lesson as if she had communicated nothing of importance, he had trouble concentrating. A faint aroma like that of dried flowers carried to him whenever she moved to refresh their tea from the large thermos or to get books from the bedroom nearby. He glimpsed a single bed, a low chest, a satin wall hanging, the latter incongruous in the Spartan surroundings.

When she came back, he took the book from her hands and set it down and led her into the sleeping room. For a second her eyes showed surprise and then satisfaction, and a small, almost secret smile ran like water across her lips.

In bed, she was all the things he wanted from a woman and more, her body an instrument of delight, her mind a channel to new thoughts. As he drew from her responses that made him feel invincible, she said in English, "I told you, I am not traditional Chinese woman."

If that was a flaw, he worshipped it. Kissing her shoulder, her neck, the flat spot between her breasts, he murmured. "I do not want a traditional woman." He wanted her, for now, for always. He started to tell her about Christine, but then decided to wait until later. Would a non-traditional woman be interested in some other woman's child?

"A traditional woman has no say. If she is lucky she learns to love the man selected for her, and he dictates her every move. Most are not lucky." She looked up at him. "Maybe you will leave me, like a Chinese Madame Butterfly."

"No," he said, "I will never leave you." And suddenly, he knew the words were true. Wherever he went, he wanted her with him. "Now tell me how to say this in Chinese." He touched her breasts. "And this." He touched her waist. "And this." He let his hands trail down her body.

After a while she quit translating, and he quit talking. He was a swimmer in a foreign sea, and she floated within reach, tantalizing but different, and he didn't care if he drowned; he needed her very much.

As the weeks went by he knew moments so precious he held his breath for fear they would dissolve like soap bubbles. Although it seemed they had all the time in the world, he knew too well time had a way of running out.

"Be careful," Freddy warned one day. "Do not get too entangled with Lin Sulin. Time's are changing."

Logan scowled, the two of them at typewriters banging out copy for Freddy's paper. He felt peeved with Freddy for his unchanging expression and appearance, his elegant clothes a stark reminder of the tattered, ragged masses that kept pouring into the city. "Are you calling Sulin a Communist? We all sympathize with the Communists in some way, don't we?" He unhooked the E that always stuck and continued typing, the sound loud in the small room.

"No, I don't mean she's a hanger-on, or sympathetic to," Freddy said, his voice just as calm and cultured sounding as always. "She's a Communist. Capital C. Watch yourself. I mean a little pink is fine, but red? The talk is she wrote articles decrying the wealth of certain Chinese who are friends with Chiang. She was teaching at the time. They forced her to resign."

Logan had seen posters plastered on walls denouncing the government, heard the talk, had seen soldiers frisking peasants, but he rationalized it had nothing to do with him.

One day he planned a dinner at his apartment, brought in pork stirred with vegetables, found a bottle of French wine, bought flowers from the stall across the city, and planned how to tell Sulin of his love. She showed up three hours late. "Where were you?" His words nailed her in the doorway.

She said nothing, merely set about warming up the food. "*Duibuqi,* sorry, I prefer not to talk about it now."

Shortly afterward he noticed people on street corners handing out flyers protesting the economy and the government. Others, who appeared too tired to protest, spouted slogans for a fee. All disappeared when Chiang's police stomped into sight.

Evidence of corruption shrieked loudly as more beggars crowded the streets, more sing-song girls beckoned from alleys, more men rode in long, black limousines. After a while, Logan went to a meeting with her and came away with the impression Sulin's friends were like any other group of idealistic people. They discussed Kant and Mill, controversial theories sometimes derided, sometimes held up as solutions to everyday problems. Mostly the talk sounded like a college discussion on a cold winter day.

"Freddy says your friends are Communists," Logan said one night after wine had flowed and talk had escalated, few disputing the most radical speakers. Communism, seldom mentioned while the war against Germany and Japan was fought, had become a word of derision in the States.

Sulin said. "During the war Communist Russia was America's ally." Her words were spoken naturally, almost as if she were saying, you eat rice today but you ate potatoes yesterday.

Logan had trouble seeing past the blurred political lines. "Are you a Communist?"

"I do not think in labels," she answered, seemingly unperturbed by the question. "I think in terms of people."

It was a logic he could understand. His mother, with her patrician ways, had routinely given to those less fortunate, and going a step further in her effort to educate him beyond what he learned in school, each summer, from the time he was nine, she had sent him to a summer camp she subsidized. He had learned to live without the many things he had taken for granted, and in college, to the amazement of his fraternity buddies, he spoke out for the disadvantaged.

Logan frowned. In college he had at times supported Communist positions merely to shock others, something the smart crowd did. His mother had been a capitalist at heart, as were all his friends. But when Sulin talked about equality and fraternity, the words echoed with a different meaning. Still, could it be that much different?

That night, afraid of what he might learn, afraid she'd leave him, Logan told Sulin he wanted her no matter what.

He told her so from half a room away, without the complications of touch and taste.

"No matter what Freddy said?" Half-taunting him, she rose to belt a silk robe around her slender body. "Words are only words. Deeds are important. *Ni dong bu dong?*"

"If communists are like you, then I want to know them." He looked past her to the spare and cold apartment made warm by her being there, the words tossed out easily, meaning only that he loved her. "I want to learn, to differentiate between labels and actual philosophy. If you will teach me."

Without artifice, without sidewise glances, without any of the wiles she used so well, Sulin said, her face solemn, "Once all Chinese love come after marriage, or never come. But with you, I know from first."

"I love you," he said, his voice equally sober.

"And I you." She ran to him, her eyes gleaming. "I pledge love for you, Logan Wainwright." She laughed, snuggled into his arms.

At times during the following days he felt as if he were disowning all he'd ever treasured, but most of the time he felt as if he were flying above the crowd, part of a privileged elite allied to a most glamorous, beautiful, knowledgeable woman. Life was a game fueled by food, wine and unending talk with smart young people and moneyed older ones. They talked and discussed politics and philosophy as if it were an intellectual exercise, his Chinese improving daily as was Sulin's English.

Slowly he learned of the pamphlets and flyers Sulin composed and others distributed secretly, tacking them against walls and fences after dark. But mostly he learned about Chinese activities from English correspondents who came back from behind Communist lines. Congregated in smoky bars, reporters who had "scooped" their competitors, spoke in clipped British accents. The reporters brought legitimacy to Mao, who was fighting Chiang and his troops. Logan went home with words like gallantry and valor ringing in his ears.

One night, late coming back to his apartment, Sulin wasn't there, but two Chinese officials with cold eyes and smart uniforms met him outside his door.

"Mr. Wainwright, Colonel Wang," said one as they approached from right and left, boxing him in. "You know Wu Huixia?"

"Who?" Logan shook his head and looked from one man to the other for a clue. "The name means nothing to me." He relaxed, took out his key, unlocked his door. It was easy to speak the truth.

"We have heard that is not so." Colonel Wang pushed through the door to Logan's flat.

Freddy had helped him furnish the rooms with couches and gilt-trimmed chairs, left over from the French. "Decadent," Sulin had said the first time she'd seen them, "but pretty." He loved her honesty. Did Chiang's people have her? They could break her slender body as easily as he bent a chopstick. "What is it you want?" Logan asked.

"Only to look around."

"Don't you need a search warrant or something. That's how we do it in America." Good god, if they had Sulin.

"Ah, but you're not in America." Moving purposefully past Logan, Wang strode into the bedroom where he gave a cursory look around before opening and rummaging through drawers, turning back quilts on the brass bed, and pulling clothes from wall hooks. Toiletries were strewn over the floor, a bottle of after-shave “accidentally” spilled.

Back in the front room, the colonel swept books from shelves, let manuscripts flutter to the floor. Smiling at Logan he took a cigarette from a pack, lit it and dropped the burnt match on the carpet. Through a puff of smoke, his eyes narrowing he said, “You don’t know Wu Huixia, but you know Lin Sulin.” His smile mocked Logan.

Wanting to strong-arm the man from his apartment, Logan pulled a cigarette from a pack and took his time lighting it. Pointedly, he placed the spent match in an ashtray and inhaling deeply he looked back at the officer. “Yes, I know her. So what?”

“She pretty lady,” Wang said in English. “Go to many parties, see many people.” He smiled. With his heel he ground out his cigarette on the rug. “Strange, how you can like such a one.”

Were they even now going through her things, ripping her clothes apart looking for hidden messages, emptying out drawers, touching her? His jaw tightening, Logan decided if they had her, they’d say so, taunt him with it. “Get out of my house before I throw you out.” He spoke softly but firmly.

“Be careful, Yank, or we throw you out of China. And you never come back. Good night.” The Colonel smiled broadly.

A few hours later Sulin came to him across the roof. Hearing a tapping on the windowpane, he opened the window, pulled her in and held her until she stopped trembling.

“The police have woman on her way to warn me. They interrogate her. Eventually, she will tell about me.”

“What can she tell that they don’t already know?” he whispered, his mind racing, planning a route home. Overland to Hong Kong, proceed from there.

"I relay messages. On radio. She, too. They can shoot her as spy."

He stared at her, unspoken words beating like a gong in his head. *If they caught Sulin, they could execute her.* In months she had made every other woman appear slight and insignificant, the same but different from Nancy, a similar delicacy, sweetness, and interest in bettering society. He could not leave her. "We can book passage on a British ship and be on our way home." In Seattle, their house would be a Mecca of intellectual enlightenment.

"To America? But my home is here."

Seeing nothing but the long lonely years without her , he looked aside.

She put her hand on his arm, the touch light as down, her look gentle. "Why did you go to war?"

"Because I had to, to make the world better, safer."

"Yes," she said as if she had achieved a major victory. "And now I have to join the comrades with Mao. Make China better, safer." His thoughts raced. Living without her was not an option. "Marry me."

She looked at him with surprise as if it had been decided already. "I doubt they take you unless we are married."

So she had planned on him going with her! The knowledge both pleased and bothered. His chances of going home diminished, he realized he had both won and lost. But the unrest in the country, in the world, could not last. In the future, he and Sulin could go back to Seattle, join Christine, be a family together.

“It is fate, Logan Wainwright,”she said laughing, the sound tinkling up and down the scale like music.

The next day he signed his name alongside hers in the marriage registry. Afterward she threw her arms at the sky as if encompassing it and him. “Mr. and Mrs. Logan Wainwright,” she cried, “Lin Sulin and her husband.” Her face was wreathed in smiles.

Still, he knew on some plane he could not quite fathom, some part of her was separate from him, more Chinese than wife. Looking out over the rooftops to the sea, he thought, tomorrow he would write to Christine. But what could he say? Daddy loves you? That he was temporarily joining the Communists, a thing that didn’t sound as bad as it did at home. Maybe not writing would be best. He would write later when his thoughts were clear, the images precise.

“Congratulations,” Freddy said after the signing, “but if I fathom it correctly, you better make yourselves scarce soon. If things go the way they seem to be, contact me at this address in Hong Kong, where I maintain an apartment.” He handed Logan a small printed card.

That evening as Logan and Sulin waited with friends, word came by messenger, from behind the Chinese lines, from high in the aristocracy of Chinese Communism. Wu Huixia, an assistant to Zhou En-lai, welcomed their comrade, Lin Sulin, and her husband, Logan Wainwright. Wu would escort them behind the lines without delay. And hereinafter, among the Chinese, Logan Wainwright would be known as Wai Liang, good foreigner.

Chapter 5

Christine

Washington, D.C., 1972

Back home Christine swirled through an almost never-ending flurry of parties. Washington hostesses vied for the honor of hosting the President and all who had gone to China. Christine had never been so busy, the administration and professors at Georgetown University lauded her, and she knew tenure would be offered. Her classes suddenly filled to overflowing, everyone wanting to sit in. Once *Pictorial Parade* showed her on the same stage with President Nixon, she became a celebrity. Her picture appeared in a group photo on the cover of *Washington Reports,* and *Capital Fancy* printed several shots from the Beijing zoo with her in two of the frames. Everywhere she went people fawned, questioned, feted. She had gone to the fabled land and returned.

It was as hard to explain China to the U.S. as to explain the U.S. to China. Life was an expanding bubble rising on the air like a Chinese box kite full of air. She had difficulty getting back into her D.C. life. Dr. Taylor had died while she was gone, and she found herself not only missing him but also filling in for him when a Chinese speaker needed translating. It was all very heady stuff. Even so she felt like an actor playing a part. Her part in the China story had been small, most of it beneath the surface, but for days images of Gang-jo rose at odd moments. She dreamed of him, wondered about her father, each man beyond her reach But most of the time she was too busy to think about either. No letters had come from Logan. No word from or about Gang-jo. She didn't know whether she had expected any or not. In time, she supposed, all memories grow dim.

And then China wasn't news anymore, the insatiable appetite for the new and different had moved on, China seemingly forgotten by everyone except a special few. The war in Vietnam was dragging on. President Nixon's accolades were forgotten as his administration came under fire for political chicanery at home. Memories of the historic trip fading, six weeks passed in a blur of days as she fit back into her old life. One day, speaking about Chinese art to a group of students, she suddenly stopped mid-sentence, realizing all the facts and the polite phrases of the past had nothing to do with the China of today, for in that gut-wrenching moment, she acknowledged to herself she was pregnant. After she dealt with the usual clutch of students who lingered after class, she allowed the night Gang-jo spent with her to race full speed through her mind. She'd never been able to tolerate the pill. In the romantic haze of all that had happened she'd submerged the memory of the bright rubber condom breaking, never admitting the possibility of his seed taking hold.

The thought stunned her. A child! She hugged herself, studied her reflection, and touched her tummy. She couldn't be pregnant; didn't look pregnant. Besides, she was single. A child of China? It seemed unreal. She struggled to remember everything. At every meeting a sense of excitement had prevailed. Everyone had known the significance of the American/Sino relations. She and Gang-jo had been no different. That night of love she'd learned snippets of Gang-jo's past. He'd thought of distant places at four years of age. He'd been the village scribe before he was ten, forced to marry at twenty-one. He'd known her father, tried to help her, but many times he had repeated the Party line and remained as unreadable and as distant as the miles separating her from him.

She mulled her options. Abortion in the District was illegal, but some women went to New York where it was possible to obtain a safe operation. She knew no one who had gone, at least anyone who had talked about it. She began a clandestine search, read phone books, talked to doctors, colleagues, asked people who might know. The answers skirted the issue but never revealed useful information.

"You aren't...?" one woman said, the Ladies Room mirror echoing her shock. "Oh, no, just wondering. I was reading a book." The woman relaxed visibly. "My maid says jumping off a roof should do it." She laughed. The word, abortion, still held connotations of illicit sex, back alley procedures, possible death. Washington insider gossip drifted from the restaurant where the word was Henry Kissinger would be the next Secretary of State. Christine watched the woman adjust her scarf, smile and exit.

Time slid by. Then one eye-opening day, she realized it was too late even for New York. She would have Gang-jo's child. She had to tell him. She sent a letter through diplomatic circles, asked him to pass on the news to her father. But weeks and then months passed, and no reply came, no notes or clandestine letters, no word through diplomatic channels came from either man.

Gang-jo was as lost to her as her father, but his child was

growing within her, and she must come to terms with it. Studying herself in the bedroom mirror, she said aloud, "I'm having a child I must raise alone." Her face showed neither joy nor anger. If she must carry this baby to term it would be hers, an American born and bred. A tear leaked, but, with determination, she willed it back, lifted her chin and stood tall.

Guarding her secret, she went on with her life. All the problems related with raising a child on her own attacked her in the night. She imagined headlines in scandal sheets. *Unwed mother gives birth. China lover has Communist kid.* Such thoughts made her smile, and slowly the idea became less problematic. She knew she could cope.

During her third trimester, her classes became more demanding, students and faculty acting as if she were, not just knowledgeable about China, but an authority with unlimited knowledge. They were also glancing at her with speculation in their looks. No one said "illegitimate" any more, but the stigma remained; she could face unexpected consequences.

She mailed a letter to Aunt Betty without re-reading it. "I'm pregnant, having a baby and getting a sabbatical, ostensibly to write a book. Would you want me in Seattle?"

"Of course I want you. Come home as soon as possible," Aunt Betty, her mother's sister, the woman who had raised her, who seemed like a mother, replied.

Spring had added bright color to Seattle's green. Annuals and perennials decorated the hills, flanked the houses, showed in the parks. She relaxed. She was back in Seattle, where her father had picked up Chinese from the Changs in the International District, where she'd first seen his letters from Shanghai, where slim, out-spoken but liberal-minded Aunt

Betty pulled her in with brief, perfunctory words of greeting. After a few angry remarks about men who impregnate women and let them fend for themselves, Aunt Betty once again handed over the two letters she'd had from her brother-in-law so long ago so Christine could reread them.

"Dear Betty, I told you I'd write when I was settled somewhere. I can hardly believe it, but I'm in China. Remember my friend from the war, Freddy Patterson? I'm working for him on his paper. Don't know how long it will last, but right now it's a challenge. I'm also studying Chinese. The Chinese I learned from the Changs doesn't go far here! Take care of Christine and yourself, and I'll be writing soon." Logan

Through the years, sitting at the same table, Christine had read much into those few sentences. Mentioning her showed he loved her, planned to come home some day.

In the next letter, he'd written: "Betty, talk about change, this is it. Makes me question everything I ever believed. Still, I suppose people are the same everywhere. It's hard to understand everything that's happened, but I'm trying. I've met a lot of interesting people of all nationalities, but I must admit things are changing fast. I remember the past, but I try not to live there permanently. Give the little one a hug from her dad. I must run. Have to interview a White Russian who speaks Chinese!"

The words gave hints of the trouble communism would bring. For a time, as Aunt Betty carried her bags upstairs, Christine stared out the window, admiring the gazebo where she'd played as a child, the green of the back yard. He'd called her "little one," as if he really cared.

The third letter, addressed to her directly, she knew by heart.

The last lines she'd always had to struggle to read, the words flowing together as if he'd hurried to finish. "Remember always, no matter what happens, that I love you, will always love you. I'm sorry I cannot write more, but I want you to know no matter what, I'll always be your father. I'll always love you." The words had furthered her sense of awe and hope when she'd gone to China.

Now, as her condition grew increasingly obvious, the days became over- whelmingly the same, she and Aunt Betty eating meals together, watching *All in the Family* on television, walking through the old neighborhood, occasionally going to the movies. She contacted a few old friends and spoke to those in charge at the University. Everyone wanted to know about her trip to China. She rehearsed the amusing, the exciting, the factual stories about the President, Mao, and others and told them at times, but until her water broke, Christine kept to herself that her child would be "part Chinese."

Aunt Betty took the news in her no-nonsense spinster way. "I'm sure you've thought through the implications, the possible complications for the child."

"Aunt Betty, it will be all right." She could afford to give her baby a good life. The University of Washington wanted her to join their faculty, and she could also go back to Georgetown. If there was talk about her pregnancy, she heard none of it.

Fifteen hours after the first pain, she gave birth at a hospital on Capitol Hill, the building wedged in between old mansions and new high-rise condos. She named her boy Mathew Joseph Wainwright and called him Matt. She had walked on a stage where no one had walked before, lived through an extraordinary time, everything speeded up. When he was old enough, her son would understand. Anyway, this was America, the great melting pot, where civil rights was a rallying cry. This wasn't China with its years of isolation. Her child would fit in, find his place in Seattle, and everything she did would pave the way. Already she knew a fierce, deep, maternal love.

Aunt Betty, on a visit to the hospital, said in an offhand way, "I hope you've gotten over thinking your father will come home any day. After all, you're twenty-nine now."

Christine glanced out the window and paused before answering. It was misting outside, rain smearing the glass. Her yearning for Logan and all things Chinese *had* bordered on obsession. It was the first time Aunt Betty had alluded to it. "*When I was a child I thought like a child*, she repeated to herself, and hugging Matt closer said, "I have a new obsession, if I can call this darling that." She exchanged a smile with Aunt Betty.

The following year, after she made sure the bond between her and Matt was strong, she resumed teaching, her celebrity status still glittering in academic circles. She was the University of Washington's China Expert. The Seattle Post-Intelligencer did an article about her complete with pictures. A television and two radio interviews followed. In addition to teaching Mandarin, she expanded her students' knowledge about all things Chinese. Her classes were extremely popular.

She bought a white frame house two blocks from Aunt Betty, remodeled the interior, put Matt's name on a list at a Montessori School and followed up on friendships in the International District.

One day when he was a toddler, she took him to visit the Changs. Past the shops with their tourist inventory of fans, bells and satin jackets, past the restaurants run by Japanese, and Koreans as well as Chinese, she hurried as if she were coming home. Her father had walked the same streets, knew the same people.

In the Chang's upstairs apartment over the butcher shop where he had soaked up their way of speaking, everyone laughed and talked and made much of Matt. Grandpa and Grandma Chang had joined their ancestors, but the other Changs were eager to share their family with a boy of visible Chinese ancestry.

Auntie Pearl, the titular head of the family now, still spoke English with little regard for grammar. "So when you go back to China?" she asked passing out almond cookies, filling cups with tea. At seventy plus she was pleasantly settled in age and eager to extend hospitality. She watched as Matt toddled between her and Christine, holding on to legs, grabbing at furniture.

"I don't know," Christine said. "I hadn't planned on going." Or had she? The ache had not quite subsided; occasionally some image from China invaded her dreams. Yet, when she awoke whatever it was drifted away, and she was left staring through the picture frames of West Lake, but nothing filled the frames.

"Too communist. Better in Taiwan." Auntie Pearl dismissed the country airily. "Maybe this one go to China some day," she said picking up Matt.

"Perhaps," Christine admitted, knowing that Mrs. Chang viewed Matt's Oriental features as proof positive of his split loyalties. She felt no such certainty. The President she'd come to admire on the trip was foundering in lies, Watergate staining his achievement. China waited like a sleeping giant behind doors that had opened a crack. "It will be up to him. As an American he'll decide on his own."

"This one is Chinese/American," Mrs. Chang corrected. "He go."

Christine smiled, but the words stayed with her. It wasn't as if she were teaching English literature. Her interest in China showed daily in class, and sometimes, because of a student's question, it expanded even while she concentrated on showing Matt all that America had to offer. She took him camping in the Olympic Mountains on the Peninsula, watched him play among the tree trunks tossed by the surf on the beaches at LaPush, and took him on the ferry to Bainbridge Island. He became her life. She had trouble showing interest in the men who showed interest in her. The older academics she occasionally dated patronized her, and men from the scientific or business community never shared her interests. She felt closest to the men in her hiking group, but all of them seemed like brothers, treating her like a favorite sister.

By the time Matt turned six, she could no longer conjure Gang-jo's features. The magic of that time seeping away, she seldom talked about it anymore. Although her interest in China, its history, its present, never waned, life was good, and she didn't want to complicate it. She loved teaching. That and Matt filled her life. But lately her teaching schedule had her running. When she finally complained, the university offered to hire an instructor to help lighten her load. She felt both relieved and a trifle concerned. An instructor teaching introductory classes, following her lead, would help considerably, but she didn't want just anyone. He or she would have to have an overriding interest in the subject., be enthusiastic as well as knowledgeable. She asked for and received the final say on the potential lecturer.

The day she carved out time to see Jason Sterns, rain streaked the windows all morning. As late afternoon gloom descended, a fine mist made unclear the trees on the quad below her office, rendering it as hazy as a Chinese brush scroll. She skimmed Sterns' file. Fresh from American University, he had two glowing references from his graduate professors, a published paper and the backing of his school, all of which prepared her for a World War II veteran who'd recently returned to school, a man with bifocals, a wife and three children. She wasn't prepared for Jason.

Only the lamp on her desk was lit and his blonde hair showed up in the shadowy room like a beacon, his blue eyes bright, his white shirt blazing, unbuttoned at the throat beneath an unbuttoned corduroy sports coat. His thighs were encased in skin-tight jeans. He couldn't be more than twenty-something at the most. Why hadn't she looked closer at his resume?

He said, "Professor Wainwright, Jason Sterns," and stood waiting, perfectly at ease, his gaze taking in the room and her.

Something about him completely unsettled her from the first. Most lecturers treated her with the utmost respect; none assumed they were her equal. While his respect was certainly evident, he smiling politely, his eyes flashed an intense inner concentration and an overwhelming interest in whatever he saw, including her. Not since Gang-jo had anyone shown her such admiration without saying anything untoward. Tall as a Viking, and fit as someone who jogged each morning, swam each night, he seemed out of place, as if he had entered under false pretenses. He didn't appear anything like the academic she'd expected, but his file certainly belied that thought.

Covering up her confusion, she said in a tone that was only a slight bit divorced from a lecture, "I've been reading your file. It's impressive, I must say. But learning to converse adequately in Chinese is not enough. To understand the intricacies of thought and expression, the nuances of meaning, takes concentration and dedication."

He nodded and again spoke politely, "Neither my concentration nor my dedication have been questioned previously." His words were firm, his smile gentle, but he didn't look aside but let his smile stay with her.

"No, of course not. Let me clarify. Knowing a language means more than speaking words in proper sequences; it means knowing the culture, the arts, the history, appreciating the subtlety of a poem, understanding the economic reality, the idiom of the uneducated." She glanced past him to the book-lined room where she had always felt so in charge before. "Knowing Chinese intimately might be compared to understanding the complexity and the involvement of the calligrapher with his art."

"I agree." He nodded emphatically. "Su Dong-po said painting could serve as a means of communication as well as expression. I've studied his words, and I believe I've absorbed his art. He successfully blended Chinese thought with Chinese locution."

Color invaded her cheeks. She'd never known any American who quoted Su Dong-po. "Yes, of course. I have a book about him here." She pulled a volume from a shelf behind her. Opening it, she used some of the paintings to illustrate her point and held the book so he could see.

He moved closer. “May I?” He took the book from her and turned the pages rapidly. “This one I especially like.” He held the page open with a finger and held it out for her to see.

Feeling as if she were losing control, she wished she could start the whole interview over. “Yes, it’s very nice. Of course it’s important to know popular history, be familiar with Sun Yat Sen, Chiang Kai Shek, Madame Chiang, the Soong sisters, General Stilwell and now Mao Tse-Tung, Deng Xiaoping.” The generalities flew from her lips before she could prevent them. My god, what was happening to her?

He indicated a chair. “May I?”

She flushed. “Forgive me. As you can see, my work schedule has been hectic.” Despite his youth, frown lines showed between his well-shaped eyebrows, the mark of someone who read a lot, deliberated often. She’d never known anyone who not only knew but quoted Su Dung Po. “Did art propel you into the study of the Chinese language?” Looking at him she would have thought Scandinavian history, anything but Chinese language arts.

He sat down. “When I learned to speak and read Spanish, I realized I had a facility for languages.”

She almost shrugged.

He smiled, added, “ I became fluent at age ten.”

He hadn’t sprawled, but she had the impression he was. She lifted her head in an effort to gain height. “Spanish can be useful, especially in the Southwest of our country, but it is hardly Chinese.” She cleared her throat. “How did, er, Spanish lead you to Chinese?” She gave him a ‘I’m the boss’ expression.

"Simple. I went from Spanish to German, French, Italian, Russian, and smatterings of conversational Polish, Greek, and Arabic to Chinese."

"Arabic," she repeated, awed now. He had to be a genius or a clever con artist.

"At school they let me study in advanced classes. Then one summer when I was sixteen I traveled through Turkey." He grinned. "I hooked up with some hippies hitch-hiking the Middle East. Learned to speak enough to get by. We ended up climbing a few mountains also."

She made a show of looking through his file. "About your Chinese...."

"People say I have a flair for languages." He shrugged. "Words always fascinated me. What is the etymology, the pronunciation, the spelling? When did certain words change, migrate from one country or culture to another? What were the influences upon it? Chinese, of course, has its dialects, its differences from area to area. As my résumé states, my study was in depth."

"We teach Mandarin." Christine felt as if the rain outside was snow and he was dealing in it, but his credentials from American University, the letters of recommendation refuted that. She turned pages, found his age. Twenty-six. His marital status: single.

"I studied Mandarin. Currently I'm studying the classic characters. The calligraphy is something, but I'm making a stab at reading it." He shrugged. "Truthfully, not that well."

She leafed through his file again. Every letter, every recommendation was specific—he was good. His age might be an attribute. Many older men would not like answering to her. Even though talk of equality infiltrated all campus circles, few men were keen to see it in their departments. She'd not come to her status unscathed. And truthfully, something about him excited her. To have someone truly knowledgeable about Chinese language and culture would please her. And in some way, not definable, he reminded her of Gang-jo. She said abruptly, cutting him off as he spoke, "Can you start Monday?"

His smile was all encompassing. "Sure. Today if you want."

She ignored that. "I'd expect you to deal in the basics, prepare your students to go on with their studies after completing your classes." She related what she'd been doing, gave him copies of her introductory material, and stood, her composure in place once again.

He took the material and said, his mouth in a smile she tried to interpret but couldn't, "I'll do everything I can to make the classes so interesting everyone will want to continue learning from you. Including me."

Shaken, she decided to wait a few weeks before visiting one of his classes to see how his teaching went. Unless he had fooled everyone, he had to be a linguistic genius. And he certainly wasn't bad to look at, but that part she'd keep to herself.

Chapter 6

Christine

Seattle, Washington - 1978

Two weeks later she slipped into a seat at the back of Jason's lecture hall and listened, leaving before he noticed her. She sent a note to him later. "I like what you're doing,"she had written. His Chinese accent was impeccable, and his method of teaching, while slightly unorthodox, seemed to be working. She stayed away again until the middle of the semester.

It was late, his last class of the day. Opening the door to the lecture hall, she heard him repeating words she'd used to him on arrival. She couldn't help smiling. It had been good to have her words, not only endorsed by him, but also acknowledged by him. Happily, she leaned against the wall. But five minutes passed before any students came out. She straightened, moved closer, ready to go in. In the faculty lounge she'd heard about Jason's popularity, but she'd not expected to see students leaving with smiles on their faces. The bulk of them didn't leave for a full ten minutes. Calling *zaijian*, goodbye, over their shoulders, some were laughing, all were apparently pleased with the class.

Entering carefully in order not to be run down by stragglers, she caught him, backpack on, leaving by the opposite door.

"Wait," she called. "I'll only be a moment. It's about a program I'm doing for the Seattle Travel Club. They want me to talk about China and give a fifteen-minute primer about the language."

He turned back toward her, a broad smile on his face.

She said hurriedly, "I thought maybe you might want to do the primer." She added the date and the time as he stepped toward her.

"I've been hoping you'd come by. Sure I'll do the primer. Glad to."

"Well, good. Then I'll see you later." She started out.

His voice stopped her; his smile held her. "I've got a better idea. I was just going to grab an early dinner. Come along and we can talk about the program."

She glanced at her watch. Aunt Betty was picking up Matt from a play date. Time would not be a problem. Still she hesitated until she saw his smile fall into slightly mocking lines. "Okay."

"Great." He stood back so she could precede him out the door. "I found this Chinese place on the Ave., China First. It's at 4237 University Way, NE. You can tell me if the food is authentic."

"It's very good. Popular, too. I'll meet you there."

In twenty minutes she had parked above Fifteenth, NE, and walked down from the side street. The usual array of people crowded the sidewalk—students, tourists, locals. A cacophony of voices met her as she entered the restaurant. She half expected to find Jason holding sway among a crowd of students at the big round table in the front window, but he waved to her from a booth near the back, standing up and calling, "Back here."

After threading her way past waiters and patrons, she slid in opposite him.

"I believe chow mein and chop suey are American inventions, so I ordered fish, steamed rice, vegetables, kung pao chicken, mu shu pork and lemon drop soup. If I goofed too badly, you can give me demerits."

"It sounds good and enough for doggy bags," she said, and it was. While they ate, Jason as adept with chopsticks as she was, she explained that soup was traditionally served last in China.

"So I learn something every day." He grinned, and then said more soberly, "Tell me, did you find China much changed from the days of the Soong sisters?"

"We were restricted in many ways; my observations aren't that relevant."

He nodded. "I've been reading history. Barbara Tuchman's *Notes From China* blew my mind wide open. Not to diminish Nixon's role or anything you saw, but Tuchman spent six weeks in the countryside, among the people. Fascinating stuff, she showed the good as well as the negative side of China today."

When she admitted she hadn't read it, he said he'd loan her the book. "It sounds as if thought and creativity have been strangled. You must have seen or heard something when you were there."

"A little." How could she talk about a father she'd never seen, a man who'd been a one-night fling?

Silence followed. With her chopsticks she picked a nut from the kung pao chicken, a mushroom from the plate of vegetables. "I think I've had it."

He nodded as she placed her chopsticks across her plate. "I'm almost there." He ate a few more bites and then stabbing her with a look said, "I also boned up on Stillwell and the

American experience with China from way back." He grinned again. "You've got me hooked."

Her smile came unbidden.

He told her about his family, mother, father, younger brother. "I was the maverick. After I graduated high school, I took off. Mr. Thumb and me."

"Mr. Thumb?'

"I hitched rides. Saw the USA and Europe. Read every book I could get my hands on. Classics, trash, porn, you name it, I read it. College came later." He leaned against the back of the booth. "Now you. Tell me about yourself. What do you do on weekends?"

Feeling skittish about sharing, she said in a throwaway voice, "For recreation, I belong to a hiking club and take the easier trails."

"Never been married?"

She shook her head.

"Why not?"

"Really!"

"Okay, sorry, out of bounds for sure. Did I tell you I bought some art? Reproduction of a carving, a couple scrolls for my bedroom, probably not authentic, but peaceful. I've got a flat here in the U district."

She told him about the few pieces of Chinese art she had and then she added, "I noticed your were wearing hiking boots. I take my son hiking with me sometimes. He's six and will be waiting for me."

A look of surprise crossed his face.

"I'm astonished you hadn't heard."

He said nothing for a while. Then he said, "I'm sure he

keeps you busy, but maybe the three of us could go hiking sometime."

"Maybe," she said standing and pulled dollars from her over-the-shoulder bag. "Here let me get my share. It was supposed to be about the program."

He smiled again. "It wasn't was it? Let it be my treat."

It was her turn to smile. She wasn't going to fight him for the check, make an issue in the middle of student alley. Matt would be getting restless, tired of the relentless quiet at Aunt Betty's, no TV allowed until after six. With a slight wave, she hurried out.

She was unlocking her car when Jason came running. Her eyes questioning, she hesitated.

"I don't have your phone number at home. Sorry, I should have asked earlier, but we got to talking and…."

Smiling ruefully, his hand on the car door, those gleaming blue eyes looking at her as if her face was an object to study, she found her pulse racing.

He shrugged, the smile disappearing. "I need your home phone if we're going to get together for a hike."

For a few seconds he seemed to have lost his supreme confidence, and she relaxed, reeled off the number.

His smile reappearing, he murmured, "Thanks," and opened her door so she could get in. She started the car and watched him wait until she drove off.

Two weeks later the seats were almost filled and people were still streaming into the Travel Club as she checked her transparencies to make sure she had them in order. Jason waved to her before he took his seat up front. A pair of ubiquitous jeans outlined his body, no guessing at his sex, and a body-hugging shirt molded his chest, his shoulders. You had to notice, she said to herself, a long time since she'd been so aware of a man. Going toward the seat reserved for her next to him, she asked, "Have any trouble finding the place?"

"No, should I?" His eyes teased her.

Feeling as ancient as Auntie Pearl, she said seriously, "I expect we'll get a lot of stupid questions tonight." She sat.

He grinned. "Stupidity was never my strong suit."

"You've passed muster," she said, trying for a light touch, but not quite making it. She realized her legs were crossed in his direction, her arm on the armrest with his. She uncrossed her legs. The room was getting warm, people still pushing in. More chairs were added, the audience jammed together as the club president welcomed everyone.

"I see there's a lot of interest in China," Christine said when she began her talk. Although ignorance about the Orient was abundant – one person even confused China with Japan – the audience was well traveled and eager to hear whatever she told them. Her slides brought ahs and ohs, the ornamental buildings of the Summer Palace getting intense interest, the photo of her with Zhou-Elai adding to it. She ended with the line, "They must think Americans do business in the john," and while faces showed puzzlement, she explained about finding telephones in the bathrooms of the hotels. Laughter led applause. She sat down smiling and watched Jason take over.

Stepping out from behind the podium, he said, "*Wo xian ziwo jleshao zixie* – let me introduce myself to you. As the president of the club stated, I'm Professor Wainwright's colleague. My students are preparing for an exam, but I'm not going to grade you." He grinned and everyone laughed and Christine thought, he's a natural, much more at ease than she'd ever been at his age. Occasionally, she still used words like hopefully to soften a sentence. He didn't. Neither did he have to be told to speak up like she had the first time she'd given a talk. "Chinese is a tonal language, with four tones, but we're not going into that. Memorize important and polite words and phrases and you'll do fine on a tour. I intend to give you words and phrases that will be helpful."

He printed in bold letters on the board. *Zhongguo* "That's China." He pronounced it in Chinese and then wrote *Meiguo*. "That's America." He had the audience repeat the Chinese words with him and quickly led them through the days of the week and the numbers from one to ten. After the audience struggled through the list, he said, "I didn't hear your voice, Professor Wainwright, " and looked from her to the audience, bringing them into it. They applauded. He grinned and she, bowing to pressure, went up to stand beside him to repeat the next set of Chinese words in unison with him.

Soon he was saying one word, she another, working through *shenme,* "what" to *weishenme,* "why, " until the audience had useful words they could memorize phonetically.

People surrounded them both afterward, thanks were given, more questions were asked and handout sheets were distributed. When only the president of the club and a few others remained, Christine gathered her materials together. "I didn't appreciate what you did," she said to Jason.

He turned off the light on the overhead machine and faced her. "I apologize. I should have asked you ahead of time."

She heard the words, *the full professor leads, the instructor follows*. She shook her head. "I wouldn't state it quite that way."

What in the hell, did she mean?

The slight lines between his eyes deepened. "Well, we pulled it off, in my estimation." He shrugged. "But it's your show. I won't presume again."

She wanted to say something else, but he was thanking her for the opportunity, thanking the president of the travel club and leaving.

At home she paid Josie, the teenage baby-sitter who lived next door, turned off the stereo and television and turned her attention to Matt who had kept his seat when she entered. Her gaze swept the sparsely furnished front room, Scandinavian furniture, beige and cream colored carpet and draperies, nothing distinctive nothing to say it was solidly hers. Matt was asking about his father again. Why didn't he have a father like Josie did? Like the other kids at school had?

How could she answer him sensibly when she'd been so asinine with Jason? For the first time in years she felt incapable. She set her briefcase on the floor, tossed her coat over a chair and sank into the sofa next to Matt. No trace of a smile on his face, his sturdy legs, hanging a foot from the floor, moved slightly. He deserved an honest answer. "Your father lives far away." She ran her hand through his silky dark hair, pretended to straighten it.

"But why doesn't he live with us?" His gaze had an accusatory quality.

Avoiding eye contact, she got up, put her books away, hung up her coat. "Because he has another wife."

He looked at her with head cocked to one side. "That mean you're divorced?"

Seeing the cogs turning in his head, she nodded. "Something

like that. Now you better get ready for bed."

He pulled his legs up, settled back against the cushion. "Why can't I stay up and watch TV. Josie watches till twelve."

"Because Josie's older than you. What are you trying to pull, mister?"

"No harm in trying." He grinned, started up the stairs. "You know, Mom, I can't make up my mind. Should I join the New York Yankees when I get big? Aunt Betty says they're the best."

"I thought you wanted to be a fireman." She wanted to hug him so hard he'd never let go, the edginess she'd felt with Jason no longer important.

Two weeks later, Jason called. "I was wondering if you'd mind if I came along on the hike tomorrow. Up the Cascade Trail."

Surprised, almost forgetting she'd given him her home phone number, she said, "I don't believe they have any restrictions." How did he know what club she belonged to? The radio announcer was saying Anwar Sadat of Egypt was flying to Jerusalem to discuss peace. It had to be a goodwill gesture. She turned down the volume. Lately she had shared with her class what she'd read in the book she'd borrowed from Jason, snippets of facts that stunned her. An officer in the Chinese Army served fifteen years before he was allowed to have his wife and family with him. People were re-educated if they held "wrong thought."

Jason's voice overrode the voice on the radio. "You sure you want me tagging along?"

"Actually everyone and anyone goes up the Cascade Trail." Damn, that wasn't what she intended to say. She sounded so damn ridiculous. "Anyway, I have to give you back the Tuchman book."

"You could bring it to school."

A short silence followed while she tried to analyze what made her say such asinine things when Jason was around.

"So, I'll pick you up at eight. Okay? Unless you prefer to meet at the trailhead."

She'd much rather he met Matt at home. "It would be a relief to have someone else drive."

In the morning, she had sandwiches, fruit and cookies in her backpack, thermoses of coffee and water, and individual packets of trail mix in her pocket when Jason arrived. She watched as he parked in front and loped up the sidewalk to knock "shave-and-a-haircut" on the front door.

Opening it, she smiled politely. His head was bare, dark glasses covered his eyes, but she was sure they were turned on her.

"All set?"

"Almost." She stepped back from the door, "Come in." As he entered, she called up the stairs, "Matt, it's time to go." She turned her gaze back to Jason. "He gets wound up in his projects. He's into model airplanes now."

He smiled. "Sounds like me at that age. I think I hear him coming." He looked up, took off his dark glasses.

She watched intently. Sometimes in the supermarket or standing in line at the theater, people stared at them as Matt, unaware of the perplexed scrutiny, called her mother. Others frowned, obviously trying to figure out the connection. Others went overboard telling her how cute her little Chinese boy was. Even in the International District some people showed displeasure seeing a mixed race child. Jason showed nothing. "Hey, Matt," he said when Matt reached the bottom step, "I'm Jason. I'm going hiking with you today." He held out his hand.

Matt smiled with pleasure, and put his small hand in Jason's large one, before rushing out the door. "Come on, you guys, let's go."

Jason turned to her, his blue eyes slightly narrowed. "Ready?" he asked.

It seemed Jason had accepted Matt totally and was slightly amused because she hadn't said anything sooner. She had to smile.

Her "high" lasted all day. The trail rose constantly, Matt's little legs churning, the others in the club passing the three of them. When Matt tired, Jason hoisted him to his shoulders and carried him to the top, going faster now, waiting at steep areas for her to catch up. The trail was slick with pine needles, the air as crisp as the Granny Smith apples she dug from her backpack halfway to the resting place. She caught her breath as she sat on one of the boulders sticking up through the soil at the turn-around spot. "We made it," she said looking with exaggerated joy down to the cedars and pines below and above to the trail that wound ever higher.

She called Matt back from his investigation of the area and portioned out the lunch. For a time no one said anything. As the lunch dwindled, Jason swore he'd never eaten a better tuna sandwich. "What do you say, buddy?"

"Mine was peanut butter, but it was the best peanut butter I ever had."

Jason and Christine exchanged smiles, laughter lurking, exploding.

Matt perched on a flat stone next to Jason. "What are

you guys laughing at?"

"About doing this again" Jason looked straight at Christine. "Can we?"

"Yes," Matt cried.

"I'll see," she said, not daring to look at Jason. How could she even think the things she was thinking? Aunt Betty would say he wasn't dry behind the ears. Who knows how the university would respond?

When Jason appeared at the door the next week, she said, "I have to work on an article. The deadline is coming up." Not quite true, but close enough.

Matt, rushed to the door and cried, "I don't have any plans."

Jason grinned and leaned down. "I guess it's just you and me, Buddy." He glanced up at Christine. "I'll take good care of him, have him home before dark."

"Please, Mom."

Slowly, she nodded.

After they were gone, she made herself work on an article about the Ming statues. Interest about China had dwindled; she wasn't sure the article would be accepted. The radio blared news about the Vietnam War; she kept thinking about Jason. When dark came and Matt wasn't home yet, she dialed Jason's number. His answering machine cutting in, she heard him say, "You know the drill, leave a message after the beep."

She blurted out something and was hanging up when Matt came running in. "We stopped for pizza on the way home. Mom, we had such a good time. You shoulda been there." He smelled fresh as the outdoors, and his eyes gleamed. She had to smile.

From the doorway, Jason turned to Matt. "Okay, pal, time to say goodnight."

Matt nodded. "Okay. Goodnight."

"What do you say?" Christine coached.

"Thanks for a nice day."

"My pleasure. Now get upstairs and start getting ready for bed. I want to talk to your Mom."

Obediently Matt climbed the stairs.

Christine murmured, "Sometimes I have to beg him." The words, 'he needs a man's hands' hung in the air.

Jason 's smile settled on her. "Can we make it a threesome next time?"

She told herself she was giving Matt an ongoing male presence like a big brother. They'd be out in the healthy air, tramping trails. "Yes." Thanking him for being such a good friend to Matt, she pretended not to see his quickly shuttered look of amusement.

Before the weekend, Kathy Feingold called. Friends since grammar school, they'd maintained a loose friendship. Sometimes Christine went without seeing Kathy for months. She supposed that was why their friendship had survived so long. Kathy said, "I'm having one of my small dinner parties, and I won't take no for an answer. Saturday, fiveish for drinks and Salmon Wellington whenever I think people are sufficiently relaxed."

She pondered pleading a previous engagement, telling Kathy, thanks but no thanks, and going up into the mountains with Jason. But a voice inside her kept saying *if only he were older.* She left a message on Jason's answering machine, her relief mixed, as she said she and Matt were busy the coming weekend.

Setting off for Kathy's, she told herself she had managed to put Gang-jo into the past, gain a proper perspective on China and realize she'd probably never see her father again. With Jason it had to be easier. Perhaps Kathy would have a bachelor in tow for her to flirt with, someone to take away this involvement that was mainly in her head.

The fine mist that had obscured the end of the block had stopped when she arrived at Kathy's, getting there late because at the last minute the baby-sitter couldn't make it, and she'd had to take Matt to Aunt Betty's.

The Feingold's brick house on Capitol Hill stood among similar big houses of an era when logging kings built mansions. Kathy had taken Aaron's name when she'd dropped out of graduate school to marry him. A turret room, a formal dining room, a kitchen where Kathy performed miracles, and Aaron, who taught physics, posted lists of metric measurements on her cabinet doors, making the old home distinctive. "Don't stand on formality, come on in," read a sign posted on the door.

Leaving her coat in the entryway, Christine scanned the guests in the living room, one step down, hiding her surprise at seeing Jason. They were gathered in little knots on Kathy's eclectic collection of couches and chairs beneath a bold and improbable collection of local artists' paintings. Old friends and acquaintances were deep in conversation, not noticing her arrival. Her glance settled on Jason who leaned against the bar at the far end of the room. For the first time he wasn't wearing jeans. Although his three-piece suit wasn't white like John Travolta's in the movie "Saturday Night Fever," it did nothing to dispel the image. Again her pulse increased, a faint flush came to her cheeks.

Catching sight of her, he strode across the room, and voices discussing the political ramifications of the women's equal rights amendment passing, stopped mid- sentence.

"Come, let me buy you a drink." His voice rang with his usual self-assurance. "I'm sure you know everyone here and can say howdy on the way." He took her hand. "How's Matt?"

"He's probably arguing with Aunt Betty about which television show he can watch," she said, aware that everyone was watching as he led her down the step to the living room. No one was speaking.

Alice Farnsworth, proprietor of a profitable tourist store on the waterfront, muttered softly, "My, my."

Christine would have pulled her hand from Jason's, but his grip was firm. The long living room with its high ceilings and long narrow windows appeared to go on forever. "He's still talking about the hike you took him on." She spoke loud enough for all to hear, wondering why she was trying so hard to make what was happening disappear. She waved to a man she knew, sent a hello to another. She heard, "Hello, Christine, hi Chris, " as Jason led her to the bar where Aaron presided. Almost on cue, Kathy came running in from the kitchen, an apron tied around her waist. Subdued conversations resumed, but it was clear people were really listening to what Christine was saying.

Kathy hugged her, said, "Aaron, give Chrissie a pinot noir. Isn't that what you and I devoured one night when we were doing a sleep-over in high school."

"I think it was something we called poison piss." Christine kissed the air near Kathy's cheek and sneaked a look at Jason who had not relinquished her hand.

Kathy raised her hands dramatically. "You're way behind. We've all had a couple refills, on the way to getting smashed. I see you know Jason." She hit her forehead with a hand. "Of course you do. What's the matter with me?"

"I'm cutting off your drinks, Bets." Aaron handed Christine a wine glass filled to the rim. "This one is the truth-teller."

Jason grinned.

Kathy giggled. "The food will be ready soon. I promise." She sketched a bow toward the room. "I even hired a girl to serve. How's that for class?"

"Hear, hear," Alice shouted, and they all took up the cry.

"Come on out, keep me company," Kathy said below the general hubbub. "You can have her later," she said sotto voce to Jason.

"I think he's gone on you," she said in the kitchen where the "girl" had plates in the warming oven, rolls heating in the microwave, and was cutting the fish into serving size pieces.

Christine shook her head. "He's too young." She set her wine glass on the counter, nibbled a cheese puff from a dish waiting to be carried into the other room.

"Are you kidding, he's teaching Chinese and the buzz is he's going to make Associate Professor before you can say jack sprat or whatever the Chinese is for it."

"Kathy, please." She took a long sip of the wine.

"I mean if I wasn't married to Aaron and slightly crazy about him as well, I'd go for that boy. He's fabulous." She smoothed her dress over her hips. "Anyway, boys like that never look at old round-faced Kathy."

"Kathy, will you stop it; he's just a friend who takes Matt hiking."

"Chris, honey, don't dig yourself deeper, I didn't see you dragging your hand away from his, and don't look now, but I think your boyfriend is following you." She ripped off her apron and smiled at Jason who was saying, "Can I help?"

Kathy shook her head and called into the living room, "It's ready folks. Take your places in the dining room or forfeit your right to sit down."

Jason tucked Christine's hand under his arm. "Can I see you in?"

She grinned. "I hardly recognized you. All dressed up."

"Look who's talking. Remind me to tell you how great you look."

"I'll hold you to it," she said, glad she'd worn her black evening pants. Fitting tight over the hips, they also flared beautifully, and the pink top, dipping dangerously low in front, had frilly little cap sleeves that made her feel ultra feminine.

"Come on you two. Time for that later," Kathy called. "Bring your drink with you, Christine. Here, I have you opposite one another at the table. At least you can look at her, Jason."

Later Christine couldn't remember who said what when, but through it all she was overwhelmingly aware that among the eight academics, plus acerbic Alice and her equally acerbic husband, Jason more than held his own. His knowledge was extensive, and his poise unlimited. In the beginning Alice pushed him into saying what musical group he favored. When he named The Rolling Stones and predicted they'd be famous for years, she rolled her eyes, and others claimed all those rock groups played so loud no one could really hear the music, if you could call it music. Aaron said he used to be a

Frank Sinatra man himself, unless you put on a Chopin piano concerto.

"Something classical," Alice added. "Leave those groups to the kids."

"I prefer Vivalde myself, but Chopin has its appeal," Jason said and proceeded to tell about the concert he'd heard at Chopin's childhood home at *Zelazowa Wola*. "It means iron will."

Silver-clinking silence followed.

Kathy changed the subject.

As the evening progressed, all of Kathy's guests in some way tried to one up Jason, push him into a corner labeled youth, and Christine listened with admiration as Jason managed to stay afloat or beat them at their own game. Whether it was OPEC or nuclear energy he knew the latest from the newly implemented Department of Energy to the whys and wherefores of Elvis Presley and his death. He was knowledgeable about welfare and the poor, the latest Supreme Court decisions, and he often added statistics to bolster his words. Openly admiring, Christine drank too much wine and found herself returning Jason's smiles and gratifying looks, aware that the flickering candlelight flattered everyone, and she felt glamorous, prettier than she'd ever been.

After pecan pie and brandy, people began to trickle out. Kathy declared Christine had no business driving and taking Christine's sequined evening bag, fished out her keys and gave them to Jason. "See that she gets home safely."

"I'll get even with you," Christine whispered to Kathy as Jason held the door for her. Outside, the night air hitting hard, she let Jason lead her to the car. "You managed to stay alive through that." She got into the passenger seat.

"I had an early start." He got in behind the wheel, turned on the lights, and let the car coast down the hill before he started it. "Grew up fast taking classes with older kids. Anyway, I wanted to impress you."

"You did." She studied his profile. "It just occurred to me, how are you going to get home?"

He glanced at her. "I don't intend to go home."

The words curled around her, took hold and didn't let go. "What are you trying to say?" she managed, her voice small. She sounded nothing like the capable woman she was. "I'm beginning to think I really had too much to drink."

"Christine, sweetheart, I started having sex when I was fifteen. I'm not going to stop now." He reached over, touched her hand. "Frankly, you've had just enough vino to relax nicely."

Oh, my, she thought, but wasn't this what she'd wanted?

He pulled the car over to the curb and kissed her, taking her head in his hands and taking her lips in a way denoting ownership.

"Oh, my," she said aloud, feeling a warm tide strike from the top of her head to her toes.

"I'm going to fuck the hell out of you," he said kissing her again and again, tipping her head so she had to face him, look into those blazing eyes, his body never touching hers, his lips finding the spot where her shoulder met her neck. "And you'll like it. No one's ever complained."

"Were there that many?"

He lifted his head. "In my mind, not one person before you." And then he added, "*wode tian xiao jiaozi*, my sweet, little dumpling."

Later, she often wondered if the Chinese phrase had done it. He was so utterly different from anyone she'd known before, exceedingly informed and intelligent, in touch with everything she liked, loved and admired, and no one had talked to her like he had or kissed her like he had either. Everything about him shouted modern America.

Two days later she took her father's letter to the nearest copy mart, made two copies, hurried home and put one copy and his letter in a file she kept on her closet shelf. The other copy she taped to the back of his picture. In his World War II uniform, his hat at a cocky angle, Logan Wainwright, too, looked overwhelmingly American, ready to do whatever he could to keep the barbarians from the gate. She took the picture into Matt's room. When he was older, she'd show him the letter. Now, it was enough that he knew his grandfather had existed. She doubted she'd ever see him, doubted that he still lived. 1972 was more than a decade ago. Whether Jason took off tomorrow or not, he'd made her see; this was her life, not what might exist in China. She smiled when the phone rang, and his voice sounded in her ear.

Chapter 7

Logan

Behind Communist Lines – China 1948

Once, early on, he had paused to look back. In the far distance Shanghai's buildings showed like cardboard cutouts against the sky, a mist of unclear shapes reflected in the rising sun. A stain of coral striped the horizon and reflected in the cumulus clouds in the west. He hurried to catch up, Sulin waiting, her glance a reprimand.

Ahead a vast expanse of land stretched, denuded of trees, interspersed with small rice and grain fields. During the night they'd passed squat houses clustered together, forming villages distinguished one from the other by the number of rooting pigs or squawking chickens. At one place they'd squatted against a wall and rested, the barnyard aroma telling him animals were nearby.

The night had held its mysteries as closely as Wu held his conversation. At first Logan had tried to engage him, never having had trouble chatting with other men, forging a place where friendship or one-upmanship established a working relationship. But Wu had simply avoided his overtures and Sulin had reiterated the need for quiet.

As the night took him from overwhelming excitement into a numbing marathon of motion, he could not tell one village, one farm, from the next. What was he, Logan Wainwright, an American, doing in this poor land, this country where citizen fought citizen, and ideologies competed? Eyes gritty from lack of sleep, dirty, disheveled, hungry and growing ever more irritated, he wondered, was this what Sulin wanted? They could still turn back, but which way? Already Shanghai had disappeared from sight, his glimpse perhaps an illusion, conjuring up the known. Frustrated, he tossed his duffel bag down, stood breathing deeply, catching his breath, and trying to channel his thoughts. Before they left, standing in that apartment surrounded by her friends, Sulin had said, "There is still time, Logan Wainwright, to change your mind." Logan Wainwright, not Wai Liang, the Chinese name someone had given him.

Now, as she urged him on with a tiny gesture, he read in her gaze the gentle con- cern, the love he had almost doubted. He wanted her no matter what, and in the weak, dust-filled dawn, chill still hugging the air, he saw another face, one he had hidden away so deeply its visage had seldom surfaced. Day taking the sky from gunmetal to pale gray, light touched Sulin with gentle fingers, erasing the fatigue that had let her fall into a deep sleep as they'd sat with their backs to a wall. Something radiant glowed from her face, some inner magic. It could be Nancy smiling at him, the same sculpted lines, the similar sparkle in the eyes, the musical voice. A surge of adrenaline rushed through him, and disregarding tired muscles, he hoisted the duffel bag and hurried to catch up with Sulin and their guide.

Wu Huixia had at all times kept a mean pace. Sulin followed closely, her body a gray and indistinct shape as she made a turn through a field during dawn, the ground rough, uneven, the air chilled Stumbling, she caught her balance, hesitated briefly. Taking Sulin's pack from her shoulder, Logan slung it over his own and smiled at Wu. This man who hacked and spit and blew his nose on his fingers was an enigma Logan tried to dismiss like he did the people who looked up from fields or stared from doorways as the morning progressed. When he had time, he would remember it all, make sense of the people, this flight. Spring, pressing hard against winter, sent tiny green shoots above ground wherever there was water, and occasional birds swooped and dipped. Plodding behind Wu and Sulin along a narrow dirt road he waited for the times Sulin glanced over her shoulder, her eyes meeting his like a love note delivered in silence.

As noon approached, the sun brought warmth, and Logan took off his coat and added it to his pack. Sulin said, "By evening you will need it again. As soon as the sun goes to bed, earth's cold rises." It was the longest speech she'd made that whole back-breaking, mind-drugging day.

But soon one day became wedded to another, Logan's curiosity rising exponentially as people and places came into being and were left behind. Down dusty one-lane roads, going by ox cart, hiking through fields, riding in dilapidated trucks or piloting bicycles held together with baling wire, he had no idea where he was. The maps of China, that had played in his mind like travelogues in Shanghai, were useless here. He could never retrace the route back.

Dominating rest periods, despite the cold, the dirt, and the blisters that developed on her slender feet, Sulin's voice rang pure as bird song.. She explained that when they caught up with the true government, they could stop traveling. He nodded. She was all that counted, and Wu, who acted as if

Logan was there on his sufferance, was just a guide. It was difficult to know his place in the scheme of politics that wound like a thread through everything that he and Sulin discussed. At times she interpreted when her rapid-fire speech with Wu left him frowning.

Backtracking and skirting towns, because Wu said Chiang's men were billeted close by, left little time for speculation. Exhausted, at night, and sometimes in the day, whenever Wu called a halt, Logan fell asleep instantly—in a field under the stars or curled up on a farmer's floor.

At peasant houses women with work-roughened hands and men, grizzled and stooped, shared their rice gruel. Once Logan tried to give his portion to the thin, pot-bellied children who watched him eat, but the people would not let him. Puzzled he looked at Sulin for explanation. He'd thought all children got the best food, were dressed in the brightest and warmest clothing and indulged to the extent of their parents' abilities. "I don't understand."

Her voice rang bell-like and clear. "They know we work to make their lives better and helping us now helps the children in the future." She gave their hosts one of the special glances Logan had come to think of as his. "They honor us because we are with the Liberationists."

It was a term not clear to him. "Even this big-footed American?" He hoped to lighten the moment, Sulin so serious, everyone with long faces, the hut so mean, the children so thin. A single electric bulb dangled from the ceiling, no more than 15 watt, he imagined, and the light would be extinguished after the meal was over.

Wu spoke slowly and with emphasis Logan hadn't noticed

before. "That you come from overseas to help in our revolution means much to them. You will explain us to the western world."

Logan made himself smile, but he felt like a fraud. He was not out to liberate anyone. He wanted to protest the word, shout that it didn't apply to him. Starting a branch office for Freddy was one thing, but writing for the Communists.... How had his innocent journalistic jottings grown into this? All the next day he said little.

One night a beaming farmer and his ever-smiling wife insisted Logan and Sulin use their bed. Logan sank with gratitude into the puffy feather comforters, cradling Sulin in his arms, luxuriating in the softness, the warmth and the chance for privacy. Aware of the family on the other side of the drawn curtain, he whispered and Sulin whispered back, her breath soft on his face. A tired longing rose and quietly he made love to her, the idea of the others so close almost an aphrodisiac; the family, a few feet away, snored and Wu coughed from the pallet in the loft above. Afterwards Sulin whispered, "Fatigue not so great after all," laughter tickling the words. He knew then that everything would be all right. He'd report the truth, whatever it was.

When they were on the road again, twice they had to hide in a ditch as Chiang's soldiers zoomed by, their American motorcycles bright in the thin, early morning sun. Wiping grass from his clothes, Logan looked after them.

"You wonder if you picked the wrong side," Sulin said lightly, as Wu set off again.

"I picked you," Logan said, taking her hand. He'd been swept up in a Great Adventure. Now that he had a way to look at it, he was no longer troubled by a lack of deep philosophical commitment and he found himself composing columns in his mind, articles to be read by Americans sitting in their sanitized homes. He would share his open-mouthed wonder at a land that seemed to go on forever, at the poverty, and the hope of the people.

At night, when possible, Sulin soaked her feet and bound them with scraps of cloth. Her courage and resilience astounded him. Everything leading to this moment, seemed placid and uneventful, his life in the U.S. incredibly privileged by contrast.

When they had been on the road for two weeks, a gigantic dust cloud appeared on the horizon, momentarily blotting out the sun. They had not spoken for hours, walking single-file, keeping to the edge of the road, so they could tumble into a ditch or field if necessary. Now Wu slowed his steps and held up his hand, and Logan glanced toward a terraced rice paddy, wondering if it would offer enough shelter. But Wu began to smile as vehicles moved ghostlike from the dust, trucks filled with men holding rifles.

Sulin let out a yelp. "Our people come to protect us!" She ran into the road and said in English. "They come because of Wu Huixia. He is high in the movement. It is an honor that he came for us."

Logan glanced toward Wu who had seemed little removed from the uneducated peasants they had met on their journey. He was moving into the street to meet the young officer who got out of the passenger seat of the first vehicle. Their greeting went too rapidly for him to decipher. He glanced at Sulin.

"They speak dialect from far province." Her eyes radiated seriousness. "Wu very important. He was with Mao on Long March. They walked for months, getting followers on the way. Mao was smart peasant and got others like him. Wu is one of the best."

Logan mulled all he'd heard and seen as he sat with Sulin, passengers in a truck cab, Wu in another. The days were warmer now, and brighter, sun like honey sweetening the hours.

That night, in the flickering candlelight of a strange mud hut, Wu shouted, "We will bring China into the 20th century," and the soldiers banged their rifle butts on the floor and roared approval. It was not the posturing of Logan's college days.

A week later they were deep in communist-held territory. "We're safe now," Sulin whispered. Smiling, at the incongruity of the words—safety and communism—Logan watched in amazement as people rushed from houses to greet them. "Comrades!" they yelled as Sulin and Logan got down from the truck and stood in the road, the people swirling around them.

No mud huts were visible, only brick houses or freshly painted wood houses, shaded by trees, fronted by flowers. The setting sun was turning the brown earth to tan, pink-tinged with dark shadows, and from behind walls and down alleys, a stream of people continually appeared to point at him, giggle, measure themselves against his height or to greet him with solemnity. Words danced and dipped and became indelibly printed on his mind, the thought intruding, *he and Sulin would not be leaving China soon.*

That night she handed Logan a well-worn copy of The New

York Times dated 1944 and read the headlines aloud. "Yenan, the Communist Headquarters, A Chinese Wonderland City."

He scanned the article that said Mao led a self-confident, self-respecting people. "It sounds great," he said, looking at Sulin. "I guess it depends upon whose ox is getting gored."

"Don't worry your mind about such things. It is enough that you are here with me." Her voice had a loving sound, and her eyes took him in like a sponge soaking up water, as if she were seeing him for the first time. "People like Chiang are called bananas, yellow on the outside, white on the in"

"And I?"

"I think you are white on the outside."

Yellow on the in, he completed in his mind, not sure it was true. "If I'm a banana, who isn't?"

"Advisors to your President Roosevelt had this distinction." Sulin riffled through old papers piled on the table in the three-room house assigned to them. "They gave him false information. But enough of that. Comrade Mao wants us to publish a magazine," Sulin explained, sorting through papers, placing them in separate piles. "And to print pamphlets, brochures, a daily paper, too." She paused in the sorting.

He frowned. Communist propaganda. If he said no, what would happen? Outside the door marigolds and sunflowers were nodding in a gentle breeze and he knew that if he kissed her on the side of the neck, she would turn to meet his embrace. He said nothing, but was this merely the beginning? Each day he waited for the other shoe to fall.

Yet, as days and weeks passed, and nothing untoward happened, his lingering antipathy to communism began to fade. Little by little, he sloughed off doubts. As he began the work that everyone expected and accepted without change, he knew a wonderful sense of peace. What he was doing was good, stories about the people, about the land, and only incidentally, occasionally something about politics. The journalists working with him were first rate, and always they allowed him to speak his thoughts, exercise his doubts, and no one laughed at his pronunciation anymore. Now, he spoke almost without an accent. He felt capable again, like the Logan who had walked with confidence and optimism along the streets of Seattle. Writing and reporting in three Mao-backed periodicals: *From the Front*, *Mao's Words*, and *The Chronicle of the People*, he helped popularize the movement and solidify recognition from foreign journalists, who knew his writing by his Chinese name, Wai Liang.

Days and weeks went by when the thought he was living in a foreign country never entered his mind. Sulin's passion and intellect was as great as his, but she also had a sweetness that he surmised surpassed his own underlying kindness. She made him feel grateful and humble. He couldn't fathom living without her.

One night, late going to bed, he pushed open the bedroom door and the light from the outer room outlined Sulin, her eyelashes paint brushes stroking the alabaster of her cheeks. He turned off the light and kneeling beside the bed where she slept, he watched the rise and fall of her breast. Her gentle breathing, her hair fanned out on the pillow, everything about her thrilled him. When he touched her cheek, she sighed and turned slightly away from him. He ran his hand over her shoulder and down, cupping a breast, feeling its nipple harden beneath his palm

Sensuous as a kitten, she moved, arched her back, and sighed.

Slipping in beside her, he put a hand on her slim waist, ran it down her flanks. Each day was filled with hectic activity and far ranging talk, all of it as basic, as fundamental as he felt now. He wanted his wife, wanted her body joined to his.

"You come to bed late" she whispered, speaking in English as she sometimes did with him. Her hand found his hip, her head his shoulder. "Too much work make for trouble." A sliver of moonlight coming in the high window cast olive green shadows over the sheets tented over his knees. "When this is over, Chiang gone, I mean to take you to Seattle, show you off."

Running her hand over his chest, she said so softly he made her repeat the words, "When this is over I will give birth to our baby."

The possibility of Sulin being pregnant stunned him. Why had he not considered the possibility? He studied her face, lost mostly in the shadows. "You sure?" The thought of another child, a daughter he'd seen much too briefly, came swiftly, unbidden, the toddler he'd half-consciously seen in every child he'd encountered.

"Really. I am with infant."

"More reason to go to Seattle."

"My child will be born in China." Her voice was firm, uncompromising as if saying their child linked them irrevocably to China.

He felt as if someone or something had hit him from behind, and he tried to articulate his feelings, but the words sounded weak when spoken. Sulin, in her fervor for the reform the new government would bring, was linked to the Maoists. He needed to forget his American daughter and in doing so allow her to forget the father she'd never known. He put his hand on Sulin's belly and said, "Do you suppose it will be a son?"

Chapter 8

Logan

The People's Republic of China – 1950's – 1960's

The following years passed so swiftly Logan had trouble separating one from another. Tapped by the Ministry of Culture, he and Sulin performed a myriad of jobs that explained the "finer things of life" to the masses. In addition he taught English to diplomats' children. Sometimes he and Sulin traveled through the country, leaving Meiling with a nurse. But most of the time they were at home in Beijing, going from three cramped rooms in those bright early years to a house with a walled garden later. It was a good and busy life, and Logan was happy. His work pleased him; his wife and family delighted him.

Later, when government decisions created hardships so severe officials doctored reports, he heard nothing about it. He was removed, special, eating well, living well. How special he didn't fully surmise. Sulin was like a moth fluttering around him protectively, Meiling a treasure, his life a role he had chosen.

As the years passed, two becoming three, five becoming six, Logan's role as teacher grew. He expanded the English lessons he gave Wu Huxia's son, Gang-jo, made them more detailed, wanting the boy to understand abstract discussions, respond appropriately to concepts that had no literal basis. When the heat of summer forced them outdoors, Logan taught in the garden beneath the shade of flowering trees, where the breeze rustled papers and the fragrance of jasmine sweetened the air.

Meiling joined the classes but unlike Gang-jo, she never sat still. Like a bird she perched here, and then there, chirping all the while. "But, Daddy, why must I learn English? I am Chinese."

Daddy! The word moved through him like an accolade, warm as an embrace. "Because English is an important world language," Logan answered, his eyes feasting on this delicate creature formed through his and Sulin's love.

"English is not as good as Chinese," Gang-jo said, for once not ignoring six-year- old Meiling's conversation.

Logan knew the boy spoke from the superiority of his twelve years. "English is not better or worse. Just different," Logan explained, walking around the goldfish pond while he listened to Gang-jo explain the matter of tenses and plurals to Meiling.

"But in Chinese we don't have them, and we do all right," she said, cocking her head to the side, unconsciously aping her mother.

Logan wanted to smile, but Gang-jo scowled in the way of the young sensing a weakness. Logan expanded on Gang-jo's explanation to Meiling. "So you see, the seeming intricacies of English are necessary." Although she was too young to understand the concept, still he enjoyed talking at her, his words hanging in the air for her to grasp later. His second daughter, who looked more Western than her sister, they'd named Weiping. Both girls partially made up for the daughter he thought about at odd moments, her image flashing like a firefly and then gone, the guilt remaining. Was she lost to him forever?

His gaze went beyond the wall. People of the community chatted with him, shared gossip, told jokes, and when he left the immediate neighborhood, people still knew him, calling to him by his Chinese name. He was the white man who had written the truth so that foreigners would recognize the greatness of the new China, the excellence of the Chinese people.

"My efforts were puny beside those of others," he would say in the Chinese way

"Ah, Mao," they would say, and their eyes would shine.

Logan had trouble understanding their adulation, but he, too, felt proud of China's progress. No longer did beggars clog busy streets, their deformed limbs thrust out, begging bowls at the ready. Prostitution had disappeared. Re-education programs proliferated. Former fancy ladies had honorable new professions; number one ladies in formerly grand houses unbound their feet. Girls stood head to head with boys. Self-esteem and knowledge expanded, people's worth to society multiplied. From everything Logan had seen, the new egalitarian system was working. He quit deriding himself about Christine. With Betty, she would have a good life. In 1957, when Logan was thirty-five, he and Sulin attended a dance program at Meiling's school. Like a delicate hummingbird stealing nectar, she moved with precision through the dance with her classmates. Even though no one mentioned it, her artistry stood out. Reciting a poem later, she illustrated the verse with movements that added to the beauty of the words. Although the other children also moved at appropriate times, their movements were choppy, their voices dull compared to hers. Logan's mind was still filled with fatherly pride when he and Sulin arrived at the magazine late.

The others in their office were already gathered around the conference table, a representative high in the Bureau of Printed Affairs among them. Everyone turned to look at them.

Sunshine streamed through the window. No clouds marred the pale blue sky, and a hum of soft voices drifted from the courtyard below. Logan knew supreme contentment and his smile reflected it, going like a summer breeze from one person to the next. But Sulin was apologizing, head bobbing, words liquid and soothing, as she said she and Logan should not have been late. Logan frowned.

The cadre leader, a man whose soft cheeks and lips made Logan think his voice would match, inclined his head and then announced firmly, his voice cracking, "Please be seated." As they sat, he said, his smile impartial, shining on everyone, "You all wonder why I am here when it is not my usual time to visit. It is because I have an important message."

The cadre's right forefinger slashed through the smoke rising from his cigarette. "China has been a single poppy, a bud that flowers alone. Now, we must let a hundred flowers bloom, let a hundred schools of thought contend." He fanned his fingers. "People like you, the intellectuals, will lead the way. You must tell us what it is we should do, what reforms must be instituted to better serve the People's Republic." He paused, and the light in his eyes grew dim. "So," he said, his gaze skimming by Logan, passing over Sulin, and touching the others at the table, "This, what happened here this morning," he indicated Logan and Sulin, "provides an excellent opportunity for discussion with intellectual input." He turned to Logan. "Let me give an example. It might be that you, Wai Liang and Lin Sulin, feel the need for more time away from the job. I would like to hear your opinions."

"We appreciate the chance to express ourselves," Sulin said quickly. "It was our fault we were late. We do not need more time away from the job."

"I see. Maybe you need more time *on* the job."

"Sometimes it would be helpful when we're on a deadline."

Her voice was so soft Logan hardly heard it.

The cadre nodded. "And you, comrade, do you feel the same as Comrade Lin Sulin?" His eyes cut quickly to Logan, slicing deeply like a blade de-boning a fish.

Logan glanced around. His comrades were smiling. Tea was being poured. The covers of magazines he'd help put out decorated the walls. How could anything be wrong? He leaned forward. "I think there should be more cooperation between schools and places of work. Time for parents to visit their children's schools, to see what the learning environment is like, get to know their teachers."

"I see." The cadre smiled, and his pillow cheeks turned his eyes to slits again.Like Mao, Logan thought, surprised and amazed that this was so.

The official leaned back in his chair as if he had all the time in the world to discuss this idea. "That is indeed an interesting thought. How much time would you devote to this?"

Expanding as he went along, Logan threw out ideas he'd never formalized before. He expounded upon the theme of responsibility between segments of the society. "I expect an hour a day would do it."

"But Lin-Sulin has testified that more time is needed to get your work done."

"I don't think she meant...."

"How can you speak for her? Are you in her head?" The Cadre lit another cigarette from the butt glowing in his fingers. He looked at the others around the table.

The editors, writers, translators, photographers and typists who put out the magazine, avoided Logan's eyes. The man who ran the printing presses, who at times had grumbled at Logan's demands for higher standards, nodded, agreeing with the visiting expert. The paste-up of the magazine's next edition had been pushed to the end of the table as if unimportant, forgotten.

"Do you think Wai Liang shows capitalistic tendencies?" the Cadre asked, examining the glowing tip of his cigarette.

The pressman squirmed. "He wants time off like people in capitalistic societies."

"His thinking is polluted by capitalistic thought," another said.

Logan cried. "I only meant...." What the hell was going on? He'd worked next to these people day after day. He'd thought they were his friends.

But others accused him now, voices rising. "He always has Lin Sulin go over his work. He takes her from her own tasks. He treats her like a lackey."

"Like a slave."

Sulin shook her head, but the talk continued.

That night Logan went home in a daze. "What kind of shit was that this morning?" he cried to Sulin when the gate leading to the street was firmly closed behind them.

"You make too much of it." But a frown appeared between her eyes and didn't leave, no matter that Logan hugged her, and she hugged him back.

Later that year Logan received word. Wai Liang had been a true comrade, and a true comrade wanted nothing but to better himself, become more worthy. To help with the Great Leap Forward, to amend his rightist attitudes, Logan was to go to the country, live with people who were the backbone of China, learn from them even as he taught them. Sulin and the children would stay in Beijing.

Grabbing the paper, Logan ran out of the house, rushed down the alley to the street and crowded aboard a bus bound downtown. Pushing his way to a seat, he offered no apologies. The waiting room at the Public Security Bureau, swarmed with people. He elbowed his way to the head of a line and demanded to see someone in charge. The clerks shouted that he should take his turn. Shoved aside by citizens jockeying for position, he lost his place. Without thinking it through, he pushed through doors to the head office.

A clerk looked up from behind a desk.

Logan slammed his hands down on the desk and demanded, "Why are you sending me to the country?"

The middle-aged man behind the desk shook his head. "I know nothing." Speaking in a soft voice he added, "Please, don't make it worse for yourself, Comrade. Whoever you are, your case has been fully documented." He fiddled with a pencil.

Logan leaned closer. "I am Wai Liang, Logan Wainwright, and damn it, you better show me what you mean."

The man's eyes flared. "Oh, are you Wai Liang?"

"Yes, damn it, that's what I said."

"You realize, of course, that I don't have to, but you being a foreign born citizen, makes this a special case." The man slid his chair back, got up and went to a bank of files along the far wall. He pulled a folder from a file and handed it over.

Logan thumbed through the papers. Testimony had been taken from everyone he'd worked with for years, as well as the cadre and current fellow workers.

The man put the file back and smiled. "It is thought that in getting in touch again with pure thought, you will mend your errant rightist tendencies brought about, perhaps, because of your bourgeois beginnings."

"Bull shit."

The man raised his eyebrows. "If you are berating me in English, it doesn't matter. I never learned the language of capitalism."

Logan stormed outside and walked home, down the street of the tailors, past the noodle shops, by the school where childish voices shouted Mao's praise. Adrenaline surged through him. At home he paced the house, going over in his mind all that had happened. He was glad Sulin was at work, his daughters at school. How could a country that had seemed so forward, so democratic sounding, do this to him? Was he at fault? Had he been arrogant, demanding?

Hands shaking, he gathered together books, and was adding stationary and writing materials to a small case when a knock came at the gate. Startled he glanced around. The gatekeeper was probably at the market, choosing the produce that would appear on their table that night. Before he could decide what to do, a figure pushed through the gate and entered the house by the front door.

Logan slumped with relief seeing Gang-jo. At fourteen the boy was slim and tall, all bony wrists and ankles. Awkward appearing, uncertain, he paused as if not knowing what to say or do. Logan gestured, indicating the boy should come in, sit down. Immediately, Gang-jo's good-looking face grew tight, hard with the harsh judgments of youth, unrelenting. "So it is true?"

"What is true?" Logan asked, continuing to sort through his books.

Gang-jo's voice shrill with anger, he shouted. "You are a rightist. I should have known. Always talking about America. Wearing those clothes."

Surprised, Logan looked down at his Western shirt and shook his head. "What are you talking about? You don't understand."

"*You* don't understand. China doesn't need foreigners."

"Gang-jo, you can't mean that. I'm your teacher, your friend. I've known your father since the liberation. You've been in and out of this house for years." For a moment the boy wavered, looking away, as if unable to meet Logan's gaze. "You know I'm not a rightist, whatever in hell that is."

"All capitalists are enemies." Gang-jo's heels hit the floor with military precision as he left.

Logan looked around, seeing the splendor of Chinese luxury in the elaborately carved furniture, the highly polished wood, the jade, the marble. Had each word he'd uttered through the years been examined ad infinitum and found wanting? Opening the door he listened to the sounds of the street, the muffled musical voices, the sibilant sound of rubber tires, the creak of carts, the braying of draft animals. Through the years he'd kept in touch with Freddy Patterson. Freddy would help him, and no matter how she protested, get Sulin and the children out safely.

He rushed outside, but half a dozen strong young men intercepted him in the courtyard. Shouting invectives, as Gang-jo watched, they overpowered him and escorted him firmly to the bus that would take him to the country.

Eight months later, standing in the doorway at home Logan eyed the living room, the loneliness he'd known encompassing him again. Other intellectuals accused of being rightists had been worked until their backs bent, their eyes grew vacant, but they had been together in labor camps; he had been alone. He tried to make sense from the nonsense that had happened, but no order emerged from the chaos. He had lived with privation and suffered invective, done menial chores and survived the boredom by reciting all he could remember of days when promise had whetted his pride and knowledge had been applauded. But now the nightmare was over. After stultifying and sometimes frightening times, the days of drudgery and degradation, he was back in Beijing, his hands calloused, his eyes glazed, not daring to think beyond the moment.

Like an outsider returning to a place he had never really known, he slapped at the travel dust covering him and repeated the poem that had pushed and prodded his mind daily for eight months, Robert Frost's *The Road Not Taken*. The fatigue of a long absence slowing his step, he looked around the formal room with critical eyes. "Two roads diverged in a yellow wood," he said aloud and doubled his fists, tears not shed before, filling his eyes. After months of making do with benches and three-legged stools and a bed without a mattress, he felt stunned by the luxury. Sulin's porcelain collection, brought from her ancestral home, was housed in a Blackwood cabinet. Similar shiny black tables were strewn between overstuffed chairs set precisely on a scarlet and gold Persian carpet. What about the Republic's much-vaunted equality? What dichotomy of being had he not seen, had he not understood?

A soft step, penetrated his clouded thinking, and the Frost poem, stopped its incessant repeating. He stared at Sulin, not ready to see her, but longing to. Her image had sustained him, and he filled his eyes with her now. She had changed in subtle ways he could not immediately identify, her silence forbidding, her beauty without dispute. Even as he said nothing, neither did she. He imagined she was holding back, as if someone were listening or perhaps watching, and this attitude saddened him further. Would she have to report to someone about him? They lived in luxury unimaginable when contrasted with the gut-wrenching poverty he'd seen. Why didn't she say something? Was he that changed? Had he combed his hair that morning or only put acceptance on his face? He straightened, seeing her completely now, seeing past the film of self-thought holding him apart. He had put his own suspicions, his anger, on her. Shame mingled with the anger. "I am home," he said, needing words to float between them, no matter their content. Hadn't he loved her always?

"So I see." She came to a stop across the room, away from him, remote, her eyes quiet, not dancing or teasing as they had done in the past.

"And you. Are you and my daughters well?" His words sounded brusque, harsh in his ears, and for the first time since leaving, he spoke English. It ricocheted from the walls and threatened to drown him with a backwash of harsh sound.

"I am well." She took a step closer. "You look as if the country air was beneficial. Your face is tanned, you hair lighter." Her smile was tiny, tentative.

"I was outside every day." Her voice, her graceful movement impressed itself on him, bringing him back, opening the way. "The country air was often ripe with night soil," he said, adding a small smile. He had not been so isolated he hadn't known. Whole classes of people had been accused, scooped up, sent away for retraining. Would there be electronic bugs in the room, sophisticated surveillance for the Westerner? He could not take a chance. He waved at the furniture "All this is too good for the likes of Liberationist fighters."

"Yes," she said, her voice loud as she enunciated clearly, each word said as if it were an elocution lesson, her eyes bright with understanding. "We have more worldly goods than we need."

Logan wanted to throw something, hit something, furious he had been reduced to posturing, Sulin forced to go along. He shouted in English, knowing he shouldn't but not caring. "Damn it, stop this idiotic talk. You are my wife! Act like it." He crossed toward her in long strides. Her hands fluttered over her mouth, her eyes grew big and tears wet her cheeks before she threw herself into his arms.

His tears mingled with hers.

"I need to forget what happened," Logan said later that

night as they sat together on the sofa, the children tucked in. "I did nothing wrong. That is the part that bothers me the most. All those months. Such a waste of time."

Trembling, she pulled away from him. "In any revolution miscarriages of justice happen." Speaking so softly he had to lean close to hear, she said, "I have asked to have your file removed from the Bureau. I believe they will do it." For a moment her eyes glittered.

He lit a cigarette, half turning from her, cold invading his body, moving toward his mind. All those months away he had convinced himself it was a mistake, some clerk doing the wrong thing, Mao and the others aghast, not knowing how to rectify it without denying the people they hoped to lift up.

She touched his arm. "It was not an easy thing to do, Logan."

He inhaled deeply, let the smoke trickle through his nostrils, remembered how she had looked when he had first seen her, the wine red gown, the pile of black hair. Now he saw the sadness in her eyes and realized again what he had seen before. No matter that their thoughts often leaped together in glorious harmony, that they shared passionate interludes incomparable in their intensity and pleasure, at times the differences in their backgrounds made words stick in their throats. What she had gone through, the suspicions, the doubts because of him, could not have been easy. "I know."

She looked down, her head tipped to one side, every line of her body seeming smaller, subservient.

He wanted to push at her, make her react in a Western way, one that would allow him full understanding and relief, but he said nothing. *The road not taken* ripped through his head.

"In any movement for change, the end result is all that

matters," she said parrot-like.

He shook his head. "Damn it, don't talk like that. Right now all that matters is that I'm here."

"Shhh," she put her fingers to her lips.

He put his arms around her, buried his face in the fragrance of her hair, and without saying another word let the things that had held them apart disintegrate. But that night, long after she was sleeping, he wrote to Christine and made sure the letter started on the clandestine route to Freddy in Hong Kong.

Logan's job at the magazine terminated, he was put to work translating approved novels. He found calm in acceptance. In the spring when the world was young again, he took the children to the park and tried hard to remember the games girls had played at home with jump ropes and jacks. Meiling and Weiping laughed and hugged him for he was clearly a male more steeped in the mysteries of boys' games. He felt delirious with love for his daughters. In the fall he took them to the circus and came home and tried to duplicate the feats of the jugglers. They laughed and ducked their heads and hid their mouths behind their hands. They were like Sulin, children of China, with actions of the present tied to the past, and the interlude in the country he pushed aside, and the road not taken stopped popping into his mind.

When winter came, Sulin insisted they all ice skate on the lake at Purple Bamboo Park. In Seattle the ponds and lakes never froze; Logan had never been on skates. The girls peeped out from layers of clothing bundled so tightly they looked like round balls. When they fell, they bounced back up. He took a bit longer. "Oh, Daddy!" they cried with delight, and he knew contentment once again and watched within a fever of love as Sulin, scarf flying like the sail on a ship, skimmed over the frozen surface. In no time the girls were aping her. Logan took off his skates and watched.

The months with the peasants buried beneath the joy of the present, China in its second Five Year Plan, the Great Leap Forward, brought Logan optimism about the future. At home he and Sulin entertained a succession of foreign visitors: minor diplomats from Albania and Kenya, businessmen and artists from Yugoslavia, and students from French African nations. When he heard rumors of political happenings in China that seemed as senseless as his time with the peasants, he kept his doubts and fears to himself. Everything and everyone was changing. Sulin no longer used cosmetics, and her clothes were as shapeless as everyone's. While her beauty needed no embellishment, he missed her sly, sidewise smiles and flirty manner. In the past she had walked and talked and moved in ways meant to excite more than platonic friendship. One night, he said, "Why do you walk like a man and look at me like one man looks at another?"

"The Chairman says women should not be coquettes. Instead we should develop our intellects in order to fully participate in the political process."

"You have always participated in the political process."

"It is better not to look different from the rest."

"You will always look different," he said, taking her hand.

She gave him the flirty look he adored, mouth and eyes teasing and then promising before she leaned against him.

"Only for you," she whispered.

One night at the ballet, after a performance more militant than entertaining, Logan saw a friend he had not seen for years. At first, among the crowds leaving the hall, he did not recognize Ma Zemin for the man had aged, looked twenty years older than his thirty some years. Bent over, he walked with a shuffling gait.

"What happened?" Logan blurted out later as the two sat together over drinks until their heads spun and the truth sneaked past defenses set up during the Hundred Flowers Movement.

Ma Zemin talked openly, without emotion. For two years he had been at a labor camp planting rice, his hands and feet constantly in cold water. At the camp everyone had spied upon one another, reporting the smallest infraction of the rules—a grain of rice spilled, a gift not shared, a thought held back, a voice not raised loud enough in praise of Mao. He had been a painter, a famous artist. His hands crippled from arthritis, he could hardly hold a brush.

I was lucky to be by myself, Logan thought, watching Ma lift his cup with both hands.

The next time he saw Ma, he called, "Ma, wait up." But Ma kept walking and Logan was forced to catch up to him.

Ma said, "I'm sorry that I talked bourgeois nonsense when I saw you."

Logan went home and put on the records Freddy had sent from Shanghai in the early years: Benny Goodman, Artie Shaw, Cab Calloway. Turning up the volume, he sat down to listen. After a while, he turned the volume so low he could hardly hear it. Then he shut off the player and put it away with the records in a box he hid behind a collection of approved magazines. What if the neighbors heard, what if they said something, what if...

One night, when the girls were sleeping, the gatekeeper and the cook in bed, he spoke to Sulin about leaving. They lay in bed, staring at the dark. "I'm tired, Sulin," he said, feeling older than his years. The glorious adventure had ended; the ship was foundering. Children with distended bellies stood on every corner. Old people in rags begged again. Once he reached down to pick up a paper bag—a rare sight on the busy road where thousands of peasants claimed every scrap of paper, cardboard, or wood for their fires—and found a dead baby inside.

Sulin's voice held a hint of condemnation. "Forty-five is not old. I am almost as old, and I don't talk like an old one." She turned toward him, the movement quiet, hardly rippling the quilts. "What is...is what is."

Her face was lost in shadows, but he knew it by heart – the smooth skin, the high cheekbones, and the almond-shaped eyes. Against the blue-white of the pillow, her hair fanned out, soft and girlish, and no matter that in the daytime she braided it or wore it bound tight to her head, he imagined he saw a nimbus radiating from her locks that had nothing to do with her looks but with her. The perceived aura both delighted and frightened him, for whatever happened, for better or worse he was bound to her. They were yin and yang, man and woman, husband and wife. Moving closer, he smiled at what he termed her oriental fatalism. "I dread what could happen; we must leave."

"Perhaps you exaggerate the danger. Anyway, who would

give us an exit permit?"

"There may be other ways." During the years he had sent stories to Freddy in Hong Kong. Freddy had published them anonymously, paid small sums for the articles, and banked the money for Logan. There was enough in the account to get away. "By water perhaps. Freddy will help."

"Is my honored husband suggesting we swim? We would only be plucked from the cold waters by British gunboats or Chinese sampans and returned home in disgrace." She attempted a laugh.

Obviously trying to lighten the moment, she'd drowned his optimism in logic. He conceded escape would be difficult, but he didn't give up the thought.

As the years slid by, changes burst upon the scene faster than he could keep track. One day he and Sulin sat in the courtyard where the pale sun could reach them. In their hands were cups of green tea, on the table shrimp balls, dumplings and moon cakes. The family of Wai Liang had never gone without like some of their neighbors. American citizens of China were showcased. That day, his daughters came home from school, Meiling subdued, Weiping in a fever of talk.

She danced around the yard, examining this and that as she spoke. "It was really exciting. We were told if enemies existed in our neighborhoods we were to rout them out. Rid society of counter-productive members. Mao wrote about it in the newspapers and said he depended on youth."

"Is this true?" Her voice even, Sulin glanced at their eldest daughter.

"Yes." Meiling shrugged delicately. "Students were told to open fire on class enemies. They didn't list enemies specifically, but some kids are sure they know who they are. Some are talking about certain teachers."

Weiping picked up and examined a cup before setting it down. "The ones who talk bourgeois nonsense. Workers, soldiers and peasants are already uniting against those who grind them into the dust. Someone said they're the true revolutionaries."

The day was so serene, a bird perching on the wall, flowers in pots reaching for the sun, the touch of unreality skittered beyond Logan, out of reach, his mind refusing to accept it. "Who is your enemy? Whom would you open fire against?" He smiled.

Seventeen-year-old Meiling averted her gaze, but fifteen-year-old Weiping named Lu Shou, a neighbor. Weiping had always been the different one, the one who looked the most like him, the one who tried the hardest always. Did she secretly hate her rounder eyes, her taller frame? His heart squeezed, held tight. "Why Lu Shou?" he asked, showing nothing of his inner turmoil.

"Only a capitalist would spend money like he does." She tossed her dark brown hair, and azure glints flashed from her eyes. "Everyone says so."

Logan wanted to warn her, be careful with your talk, but would she listen? Lately youth looked at age with anger, not respect. "His wife. Is she, too, a capitalist?" Logan watched closely this child-woman who could betray them all. By extension was Weiping condemning him and Sulin, too? Examining one of Sulin's porcelain cups, she frowned, muttered something he couldn't hear.

"If Lu were a true backer of the party, he would share his

money with the people. She is his equal partner. If she did not approve she should have left him. The Lus are too privileged." She set the cup down, looked around, her frown growing. "These cups?" she asked.

"Everyday pottery," Sulin said, her voice holding a hint of exasperation.

Logan knew better. "What about Lu's son and daughter?" He kept his voice neutral.

"They should be questioned to determine the amount of their guilt. Looks can be deceiving, but looks can also point to guilt. Now, may I be excused? I need to write my criticism."

"Criticism? Of whom, of what?"

"Of the neighborhood. We each report on our own neighborhood. It's the only fair way."

While he mulled over the words "criticism," and "fair," she left.

"Excuse me," the older of his two daughters started into the house. Judged one of the better tellers of tales, Meiling had been tapped to make individual appearances in the city. Soon she would travel with her story-telling group to outlying districts. "I must leave for my study meeting. My story group is doing the "Rent Collection Courtyard."

"Eat something first," Sulin suggested.

"I'll get something later. Goodnight Mother, Father."

Proud of Meiling's accomplishments, Logan smiled. But Weiping worried him, her impulsiveness long noted. He told his fears to Sulin.

"A wise person does not pull a donkey in a direction it doesn't want to go," Sulin said getting up to set a row of small clay pots in front of a large ornamental stationary pot. The fountain, which they'd turned off months ago, had a water ring halfway up the tiles and sand had settled on the bottom. "We must be careful with her. So young to have such power thrust into her hands. Maybe if you talk to her, in some way temper the thrill she's feeling..." Sulin looked at him with a pleading expression.

Logan felt duty-bound to say, "I will talk to Weiping."

Yet, as the days went on, his work translating a novel extolling the wisdom of the state gave him temporary escape, the walls of the compound isolating him from the city. At times Weiping reminded him of a younger Sulin in the way she spoke, phrased ideas. Then he was given an ancient text to translate, and plunged into the past, he forgot his worry, his hours occupied with subtle shades of meaning translating words and concepts.

In July 1966, when the air stood still and flies grew too turgid to move when swatted, word came that Chairman Mao swam for an hour in the Yangtze River. Buoyed by the current, cheered by the multitudes, the aging Mao's feat became a rallying cry for the nation. "Seventy-three, and he swims with vigor. See how he takes the current! See how he floats, see how he always rises to the top, a true leader." Banner headlines announced his feat. Voices shouted on the corners, bellowed from the radio. Free newspapers were printed in red ink. Articles claimed Chairman Mao had showed the way – action rather than inaction.

That night people everywhere set out red lanterns that glowed like fires sparking the night. Drumbeats boomed, waking Logan from a fitful sleep. Cymbals clanged, firecrackers popped, and underneath the tinkle and sparkle the collected voices of the city murmured, indistinct, menacing, like a sleepy dragon ready to unwind. The Cultural Revolution that had crouched like a paper tiger just out of reach, had gained flesh, was moving and hungry, and somewhere out there among the people who espoused its tenets were his daughters.

Logan stopped wearing Western clothing, pushed foreign books to the back of shelves and burned letters he'd kept from Freddy Patterson. He spoke no English to his daughters, only secretly to Sulin who curled closer to him at night.

As the storm against intellectuals, people labeled "capitalist roaders," or spies and anti-revolutionists raged, Logan seldom left the compound, glad to work at home translating the minor novels and plays Sulin brought him.

When Meiling was ordered to go to the far provinces to do her story telling, Logan feared the art and beauty of her performance would be lost in political messages, and she would be lost to him in the revolution. Hugging her, he held on too long, felt her draw back. When she reached the front gate, he ran after her. From his shirt pocket he took a scrap of paper and a pencil and wrote Freddy Patterson's last known business address in Hong Kong, Betty's address in Seattle. "Don't say anything, but memorize them in case some day you should need them. Betty is your Aunt Betty. She cares for your half-sister, Christine."

Solemn eyed, she stared at him. Would she repudiate him later, cry out some horrible denunciation? Pushing down the impulse to follow her into the street, down the block, he went inside.

The next day Sulin came home from work very late, her clothes rumpled, her lips swollen.

"What happened?" he cried, running to meet her.

"The Red Guards are children who don't know what they're doing." She went past him to the table. Her hands shook as she poured tea from the thermos. The cup showed a pastoral scene, rice fields climbing a terraced mountain.

"They attacked the magazine, arrested the editor, took him away because we print English editions." She moved from one side of the room to the other as if ridding herself of the memories as she talked. "They hung huge character signs in the office: *English: the language of capitalist foreign ghosts. Intellectuals: pawns of the imperialist West*!" She laughed, the sound bitter. "Posters covered the walls and hung from the ceiling. I had to thread my way through them to get to my desk. They were waiting for me there." She started to cry, knuckled her eyes and mouth.

"Sweetheart, sweetheart." He tried to take her into his arms.

"Let me finish." She lifted her head and, lips trembling, said, "They made me kneel in the corridor and explain my crime of wrong thinking."

"Wrong thinking?" Logan whispered.

"I did not answer fast enough," she said as softly as he.

Anger ripped through him. He wanted to run out into the street and hit the first passerby.

That night when Weiping came home long past her bedtime, Logan met her at the gate. "Get in the house. Now."

Scowling, she touched the red band on her arm. "You can't tell me what to do any more."

"Are your mother and I the enemy, too?" He put out a hand.

She ignored it. “You think because you hide the good furniture, give up your Western clothes, you have made amends. Well, it doesn’t work that way, Father.” She glared at him.

For a moment he glared back, sadness constricting his heart.

“Now, let me by so I can go to my room.” Weiping spoke in a loud, impolite voice. “Oh, and leave the gate unlocked. My friends may need a place to sleep.“

Later in the privacy of their room he said to Sulin, “We must leave tomorrow. We still have a little money. People can be bribed, the path made clear.”

She shook her head. “Dear husband, I can never leave our girls. When this craziness is over, they will come back to us. You will see.” Gazing steadily at him, she asked rhetorically, “When the Ku Klux Klan lynched people, did you leave? When the Great Depression left people starving, did you go to another country?”

He did not say these things had little affect on him, that he had never known anyone who belonged to the Klan or who had starved during the depression. His deep love for America had never changed, so how could he fault her for her loyalty to China? Unable to swallow the lump in his throat, he went into the backyard and listened to shouts echoing from all sides. To the south a fire lit the sky. Palming a cigarette, he smoked quietly as footsteps pounded down the alley, grew closer, cloth shoes thudding, voices raised angrily. He put out his cigarette. Two doors down, fists beat against wood. Voices demanded entry.

“A minute, a minute,” his neighbor’s ancient gatekeeper cried.

Logan looked over his back wall in time to see a tangled mass of young people smash the old man down. His legs buckled, his body collapsed, and he fell clutching his chest as the Red Guards ran past him into the compound.

Logan ran out his gate and down the alley, hurried to the old man, lifted him up, felt for a pulse. "I think he's dead," he whispered as Sulin appeared at his side.

The Guards were shouting, "This is the house of a traitor! His short wave radio opened his children's ears to foreign propaganda!"

"Hurry," Sulin urged, tugging at Logan until he left the old man and followed her back to their own courtyard. Once it had been beautiful, before beauty meant decadence, and they'd been forced to abandon its upkeep. "We must wake up our gatekeeper and the cook," she said. They had come with her from the past, old family retainers who had tended her when she was a baby.

"It is no longer good for you to stay here," Logan explained when the old ones came out rubbing their eyes. He pointed toward the neighbors' house where muffled sounds and loud shouts continued.

"But where will Old Wang go? My wife and I have always been with Mistress's family."

"You must go back to your village, to your people."

"Mistress is our people."

"No," Sulin corrected, "you should not call me mistress. It is not the new way. It will bring trouble to you and to me."

Pulling a bundle of yuan from his pocket, Logan said, "Share the money with the people in your village. For your own good, for everyone's good, you must leave."

"But who will answer the gate? Who will cook the meals?"

"We will manage." Sulin spoke harshly. "You must obey."

Rounding up their belongings, tying them into bundles, she shoved the two old ones toward the gate, pushed at them with her hands and her words. Afterward, she sobbed. "It is as if I turned my mother and father into the streets."

Chapter 9

Logan

The People's Republic of China – 1960's

When the Red Guards pounded on Logan's gate, he telephoned Sulin's office, heard her hesitant hello. He said, "They are here. Don't come home," hung up and went out to open the gate.

They appeared to him through a prism of unreality, as if an unknown director called for action in a movie not yet written. They were a mirage, unreal, a cohort stirring the dust with their restless feet, stirring the air with their voices. He was a traitor, worse than a cockroach feeding on the food of others, telling his elitist lies. Teenage boys and young men welcomed him with their fists, and he found the anger, the pride that he'd known long ago and fought like an abused citizen until they beat him to the ground where he railed at them in Chinese and English. But they were too many and too young.

Daylight hovered above him as they dragged him inside, sun fading away as he bumped across the threshold, words pushing at his throat unsaid. Why were they doing this? Shouting he was the son of a toad, a foreign devil, they kicked and pummeled him until blood ran and pain assaulted him like an animal tearing at his guts, laying open his skin until his body throbbed with unceasing, unrelenting aching until the light and the pain disappeared into a black welcoming night.

When he regained consciousness dark had descended.

"Ah, you waken." A smooth-faced man in his mid to late twenties bowed slightly. "Permit me to introduce myself. I am Pao Ching."

Through a blur of blood and sweat, Logan eyed the shorter, younger man. He was the one standing by while the others had beaten and pummeled him, the one who had waited until they had dragged him upright so he could shout accusations and punch him into insensibility. He was the one who smiled while he hit.

"You don't deserve to live. But we are magnanimous. In the morning you will see how just we are."

Logan heard the blow coming before he felt the impact, the pain ripping past barriers extending to a place he'd never known. He sagged against the ropes holding him, and again the blackness came.

In the morning he heard the words before consciousness came fully. Wai Liang was a traitor, a mud ant, a nothing. Then his bindings were dropping away, and Pao Ching was saying, "We will be back. Stay here. Do not leave, you miserable worm. Understand? You are a mess. Is this a foreign trait? You should clean yourself, make yourself presentable for when we return." As he heard the door slam, the gate clang shut, Logan rubbed life into his numb and swollen wrists and ankles and pushed himself shakily to his feet. The room shifted and then steadied slowly. Hobbling to the bathroom, he felt old and decrepit. His nose was sore but not broken, the cuts would mend, the bruises would go away, the aches would subside, but he would never forget.

For an hour, he watched the door. When no footsteps sounded, when no one came back, he hurried to the phone, but the line had been cut, the telephone smashed. The shadows lengthened and the chill of night invaded the house, but no Sulin appeared, no Red Guards returned.

He fell into a death-like sleep, waking three hours later, strange voices intruding. Cautiously, he went outside, sticking to the shadows, walking carefully, his feet and legs sore, cuts bleeding again. A small crowd had gathered and were pointing at his house and pelting it with trash.

He hurried back inside. In the middle of the night, when the street was deserted, he went out to see. A huge poster with high Chinese characters hung at his gate. It read, "House of a Traitor." The red paint spelling out the words had dripped like spilled blood. He tore the poster down.

Later, when the gate creaked open, he peeked through a window. Weiping, looking anxious but well, hurried up the walk. Oblivious to pain, he ran out. No matter that she wore the hated red armband, she couldn't be like the others. "Thank God." He gathered his youngest daughter into his arms.

She shrugged out of his embrace. "I cannot stay. I thought you should know they hold Mother at work. She was condemned as an elitist writer. They say you are a spy."

"Nonsense. You know better than that"

She avoided his gaze. "It is better if I stay away. The whole city is upside down. Yesterday I met students from Shanghai." A small smile crossed her lips. "Red Guards can go anywhere without money. The trains are free for us." A proud look settled on her face.

Logan stared, shocked at the far-reaching affects of the Cultural Revolution. It had taken his daughter at fifteen and turned her into a parrot for the movement. "What do the leaders of this craziness plan for your mother and me?" The words came out before the wisdom of silence occurred.

Weiping's lips curled as if his question disgusted her. "How should I know? The accused appear at Struggle Meetings where they examine their conscience, acknowledge their wrongs."

"Your mother and I have done nothing wrong."

She shook her head. "Father, to think that way is wrong. I fear for you." Tossing her head, she ran out, into the street, away from everything he had taught her.

The next day Pao Ching and two others returned. They tied his hands behind his back and loaded him into the bed of an open truck where he shared standing-up space with men and women wearing dunce caps and signs draped around their necks. One read, "Bad Thinker, Revisionist, Defender of Old Ideas." His said, "Traitor." He recognized no one, and no one took notice of him, their gazes on their feet as if the fight had been drained from them.

I'll be damned if I'll hang my head, Logan thought as Pao Ching climbed into the cab and the truck moved forward. Each bump in the road throwing him off balance, Logan fought to stay upright. He found a place against the side and held it as the truck bounced and jerked. The closer they got to Tiananmen Square; Mao's picture was seen everywhere, bigger than life, immense. His sayings were painted on buildings, displayed in windows, his poetry blared from radios. People clutching his red book of quotations in their hands surged through the streets, shouting. They jeered at the truck with Logan in it and pointing their fingers, shouted, "Repent, repent."

Above his head, floating high over the street, a banner proclaimed in Mao's words: "When we die for the people it is a worthy cause." Was he being taken to a guillotine like the aristocrats during the French Revolution? If he were to be executed, was this the last he'd see of the world, this street, this place? An ache, a longing for a quiet meadow, a pristine mountain, gripped him, but he couldn't conjure Mt. Rainier, Puget Sound, the cool, green grass, his mother's face, Sulin's.

Loudspeakers boomed revolutionary music. Fixed to walls and buildings and swaying from clotheslines, posters attacked bourgeois leaders. Names were spelled out in huge characters, and near the place where the truck stopped on Dianment Street Logan read his name.

How could young, uninformed people, some barely out of childhood, take over a country, hold him hostage and pervert the China he had accepted without the backing of the leaders? It couldn't, he thought, his outrage bringing him strength.

"Come," Pao Ching cried, leading him away from the others in the truck.

Logan followed him inside the building that had been constructed before the Chinese love affair with the Soviets had ended. The large meeting room was packed with people sitting on the floor, on benches, and leaning against the walls, facing a table and three chairs placed in the center of the room. On the far wall a giant painting showed Mao's round face in accepted lines: fatherly and loving.

Pao Ching tugged Logan toward a bench, and three men in quasi-military uniforms entered the room from the far end of the hall and sat down at the table facing Logan. Dun Zeng, the man in the middle, was universally known, a man who had held numerous government posts. A murmur passed through the room until Dun Zeng lifted his head and looked around. Soon, no one spoke.

The other two men at the table shuffled papers, the older of the men looking bored and taking no notice of anyone. The younger man scowled and looked up often, his gaze stabbing here and there as if attempting to convince people of his importance. Wu Gang-jo!

Logan stiffened. His former student, son of Wu Huixia, pretended not to see him. The boy, who had ingested learning as easily as he had swallowed the lotus seed soup Sulin's cook prepared, was a handsome young man. Could he have so easily forgotten the past when they had discussed the world beyond China's borders? Could he have submerged the memories of sitting at Logan's table, laughing and joking with Logan's daughters, complimenting Sulin, devouring Logan's knowledge? Yet, there had been hints, and how could any young person fight the rising tide of their peers?

A murmur rose, subdued whispers like a wave washing through the room. Carrying a low stool, a square-shaped woman entered through an inner door, passing peasants who pulled in feet and legs, pressed closer to one another to make room so she could pass. The woman set the stool down and left.

A few minutes later she returned, prodding a prisoner, a smaller, finer-boned woman, in faded, worn blue pants and tunic, ahead of her. The prisoner settled on the stool like a stem holding firm to the last flower petals of fall.

Logan absorbed Sulin's presence. Like a moongate seen through flat light without dimension, the animation that had proclaimed her superiority was gone. No light flashed from her eyes, no emotion, showed on her face, yet grace shrieked from every line of her body. Stricken, he cried out her name, his voice loud.

For an instant her head came up and the dull pewter of her eyes flashed like polished silver as she searched the crowd. Turning her head in all directions, she probed the room, her shoulders hunched, her body drawn in upon itself as if she were protecting herself from the multitudes.

"I'm here," Logan shouted in English from his bench several paces behind her.

Instantly, Pao Ching pulled his arm up and back until his shoulder blades burned with pain. Still he saw her lift her head, and turning swiftly, locate him. Lifting an arm in greeting, she was fragile as a flower in a windstorm, beautiful in vulnerability laced with inner strength, her eyes glittering briefly before a Red Guard shoved her head toward the floor.

His heart fibrillating dangerously, Logan watched the woman, who had been friend, lover, companion, wife, fade like a flower past its prime. Noting each drooping line of her body, his heart lurched. She'd always contained a center of resilience, strong as alabaster or marble. Now it seemed the inner core was fractured and the outside splashed with cheap paint. Always fashionably correct, and in the past elegant and fastidious, her torn and dirty clothes were the consummate insult.

Dun Zeng gestured, indicating Sulin should stand. She rose and bowing low to the portrait of Mao she said to Dun Zeng, "I beg the Chairman's indulgence and for-bearance." Her voice sounded dull, defeated, far from the ringing musical chant he was used to.

Logan had to bite his lips to keep from crying out. He

wanted to protest, tell her not to confess, not to corrupt her innocence.

Dun Zeng listed her crimes, reading them in a loud, matter-of-fact voice from his place at the table. She wrote articles for foreign consumption. She married a foreigner. She was a friend of rightists. She was an enemy of the Party.

"Traitor!" a man yelled from the sidelines. "Dirty revisionist, capitalist roader."

Soon a din of voices shouted political phrases and branded Sulin with foul names. A man nearby spat into her face. Gutter language bombarded her, knifed into Logan, He wanted to fight them all, grab her up and run from the building. In his mind a safe place waited where warm breezes teased flowering mountain meadows. He wondered if he were hallucinating.

Shouts of abuse became one voice, a din ricocheting from the walls, insensible, unclear.

Dun Zeng rose, and as suddenly as the attack started, it ended. In the ensuing quiet, he read from a sheaf of papers he called The History of a Traitor. He paced from one end of the table to the other, pausing at times to look down at Suilin.

The traitor Lin Sulin was a daughter of landlords who had also been sons and daughters of landlords. They had enslaved the Chinese people until the glorious Communist Party and their beloved Chairman Mao had set them free. It was clear that Lin Sulin was an enemy of their beloved leader. Had not her brothers supported Chiang Kai-shek, a toady of the West? Everyone knew imperialistic, capitalistic America was arming Taiwan. Lin Sulin had married a foreign devil from the United States, China's sworn enemy. China must be protected from her kind.

People roared, “Lin Sulin is a traitor.”

Dun Zeng held up his hands, and the roar subsided. “But the Chairman is magnanimous,” he said, looking out at the crowd, his face transformed as he smiled. “If the comrade confesses, admits to her wrongdoing, Chairman Mao and the Communist Party would be pleased. Wrong thinking and acting can be rectified, a person restored to his or her proper place in the People’s Republic of China “ He took his seat, leaned across the table toward Sulin and spoke softly. “You may speak now, Lin Sulin.” He smiled at her.

As if given an injection of adrenaline, she rose and turned, facing first one and then another section of the hall, her body straight, her eyes direct. “Thank you, Comrade, and you who have my welfare at heart.” Her voice rang sweet and clear. “Foolishly, I wrote articles in English and French, but I did so thinking I was helping our great Chairman Mao. My dedication to the People’s Republic cannot be questioned. Was I not part of the Liberation Army? Did I not join with the comrades despite the pleading of my brothers who were with the Kuomintang backing Chiang?”

A whisper rippled through the listening public. “This is true,” someone said.

Dun Zeng rapped for silence. “What a sorrow. You who were there in the beginning spoiled your record.”

“The record will show, Comrade, I joined the party of my own free will. I could have joined my brothers and gone with Chiang Kai-shek. But instead, I, and my American husband, who saw the sins of the West, joined our glorious fighters for true freedom. If I had really wanted to be part of the Western culture, part of the capitalist society, I could easily have gone with Chiang."

Murmurs rose from the crowd, and here and there heads nodded, voices murmured, "I remember."

Dun Zeng gaveled for silence. "As our Chairman has written, mistakes are inevitable; it will be well if we seriously correct them."

Sulin nodded. "All people in the revolutionary ranks must care for each other, must love and help each other."

A swell of approval passed through the hall. "She speaks true. Her words are Mao's words."

Dun Zeng smiled. "Lin Sulin's confession, written in the past week at her place of work, made these things clear, but it is always good to hear them again."

Logan felt hope. Sulin's hands, so eloquent in their movements reached up to push back a stray lock of hair, and they were shaking. Quickly, she clasped them behind her back.

Her interrogator went around the table and, standing over her, said, "It is clear that the Comrade was confused, and now sees the folly of her former ways; but good is often offset by evil. We offer first this address, written in the hand of Lin Sulin's husband. An address to a foreigner in Hong Kong."

Logan's heart raced, he closed his eyes, momentarily shutting out the room, the close unwashed smells of the crowd, the cigarette smoke collecting like fog near the low ceiling. He knew raw, unvarnished fear, and he could have caused it.

Dun Zeng held a sheet of paper high above his head. "We also have this letter written by Lin Sulin's husband, the foreigner, Logan Wainwright, also known as Wai Liang. He wrote to an American in Hong Kong, and I read the damning words, 'Deposit for me in the Bank of Hong Kong payment for the article. One never knows when it will be useful.'"

Dun Zeng appealed to the crowd. "I ask you, is this not the mark of a traitor?"

Again his words were drowned out by the clamor of the people.

Logan jumped to his feet, shouted above the din, "Let me see the letter. If it is mine, I will answer for it, not my wife." He glanced at her, telling her silently how much he loved her, telling her he knew what she was doing for him.

Pao Ching signaled, and the Guards beat him down, stuck a dirty cloth in his mouth and tied another around his eyes. Words without leavening crashed against his ears. Lin Sulin should have known better than her husband. He was a foreigner, spawn of the West. Such a one was filled with Western thought and would naturally make mistakes. But she was Chinese, and as such she must answer for them both. In the countryside where she would live and work with the peasants, she would have time to contemplate the great wrongs she had done to China.

And then he felt her hand on his cheek followed by scuffling sounds, as if she were being pulled away. Thrashing, he fought until they dragged him outside and pushed him into the back seat of a car and slammed him with their fists until he had no more fight left.

When realization returned he knew the car had stopped. People had gotten out. Someone had removed his gag. His hands were untied, his eyes no longer blindfolded. Blinking to clear his vision, he looked around. Could it be true? This looked like his compound. Beyond the gate his house appeared as he had left it, no poster hanging from the gate.

Pao Ching said, "With Lin Sulin gone, we will be short-handed. You will need to do the work of two. We will bring you assignments. Don't forget, you are under house arrest." And then he left.

Full of thoughts that had nowhere to go, Logan went inside and dozed off and on during the rest of the day and night. The next day they brought him assignments, some rice, some beans, a squash. Each day he typed inflammatory phrases and untruths and tried not to think of Sulin. An aristocrat's daughter, she had never worked with her hands, knew nothing about the chores of a peasant.

A few weeks later, after dark, a knock came at the gate. Logan pictured someone banging the brass rings, jiggling the handles. Should he ignore it? If it were the Red Guards, they'd come in anyway. But maybe it was one of his daughters. He hurried out.

Wu Huixia, Gang-jo's father, stood at the gate. Wearily, Logan offered him tea.

Wu Huixia spoke of the weather first, the forecast for rain second, and then added, "As a foreigner who chose to become Chinese, you are an honored guest. You could not be sent to the country again."

Logan stared at him. "Was there nothing you could do for Sulin? I thought you were her friend. Have you forgotten I educated Gang-jo at your request."

Huixia shook his head. "I have always appreciated your teaching him." He settled deeper into his chair, and for a time he looked past Logan before he spoke. "When my father was beaten to death for not paying taxes due on his donkey, I joined Mao. When we made the Long March and set up headquarters in Yennan, I was fifteen. When I was twenty-six Mao said a man shouldn't remain single. Ai-Min was sixteen years older and schooled in the ways of politics. When Mao talked in riddles or poems, and Zhou spoke in words better understood by learned men, she explained their meaning to me. She said it was my duty to impregnate her. I did not know she was too old for child-bearing, that she would not survive. She died when Gang-jo was born."

"Why do you tell me these things now?" Logan eyed the house that had been ransacked, holes gouged in the walls, dishes broken, his clothes destroyed. He had cleaned up the mess, patched the plaster, but the pain remained.

"Because when my son was born, I named him Gang because he had need for bravery, and I added Jo, for America's General Joe Stilwell who served in China. It was 1944 and during the war Americans came in droves to see us. Your President Roosevelt, who was tired of Chiang's high-handed ways, sent Vice President Wallace to pressure Chiang, hint that if he did not do what the Americans wanted they would deal with us."

"In 1944 I was home recuperating from a bullet, " Logan said remembering it all in one quick moment, that idyllic time with Nancy, the birth of their daughter. Barely retaining his patience, he tapped his foot.

"What Gang-jo had to do at the Struggle Meeting was not his choice."

Logan frowned. Gang-jo had juggled papers, handed the proper ones to Dun Zeng; he had never spoken.

"I chose a road that did not always run straight," Wu said, not meeting Logan's gaze, his leg twitching. "I set my son's feet on the same path. He is young and doesn't see the intersections yet."

Logan rose and looked toward the door. "You have said nothing about Sulin."

Wu Huixia got to his feet. Going toward the door, he said, "I know nothing, but I will see what I can do to help. At least locate your daughters."

The following week Logan came from his bedroom to find Meiling and Weiping in the kitchen, the two sisters putting together a meal of cabbage, sweet potatoes and rice. Logan felt as if he would burst from love and suppressed anger. He closed his eyes, and searched for words to bridge the distance between them. None came. He made do with "Welcome home."

Meiling came to him first. "Wu Huixia told us about Mother." Then Weiping said, her gaze on her feet, "It was not her fault she was born into a wrong family." Fighting tears, he embraced them in turn and watched and listened as, in a subdued fashion, they discussed the process of cooking. Twice Meiling looked up to inquire about his health, his day. Weiping said, "He is lucky."

The words ricocheted from the walls, repeated in his mind. He wanted to admit his guilt, explain that he was only trying to help, but words stuck in his throat. He wanted to say, tell me what happened to you, talk to me about your mother, about what has happened to us. Instead he said nothing, and neither did they, and the gulf between them, once paved with love, grew wider. Each day Sulin didn't appear at the gate, greater cold entered his mind. He tried to thank Huixia for bringing his daughters home, but Huixia brushed the words aside.

Three years later a truck loaded with squawking chickens, stopped in the road and tooted the horn. A man got down and banged on the gate.

Logan went out.

"The traitor Lin Sulin is no more. Comrade Lin has returned," the man said handing Logan an official-looking paper. He glanced at it but didn't read it, for from the back of the truck, among the squawking hens, a figure climbed down. Her hair was white, her eyes sad, but it was Sulin. He ran to her, tears streaming down his face and heedless of anyone watching, he threw his arms around her and led her into the house.

She was all he had, she and their daughters, but she was as quiet now as they, seldom initiating conversation, her feet no longer tapping rapidly, but walking slowly, deliberately. Only at night, in the privacy of their room, her whispers, her smiles once again gave him muted optimism. At times, he reestablished rapport with Meiling, talking of pleasant moments in the past. But then she married a floor man in a textile factory in Tianjin and went to work in the sewing room. The two of them lived in factory housing, and when Meiling had her one child, she would bring it to the nursery and later to the preschool and kindergarten on the factory premises. Her story telling was as lost as Sulin's laughter.

Although she spoke politely, his youngest daughter understood nothing he said, and he didn't understand her. When he congratulated her for her excellent grades at People's University, she said she hoped he wouldn't embarrass her by mentioning it again. To do well brought good to the country. Eventually, he quit trying to communicate, and the heaviness in his heart grew. He knew he'd never leave Sulin.

In spring, the season that the 8th Century poet Tu Fu called "the season of falling flowers," his garden bloomed; birds came, and their singing lifted his soul. Life became pleasant; he felt useful, needed, and almost fulfilled. Once again he thought of the daughter he'd left behind.

Chapter 10

Christine

Seattle, Washington – Late 1970's

Christine was surprised at how easy it was not to object when Jason moved in. One day she came home to find his clothes in her closet, his books in her study, he and Mathew gone. A note on the table said he and Matt were at a ballgame at Matt's school. "We'll bring home some take out, if you'll make a salad to go with it."

Why not? she asked herself. Matt fretted when Jason didn't appear. The two of them routinely did the "manly" things Christine had thought she'd have to farm out to Big Brothers. Anyway, Jason spent at least four nights a week with her and Matt. . Kathy claimed she had played fairy godmother, and her group took for granted inviting one meant inviting the other. If Christine was shopping at the Pike Place Market, Jason would be there joking with the farmers, playing catch with the salmon tossers, buying loaves of bread, bouquets of flowers. He escorted her to the Group Theater and talked about the socially conscious plays with her afterward. After the first few times she ran him off early, he spent the nights. She admitted waking up next to him was an addiction she didn't want to cure.

The first time she took him to the Changs, steering him by the markets where chickens and ducks hung in the window, the Dim Sum place that served lunch only, and led him up the outside stairs to the apartment where Old Auntie held sway, she wondered: would he understand these people who had fostered the Wainwright link to the Orient?

Old Auntie had tea ready almost before they were inside. "Where's my boy?" she asked, ignoring Jason, as if to say, what could she want with a man who was not only Caucasian but also blonde?

"Matt's in school. I brought Jason to meet you. He teaches at the university, too."

"He's not Chinese," she said in Mandarin to Christine. "Matt Chinese." She added in Pidgin English.

Jason lowered his head in a gesture of respect and said in Mandarin, "It is my honor to be here. I am only a lowly teacher of Chinese speech."

Auntie's frown slowly disappeared. "You speak good. Better than my miserable English." She handed him a cup of tea. "You good friend Matt's mother?"

"This measly man is not worthy of this woman, but she is a most generous woman, and helps me with my poor Chinese."

Even Auntie cracked a smile. "You know old ways. Is good." She glanced at Christine and nodded and then led them into talk about the past, a past where Christine had often gone in imagination. She saw again the grandeur but not the squalor.

Old Auntie shook her head. "Not all good, but not all good here, either." But she smiled as Jason waited on her, listened respectfully as he talked about the differences in the Mainland and Taiwan, told stories even Christine hadn't heard. Obviously, he had boned up on ancient history before their visit.

When Christine and Jason left, Auntie whispered in

Christine's ear, "You marry that man, he good for Matt. Almost Chinese."

Christine conceded they were good together—at the university, socially, at home.

"He young. Vigorous man. Good for woman."

Christine blushed. In the bedroom his virility and stamina made for perfection. Inexorably, he drew her into his more playful moods. She hadn't felt so lighthearted in years. His keen mind was at least equal to hers, and always their mutual interest in China made for a closeness she had thought impossible. Still, she shied away from the thought of marriage. Would she be cheating Matt of his real father?

Conflicting reports about China filled magazines and talk shows. People on tours came back enthusiastic about food, the terra cotta warriors in Xian, the scenery in Guilin. But underground books and papers painted a different story. Talk of governmental abuses trickled out, and Christine cautioned her students to be critical of all reports.

One day picking up Matt from school, she urged, "As soon as we get home, go wash and don't dawdle. Jason should be here soon." It was their pizza night, an outing rapidly becoming a tradition.

At home Matt was pounding up the stairs when the bell rang. Had Jason forgotten his key? She dropped her book bag in the study and hurried to the door. Aunt Betty stood on the other side of the screen, her face etched with extra lines.

Christine frowned. "What is it?"

Betty held out a flimsy envelope. "This letter came addressed to me, so I opened it. But it's for you. From your father."

“Oh, my god!” She backed to a chair, the image of the man outside the theater in Beijing invading her mind, the scene repeating. Hands shaking, she slit open the envelope and pulled out the single thin sheet. “Dear Daughter: I do not know if you will get this. I do not know anything for certain anymore. But I want you to know I love you, even though I don’t know you. Your mother was a lovely woman, and no doubt you are, too. I will try to get this to Hong Kong and to you. Your father, always.”

She read the words through twice before looking up. *I do not know anything for certain anymore.*

Aunt Betty said, “It was sent long ago and probably around the Horn subsequently. Look at the envelope. It’s really a mess. A wonder it even made it here.” Concern etched her face.

Christine touched her dark hair, so pale compared to the ink black of the Chinese, the ones who were doing god-knows-what to her father.

“Your father was a good man, devastated when your mother died and for a long time.... Christine, are you all right?”

It was the last she heard. When she came to she was in bed, Jason leaning over her. Seeing him through a fringe of lashes, she fought for comprehension. “Where’s Matt?” He was Gang-jo’s son, and Gang-jo had tried to help her, undoubtedly at great risk to himself.

“Aunt Betty took him home with her.”

She glanced from Jason to the cloudy overcast sky outside, the sun not visible, hidden for days. “I had a letter from my father.” She explained how she’d put her father on a pedestal marked China. She attempted a smile, but it fell short. “I think I saw him there. He sounded so American. And now...”

Suddenly, the tears she'd fended off flowed. The story she'd never told, but that she'd revisited often, came flowing from her lips, bearing a repetitive rhythm, the words holding a measured cadence.

His shoes and jeans falling where he stepped out of them, Jason got in beside her, held her, and whispered encouragement.

Finally, emotionally exhausted, she lay quietly and quiescent in his arms.

"Marry me," he said. "I want to be with you always."

Through red eyes she peered at him, and sighing, picked up the letter from the bedside table. A stray lock of hair fell over her forehead, and she pushed it back impatiently. "I don't know. I used to imagine what it would be like to see my father. A movie with an orchestra playing in the background, a rosy dawn, sun coming up, enhanced color. When I think I saw him there was only the awful feeling I could do nothing; he could do nothing. Not anything. Now this." She put the letter down again. "I wonder if he's suffering. If he's alone." Her voice caught and she said, "Marriage is a big step. I have to think about it." A cedar tree brushed the house. Everything was so typically Northwest American—hilly city, water lapping at houseboats on Lake Union, people hiking the mountains, picnicking in the rain. She and Jason zipped up and down I-5 in small automobiles. Went to the Seattle Center for the Bumbershoot Festival. Her town was different from other American cities, but what was typically Chinese? She used to think she knew, but China had changed when no one was looking, when the world had been knocking futilely at the gates.

Jason's smile was gentle, his lips on her forehead a feather touch. "Matt needs a father. Hell, in ten years he could be humping some teenaged Lolita." He grinned at her.

She couldn't grin back. "In ten years I'll be mid forties." Kathy might applaud, but no one else would. It wasn't the way things were done. The man should be older than the woman. Any amount of male seniority worked, even twenty years. In fact men smiled and said, "You lucky devil."

"So? I'll be mid-thirties. For Christ sake, look in the mirror, Christine. You're one hell of a good-looking woman. You've got a mind that doesn't stop. And your body... Sweetheart, I get a boner just thinking about it."

She had to smile. "You just proved my point. Boner, for god's sake. Who ever heard of that?"

"You just did." He shook his head. "Language changes but some things don't. I want to marry you, and age has nothing to do with it. I know you love me, why not go for the whole show, boner and all?"

Smiling, she put her head on his shoulder. Couples had started to eschew marriage, were living together, saying commitment was enough. But commitment wasn't what she wanted for Matt, and Jason knew it.

"Would it help if I said *ai?*" Using the Chinese word for love, he proposed to her in Chinese and followed it with Russian, Spanish, and French.

She had to laugh. "Let me think about it, you brainy one."

In the morning, she drove to Green Lake and walked the three miles around it, her mind going rapidly. A brisk wind pushed against her, and choppy waves knifed the surface of the lake. But the ducks gliding the water barely moved, and way below the surface, she knew it was calm. Just as deep down inside she was unchanged. She stuck her hands into her pockets and leaned forward, passing a woman pushing a stroller, an old man, legs splayed, feet turned out, moving stiffly. Would her father be like that, old before his time? With Jason she could continue the good life she had—season tickets at the Act Theater, member of the Wing Luke Museum, supporter of the Minority Playwrights' Festival. But at the library Matt chose books with pictures of children with his eyes; he went to the Changs as often as he could. He deserved a father, and Gang-jo was as lost to Matt as her father to her.

She could stay single, dream of a reality that had never been, or marry Jason. He wouldn't hang around indefinitely. She'd seen how female students looked at him, she'd seen how all women responded to him, and she'd seen how Matt had bonded with him. As the sun, trying to peek through cloud cover all morning, burst forth, she knew what she had to do.

"Yes, Jason, yes," she said bursting through the outside door an hour later, catching him sprawled on the floor with Matt, helping him put a train layout together.

Nodding at her, a secretive smile on his lips Jason leaned toward Matt. "How'd you like me to stay here always?"

Matt looked from him to Christine. "Are you two getting married?'

"Yes," she said. "Would you like that."

Matt pushed a piece of track into place. "Sure." He grinned at Jason. "I need help putting this thing together."

Chapter 11

Christine

Seattle, Washington, 1980-1989

Night wrapped the half-hour ferry ride from Bainbridge Island to Seattle in glamour. During the past few days, she'd slept little, but she felt wide awake, alert, aware of her body as she'd never been before, her mind zipping along in concert, the honeymoon holding her in its spell. The rented house, hidden among evergreens, had been a respite from the academic world, the demands of their equally demanding lives. Picnics on the strip of beach broken by seafood at a restaurant in town had been wedged in with reading and talking. One night they had skinny-dipped and shivered up the steep stairs of the bluff. Inside their hideaway house, Jason had blown life into the coals of the fireplace and in the flickering light, they'd spent the night.

The moon shimmering the water, the ferry moved slowly closer to Seattle, and she stood with her head resting on Jason's shoulder, China the farthest thing from her mind. The recent days were warm in her memory, and the city's skyline showed like a drawing in black and white. To her left the Space Needle reached into the night sky, the revolving restaurant bright against purplish black, and to the right the aging Smith Tower's upper story lights vied for attention. In between, newer buildings added to Seattle's growing downtown.

"When you going to tell me about Matt's father."

Jason's words startled her. So many times something had kept her from speaking. But what could she say? That she had been swept up in the adventure, the historical significance of the moment? That Gang-jo had been fascinating in a different way? That everything at home was upside down, boys burning draft cards, going off to Canada, women sleeping around in unspoken protest. In the District of Columbia, she had felt above the crowd the ten months she had lived with Brewster. They'd parted when he was posted overseas. There had been no one else. Sleeping with Gang-jo had seemed even more daring than living with Brewster. She'd felt it proved she was a woman who ran her own life. She'd felt empowered letting Gang-jo come to her room. Would she have gone to his room if he had asked?

In as few words as possible, she told about that night, tried to divorce it from the historical aura enclosing it.

For a while Jason said nothing, then he asked, "What about birth control?"

"It's obvious it didn't work." Knowing Jason watched her intently, she kept her gaze on the approaching city, Seattle's lights reflecting like pearls in the water. "And abortion was illegal."

He shook his head. "What a bummer."

Arms resting on the railing, she kept her gaze steadfastly ahead, "I had trouble believing I was pregnant; it seemed unreal. Soon it was too late, but by then I began to think in other terms." She watched the ferry dock draw closer. "And now I'm glad."

"That's all?"

"Of course, what were you thinking?"

"Maybe you loved that guy. Stuff like that. Nothing important." He leaned on the rail next to her, his arm touching hers. "Sweetheart, I sure as hell don't care how many one nighters you had. I certainly had my share. I'm thinking of Matt."

She didn't have to mull through that one. "He loves you."

"Christine, he's *my* son. But he needs to know about his biological father." He kept his gaze upon her. "You, of all people, know that."

Hearing the slight reprimand, she looked up, "How do you tell your son he was a one-night stand?"

"You don't. But you sure as hell tell him. I figured it's time you faced it because, lady, you're saddled with me for life, and I guarantee it will be one fascinating day after the other."

She laughed, and married life, while not endlessly fascinating, was as pleasing as Jason had indicated it would be. Jason's star rising, her own winking steadily, their private life great, she wondered if some aberration would interrupt the daily rhythm. On a Selectric typewriter, Jason wrote two books showing the connections between various languages and tied the languages together with a theory connecting speech to migration patterns in a new way. His thinking propelled him into forums led by well-known linguists. Defending his ideas, he drew the attention of the media, and television interview shows followed. His wit, his charm, his looks and knowledge made him a talk show favorite. He was a full professor by the time he was thirty.

When he turned thirty-one they moved to a house on a hill overlooking Lake Washington, a house luxurious enough and big enough for his new status. He had a sense of ease about him, a composure far surpassing his age. She felt very lucky.

Her father and Gang-jo were of another world.

Weeks later, Mt Rainier showed like a snow cone above the skyline of Seattle. Surely it boded well in a city where clouds hovered like sun in the desert.

Pushing thoughts of China aside, she said nothing to Matt about his father until he was fifteen. In a few prepared sentences, she explained, stating facts she'd memorized, aware of the stilted teacher-lecturer sound in her voice. The air, thick with unshed rain and unspoken words, Matt sat quietly at his desk during her recital.

Afterward he stirred, muttering, "I figured out something like that long ago." He seemed slightly embarrassed, fiddling with his pencil, gazing out the slider and beyond the deck to where a sailboat plied the lake. He had his father's height, his high cheekbones, his eyes, but he was thoroughly American, playing football, organizing a band, he the lead guitarist. He ate popcorn at the movies, and had music going at a high decibel as he studied. His room was plastered with posters.

All these thoughts raced through her mind as she turned the stereo down. Pink colored her face. "Long ago?" she repeated.

He shrugged. "A couple years anyway."

"I suppose I should have said something earlier. I wanted..."

He interrupted. "Mom, look at me." He faced her frowning. "I look more like Old Auntie Chang than you. I used to think I was related to the Changs. Then I figured out the math."

"Math?"

"The right amount of time between your China trip and me." He glanced at her.

She took a quick, deep breath. His room had the faint smell of dirty socks, and she found tears in her eyes because everything seemed so homey and American and yet wasn't. "Matt, I'm sorry. I should have said something sooner, but you seemed so happy, I didn't want to upset you." She put her hand on his shoulder.

He didn't brush it off. "Mom, I don't know that guy. Some Chinese who's never been around? Why should that upset me?"

"Are you being facetious?" Her voice had a scratchy sound.

He shook his head. "Heck no. Jason's been my Dad since I was little. He'll always be my dad."

She felt like the luckiest woman in the world. Without planning to, she told him about her father, about the letter that had come from China, about wanting to know what happened to him.

Matt swiveled his chair around and got up. Already he was taller than she was. "Tell me his name."

"Your grandfather?'

"Well, sure, him, too, but I was talking about my biological father."

"Gang-jo," she said, and for the first time in years he became more than an abstract thought. He'd been more than likeable, charming in a foreign way, and always she'd been aware of what he might do to help her find her father. "I never saw or heard from him again."

She waited, but Matt said nothing more, and she didn't know what to say. After an awkward silence he said he had homework, and she left.

A few days later he announced he wanted to learn to speak

Chinese. Christine whispered concerns Jason shot down with two sentences "Let him sit in on my classes. If he's serious he'll stick out the semester; if not no harm done." Afraid of where this was leading, she couldn't say no, but she threw up stipulations: all A's and B's in his high school classes, no goofing off in Jason's. When Matt began speaking in simple sentences at home, she was pleased.

One morning, on impulse, she wrote to Wu Huixia, reminding him of her visit with President Nixon, suggesting he might want her to return to China to lecture. "I am a full professor now." She needed to know about her father, about Gang-jo. Still, she said nothing to Jason.

Two years later, like a bolt from unseen lightening, a letter came from Wu Huixia with an invitation.

"I in my capacity am with delight ask you return to China. We would be glad to host Christine Wainwright lecture at university. Our students would be please to have Chinese speaker from America address them. Please contact me about arrangements. We proud to give you and your family flight on Chinese Airlines. When you arrive Beijing, a car will take you to Friendship Hotel."

The thought of returning to China filled her mouth like dark chocolate leaving a bitter aftertaste. Going there had been exciting, but now her thoughts were far from clear. Fear of what she'd find took the sheen from her excitement. Yet how could anyone ignore a country whose scholars had brushed poetry onto parchment before Cleopatra took her barge down the Nile? She sent a note of acceptance even as a growing sense of unease riled her stomach. Wu Huixia had to be important in the government for her letter to reach him. Such people had access to facts others never knew. But what good would going there accomplish? Would she see her father? What about Gang-jo? Did she want to see him? Would Matt? If either one was available, Wu Huixia would know. Daily, she read and heard about the growing student movement in China. But it seemed remote, her life with Matt and Jason taking precedence. What guarantee did she have that Huixia would lead her to her father and Gang-jo? None. Still....

"You've been invited to China?" Jason stared at her, shrugged out of his backpack and took books and papers out, strewing them over the kitchen counters. Surprise laced his words, lingered in the stiffness of his stance. "I thought you hadn't heard from your father again."

"I didn't. I got a letter from Wu Huixia. He wants me to speak in Beijing." She had planned they'd eat at one of the seafood restaurants on Lake Union. Abruptly, she changed her mind. She needed to be home, to think this through, to hear Jason out.

"So he wrote to you." He was riffling through his pile of mail. "Just like that." He grinned. "You must have made some impression when you were there."

She got celery, carrots, onions, broccoli and Napa cabbage from the refrigerator, began cleaning them in the sink, avoided Jason's probing gaze. "Actually, I wrote to him first." She set the cleaned vegetables on the built in cutting board.

"You what? " He tossed his backpack toward the window seat and tipping his head to the side said, "What the hell's going on? You mean I'm just hearing about it?"

She began chopping the cabbage. "Nothing's going on. I'm going to China."

"Just like that." His voice was flat.

"Jason, I see it as a chance to see my father." She raised and lowered the chopping knife rapidly, watched the growing pile of bite-sized cabbage. "I've waited too long. I should have gone long ago."

"You should have told me long ago." His voice carried an edge.

"I didn't think it would matter. The students are staging Democracy Salons. You know it's where students, and anyone who wants to attend, talk about democracy. It should be a great time to be there."

"I'm aware of the Democracy Salons, Christine." His tone sharpened.

"The thirst for knowledge about the West is insatiable. My father…." She let the sentence trail off as he reached past her, pulled a Rainier from the refrigerator, drank from the bottle.

"The man you've never seen."

"I told you I think I saw him when I was there."

He shook his head. "Aren't you being a bit obsessive?"

"Obsessive? I'm talking about my father, for god's sake." She bit her lip, felt a tear hit her hand.

"You crying?" His voice lost part of its sting.

"I don't know. I guess so. I know I've already accepted, and I want to go and I'm sorry I didn't tell you sooner." He shrugged. "You know I can't get away now."

'I know." Guilt bore down hard. She'd never planned on Jason going with her.

"That's beautiful. And you didn't once think of telling me."

She got down the wok, turned to look at him. "I'm sorry,

Jason. I didn't think you'd be interested."

"Not as interested as you, that's for damn sure. You're all wound up in China; I speak the language. And why in hell you want to go back where Mao played a cat and mouse game with you is beyond me. Aren't you just a little afraid?"

"Mao's dead, and Deng Xiaoping is the one who's always reached out for trade with the West. As for you just knowing the language, that's not how it's sounded to me."

He shook his head. "Oh, shit. Just remember, I don't like being out of the loop." He finished the beer, reached for another. "Don't ever treat me like that again. Are we agreed?" His eyes were hard, his chin up.

We almost had an argument, she thought knowing it had not really been settled, After that she seldom spoke of her upcoming trip, and he never asked, he as coolly polite as she. Quietly, she began the paper work necessary for visiting China.

As pictures from China appeared in the American press, each day after school Matt rushed in with enthusiasm, talking before he located her if she were home, or meeting her in the hall if she came home later than he did. One day he had photographs of Chinese students in American jeans speaking out about freedom and democracy, images he shared with her.

"Gosh, it's fantastic. Really great. I mean they're acting just like us. I've been in contact on the Internet with some of the students. They're really cool."

"You have?" She couldn't keep the amazement out of her voice. She used the computer to compose handout sheets, work out lesson plans, not to contact people overseas.

He threw out names and happenings as if his knowledge

was long held and the students old friends. “They want to know about America.” He grinned. “Makes me feel like an expert. Can I go?”

Her heartbeat escalated.

“I really want to go.”

His boyish enthusiasm made her smile. Most of the time he and his buddies played it cool, wearing sunglasses when the sun wasn’t out, pretending to knowledge that they didn’t possess. Already he was taller than her, his neck thick, his shoulders widening, his hips slim. Like Gang-jo. “I’ll think about it.” The rhododendrons were blooming; azaleas brightened the hillsides, and the slight cooling of Jason’s attitude toward her had reached a plateau, stayed there.

A few days later she was going over papers in her office when Matt rushed in to tell her the former Chinese Communist Party secretary had died. He spoke as if it were of monumental importance to him. She glanced at the calendar where she penciled in important dates. It was April 15, 1989.

“He’s the one who befriended the students,” he explained when she didn’t respond immediately. “They’re not happy about it,” he added slouching in the doorway.

“So I gather.” She set aside the papers she’d been going through.

“Mom, China’s supposed to be a communist country, and the students say they will never ever stop calling for democracy!” He stared at her with eyes wide open. “It’s a big deal.”

“I wish some of my students had your overwhelming interest.” She shivered, feeling as if a cold wave had caught her and was dragging her from shore while Matt was jumping in with both feet, breasting the waves before she could begin to stroke. How deep was his identification with the Chinese students? Not once had he mentioned his father, but he had to be thinking of him.

"They're calling for an end to corruption, bad management, bad leaders. Whatever that means. And they're naming names." Brimming with energy, he paced the room.

She set down her pen, moved a book, felt her stomach gurgle. Was Matt caught up in the excitement of the moment as she had been years before? With the one child China policy, Gang-jo might be more interested in his American son than was comfortable for her, but could she keep Matt from him? And did she want to?

"I want to go with you." His voice deepened.

She took a deep breath. He was sixteen, going on seventeen. How could she deny him this opportunity? "Okay." Rewarded by his broad smile she partially relaxed.

Later, in her sparkling, all electric American kitchen, she said in an off-hand way as she and Jason worked together on a pick-up dinner. "I worry about what this trip will mean for Matt." The sun was setting over the Olympics, turning the distant mountains pink, the clouds a rainbow of color, but she felt colorless, washed out. "Seeing his father."

"If you're thinking of me, Matt and I are pretty tight. And if you haven't noticed, he's very much American, not Chinese." He got spinach greens and red onions from the refrigerator, handed them to her. "I'll start the charcoal. Rib steaks okay?"

"Yes, sure. I'm not worried about you and Matt. But Wu Huixia's son...."

He turned from the door leading to the deck where they would be eating later, the redwood furniture already set with pottery that blended in with the evergreens shading the house. “You worried Matt might want to stay? I’m wondering about your own reaction. You’ve invested a lot of yourself in China.”

“My father. You know how I feel about that.”

“I’m talking about Matt’s biological father.” His eyes shadowed, the light he usually turned upon her invisible, he spoke soberly, no humor or high feelings in the words. “Maybe you want to check him out again.”

“Don’t be ridiculous.”

“Then why don’t you say his name?”

The seriousness of his pronunciation caught her. Startled she stared at him and wondered. Was it a Freudian slip? Did she subconsciously want to do what Jason accused her of? “Gang-jo’s his name, as you know.” She breathed the name out. “I worry about what’s happening, I don’t worry about him.” She shot a glance at Jason. “The students, the whole democracy business. It’s no small thing.” Was she parroting her own son?

“No,” he agreed. “And Matt needs to go, if only to get it out of his system.” He shook his head. “None of this is about the students, and you know it. ” He shrugged. “And you need to go, too. And you know why.”

She bristled. “No, I don’t.”

“To see Wu Gang-jo.” For a while he returned her look, and then he said, “Come on, let’s get this meal going. Your man’s famished.”

She could see despite his light tone a small crease between his eyes. Rapidly she said, “Tomorrow, Kathy’s hosting a farewell luncheon, and everyone who had been or thought of going to China is attending." She was relieved when Jason said something about Kathy and let China drop in favor of gossip.

At lunch at Julia's 7 Carat Café, just up from the houseboat community, a couple who had traveled the People's Republic on their own, talked about standing in several lines to change money or book a seat on a plane. Others gave similar tips. Christine came away with a stomach full of grilled vegetables, tofu and a list of no-no's—don't book hard seat on the train, don't expect to do anything in a hurry, don't stay at a Friendship Hotel, and don't be surprised at anything, but be prepared for culture shock. She didn't believe the last. Hadn't she been one of the first behind the bamboo curtain? As Jason kissed her goodbye at the airport, he said, "Have Wu Huixia lead you to your father. Matt's father, too. The first for you, the second for Matt. I'm sure you understand." His words left an unsaid threat in her mind.

Chapter 12

Logan

The People's Republic of China - 1989

As students set up a tent city in Tiananmen Square, Logan felt a sense of *deja vu.* During the summer he attended some of the university meetings, staying in the shadows, questioning the wisdom of being at a Democracy Salon. Going to Tiananmen seemed to be the current "in" thing for American tourists. American journalists, professors, and tourists argued (politely but condescendingly he thought) the philosophy of freedom with Chinese students. The students wondered if democracy led to anarchy or free speech to libel? All the talk seemed a harmless exercise until the students, grasping the true meaning of democracy, radicalized the talk and posted militant expressions of freedom wherever they could. Logan wondered if his surreptitious attendance had been a mistake.

He tried to stay uninvolved as more and more Americans mingled with the students, bought sodas from vendors, and raised their fingers in a V. Taking a big chance he talked to a few, but nothing they said made the Seattle of his memories come alive. Photographs of student ringleaders popped up all over the world, and Logan slept fitfully, sure the attempts at reform would be squashed soon. He didn't attend another salon.

At home, working in his walled garden, watering the roses that bloomed despite the weather's best attempts to keep them from growing, he pondered the pattern of his life. Since he and Sulin had retired, he spent much time reading and listening to music or contemplating the past as he fertilized and watered. He often imagined a world other than what it was. He had asked again for permission to travel to America, and once more been denied. That made three times. The pain smoldered within him. What would he have to do to gain official trust? The student movement threatened to restrict him further.

He was deepening the shallow ditch around the bamboo tree when Wu Huixia sent word: he wanted to see Logan the next day on a matter of utmost importance. "Tell him I'll be there," Logan told the messenger and tried not to fathom what the summons meant.

Soviet leader Mikhail Gorbachev was in China and reporters from all over the world were converging on Beijing. They gathered because of the Premier, but they reported about the Chinese students, and Logan imagined the gathering consternation among Deng Xiaoping's inner circle.

Getting a watering can, Logan filled it and poured the water slowly around the tree. If only difficulties would disappear as rapidly as the water absorbed by the dry soil.

He was on hands and knees, moving to his herb bed when Wu Huixia arrived unannounced. Seeing Wu, supported by his chauffeur, coming along the stepping-stones, Logan smelled trouble and rapidly inhaled the fragrance of rosemary, breathing in the pungent aroma before Wu reached him. Unless something was wrong, why else would Wu Huixia come to him? His visits had never been purely social.

Logan put down the trowel and rose as Wu stopped within speaking distance. "This is indeed an honor," Logan said. "I welcome my old friend. But was I mistaken, did I miss the day of our meeting?"

Wu shook his head. "This old one became eager to talk to Wai Liang again."

"I am glad." He brushed the soil from his hands. "Please sit down. That chair is more comfortable than the bench. I have found it good on my back." What in the devil was Wu up to?

Wu Huixia eased himself to the wrought iron chair and waved the chauffeur away.

As the man went down the walk, Logan spoke all the mandatory polite phrases. The familiar pattern allowed him to think, rinse his hands with the garden hose, dry them on his handkerchief and not miss a beat of the conversation. Nodding sympathetically about Huixia's stiff joints, he sat on the bench, his heart thumping erratically.

When his driver was out of sight, Huixia leaned forward, hands folded on his cane. "You have been to the meetings on campus. Have you been to The Square?"

"I've heard about it." Emboldened by the lack of government interference, students were being joined by throngs of white-collar workers and laborers, even literati. Rock stars sang, people danced. Laughing at tradition, young people held hands, kissed, and fell in love while Western reporters called the happenings the "Chinese Woodstock."

Huixia's eyes narrowed. "The students are like a fly on the back of a giant panda, but foreign journalists report as if the students are wise and we are stupid. We must do something to contradict this notion."

"They write what they see. Perhaps if Deng Xiaoping or

you talked to them.... He was very popular when he went to America."

Huixia shook his head impatiently. "They would laugh because I know little English, and Deng says a child who sticks his hand in the fire should get burned. If the fire turns out to be water it is because a wiser person put out the fire." He shook his head impatiently. "But why dissemble? We must get Americans to accomplish what we want done and not know they are doing it." Leaning forward, he pinned Logan's gaze with his. "I have thought about this at length. I invited your daughter to China."

At first Logan did not comprehend. His daughters were no longer in Beijing. He seldom saw them. "What?" he said at the same instant it came to him, Huixia had said his daughter was coming to China. "Christine?"

"Yes, your American daughter. She and her son are coming to China. I thought if we brought a Chinese speaking American here, have her speak at the university, we would show that the Chinese government does not fear democracy. Seeing our display of good faith, the students and the radical professors, would be amenable to listening. I thought maybe she might be effective on television."

"Christine is in China?" For years he'd been plagued by the image of his daughter getting in a car outside Mao Tse-Tung's house. He'd almost called out. Then guards had materialized at his side, held him back. He'd been chastised for trying to make unauthorized contact, and made to repeat his loyalty to China. He'd never told anyone about Gang-jo's part and he'd never spoken about that night to Wu Huixia, but for months he'd scanned forbidden Hong Kong newspapers hoping to catch a glimpse of the Americans and Christine. But he never had.

"I hoped to get the students to return to their campuses, stop this nonsense. Now, I'm not so sure."

"I see," Logan said softly, a new refrain racing like an old song along a well-worn groove. He would see his daughter again. He shrugged, and keeping his voice neutral, he said, "I want to see her."

"Ultimately, student demonstrations are of little consequence in the broader scheme of China, but now that we are part of the world press, it is a problem." Huixia looked away from Logan, and when he looked back he was nodding as if affirming to himself his decisions. "Your daughter has never said anything unfriendly to or about us. It's important having Americans helping us and not knowing. This just adds to it." He chuckled.

In every syllable of Huixia's words amusement spilled like sunlight undiffused, harsh with brittle brightness. Logan tried to erase the frown building on his face and control his erratic heartbeat. Huixia would use his daughter to further his own political ambitions. In the depth of night, when darkness let in thoughts denied in daylight, he acknowledged ambiguity of thought, but now he carefully showed nothing of his mistrust.

Huixia leaned forward, "You see, old friend, the students must be stopped. First they laid wreaths, then made speeches, and now their tents and banners flap in the breeze, their amplified voices beat at the walls of the Great Hall of the People. It is not acceptable." An expression of barely suppressed anger showed momentarily on Huixia's face, and the light seemed to change and refract, bend back on itself as if forced through a prism that twisted it out of shape before Huixia smiled, the sagging skin of his face tightening momentarily. "This new generation I have trouble understanding."

Logan said as calmly as possible, as if there were no need to hurry, as if his heart were not making itself felt in his chest, as if his thoughts weren't going in all directions, "What is it you want me to do?"

Huixia rose. "The idea of using imperialists is not without risk, but already demonstrations spring up in other parts of the country. Students show signs of restlessness in Wuhan, in Shanghai. They make speeches in Xian. One cannot bait a bear forever. We tire of their posturing." He pushed to his feet. "I want to put you on television first. Throughout China many people know your name, have read yours and Comrade Sulin's writings. We will educate the rest, and you will pave the way."

A muscle jumped in Logan's cheek.

Huixia's eye narrowed. "You will be admired because you became a Chinese citizen. Your daughter will be China's American friend, the people's friend. We'd please everyone. Your daughter will undoubtedly be flattered as American journalists beg for pictures and interviews. The students will be impressed, and hopefully we will get them back on campus." He paused no longer than the smile that crinkled his eyes and faded as quickly. "Make no mistake. The government will not back down. Ever." He spoke quietly, but forcefully, and at the end of the short speech he turned his back on Logan, looked toward the gate and waved his walking stick in the air.

As the chauffeur entered, Logan said, "When do I see my daughter?"

Huixia interrupted, "Don't bother me with petty details." Looking at Logan over his shoulder, he huffed, "You will be advised."

Logan watched Huixia shuffle toward his car. Would he and Christine and his grandson truly make a difference? Perhaps. He and Wu Huixia had no choice.

He wiped his forehead, surprised to find he was perspiring. Glancing once more at his garden, he walked slowly toward the house. Would it be wise to tell Sulin? Whatever eventually happened with his daughter and grandson, if things did not go right, he did not want Sulin taking the blame. Better if she knew nothing. For a moment Logan allowed a small surge of excitement to fill him. His daughter had tried to see him before. He had tried to see her. Now it would happen. But if he and Christine talked to the nation and the students did not leave Tiananmen Square there'd be a bloodbath, and it would not matter if Christine was there or not.

Chapter 13

Christine

The People's Republic of China - 1989

On deck, floating down the Li River, Christine dozed off even as the head of the Karst Institute explained the geology of the region. The trip had been a long one, flying from Seattle to San Francisco, to Hawaii, and then on to Shanghai and Guilin. Jerking awake, she muttered, "sorry," to the geologist, his explanations floating like dandelion fluff past her ears. Pastoral beauty insinuated itself around each curve, but she was too tired to appreciate the spectacular scenery. A contingent had met her and Matt in Shanghai, whisked them to Guilin, deposited them in a hotel and rousted them out early the next day for an excursion, and all she could do was worry. She was to have gone straight to Beijing. Why the change in plans? She'd been prepared to talk about the subtleties of the English language and how best for Chinese speakers to study it. She hadn't been prepared to watch fishermen casting nets, women washing clothes in the river. No matter that the soft-sculpted mountains rising from meadows were spectacular, sentinels hanging over the small city, they had not been on her agenda.

It's gorgeous," she said as the sky washed everything in soft tints like a watercolor painting or a delicate scroll, a romanticized version of reality. She'd never thought such scenes could actually exist. Matt was busy with his camera, shooting from all angles. “When are we going n to Beijing?” she asked the young men who hovered over them, no one else except the captain and crew on board.

“First you see beauty of Guangxi Province. Very nice place.”

“It’s unreal,” Matt said shaking his head and repeating, “unreal,” referring, to the change in plans as well as the scenery. The hovering Chinese, their understanding of English limited, exchanged glances as if to say, the mountains are very real. When Christine insisted upon knowing her agenda, they said, “Tomorrow, very nice tour.”

“Sounds like the run-around,” Matt said when they were once more in their room, a Howard Johnson look-alike, utilitarian, but hardly luxurious. “Maybe they don’t want us in Beijing. Isn’t that where I might see Wu Gang-jo?” His words echoed.

Gang-jo, not my father. It had a safe ring. “You want to see him?”

“Yeah, sure.” He shrugged, saying, as if he needed an explanation, “After all, he’s my father.”

She called home, left a message for Jason. “We’re here. Very jet-lagged, but okay. I’ll call later.”

During the next two days as they were taken to caves containing ancient Buddhas, given a tour through a factory where workers lived in a Soviet style apartment building nearby, Matt asked about the democracy demonstrations, but received no answer. Although he played the radio dial, and the television in their room, they learned nothing. The factory tour produced four-and-five-year-old children from the factory day care, the children singing and dancing with fervor. Christine praised their voices and poise and didn't mention Beijing, but once back in their room, Matt switched on the TV. A man was lecturing about the classic four-volume book, *A Dream of Red Mansions* written in the mid 18th century and currently being translated into English. No news program or announcer mentioned the democracy demonstrations.

The day she was told they would leave for Beijing, Christine packed and then sat in her room with her shoes off waiting for the car and driver to take them to the airport. At ten-thirty she had Matt carry the suitcases downstairs and tried to stave off a mixture of concern and consternation when he wasn't back in a few minutes. A half-hour later he came running in.

"You were gone so long I almost sent out a posse."

He held up a hand. "I was using the hotel's computer to contact Beijing. The students I've been e-mailing from home. Mom, the party secretary, Joe something, apologized to them yesterday." His excitement spilled over into his eyes. "Isn't that something? People are listening! It's like a revolution!"

She nodded. Zhao Ziyang, the party secretary was the country's leading liberal. She kept her tone neutral "What did he apologize for?"

"For being too late to respond to the students' demands. He was on their side, but…listen to this, he's not been seen since. Nobody knows if that's bad or good." He paused, looked at her. "Do you think that's why our flight was changed?"

For a moment, she wished they were home, that Jason was with them, that they hadn't come at all. "I don't know, Matt. The Chinese always play it safe; even with the doors open, they keep their windows closed. Unfortunately, I can't see in." She shook her head. "The students may be in a no-win situation."

"But, Mom, how can the government stop a grassroots movement? None of the big shots said anything publicly so far. Isn't that a good sign?"

"Don't forget this country has been led by an iron fist. I guess we'll find out soon enough. They don't have Mao anymore, but the old guard is still there." Zhao's disappearance could mean anything from prison or house arrest to just keeping him out of sight for a while so they could deal with his recalcitrant views later when the world's attention was diverted. She put her briefcase near the door. Her passport and visa were in the hotel safe, her purse held essential toiletries and cosmetics.

At six, Matt, went to the noodle shop near the hotel and returned with enough food for three. Proud of his ability to communicate in Chinese, even though he often had to repeat himself and pantomime, every success left him looking like he'd aced a class. "What time did they say we'd leave?"

"They didn't. A delay would mean loss of face."

Matt was slurping the last of the noodles when an official called to say Christine Wainwright and her son should be ready to leave for the airport in fifteen minutes.

It was close to midnight when the lights of Beijing showed below. Gritty eyed, they were hurried to an official car and driven through quiet night streets. She saw little, the dark pressing against her, the lights dim, her chief concern that the people who met them had her luggage and not someone else's and that they left them at the hotel where she'd booked several nights. It had been touchy enough convincing Wu Huixia a Friendship Hotel wasn't necessary. She needed a measure of control, needed privacy, needed unscheduled time.

After explaining her reservation in Chinese and English to the man at the desk, she hurried Matt up to the room they shared, fell into one of the twin beds and into a stupefying slumber.

In the morning a cacophony of noise rose like discordant music to her hotel room. With dawn seeping in around the draw draperies, Christine slipped from bed and hurried to the window to look out. No sun shone and smoggy air was settling over the intersection where a mass of people on bicycles moved steadily forward, men and women clogging the thoroughfare as far as she could see in either direction. She assumed the adults were on their way to work, the children to school. The children, most of them dressed in red, were bright spots in an overwhelmingly drab, colorless scene, a sea of traffic clogging the street, filling it completely, the people in uniform blue. An occasional car, surrounded by cyclists, busses belching smoke, and a few old trucks tooted their way past bicycles and occasional pedicabs. Progressive waves of humanity added to the congestion. People crowded the sidewalks, poured into the stores, and pushed on to busses jammed tight with passengers sitting and standing. The only people she'd seen in Guilin were officials, hotel staff, and the people at the factory. Now, people flowed by without interruption.

"Matt, come see," she insisted as he began knuckling his eyes, her voice echoing shock. She had been kept from the people in 1972, now they assaulted her senses. A government car, flags flying, jostled for position with a bus whose door was wedged open, people clinging to handholds. On the street, men carrying briefcases watched expressionless as the government car cut off the bus. "Good heavens," she said to herself more than to Matt, but hearing, he came to stand beside her.

"Split second timing," he said.

She touched his arm. "Look." At the corner a crowd of pedestrians adroitly avoided a motorcycle zooming by. "I can't believe it," she whispered.

He shook his head, awe in his voice. "I've never seen so many people in my whole life."

She smiled and ruffled his hair, which he immediately straightened. "Toto, we're not in Kansas any more, but like I said, it was different before." She pointed to a few young men and women in jeans hurrying by. "You think they're part of the protesters?"

"Mom, how should I know?" Matt headed for the bathroom but hesitated in the doorway. "What time is it?"

She glanced at her watch. Although there was no clock in the room, the bedside nightstand held a telephone. Another hung on the wall in the bathroom. "Almost eight." In the final letter, Wu Huixia had said to call in the morning early. She gave the operator the number, watched Matt shut the bathroom door.

Wu answered immediately, welcomed her back to China.

"*Xiexie*," she said thanking him for the welcoming committee and assistance the night before, thanking him for the Guilin stopover. "I was very impressed by the beauty of the area and the poise of the children at the factory's nursery."

"A chance to see a different part of a foreign country and rest a bit is always welcome. You and your son are comfortable here? The hotel is sufficient?"

"It's fine. We're fine, but I'm afraid we just woke up."

"Ah, yes. You have had a long trip from America."

"Yes, but we're anxious to go the University. What time…."

He cut in quickly, but politely, his voice sounding much as it had before. "There

has been a change of plan." He added something about letting her rest from her long journey before further plans were made.

"We're too excited to sleep, and eager to go on campus."

"Yes, of course. Everyone is looking forward to meeting you. I trust you had a good flight and have everything you need."

"Fine, *xiexie*."

"If you need anything, the concierge will help you. The hotel is very Western. A better location than the Friendship Hotel, I suggested. Extend my regards to your son and I will call in a few days after you are adjusted to the time changes. In the meantime the manager at the hotel should be able to help you with anything you need. But please feel free to call at the number I gave you. I remember with delight your previous visit."

She waited for him to say when she would lecture at the university. She started to say, tell me about your son, tell me about my father, tell me what is going on, but Wu Huixia with a plethora of polite words had hung up. "I'll get dressed and we'll go eat," she said to Matt who had come out of the bathroom looking as sleepy as when he'd entered.

He crawled back into the twin bed he'd just left. "I'll eat later. First things first, Mom."

She took a shower, dressed in a white pants suit and found her way to the hotel restaurant. After fried eggs, rice, and tea she asked for directions to Tiananmen Square. The waiter, pleased with her fluent Chinese, provided a map and verbal directions.

After leaving a note for Matt, she walked to The Square, knowing he'd head there as soon as possible, and she had to know what was happening before he became involved. The sun had filtered through an amber haze, and without a mitigating breeze, it was already hot. Near The Square, big character posters in bright colors or stark black caught her attention. Some had been printed in pinyin, the Chinese writing using the Western alphabet. She passed an immense bike rack, and jostled by others hurrying into the Square, she stood just inside and gazed around struck by the vastness of the space. She'd read it was the largest square in the world, but the words couldn't compare with actuality. Nothing familiar met her eye. She remembered neither Mao Tse-Tung's visage staring down at her, nor the statue of the martyrs off in the distance. Back then she'd been ushered into and out of limousines, into the banquet hall, up to the stage, and eventually she'd ended in Gang-jo's embrace. The Square, filled now to overflowing with hundreds of students and tourists shoving and pushing, smiling and apologizing, was totally different. Young people, undoubtedly students, called, "Hello, *Ni hao*, American?" Sweatbands surrounded their heads, jeans and T-shirts hugged their skinny hips, their slowly maturing chests. All smiled a welcome.

"Yes, American," she replied and was instantly bombarded by young men and women with questions, the questions proliferating when they learned she spoke and understood Chinese. The boys resembled Matt, but on the whole were smaller, less worldly wise, but equally self-assured. Their purpose, jelled in adversity, fueled by idealism, they talked liberty, spoke about democracy and wanted to know, was it true Americans had free speech? Was it true Americans could live where they wanted to, move around from state to state without internal passports? Thirsting for affirmation and knowledge, they were eager, alert, and admiring. It was not hard to lose oneself in playing teacher, friend, and observer.

Seeking to explain nuances, Christine found herself questioning her own knowledge, her own belief systems, and, as the questions multiplied, she felt a thrill pass through her, and proudly, she fleshed out the basic rights of American citizens and explained the documents upon which they were based. More and more students crowded around. The frustration of Guilin, the far from satisfactory exchange with Wu Huixia seemed unimportant. Throughout the Square, the air was thick with voices all speaking at once, music playing, speeches given. Photographers clicked pictures and everyone was smiling or nodding agreement, or apologizing for having so many questions. Riding the cusp of adulthood or teetering beyond it, all the youth made clear their idealism, their energy, and their desire for change. She nodded approval, felt revived, revitalized.

A television crew from the United States was filming a couple from California. The man's T-shirt read: Confucius Says Democracy Now. The woman wore big-mirrored sunglasses and designer jeans with flower embroidery. Later, two-minute snippets of the interview would be shown back home. But similar scenes were taking place all over the Square, gray beards from Wisconsin, reporters from CNN, a freelance journalist from Berkeley exchanging thoughts and ideas with one another and with the students. Christine wore a continual smile as she circumnavigated the Square.

Near the students' headquarters tent, close to the center of Tiananmen Square, a boy, undoubtedly older than he appeared, stood on a box and read off a list of grievances and government abuses. Hearing him speaking through a bullhorn, Christine was glad Matt had opted for more sleep. She feared the government's response; she feared Matt's idealism, and reminding herself she owed her trip to Wu Huixia, she went back to the hotel. Matt was just getting up. He said no calls had come while she was gone.

The next day she called Wu Huixia's number again, let it ring and ring, but there was no answer. "That's strange." She walked to the window, looked out, continued speaking, airing her frustrations to Matt. "According to everything I know, once you're admitted into their extended family of connections, the Chinese feel responsible for you. It can be a bit stifling. As you know, they certainly hung onto our hip pockets in Guilin." She moved from the window to the door and back. "They don't understand the American concept of privacy. At least there's no word for it in the language. But they seem to have forgotten us."

Matt, stopped fiddling with the radio he'd brought from home. He looked up. "You have any other numbers you can call?"

She shook her head.

Turning up the radio volume, Matt said, "Listen to this. They're talking so fast I can't get it. They sound really excited. What are they saying?"

"Turn it up a bit." She cocked an ear. "University classes are being cancelled. The announcer's reading a list." Scowling, she glanced out the window again. Young people were passing in droves, some carrying signs extolling democracy, all were animated, exhilarated, calling to one another, shouting slogans. Matt looked as if he were contemplating joining them. Quickly, she said, "Let's go for a walk. Okay? There are places where it's not so crowded. Where it isn't so modern. Really different."

He shrugged. "Okay."

She led him away from the Square.

Past the Ninzu and Yanjing Hotels, she kept going until they were on narrow streets where occasional small trees added a touch of green and alleys wound snake-like through the city. "Alleys are *hutangs,* and we're likely to find some of the oldest dwellings on them. Some are quite nice, but most houses are just shelter." She chattered, trying to take his mind away from the Square.

"How do you know. You see them before?"

"No, but I read about them." Read about the big courtyards, the many rooms of the Mandarins, the array of servants, the women with bound feet. She lowered her voice on a two-block, dead-end alley where a few people were emerging from houses. Washing dishes, a woman squatted in front of a large kettle filled with water, drying them in a rack set on the strip of walk in front of her house. "They sometimes cook outside, too," she whispered. Poverty shrieked in ways she could see shocked Matt who gazed at his feet as if embarrassed. At the end of the block, two men, emerging from a bathhouse, paused to light cigarettes. Spying her and Matt, they stared.

A child in split pants ran to his mother, his eyes big. Shouting *meiguo* in a loud voice, he pointed at them.

"*Maiguo*, American," Matt said frowning.

He'd said little since arriving in Beijing, shaking his head at times, frowning often. She surmised the crowds overwhelmed him. "The little boy probably hasn't seen foreigners before. Especially ones carrying expensive cameras, and wearing expensive watches." Matt's caught the sun's gleam like diamonds. "I expect we stand out like the proverbial sore thumb."

She addressed the woman whose child had spoken. "*Shi de*, yes, we are Americans." She smiled, said, "My son and I are visiting China."

The woman looked from her to Matt, and finally she pointed at him. "He is Chinese." It was a statement, semi-belligerent. "You say that one is your son. Not possible. You are not Chinese. You adopt Chinese baby."

Christine shook her head. "No. He is overseas Chinese. My son." China declared all Chinese, even those born other places, were citizens of China. Hopefully Matt couldn't follow the rapid-fire exchange. He was standing close to her but looking around, watching the people who filtered from the houses, hurried from the bathhouse. The group was older than the students in the Square, most smiling, some not, all showing undisguised interest. She started to turn away, but a man of middle age called out.

"Does everyone in America have a car?" His tone implied he didn't quite believe it. He wore soft shoes split along the seams, a shirt frayed at the collar, shapeless and faded pants.

"Most Americans have cars, but not all," Christine said,

hoping to take their minds off Matt, her loud-voiced Chinese surprising those at the edge of the growing circle. "Some people, like the people who live in New York City, have no need for one."

"Do you have a car?" The man pointed at her.

"Yes."

A murmur and exclamations rose, filling the street. The two men from the bathhouse moved closer, their heads tipped to the side considering, taking her in, studying Matt.

A woman, with gray frosting her midnight black hair, edged forward. She cried, "Is it true everyone in America has a television?"

"Just about everybody." Christine glanced around. "Do you have televisions?" She'd seen an antenna.

With a work-worn hand, the woman, who had pushed to the front of the crowd, thumped her chest. "We do." She pointed to a roof halfway down the *hutang*. A smile transformed her face and people in the circle made way for her to step closer, their gesture that of lesser beings to one in a higher position.

"I put it up," a man said nodding his head in affirmation of a job well done.

The woman lifted her head high. "The television belongs to me and my husband. The others come to watch. I charge a small fee. Like Americans." She grinned, went into a long and proud recital about how Deng Xiao Ping had told people to start a business.

A thin man in a green army uniform shouted, "You gobble like a turkey eating all the grain. Let someone else talk." He squared his shoulders. "I serve with the military of the

People's Republic of China."

Seeing his pride, Christine nodded.

As if given permission, he cried, "I heard some people have two cars." He thrust his head forward. "Do you?" Sucking on a cigarette, he let the smoke trail from his mouth as he talked, his face unsmiling.

He could be trouble. She hesitated a split second. "That is true. *Shi de.* I have one; my husband has one." She spoke rapidly, and shifted her weight from one foot to the other. No matter how classless a society claimed to be, classes existed. Would his barely suppressed anger be at her or at his country?

"You are rich." He endowed the last word with venom.

"No, in America we are middle class."

His eyes shifted away, not knowing the term. She wondered if she should try explaining, using the television woman as an example. But the man turned back to her, his face and voice holding a baiting quality, he spoke slowly and distinctly, no trace of a regional dialect.

"And your son, does he drive?"

The previous year, when snow dusted the hills, Matt got his learners' permit. For weeks she sat in the passenger seat as he steered slowly and sedately to the store and waited proudly while she shopped, hoping, she supposed, his friends would notice him. She had promised him a "junker" when he was sixteen. He got his drivers' license late last year, and his first car for his birthday.

"I drive," Matt cried and added proudly, "I have my own car."

Everyone stirred, shifted, exclamations exploding from hitherto silent mouths. Someone said, "Too rich." Others echoed the words admiringly, and ahs of agreement rose. A woman holding a child reached out and touched Christine's linen jacket and said, "Democracy." But the military man cried, "Capitalist," in a loud and unflattering way.

Christine said quickly, "Thank you for talking to a stranger," and taking Matt's arm said, "Let's go."

He called *Zai jian* as she propelled him from the alley.

"So they're eager for our life," he concluded after she filled in the gaps of his understanding.

"Not all."

"I'd say the majority," he said.

The next day he slung over his shoulder the guitar he'd brought from home and glanced at her with a determined look on his face. He was almost as tall as Jason, beginning to be as filled out. "I'm going to The Square," he stated as if ready to launch into orbit. He fingered his guitar.

She wanted to say, be careful, don't be caught up in something bigger than all of us, but she couldn't. He was so essentially American, so confident in his decisions. Still, something about the way he stood, his head high, reminded her of Gang-jo, and a ripple of apprehension surged through her. "You know the way?"

"I studied the map you have."

"Okay, but come back in time for dinner."

"I will. Bye, Mom." He waved a hand and went out the door.

She heard him go down the hall, watched from the window as he threaded his way on foot through the growing number of students on bicycles heading to Tiananmen.

She was just about to place a call to Jason when someone from Wu Huixia's office called to say she'd be hearing from someone at the University that day. She'd barely hung up when the phone rang again. "*Ni hao*," she said to be answered in broken English.

"Maybe Professor and his son maybe want to visit campus. Much pretty."

"Yes, so I've heard. We'd like to very much. You are from the university?"

"University, yes. I privilege to work University. In morning we call, make plans."

She tried to interject a word, but again someone hung up before she could ask questions.

In late afternoon, Matt returned ecstatic, and she put the call from her mind. Everyone liked his music. The people were "cool." He talked about it all through their evening meal in the restaurant, not even commenting on the huge fish with head and fins intact, its glassy eyes staring up from a platter between them.

In the morning he left for The Square right after breakfast. Christine hurried over later to find him perched on the edge of the Statue of Martyrs strumming his guitar, humming softly and singing for dozens of students. "Right on," he cried when they asked about America, their words awkward but touching in English, his Chinese interspersed with American comments and gestures. His smile was infectious. "Hey, comrade," he cried, and when students admired his clothes and haircut, he said, "Hey, man," or "Okay, dude." And slapped a high five at everyone within reach. American tourists smiled, called him a good will ambassador.

She went back to the hotel, proud of him, but uneasy, too. Daydreaming she almost missed the soft knock at the door.

A young man in a blue Mao suit delivered a message from Wu Huixia. He was hosting a banquet for her. A car would pick her up, take her to a special location on a lake, and they would very much like to include the professor's Chinese son.

That night everything about the evening reminded her of her first trip, she and Matt handed into a large Russian car with curtains fastened in place. The young man accompanying them looked over his shoulder from the front seat and kept a stream of conversation going. "Your home in Washington is near White House? Yes?"

She explained about the two Washingtons and went over in her mind how to broach Wu Huixia about her father and Gang-jo.

At the small guesthouse, Wu Huixia stood in the door of an anteroom his hand outstretched while saying in English. "It is privilege to have Professor Wainwright again."

He seemed smaller, less formidable, but his voice was strong and he projected an old image welcoming her and her son to Beijing, the walls of the entry room decorated with framed calligraphy in the classic style. Not mass-market replicas, they were signed masterpieces. He shows me his wealth as well as his position of power, she thought while mouthing the polite phrases necessary, introducing Matt who had donned a pair of slacks for the special occasion.

"Please come in. We have shark fin soup. Very special," he said to Matt and pointed toward the next room.

A smiling young man gestured they should follow him.

"Shark Fin soup is extremely expensive," Christine whispered to Matt as they were escorted to a seat at a round table. Four smiling young men standing at the far side of the table were introduced. One man was from the university; the others were not identified by position.

"They kill the whole shark for the fins," Matt muttered.

She scowled at him.

"Okay," he whispered, "I'll zip my lip."

During the meal much laughter and constant smiles were directed at her, and Christine wondered: were they hoping to placate her? She'd been kept waiting for days, but China had marched to its own drummer for centuries. Now, the student demonstrations were growing, and whatever happened, the government would want her on their side. It was not a pleasant thought.

After lotus seed soup and more talk, Wu walked her to the waiting car, the younger men busy telling Matt the Chinese words for stars pricking at the hazy sky. It was the most private moment she'd get. "I'm sure you know Wai Liang, Logan Wainwright. He's my father."

"It is a fact long understood."

She steeled herself. "When can I see him?"

Wu slowed his steps. "I will notify Wai Liang of your presence in the city. No doubt he will contact you before your visit is over."

She said nothing about Gang-jo. Was it because the young men with Matt joined them at that moment, or was it because Gang-jo could raise issues she didn't want to address yet? She didn't know.

Chapter 14

Logan

The People's Republic of China

Normally Logan's sixty-eight years seemed an abstraction, not something to deal with, but lately he felt dulled by fatigue and overwhelmed by recent events. Summoned once more to Wu Huixia's office, he acknowledged his frustration and worry. So the end begins, he thought, knowing that if things had gone according to plan, he would not be mounting his bicycle at his home in the outskirts of Beijing but watching a ceremony dedicated to peace, a ceremony featuring his own daughter.

Skirting the main roads, he peddled toward the Square. An unrelenting heat poured from the sky, singeing the city. Tasting the dust and once more recognizing the ambiguity of his position, Logan looked around. At first everything seemed the same; the walled gardens of the suburbs opening onto the hutangs were filled with the usual busy traffic. Old folks gossiped across back fences, young people hurried to school or work, bicycles with carts hauled produce, and the occasional truck or car, horn blowing, scattered everyone.

He peddled faster. Threading through a maze of alleys that led to ever-broader streets, his mind worked at a furious pace. The student movement's similarity to past uprisings frightened him. The 100 Flowers Era, the Cultural Revolution, and the Great Leap Forward had begun with lofty visions that had shattered beneath the fists and iron will of totalitarian government. Would this democracy movement share the same fate?

As he drew near The Square, pedestrians and bicyclists clogged the width of Chang'an Avenue. Tourists leaned from the windows of the luxury hotels, Chinese gathered in courtyards and choked the sidewalks and streets. He felt a momentary resurgence of hope. Every day teachers, intellectuals, journalists, peasants, and policeman joined the student demonstrators until even Tiananmen Square wasn't large enough to hold them all. In groups of thousands they marched in one gate and out another to be followed by yet another group. Now he saw what he'd heard was no exaggeration.

Easing into the student-monitored traffic, Logan's admiration for the protesters swelled. The students were guiding cars, trucks, bicycles, and pedestrians, making it possible for ambulances to speed away. "Why the ambulances? What is it?" he asked a middle-aged man who had come from Tiananmen.

The man looked at Logan with surprise and said as if eager to share his knowledge. "The hunger-strikers. They make a statement for democracy. The ambulances take some of them to the hospital."

"Thank you. I didn't know." How could such dedication be questioned? Once he, too, had been fired with the passions of youth, the promise of a better tomorrow. Spying Wu Huixia's building ahead, he maneuvered out of the main flow of traffic, and hurried to Wu's office. Easing himself into a chair opposite the old manipulator, he waited, making the other man speak first. Their long acquaintance, built on mutual need and support, had nothing to do with real liking. Yet, he did not dislike Wu; they had been linked for too long. More extensive than kinship, guangxi was a network of friends and families obligated to help one another.

Looking like an aging Buddha, Wu Huixia folded his hands over his stomach and spoke a few quick polite sentences.

Logan shook a cigarette from his pack and contemplated it, as if the answers were there and watched as Huixia lit a kitchen match on his thumbnail and held the flame across the gray metal desk.

Logan inhaled deeply, and smoked quietly while Huixia talked about the students. Government-sponsored counter movements had begun, he said, adding peasants had been bussed in from the countryside. Sulin had told him, for ten yuan each they yelled pro-government slogans, shouted anti-American sentiments and burned effigies. It was how things always had been done, but Huixia worried a pen, played with a calligraphy brush.

Logan spoke carefully. "I take it I won't be appearing on television."

Huixia sighed. "For years I walked a rope that tightened and alternately grew slack. Now, I know how to balance. Thousands of troops pour into the city. Now, they are on the outskirts of the city." His voice, though strained, rang clear. "No, you won't be on television."

Neighborhood talk hinted the busses following the troops were filled with gas masks and machine guns. Logan felt as if a band were tightening around his chest. "They plan to stop the students protest?" *Fire on them, do god knows what.*

Huixia made a vague gesture. Raising an eyebrow, he added, "The government will do nothing that is not necessary. You must see they can do nothing else."

They instead of we, Logan thought, the words echoing in his mind. Was Wu Huixia trying to tell him something? He wanted to speak freely, but the ambiguity inherent in the meeting made him cautious. If someone was listening to their conversation, to say the wrong thing and then have to defend it later, to have their words analyzed until no syllable escaped notice, was not acceptable. Yet, he had to know; was Christine in the city? Steeling himself, he spoke in an offhand fashion, but his heart raced. "Is the American in Beijing?" *My daughter.* Images of the Seattle he hadn't seen for forty-six years rose tantalizingly before his eyes.

"Yes, the American woman and her son are here." Huixia mopped his forehead with a handkerchief. "I admit it was a mistake for me to invite them. I only thought to help China."

Word was that tourists were looking for early flights to Hong Kong. Cracking his knuckles, a thing he had not done since his youth, Logan put a hand to his chest in a vain attempt to still the awful drumbeat beneath his flesh. He'd never heard Huixia admit a fault before. Was it because they were both getting older, the measure of their days dwindling? "I want to see them."

Huixia jerked his head in the direction of The Square and pushed unsteadily to his feet. "It was not a bad idea, awards, commendations to Americans who saw the worth of both countries, you and the Americans on television, but it came too late." He shrugged, his eyes narrowing slightly, his nostrils flaring. He took an envelope from a drawer and tapped it against his hand. "The government does not condone what is happening in the Square, you understand that." He handed the envelope to Logan. "Here are tickets to take the Americans home. If you will be kind enough to deliver them." His brisk tone belied the fragility of his body.

Logan kept his voice calm. Any number of underlings under Wu's command could have delivered them "When?"

"A day or two before their departure date which is soon."

Logan turned the envelope over in his hands. The name of Christine's hotel was printed on the flap. Mentally he walked into the lobby, went to the desk, was directed to her room. The need to see the daughter he'd never known flooded him. If he went now, camped on her doorstep until she left, would he be called down for it, Sulin made to atone for his misstep? Maybe he should get someone else to deliver the tickets. But if he did that, he'd live with added guilt the rest of his life. Sighing, he got to his feet and went to the door, wondering if he could in some way say thanks.

Wu Huixia looked up from the papers he was shuffling. "Wai Liang, why are you dallying? I have work to do and cannot waste any more time with you."

Logan left, passing the guards and going by the lone cypress in front of the building. It formed a lacy pattern in the sky, its leaves moving delicately in a sluggish breeze. It looked so innocent, so beautiful in its simplicity, hugging the earth for sustenance, lifting its leaves to the sun. Tears collected in his eyes, tears of anger and love. The students reminded him of his younger self, their wide-eyed idealism soon to be broken as he had been broken. His daughter and his grandson must not be caught up in the chaos that would follow. No matter what it might cost him, he would go to the hotel, spend all the time he could, beg Christine's forgiveness for leaving her behind. But first he must let Sulin know he was all right. Shoulders squared with determination, he started home.

Chapter 15

Christine

The People's Republic of China - 1989

Each day as more people flocked to the Square, many in a party mood, laughing, singing, and swarming around Matt and his guitar, Christine watched with a mother's pride. From all over the world tourists converged on the Square, and he became the center of much attention. His songs, his expressions, his clothes were mimicked by students and admired by onlookers. The democracy movement leaders loved him for many reasons, not the least was he wasn't afraid to air his fledgling Chinese. Others, not hearing him speak, assumed he was a Chinese citizen. Foreigners took videos of him. Reporters from Taiwan, Singapore, Sweden and Germany interviewed him as well as the students. He was tremendously American: Open and friendly. Everyone appeared to love him.

Christine noted when dumpling and noodle makers set up shop, and government agitators began to appear. It was slow, incremental. The overwhelming support seemed to be with the students. CNN filed ongoing reports, stories from other broadcast journalists kept the world appraised. Christine observed with mixed feelings Matt's increasing involvement with the students. He bought food and distributed it free, gave most of his clothes to those in need, and spoke out whenever he could. At night, in their room, he composed a song he called, "Democracy Now," and played it and sang it to much acclaim in The Square the next day. Whenever he appeared, someone always requested his song. The protests and demonstrations grew larger daily. Students from all over the nation, including the prestigious Fudan University in Shanghai, joined delegations of students from both People's University and Xunghin in Beijing. Matt became acquainted with most of them.

With classes at the university temporarily on hold, and no further word from Wu Huixia, Christine grew anxious. She scoured the phone book the manager permitted her to look at after much persuasion and a bribe. No listing existed for Wai Liang, Logan Wainwright, or Wu Gang-jo. She hadn't realized how hard it would be to locate someone, sure Wu Huixia would open doors, help her. The phone book listed businesses, the airport, schools and a few government organizations, but very few residential numbers.

One day when she returned from The Square ahead of Matt, the manager came running from his desk as she entered the hotel. "Miss Wainwright, Comrade Wu Huixia here when you gone. He said sorry to miss you. He leave a note." Clearly impressed, he gave her a folded square paper.

"Thank you." She waited until she was in the elevator before she unfolded the note and read: "I very sorry miss you and remember with much fondly your previous visit. Chinese government pay hotel for inconvenience cause Christine Wainwright and son. Wai Liang, once known as Logan Wainwright, deliver airline tickets before departure three days. With Much Regret, Wu Huixia.

Standing at the window in her room, watching the people pouring by below, she read the message again. Her father was coming! She'd see him, talk to him, be with him. She'd see him in two, possibly three days! Wu's note hinted her father would bring the tickets in time for their flight. That could mean any day. Surely there would be time to talk. Should she ask about Gang-jo? What would be best for Matt? He had to meet his grandfather. Anyway, Matt and Jason were close; why disturb placid waters? But Gang-jo was his birth fathers. She'd closed the door to the past, but what if it swung open again? She'd never blamed Gang-jo for her pregnancy. She'd been just as moon struck or whatever as he. Would the powerful attraction between them still exist?

Folding her arms on the windowsill, she watched impatiently as people filled the street and streamed by. Matt was at least a half-hour late. It wasn't like him. She concentrated on the view past Jianguomen Bridge to the entrance to the Square and drummed her fingers on the sill. Where in hell was Matt?

She leaned out, craned her head. Underneath the laughter and chatter of people calling to one another, a low rumble sounded, like a dragon stirring after a long sleep. Daily the Chinese students had grown more demanding, and daily the modern hotel where she and Matt stayed, had grown more confining. She should have stayed with Matt. The stream of people going to Tiananmen had brought a festival spirit to the city, an atmosphere that he loved. Still, she'd expected him back by now. No matter that he had only a beginning knowledge of the language, his easy way of becoming everybody's friend put Matt at the center of any international group. He'd never been this late before. Dark had descended. At home he would have called.

She penned a note, placed it on Matt's bed and hurried to

the lobby. The likelihood that her father would come while she was gone was slim. Wu's note had made that clear, and she knew exactly the spot in the Square where Matt usually sat. She could check it out and if he wasn't there she could be reasonably sure he was on the way to the hotel.

She emerged from the lobby into a small crowd of people in blue tunics, 1972 coming alive in her mind again. Although Matt had said nothing about Gang-jo, surely his wanting to see him remained unchanged. She paused, questioning herself. Should she go back inside? No, she couldn't wait; she had to look.

In the dark street beyond the hotel, lights bobbed, and a loud creaking sound carried to her like a cart rattling over uneven pavement. As she argued with herself, a Chinese man wearing a 49ers T-shirt materialized out of the shadows and clapped his hands in glee.

"What is it?" Christine asked in Chinese, moving aside so bicyclists and pedestrians could speed by. The man looked at her for a few seconds before replying. She imagined he was taking in her sleek American appearance, her Caucasian eyes and white skin, and wondering why she spoke his language so well.

He said, "The students from the Academy of Fine Arts made a statue. See, each cart holds a section waiting to be put together at Tiananmen. It's an Image of Freedom, like the one in New York." His smile was broad, his voice filled with pride.

Squinting into the dark, Christine identified a white plaster arm bearing a torch. A thrill ran up her spine. "You mean the Statue of Liberty."

He bobbed his head enthusiastically. "Yes, yes, that's it, a goddess of liberty, nine meters tall!"

Thirty feet! "Marvelous," Christine called stepping off the curb into the flow of people swarming toward The Square. Laughing, all talking at once, they smiled at her and propelled her with them through the Gate of Heavenly Peace and toward the center of Tiananmen.

In fascination she gazed at the people surrounding her. Workers had joined the students in droves. A man wearing a leather apron saluted her, an old woman with a kettle of noodles held out a plate, and a man pushing a wheelbarrow forced her aside with polite phrases. A din of voices beat the air, reverberated, became one voice. No wonder Wu Huixia didn't know what to do with her, there had to be no students left at the school. How could she ever find Matt in the crush?

Catching her breath, she glanced above the middle portal of the massive stone entrance to the defaced portrait of Mao Tse-Tung. To her left sprawled the Great Hall of the People. Near there, reporters from Europe focused on a student shouting through a bullhorn. Listeners crowded around: Chinese in Western dress, peasants from the provinces, young people in modern clothes, everyone but Matt.

She let herself be pushed along. Speakers popped up everywhere and all had their listeners, their admirers, even as the main body of demonstrators congregated near the Martyrs Monument. Flags and banners fluttered; signs identified groups. All brought a look of permanence to the largest Square in the world. Edging by flapping canvas shelters and homemade bedrolls thrown upon the ground, Christine pushed and shoved her way toward the monument. Matt usually stationed himself near the center of activities, this time she didn't spot him.

As she zigzagged past nylon tents spread out in a rectangular pattern, the bicycle carts carrying the statue entered the Square.

"Instant New York City," an elderly American cried. Other Americans agreed, heads bobbing in satisfaction.

Muttering, "*Duibuqi*, excuse me," Christine elbowed her way toward a group of fair-haired young people and hurried by when she saw Matt wasn't among them.

A thin Chinese student, emerging from his tent, looked around with sleepy eyes. "Ah, ha, the lady is here!" he cried, and for a moment Christine thought he meant her. Then she saw him point to the carts bearing the statue. His arms, thin as willow branches, moved gracefully, the gesture underscoring his pride and determination.

She asked, "How long will it take to put it together?"

His eyes blazing, he cried, "It does not matter. We will work until she is upright in all her glory."

Christine nodded understanding. She had once been young and determined, full of idealism.

As she circled the crowd of sweat-banded young people assembling the statue, she felt the air of hope and resolution gripping them. Their cause had a rhythm, a cadence of its own rumbling beneath the timeless beat of Beijing. If China joined the world community, became a part of the whole, trading on an equal basis, participating fully in world affairs, its influence would not be a small thing. She wondered if Gang-jo was still an interpreter.

For a while the thought made her pause while a wild, improbable but totally possible future flashed in her mind.

China would speak, and the world would tilt in its direction. Would Matt be drawn by this hotbed of idealism boiling in the Square? At home he listened when she discussed political matters, but he had never seen a movement take shape and grow. Here the dragon slumbered, waking occasionally to breathe fire and belch smoke. Now it peered from red-rimmed emerald green eyes and switched its tail as the Chinese version of Yankee Doodle sounded. What young person could resist? Matt would be savoring the excitement, listening to the rhetoric with ears ready to hear. Would he be ready to leave, not only now, but also later

A pick coaxed "Born in the U.S.A" from a guitar. Forgetting her plan to cover Tiananmen in a clockwise pattern, she hurried toward the sound and plunged into the group surrounding the musician. But it was a stranger, not Matt.

"I'm looking for my son. Taller than me. A guitar player."

"Like Bruce Springsteen?"

"Yes!"

Over and over again she repeated the words. Always came the same reply: "Sorry." After a while she quit asking.

A girl with shining eyes buttonholed her about Hollywood. As Christine answered, the talk expanded, took different routes, another crowd gathered. For a while she felt a part of the China that had so filled her mind as a child, and she relaxed into the easy camaraderie, the dream. All week old dreams about the father she'd never known had risen in a fresh guise. Would meeting him add luster to the trip, make clear what was happening? China was an enigma within a puzzle, and her father an unknown element.

Suddenly, her legs felt like liquid, and an overpowering

fatigue hit her. As she had circled, time had slipped away. It was almost midnight, the crowds had thinned, the murmur of voices quieting to a steady drone.

Here and there people balanced on their haunches tending fires, heating food. A woman had set up a small restaurant on boards balanced on tin buckets. Christine dug into her slacks, found a *yuan*, bought some tea and rice. Surely she would run into Matt now, and they could walk back to the hotel together. But maybe he was already there.

Holding the bowl at chin level, she shoveled in the food as she moved toward the exit, the food reviving her. From all around she caught a new sense of excitement. Stars winked the sky, the yellow dust from the Gobi settling, the wind not blowing. Turning, she saw the stark white goddess loom above her. Awkward but appealing, it was a reasonable copy of the Statue of Liberty, rising above the Martyr's Monument, dominating the Square. The woman's arm, extending toward the bright full moon, held a torch aloft as if proclaiming freedom.

Goose bumps raced up Christine's spine, tingled her scalp. China! A country so enormous no one could contain her. China! A misguided, often gallant giant. A lump filled her throat, tears dimmed her eyes.

A hush descended. Chinese and Westerners, wearing solemn but beatific expressions, moved as one, all eyes on the statue. Linking hands with the people near her, she stepped closer. Suddenly, in that silent moment before the cries, the shouts, the chants, the unfurling of banners, Christine had a realization so strong she wanted to shout it. Boundaries and stiff national pride meant nothing when people realized their common humanity.

Looking from one person to the next, the old, the young, the ragged and well-dressed all wearing joyful expressions, she knew a moment of peace, of hope and exhilaration that shut out, made little of the strange week. A roar, deep and loud and spontaneous, rose and thousands of voices, sounding like one, cheered. Without knowing when it happened Christine cheered, too, waved her arms, hugged people, and shouted. A gleeful dance of freedom developing, she wondered: Had she witnessed a symbolic link to America, to democracy and true beginnings?

She felt far younger than her forty-five years, and hoped to be able to share this moment with Matt. Her dear son was so much luckier than the dedicated radicals of the People's Republic.

A man shouted in her ear, "Tomorrow, we make an Eiffel Tower." His smile reminded her of Gang-jo. Would she recognize him if she saw him? They'd both been so full of themselves, so in charge, so sure they could control it all. How different the times had been, young people in America riding the crest of a movement that was theirs while the Chinese had been boxed in by a system that said they were the world. Someone touched her shoulder.

She whirled around, expecting to see Matt.

A young man, thin and intense as the others, interrupted her reverie. "Is your name Wainwright?" He wiped sweat from his eyes with a red bandanna.

"Yes, I'm Professor Wainwright" How did he know? Was Matt nearby grinning at the scene, egging the man on? Sweeping a gaze past the young man, she searched the periphery. Next to the wall, a Chinese girl sang in bad English, "We

Shall Overcome." As if magnetized, her feet moved in that direction. The young man with the red bandanna stopped her, shouting in English, "Your son shout at police on avenue. They take her away."

Christine stared at him and shook her head in denial. Her son climbed the hills of Seattle, played guitar at the Bumbershoot Festival, crewed on Opening Day. She shouted, "How do you know it was my son? How do you know my name?"

"He say her name Mathew Wainwright. I hear. I learn much English in school."

"What are you trying to say?" she cried in Chinese. "How do you know it was my son?"

"You speak Chinese. Good. Your son wore a red shirt that said Huskies and a Seahawks cap."

Hearing the ring of truth, her heart thudded hard as the cries in the Square escalated, rumbled, angry voices suddenly shutting out the rest. What was going on? The boy's words could mean anything. Shouting at the police was the way of youth. She'd go back to the hotel and find Matt sound asleep, his mouth slightly open, sweat and man smell coming from him. "Tell me exactly what happened," she demanded, her gaze skimming the crowd.

"The police took your son to jail."

The words cut through the noise of the Square, slapped her with their ramifications. "No," Christine shouted shaking her head. Not her son in some smelly, dank cell watched over by illiterate guards. "You're sure?" she demanded.

"I saw them take him."

No need for alarm. Matt would prove who he was and they'd release him. But did he have identification with him? In

Beijing's celebratory mood he could easily have forgotten it, and the hotel held his passport. She'd go there first, probably find him in their room. But if not, she'd go to the police station. Surely someone would point it out to her.

She pushed her way to the nearest entrance and saw the students erecting a barricade with anything they could get their hands on, overturned cars, pedicabs, boxes, trash, rubber tires. Working her way around a pile of splintered wood, she emerged outside the Square. From several blocks down the avenue, the sound of marching carried, and she glimpsed a shadowy contingent of soldiers moving toward Tiananmen. All week tourists in the hotel had passed on stories of confrontations between students and police, but this... She shook her head, trying to comprehend what was happening. A quarter of a block away a big government car parked and two men stood in the headlights. One was a civilian in Western dress. The other wore a military uniform covered with medals, but the civilian seemed to be in charge, the soldier nodding what seemed like agreement. A match flared, and the civilian's face was momentarily illuminated, a cigarette lit. Christine clutched her chest. My god, was it Gang-jo? That handsome sculpted face, the wide mouth were like his. Involuntarily, she took a step closer, blood racing, her mind spinning. Could it really be Gang-jo? His voice suddenly rode the air, his hand and arm pointing toward the troops. The other man nodded again, and this time he made a backing-up gesture toward the troops who halted. In all, at the most, three minutes had passed, and now the two men stood quietly talking. She could approach, interrupt, or go on.

At a trot she started for the hotel.

Chapter 16

Christine

The People's Republic of China - 1989

Confused, angry with herself for vacillating, she didn't look back. Jason had left a message at the hotel. "Christine, I can't believe you've forgotten about the time change. Call me at a proper time, damn it." Was he still half angry with her? Now, she wondered, had she let Matt down by not seeing if it were really Gang-jo? She'd never know. But finding Matt came first, she told herself, her breath coming fast now. Quiet prevailed once she had the Square completely behind her. Suddenly, gunfire blasted into the calm.

"Damn," she cried as a surge of people raced by her. Hugging buildings, vaulting walls, rushing along with the runners, a terrible fear gripped her. Matt could actually be in jail. Night held a hard gray darkness impossible to penetrate until fire's red glare brightened the sky. Voices shouted. Shots escalated. The smell of smoke quickly made it difficult to breathe.

She should have kept Matt with her. She shouldn't have dallied in the Square. Fighting down panic, she made herself plan. If necessary she'd bribe the hotel manager. Dollars should wring telephone numbers and addresses from him

Nanheyan Street marked her hotel's western boundary. Bursting into the lobby she bypassed a group of Americans, Germans, Swedes and Brits all talking excitedly. Avoiding eye contact, she pushed by to the elevator. Matt had to be in their room. He would greet her querulously, disturbed when she wasn't where he'd expected; but the room was dark, no sign of Matt anywhere.

Back in the lobby, she hurried to the registration desk, banged the counter bell and glanced toward the back where the manager or an attendant stayed. No one came out. She slammed the bell again, a scream of frustration clogging her throat.

"Professor Wainwright?" came from behind her. She spun around, her nerves jangling.

A tall Caucasian man, with blue eyes and a face that at once was unknown but familiar, smiled at her.

"Yes, I'm Professor Wainwright," she said, attempting to calm her inner trembling. Where had she seen him before? Had he overheard her talking in the Square? Could he be from the University?

"You *are* Christine Wainwright from Seattle, Washington?" The words came slowly, as if kept in the dark for years and allowed in the light for the first time.

His voice, emphasizing the word "are," his head jutting forward slightly, as if to increase his knowledge, had her staring, looking up at him. She saw the outline of her own face, her coloring, her eyes. The knowledge growing within her like an unchecked weed, she whispered, "Are you…?"

"I'm Logan Wainwright, your father."

The man's thick gray hair fell toward his forehead, a good-looking man she could imagine in uniform, with dark hair, without lines in his face, a man tall and handsome. Every day during childhood she had looked at and talked to his picture.

"Oh, thank god." Other words locked in her throat. She had waited forever, the idea of the meeting playing itself out in scripted scenarios, their love for one another surmounting all difficulties. But not now, now when she needed time and room to find her son, to find Matt the grandson, this man didn't know. She took a step toward the stranger, hands held out in an unconscious plea as she blurted, "I heard they took Matt to jail, and I've got to get him out, and the manager's not here." She glanced toward the desk. "You heard me ring the bell..." Her words were rushed, her movements jerky. She stopped, and shook her head. "Matt's so young," she said slowly. "He acts as if he knows it all." She attempted a smile. "Don't they all at seventeen?" Seeing her father shake his head, she added quickly, "My son, your grandson, Mathew Wainwright. He was at the Square."

He nodded, spoke calmly and quietly. "Tell me slowly what it is you need."

It was clear she had mangled the telling. She closed her eyes a second and when she opened them she pushed words from her mouth one after the other, none betraying the tumult churning inside her. Finishing, she held out a hand, palm up. Help me, she wanted to cry, but no words followed. Fear filled her eyes. A tremor passed through her.

"There, there," he murmured, and taking her arm, steered her toward an empty couch flanked by two tables with vases of fake flowers. "You've had quite a shock" He sat next to her. "How can I help?"

"How," she echoed wanting to cry for so many reasons. How many years had she waited for this moment, and now it seemed anticlimactic, one need lessening the importance of the other, a roomful of people pretending not to listen, the muffled sound of shooting continuing. "I want you to find Matt."

"I'll try very hard," he said, taking both her hands in his.

"I'm sorry, sorry," she cried. Why did this moment have to be so damn pedestrian, so loaded with complications? "I thought it would be different when we met. I planned words to say, but I can't remember them." Tears escaped her eyes.

He leaned closer. "It's all right. I planned words, too. For many, many years."

Without planning it, she threw herself into his arms. Whatever had transpired, whatever would transpire meant nothing, only that he seemed strong, and his voice was even and his eyes were warm, and he was her father. "Daddy," she managed. "Oh, Daddy, please find Matt."

He patted her back, a sheen of unshed tears filling his eyes. "There, there, it will be all right, Christine. I guarantee it. I will find your son. Matt?"

"He's a good boy, never in any trouble. He's never been in a jail before." Saying the words hurt like burrs pressing into her flesh. Her American son in a Chinese jail!

"My dear daughter, I'm so sorry this has happened." Logan's mouth curved upward, his eyes warm and appealing. "You are exactly as I imagined, beautiful and caring. And now very worried. Does my grandson favor his mother?"

She moved slightly away from his comforting bulk. "No. But he has your height." How to explain? She couldn't. Not now. Not here.

"If they have him, it will be at the jail closest to the Square. I'll go there first." His voice radiated confidence.

She wiped away tears, her voice gaining solidity. "Give me a moment. I'll leave a note for him." She rose. "In case they told me wrong and he isn't in jail but on his way home. I'll only be a minute." She started for the elevators.

He stopped her. "It would be better if you stay here."

She frowned. How could she do any more waiting? She shook her head vehemently.

"In case he returns before I do."

"Of course. I don't know what got in me." His concern for her palpable, she turned slowly back toward him and put a hand on his arm. "Sorry. It's just that...Thank you for being here...Daddy." *Daddy, like a child*, *Daddy like she'd always wanted to say*. "Seeing you is like a dream, but I'm very worried about Matt. Please hurry. "

"I'm on my way," he said getting up.

She watched him go rapidly toward the door, his voice echoing in her mind. Like a camera she recorded his essence, a man with broad but slightly stooped shoulders, no trace of dark hair, his khaki pants and shirt fashionable but faded, his feet in western shoes, well-polished, the idea of him lingering. When he opened the outside door, the sound of gunfire entered like exploding firecrackers, and she jumped, the incongruity of the sound in the western-style lobby startling. She called, her voice loud, "We have so much to talk about, so many years...."

For a moment he paused, his eyes locked with hers.

She couldn't look aside, and the urge to cry out; race to him, be comforted was strong.

"I loved you always. Remember that, Christine." His voice brimmed with emotion.

"Me, too." She lifted her head, forced a smile.

Firming his shoulders, Logan went out, calling over his shoulder, "If the telephone lines are working, I'll keep you informed."

"Yes!" she cried, but soon he was swallowed by the dark. Turning back to the room, a feeling of hope rose and then plummeted as a middle-aged man in designer shorts and shirt burst into the lobby from outside.

His eyes twin mirrors of shock, he shouted in English, "My god it's hell out there." His gaze traveled from Christine to the tourists congregated around the plush overstuffed furniture, all of them watching, listening. "They were coming from all directions. I thought I'd get shot any minute." He threw out an arm to balance himself against the wall. His breath was harsh; sweat beaded his forehead. "Four civilians were already shot. Christ, I'm lucky to be alive." He pulled a handkerchief from his pocket and wiped his brow as he literally fell to the couch.

An elderly British woman in a Chanel suit said, "This is beastly, isn't it? I expect I should introduce myself. Penelope Norton-Smythe."

No one responded.

The woman indicated the man behind her. "My husband Dr. Norton-Smythe, paleontologist."

"Good show, actually," slurred the elderly gentleman perching on the arm of her chair.

Christine went to the door and peered out. It was impossible to see beyond the green streetlights that lit Chang'an Boulevard. If she had confronted Gang-jo, could he have done something? Skirting the group, she hurried to her room.

When her father called, she needed to be near the phone. She lay down, but as sporadic gunshots continued, she got up and knelt by the window. An occasional flash lit the sky and rushing footsteps and muffled voices sounded; but she could see nothing else. Keeping a vigil, she played and replayed the evening, told herself Matt would be fine. American power would prevail. The Chinese could not let anything happen to visitors from overseas. But Matt didn't look like a tourist. She should have told her father, but how in that horrible, wonderful moment? Sleep overcame her.

Two hours later a loud booming shook the hotel. Bolting upright, she switched on a light, but gray day had arrived and Matt's bed was still empty, and her father hadn't called. Nothing had changed. She washed in cold water, put on a clean shirt and went downstairs.

"Artillery fire. I'm not sure but I think it was near the Square," Dr. Norton-Smythe called from the lobby. He reclined in the chair where his wife had been the night before. "Come keep me company."

Stroking his small white mustache, he looked stereotypical British, but Christine noticed his pants and jacket were wrinkled as if he had been up all night. "You don't think it was near the jail?"

"My dear, I have no idea where the jail might be, but I am going out to reconnoiter. Penelope is packing, holding out only what we'll need in the next few days. Several people have already gone. I'm going to attempt to find a taxi, but I doubt I'll be lucky. Haven't seen one in hours. This has the feel of India during their fight for independence. Quite a conundrum that. Not that I'm irrevocably colonial."

"I tell him it's dangerous and we should just stay put," Penelope said entering the lobby. Her classic dressmaker gown had no wrinkles, her hair was properly in place, her make up had been applied with a light hand, but powder caked in facial wrinkles, and her voice cracked. "He insists we should get to the airport to book a flight. Don't want to be lifted out by helicopter. Like they did in Vietnam. But I say, a man his age shouldn't be running around outside in whatever is happening." She cleared her throat.

Christine said flatly, "My father hasn't come back with my son."

Dr. Norton-Smith shook his head. "Bloody bad news. But I'm sure they'll turn up soon. Your father looked like a capable chap." Rising, he smiled at Christine. "Penelope apparently doesn't think I am. But I assure her I'll be fine. I'll go by the Foreign Students Club and skirt the barricades. We have to know what's happening if we're ever going to get out of here." He waved off his wife's further protestations. "Cheerio."

As he went out the door, Christine leaned on the bell and finally roused the hotel manager. He got her a thermos of tea. Back in her room, she poured a cup and went to the window in time to spot Dr. Norton-Smythe, a stick figure below.

Far down the Boulevard a line of trucks approached in a steady, stately, parade of power. "Oh, damn." She hit the windowsill with her fist. People were everywhere again as automatic bursts from machine guns came. Automatically, she jumped back from the window, let the curtains fall into place. Her son was in jail, and all hell was breaking loose, and she didn't know what the hell to do. She wanted to call Jason, hear his comforting voice, but she had to leave the phone free.

Still, a quick call. She picked up the receiver, found the line dead.

She went back to the window, alternately watched and dozed to awake at gray morning again. Her eyes burned from lack of sleep and worry made her frown. Pushing herself, she went down to the restaurant, but no one was in the dining room, no one was in the kitchen. No maids waited ready to make the beds, clean the bathrooms, provide clean towels. The hotel manager wasn't in his room behind the desk. Searching for him, she bumped into Dr. Norton-Smythe.

"Sorry, my dear," he said making sure she had her footing. He'd had no luck finding a cab. "It appears the government's determined to fight this democracy thing."

From down the hall, the manager appeared, smoothing his hair, buttoning his coat. "Excuse me. My clerks have not arrive, and I have to spend the night. I am sorry for inconvenience, poor service."

Norton-Smythe pulled out his wallet. "We need food and your excellent restaurant is unstaffed. Quite disgraceful really, but partially understandable."

The manager half-bowed, "Please, please. We are very sorry. Most unfortunate."

"Can't be helped." Dr. Norton-Smythe fingered his mustache and sniffed. "I won't report this to Mr. Nye at the Friendship Bureau, so my good chap, if you could scare up some fruit, biscuits, anything to stave off hunger until you get your staff back, my wife and I and Professor Wainwright would be most grateful." He dropped a stack of yuan in the manager's hand. "Oh, yes, deliver it to our rooms, please." He called the last over his shoulder.

A short time later the manager brought a tray containing an apple, two croissants, two pats of butter and a chocolate bar. Christine ate it all before once again prowling the hotel. In the foreign currency store a clerk stood as if frozen in time, fingers poised, ready to convert dollars to yuan for non-existent customers. She'd seen no one else. Most everyone had left when the counter democracy actions began. The corridors and elevators had a hollow, empty feeling, the shops and the post office were closed, and she saw no one. The shooting had escalated now.

She peered out the main door. A rosy glow colored the sky in the east and tinged the clouds with pale pink. Peaceful appearing, tranquil looking if she could forget those small tanks rumbling down the street. A random shot slammed into the side of the hotel close to the door. She jumped back. A volley followed as she scrambled back from the exposed glass, heard it tinkle, saw it shatter. A helicopter whirred overhead. Then nothing. She should have insisted on going with Logan. Certainly he'd have been to the jail by now. A hollow feeling invaded her stomach, spread through her body. People were running along the sidewalks closest to the buildings.

"It's World War II out there," Penelope cried, entering the lobby, her upper-class voice rasping. "Everybody's shooting at everybody."

"I went out again, " Dr. Norton-Smythe confessed.

"Foolhardy man." Pride showed in Penelope's eyes.

"I went out the kitchen door, talked with people who'd been at the Square. They say Deng Xiaoping's personal regiment is going to attack the students. I smelled tear gas." He poured tea from a thermos sitting on a table in the lobby. "The student barricades won't hold the soldiers back for long. I understand they can get to the Square through the museums, the Forbidden City or the Great Hall of the People." He set his cup aside and said quietly, "Those poor children are fighting a losing battle."

Christine pressed her nails into her palms. She had to get Matt and get the hell out of China.

The manager gestured to her from behind the desk.

She hurried across the lobby.

"I have telephone message for you. Someone said not to worry, everything fine."

She leaned against the counter with relief. "Who was it? What else did they say?"

"It was a man. He speak Chinese. A thousand pardons, please, that all I know. Telephone line out again."

"Thank you." It had to be her father. She went back to the window in her room. Opening the draperies a crack, she peeked out. Smoke and the smell of cordite drifted in. The barricades were burning. Black smoke spewed upward from tires and plastic, gas and oil. Although the streets behind the hotel were relatively clear, troops were moving in fast, and she feared her father and Matt wouldn't be able to get through.

Clouds were gathering, and a whiff of rain hung in the air. At three-thirty thunder rolled, and hard, pelting rain beat at the hotel. She welcomed the storm. Perhaps nature would temper the violence. For three hours she watched the storm compete with occasional bursts from automatic weapons, rain filling the gutters; thunder rumbling and crashing.

Around six the rain stopped and the sun appeared like a blood red patch in the western sky. Christine packed a small bag for herself and Matt, ready to leave the moment he appeared. If necessary, she'd leave the larger suitcases.

The manager, fueled she supposed by Norton-Smythe's yuans, announced the restaurant had reopened. She went down. As if to make up for earlier shortcomings, candles graced each table and gladiolus stood in silver vases. A sprinkling of guests dotted the dining room, all of them tense, gallows humor jumping from table to table. She forced a smile as everyone joked about the menu—rice and other things, meaning broccoli and a small slice of pork.

In a fog that filtered out everything unimportant, Christine opened her wallet, studied Matt's pictures, ran her fingers over the plastic sleeves containing school photos—he in his basketball uniform, with the band, clowning around after practice, with a girl at the prom. All so ordinary, so American. Except she hadn't told Logan that Gang-jo was Matt's father. Head throbbing, she went to her room, tried to call Jason, but she couldn't get an outside line. She fell into an exhausted sleep.

Chapter 17

Logan

The People's Republic of China – 1989

Logan took his bicycle from the rack near the hotel. The air was thick with smoke, the streets leading from the Square filled with people going in all directions. Dim shadows, they were sometimes highlighted by flames illuminating green uniforms, T-shirted youths. A hum of voices, commands, screams, and gunshots blended together. He started toward the jail, feelings as contradictory as his life in China pulsing through him, his thoughts bittersweet.

For so long he'd held in his mind the moment when he would see Christine. Always it took place in a quiet spot, the two of them with glasses of soda, or flutes of wine, American music purring, the air light, the day warm with a cool breeze, the green of Seattle surrounding them. Now, she'd been drawn tighter than a guitar string, and he had been little better, here in the midst of a movement bound not to succeed.

He expected he'd have to barter, trade, bully the often-unrelenting police who followed orders rather than buck the system. He had to take risks for a daughter whose love he might never keep if he did not succeed. Yet, there had been that moment at the end of that hurried exchange when she'd called out to him, perhaps seen past her own dilemma. Oh, how he'd longed to explain himself to her, how he'd wanted to paint the pictures that would show him, not as a old man, but a young man, not nearly as idealistic as those young people in the Square, but close enough he could relate. His grandson had probably been caught up in it. An American full of his democratic principles bonding with the students, but feeling none of the intense sense of accomplishment, of need, of impending martyrdom they undoubtedly felt, not unlike he had been so many years ago.

Veering from a main street into a *hutang*, he relived the past. The way was narrow, filled with bumps and made narrower by household goods intruding into the space. Two old men in plastic chairs leaned against the back of a house, their feet stretched out before them, hand-rolled cigarettes clutched in their fingers. He called out to them in Chinese and listened to their complaints as he pedaled by. A sense of loss as well as descending gloom filled him. In the modern luxury of a hotel made for Western tastes, Christine had to believe all would end well now he had interceded. But would it? Within days she would be home again in America, telling the story to an attentive hushed audience. It would be a great adventure. She might even write a book, scholarly and popular at the same time, relating her experiences, delving also into China's past. Unless he could persuade Sulin to leave, he would still be in the China Mao had started on its present path.

Resting his head against the side of a building, he closed his eyes and fended off nausea that spread up from his belly. Pushing away from the building, he took a deep breath. He had no choice but to do everything he could to free the grandson he loved but had never known.

Emerging from the alley, his bike began to slow down. Having a hard time controlling it, panic shot through him.

Helluva time to have a flat tire. Fighting the bike, he pulled to the side, clear of the steady stream of people running by, no one speaking now. All had a blank look of disbelief that spread like a miasma covering the street. Losing time, and angry with himself for it, his hands became clumsy, his mind distracted. He dropped the patch, had trouble finding it, the meeting with Christine uppermost in his mind. Always before his body and brain had meshed, doing whatever was needed with little effort. Now, his hands refused to cooperate, his mind stay focused.

Thoughts of his grandson pressed against him. What would he look like, be like? What were American boys like today? The tourists he sometimes saw were mostly older people with money to spend. What if Mathew had been lumped in with others from the Square, sent to another part of the city or shipped to the country? So many possibilities, so little choice.

At the jail a confusion of voices assaulted him, people jammed together. He scanned the room, the lines, the guards, the hall leading to the jail cells. Head high, he told the nearest guard in a quiet but authoritative voice, "I am Wai Liang looking for my grandson."

The guard shrugged. "Everybody is here for somebody. You have I.D?"

Logan nodded, produced it. Years ago, his name had brought instant recognition. Now it apparently meant nothing for the younger man looked from the ID to Logan and gestured toward the longest line.

When the guard turned aside, Logan shoved his way to the counter determined to gain attention. "I am on an errand for Comrade Wu Huixia."

A clerk, stamping dates on a stack of papers, looked over his wire-framed glasses. "Easy to say." He either had pull or high scholarly scores for glasses were seldom issued unless you had severe visual problems.

"Comrade Wu gave me these airline reservations to deliver to the Americans, Christine Wainwright and her son, Mathew Wainwright." He pulled the papers from his pocket, glad now he'd forgotten to leave them with Christine. "I was on my way to their hotel when I heard the young man, Mathew Wainwright, is here, taken from Tiananmen Square."

"Americans? We have no Americans here." The man waved to the next person in line and said to Logan, "Move aside."

Logan braced himself. No one would push him away. He'd made up his mind.

"I said move, or I'll call the guard and put you behind bars." The man's eyes were big behind the lens of his glasses.

Determined, Logan said evenly, "Call Wu Huixia. Tell him what you told me. He will verify who I am. The guard has seen my ID."

The clerk shook his head. "You are like a bee buzzing your lies. No one calls Wu or any of them."

People nearby agreed. They smiled as if to say what planet was Logan from, a man who spoke Chinese like a native had to know no one contacted the rulers.

"Besides, we have no Americans."

Logan leaned closer, took a large gamble. "You have my American grandson. It is not true no one calls Comrade Wu. I do. Here is his private number." He wrote it on a scrap of paper and handed it to the clerk.

Color drained from the clerk's face. He worried the pen in his hand, and a troubled look entered his eyes. "How do I know you're telling the truth?" If he called and bothered Wu and the story was true, he would be in trouble for taking the big man's time. The same if it were false.

Logan pressed his advantage, not at all sure what Wu Huixia would say if he was contacted. Too much had happened lately. Everyone would be looking for scapegoats, running for cover. "I suggest, comrade, you release the American, Mathew Wainwright, into my custody." Recognizing that longing and need also gave him an edge, he pointed to the papers he'd placed on the counter. "Of course you recognize Wu Huixia's chop, his mark. See, there is his signature." He held out the airline reservations, the note to the airlines.

Frowning slightly, the clerk handed the papers to the female clerk who had been listening, and she disappeared into a small office at the side. Coming back out, her fingers near the red characters that indicated Wu Huixia, she looked past Logan as well as the clerk. Her manner verified she knew the dilemma they all could be in, but she had to acknowledge Wu's chop. She muttered, "We have seen this before." People within hearing shifted uncomfortably. It was not rare to have prisoners booked at Wu Huixia's request.

Logan lifted his voice. "Comrades, I am waiting. Release Mathew Wainwright now, please."

Without glancing at Logan, the clerk motioned the guard over. Heads together, they checked lists and whispered. Finally the clerk, looking past Logan's shoulder said, "We did not take everyone's name. The business at Tiananmen happened so fast, we registered the ringleaders only." He adjusted his wire-framed glasses and squinted. "It will take a few minutes. One moment, please."

Logan waited by the counter, not letting the clerks and guard forget he was there. People came and went. Voices rose and fell. A half-hour passed without a sign of Matt. Logan cleared his throat, reminded the workers behind the barrier of Wu Huixia, repeated Matt's name. Holding his head high, confidence in his stance, command in his voice, he managed not to betray the growing weakness in his body, disgust for the system riling the juices in his stomach. His ears rang, his scalp tingled, for the clerk had stopped looking his way. Had Wu Huixia changed his mind, issued contradictory orders? Pain knifed into Logan's chest, made it difficult to breathe. While he contemplated what to do, someone called out, "Here is the American."

Logan peered down the dim hall, the promise of seeing his grandson lessening the persistent pain ravaging his chest.

Two guards rounded the bend in the corridor, a young man between them.

The boy was Chinese. Someone else was being released instead of Matt. Masking his disappointment, Logan strained to see. Maybe Matt was walking in the shadows of the dark-gray corridor. But the hall remained empty except for the two guards and the defiant figure between them, a boy wearing faded jeans and a bright red shirt. He walked with his head high. Despite his Oriental eyes, his walk was American, jaunty, confident. It had to be his grandson!

Logan took a step toward him. "Mathew Wainwright? I have come for you."

The boy's alert but wary glance touched Logan. As if relieved to hear an American voice, he relaxed in a way only Americans do, Logan thought watching intently. He seemed charged with energy and optimism, never really doubting everything would be all right.

"Great! You from the embassy?"

Logan took a step closer. He would explain his relationship later, away from everyone who watched with unfeigned curiosity. "I've come to take you to your mother. Are you all right?"

Matt grinned. "They didn't beat me if that's what you mean, but I can't say much for Chinese hospitality. What's going on? No one will tell me anything." He moved away from the guards who undid the gate and waved him past the counter.

The words, "my grandson," repeated in Logan's mind like a litany that would make everything right. A muscle jumping in his cheek, Logan had to fight the impulse to embrace the boy. "Come," he said, and making sure Matt followed him through the crowded anteroom, he went outside.

Standing for a moment near the door, he reconnoitered. Small arms fire repeated, smoke billowed into the sky, and as he paused, the boom of bigger guns reverberated. Up the street, he detected a line of soldiers marching in the direction of the Square. The streets were a war zone, the air thick with the smell of sulfur. He could not risk going straight to Christine's hotel. Disregarding the people milling around in front of the jail, he led Mathew to the sidewalk and said softly, "Your mother sent me. I'm your grandfather, Logan Wainwright." He darted a glance at Matt.

Eyes widening, the boy's mouth flew open.

Logan said quickly, "Don't say anything that might be overheard. We need to get away from here. Can you ride a bike?"

Matt's smile flashed. "Sure. Why?" But his voice was too loud, his eyes full of wonder as he rocked back on his heels and hooked his fingers in his belt.

Logan wanted to shout to the crowd, "See, I, Logan Wainwright have a grandson who's as Chinese as any of you." Instead, he considered. The pop pop of gunshots were coming closer together. "This is standard transportation," he said unlocking his bicycle and freeing the front wheel. "You have any money, I'll buy you a bike. If not you'll have to ride on my luggage rack."

"Twenty, thirty dollars U.S., a couple *yuan.* After they put us in a big cell, they didn't know what to do. I wasn't even searched when I insisted I was American and only spoke English."

"You're lucky. Prison guards aren't known for generosity. Excuse me a second." Turning aside, Logan bargained quickly, bluntly in Chinese with three men leaning against the outside of the jail. Turning back to Mathew, he pointed to one of the grinning workmen. "Give him the American dollars. You just bought a bike, and he made a month's wages."

Matt handed over a twenty and a ten, got on the bike the man pushed forward, a simple model without gears. Clearing his throat, he said, "This is unbelievable. My grandfather busts me out of jail and I buy an old bike. You really are my grandfather?"

Logan smiled, nodded. For a moment they exchanged glances, and Logan felt warmed by Mathew's smile. He mounted his three-speed model. "You really okay?"

"I'm glad to be out, but it was no big deal. A dude from Shanghai taught me some new swear words. I improved my Chinese." He grinned.

Aware of the boy's bravado, so much like his own when he was young, Logan said, "Let's go. We can talk later." As they shoved, off, he asked, "No other Americans in jail with you?" "Just me." Matt laughed nervously, "It was weird. According to what I heard, they put me in because of some mix-up. The guard who *thought* he could speak English kept saying, 'You Merican?' and I kept saying, 'what do you want me to do, show you my birth certificate?' I was born in the USA. How much more American can you get?" His smile grew. "I can't wait to tell the guys at home. It'll be a blast."

So that was the current idiom. Blast. The boy was going to be all right. Logan glanced back. Another black cloud of smoke rose above the Square.

Matt frowned. "What's that?"

"They're burning tires. Hurry up, let's get out of here." The pain was kicking up again, slamming into his chest. "We can't waste any time." He pedaled faster.

Matt caught up, his eyes troubled, "I thought the hotel was in the other direction." He cocked his head to one side; his gaze direct, challenging. "You're sure you're my grandfather?" At the same age, Logan had been ready to question everything but hadn't been sure how far to go. "I just saw your mother at your hotel, but soldiers are thicker than flies between here and there, so we're taking a round-about route, going by my house first." He smiled reassuringly.

Matt nodded, then said, his voice carrying a what-do-you-know sound, "I can't believe I'm really with you. My grandpa grew up in Seattle. What part did you live in?"

Grandpa. It sounded good. "On Capital Hill, in a big old house with a view to the Sound."

Matt smiled, "That's what my Mom told me."

Logan thought, it's happening, my grandson and I together. After a while, as they maneuvered down *hutangs* and roads where no shots were being fired, Logan glanced over and caught Mathew frowning. "So your mother talked about me?"

Lines appeared in his handsome young face. "A few times."

"I first learned about China from the Changs, so when the war ended and your grandmother died, I came out here. I was full of idealism and got caught up in their revolution." He waited until a pain passed before adding, "Your mother was two, and I loved her very much. Still do. You, too. I promised her I'd look out for you."

Matt hesitated a beat before he said, "How come you never came back?"

The sadness of not being able to explain enveloping him, he said, "In China it is never easy. So many times I wanted to come home, but it never worked out."

Matt shook his head.

"I can see you're tired. We'll talk later."

Matt grinned sheepishly. "They didn't let me sleep in that fleabag, and this bike doesn't have any gears."

"Want to stop, rest a bit?"

"No, I'm okay."

"My house is away from the problems. I'll call your mother from there, get you back there as soon as possible." He pedaled past several small cinder block houses and a small park with chess stations. The street was quiet, only a few people sitting in doorways and in a tiny yard outside a tiny house, an old woman, balancing precariously on once-bound feet, pumped water from a well.

Matt's eyes went big with wonder.

Logan had trouble smiling. Throughout his years in China, multitudes had been sacrificed for an ever-changing dialectic. The government would shift the blame now, and officials and citizens would be imprisoned, banished for years. Fear pressed relentlessly against his chest. Would Huixia be blamed for the student rebellion? If so blame would spill over on Logan, and Sulin could bear the brunt of the government's anger. He glanced at Matt who struggled to keep up, clearly more tired and stressed than he admitted.

Pain shot through Logan, traveled from his chest to his jaw. Gripping the handlebars hard, he thought of Sulin. Through the years she had become his reason for living. Just thinking of her brought a sense of peace.

He pushed harder, hardly seeing the people who watched wordlessly from doorways as he and Matt passed. He must convince Sulin to leave China with him. He'd not supported the students, but now it could be said he'd interfered in a time of crisis. Men high in the government had paid with their lives for lesser offenses. His heart beat ever more wildly.

He would tell Sulin about the Changs and the International District. There she could hear and speak Chinese, and on Sundays Christine and Matt could come for dinner. The pain lessened. He smiled at Matt and felt a warm glow as the boy smiled back, his handsome face accessible, relaxed.

"Hey, Grandpa, how much further?"

Once Logan had been as young as Matt. Was his grandson as idealistic, ready to fight for his concept of truth? Now, Logan merely felt sad and incredibly tired. "We're almost there, son." Coasting now, he turned down the block to his house, knowing in his heart Sulin would never leave China.

As soon as Matt was resting comfortably, Logan dialed the hotel, but no one answered. He closed his eyes for a second, realizing how very tired he was and how he hardly knew how to respond to Christine. Looking up from his favorite chair, he saw Sulin holding out a cup of tea. The clamor in his chest quieted slightly. He smiled, noting that the usual sounds of traffic were absent, an unearthly quiet prevailing.

"All the main roads have been closed off," she whispered. "Everyone's talking about it." For years she had made her inspections, pausing at front and back gates to talk to neighbors, calling across garden walls to those living on either side.

"We must speak," Logan said settling against a cushion with a sigh.

She tipped her head to one side. "About the boy?" She pointed toward the next room where Matt slept.

"Partly. I am taking him to his mother."

"You are taking him to his mother, your daughter," she corrected softly.

He nodded. "It is a small thing to do." The first time they had talked about Christine, Sulin had looked at him with eyes neither warm nor cold, merely accepting.

"A grandson is not a small thing," she said sitting down

across from him in the chair that had come to be hers.

Both chairs had high straight backs, were heavily carved teak, bought when the buying of goods was no longer suspect. But one didn't slouch in such chairs even though they had been made comfortable with cushions. It is a commentary upon my age, Logan thought, or maybe the balancing act he and Sulin constantly played, covering up the bare bones of Communist life with frills that made it palatable. "No, a grandson is not a small thing. Neither is what is happening. Sulin, it is not safe for us here."

"In Beijing?"

He knew she was stalling for time. "In China."

"What would you have us do?" Her voice, so soft, so mellow, moved across his consciousness like the stroke of her hand.

"I believe Huixia will get me tickets out of the country, visas and necessary papers."

"Leave China?"

Logan nodded. "Go to America. Perhaps Canada first. Depends on the visa situation."

"I know even less about Canada than I do about the United States," she said.

Logan leaned forward, spoke softly. "It is not that different. And after a while we will go to the U.S. That I assure you."

"Oh, Logan, you don't see, do you? China is my home. This." She waved a hand around her, indicated the outdoors, the street, the neighborhood.

"But...." He let the word dangle, seeing in that instant all they had shared and all they had not. Despite re-education and banishment, they had lived a life patterned on the upper classes everywhere. They had merely spoken the words of the proletariat. He needed her to see that clearly for her own protection.

"We have had this conversation before," she said even more softly than he had spoken. "I think about that boy who sleeps in the next room. He is an American. And you... you cannot forget your mother country. You talk with pride about its beauty, its bounty." She leaned toward Logan. "Even its warts."

Hearing the truth, Logan nodded, the sadness and finality of the words like a vise tightening on his chest.

"Yes." She spoke quickly, urgently. "No matter that you have become Chinese, if I had never met you, if you had married another Chinese and made this your home, I would have known you were more American than Chinese, no matter what citizenship you claim. My dear, you are so very American, it is visible to everyone."

Logan pushed against the chair back, gripped the arms while Sulin's words echoed through his mind. From the first time he'd seen her, he'd loved her. "Are you saying in a roundabout way that you won't go?"

She waved a hand, the graceful gesture so much a part of her that he had become accustomed to it as he had become accustomed to her, accepting her love, her ministrations, her companionship as a given. Now he watched intently as she got up and moved to the door and looked in to where Matt slept. Her hair was snow white, her face lined, but she was still slight, her movements a poetry of motion. Could he exist without her? They finished one another's sentences, laughed at the same jokes, knew passion together.

She turned. "I am saying, when the children were on their own and I had gained my strength back after the Cultural Revolution, I would have gone. But then, you said nothing."

"Then the problem was gone, the good times were here. People came to China from all over the world. China truly seemed the center of the universe." American travelers had flocked to the People's Republic during the late seventies and throughout the eighties. He had been sure China was moving toward a much more democratic society.

Sulin cocked her head, "Are you then, China's fair weather friend?"

Yes, he wanted to say. What was there to admire in a leadership and political system that consistently erred and then blamed the people? Instead he said, "During my last years I want peace and quiet. I want to live without fear."

"And I." She picked up an envelope from the table near the outside door. "Meiling wrote. Her company is doing Swan Lake for the first time. Our granddaughter will dance dual roles. It should be quite an occasion. I promised we would be there."

His face felt as if it were twisted in several directions. His skin hurt, his jaws ached.

Moving around the room, Sulin continued, "After a long visit with Meiling, I thought we might go on to see Weiping."

He got up. "You think they would not catch us, make us recant, confess, send us to the country for whatever trumped up reason they want?"

"I have been to the country," she said softly.

He flinched, remembering how she had taken punishment for him during the Cultural Revolution. Afterward, she had never accused him, never cried about the unfairness of what had happened. The past was a stone tied around his neck dragging him down until he could go no deeper. "You are saying they will do nothing to me."

She shrugged.

"You are thinking the Chinese people are good, the system is bad?"

She shrugged again. "Everywhere around the world they refute communism. Perhaps, in time we will, too."

He steadied himself against the wall. If necessary she was prepared to take again the punishment she thought they would not mete out to him. He felt unworthy of such love.

"The years go quickly, Logan. I would like to end my days on Chinese soil." She brought her gaze to his. "But wherever you are takes precedence. Yes, I will go with you to America." Her smile flashed, warm and giving. "It will be a good life, and I will be a good American."

Filled with the glow of her love, he went to her, touched her face lightly. She was China, the real China, self-effacing, beautiful, and powerful. "I love you very much. Have I said it lately?"

"Yes." She cocked her head to one side, looked at him coquettishly as she had done so long ago in Shanghai. "But a woman cannot hear the words too often."

He touched his lips gently to hers.

"Oh, my dear, dear husband."

Blinking, he said, "I must see Wu Huixia immediately. And we must be ready to leave on a moment's notice."

"I understand," she said, "But I will pack, two bags only. We will need the rest of our belongings when we return."

He left the room before she could see his tears. She knew

as well as he they would never come back. "Matt," he called, standing in the doorway of the room that Meiling had used as a girl, "it's time to go."

The boy was awake. Pushing himself up from the bed, he said, "I couldn't help hearing what you said. I understood enough to know you're coming to America, aren't you?"

Logan nodded.

Matt swung his feet to the floor. "That's cool."

Logan wanted to go forward, hug the boy, but he was extremely tired. He leaned against the doorframe, willed his energy to return.

"It'll be great having another man in the family. Jason raised me, and he's really like a father to me." Matt put on his Reeboks. "Now all I have to do is meet my birth father, and our family's complete." He finished tying his sneakers and looked up, turning a sober face toward Logan again. "Do you know my father?" His voice sounded hopeful.

Logan tried to ward off the dizziness that struck him. "I'm not sure."

"I've thought about him a lot. My mother said he was at meetings with her when she came with the President. He spoke Chinese and English. Knew all the big shots. She says I look like him." Matt's glance touched Logan again. "And a little like you." The smile had a touch of youthful shyness.

Logan's heart beat wildly, the words about Matt's father digging into the past, laying it open. He took a deep, hurtful breath. "Is his name Wu Gang-jo?"

Matt smiled. "Yes, do you know him? When things quiet down, I plan to look for him. Maybe you can help me."

A roaring sound filled Logan's ears, loud as the surf at La

Push, Washington, where he had gone as a child, giant waves tossing logs and debris on the wind-raked shore. The pain that had fluttered intermittently in Logan's chest spread out and up. Grabbing the back of a chair, he saw his knuckles go chalk like, his skin seem translucent, veins distended. He admitted now, he'd never forgiven, couldn't forgive what Gang-jo had done to Sulin. His American grandson fathered by Gang-jo was some kind of joke, not real. "No," he whispered, waving vaguely in the direction where Matt stood smiling and dreaming his dreams. Had he Logan Wainwright, ex-soldier, ex-idealist, ex-American spoken aloud? He didn't know for the floor was rising to meet him, and Matt's voice was coming from far, far away.

"Grandpa!"

As if from the depths of a tunnel, Logan heard and saw Matt, and he wanted to reassure the shining American boy, but words wouldn't come. An overpowering weakness and pain, so vast he could not hold it back any longer, slammed him into a dark place. Words echoed, dimmed, sorted themselves out. Was that Sulin speaking? He swirled in a dim gray cloud while beyond it she hovered, she and Matt voicing words of concern. The sounds reached him from far away and he heard them with a mounting sense of unreality. What was he, Logan Wainwright, doing on the floor, unable to move? He was young and strong and wore a long white scarf with a fringe, and when he entered a room everyone knew it.

Forcing his eyes open, he framed Sulin in his sight, seeing her as he always had, a woman filled with beauty. Memories of the past mixed with the present and telescoped rapidly until he lost track of time. From some space he hadn't known existed, a place where life had ended but death was still at bay, he recognized that Sulin and Matt said things, good things, strange things, their voices excited, pleading. His grandson was Gang-jo's son. But Gang-jo was a boy learning English at Logan's table.

"No," he muttered, pushing the word from deep within his chest, expelling air in a rush, the sound echoing on the walls beyond him. At long last he and Sulin were going home. He could not lie here on the floor. He should be moving, getting ready.

"Shh, it's all right," Sulin said leaning over him. "I'm here, my love."

Slowly, the scene became clear. "My grandson," Logan said, and the words hung suspended in the air above him.

"Yes," Sulin said. "Rest now, dearest. I will see that he gets to his mother."

"Thank you," Logan muttered during a momentary lull in the pain that wracked his body, dulling his mind. It no longer seemed important to get away. All his life people and places had changed and shifted, and nothing or no one was important any more, no one except Sulin. Only she had remained constant. Now, her hands touched his face, the sound of her voice soothed his ears, the words unclear, like a wind sighing gently in the heat of summer, so fragile, but so enduringly familiar. She had been there for him always. The pain rushed through him, pushing at his chest, tearing at him with clawed fingers, before dimming, and it didn't matter for he felt warmed by love and very tired. As Sulin placed his head in her lap and leaned over him, he said, "I'll just take a short nap." Immediately, he felt a sudden sweet peace. And then he knew no more.

Chapter 18

Christine

The People's Republic of China - 1989

Christine prowled the hotel until Dr. Norton-Smythe insisted she sit and think about logical alternatives. At one time she would have resented his interference. Now, worry furrowed her brow. Logan had gone for Matt June 2nd. The next day the fighting escalated, and now, on the 4th, the city had erupted, and she'd heard from neither Matt nor her father..

As the day dragged on, the temperature climbing to ninety, Norton-Smythe's words droning in her ear, telling her teachers, intellectuals, journalists, peasants, and policeman were all part of the protest now, Christine interrupted his flow of words. "I'm going to the American Embassy. I should have thought about it earlier."

He patted her knee. "Don't beat yourself up, my dear. Just find a cab and go."

She left messages for Mathew and her father and hurried out.

Staying close to the hotel, she circled the building looking for non-existent taxis. Finally she flagged a pedicab driver and settled back in the padded seat as the man took off at a trot. Thin, wearing shorts and tennis shoes that had seen better days, the stringy muscles in his legs contracted and let go in a noticeable rhythm. Except for age, he was not that different from the young man with the red bandanna who had told her about Matt. Had she misunderstood and sent her father on a wild goose chase? A cramp hit her stomach, and a taste of bile rose in her mouth.

By-passing a barricade of handcarts and a bus with its tires slashed, the pedicab went down streets abnormally quiet, almost free of traffic. Pedestrians were few, all hurrying. As she spied the American flag, Christine jumped down, handed the puller a handful of *yuan*, and rushed inside. Too late, she realized she'd not told him to wait for her.

Inside the Embassy, she poked at her windblown hair. Nervous energy driving her, she pushed past people. If she stood still, she feared she'd go up in smoke. Both westerners and Orientals stood in the line she bypassed. Going directly to the receptionist's desk, she leaned over it, spoke earnestly and fast, her voice cracking with emotion. "I have to see the Ambassador."

The receptionist tapped her bright red nails on the desk. "I'm sorry, the Ambassador is in a meeting, and you must take your turn." She swiveled slightly away, busied herself with files.

Christine leaned farther over the desk until her face was close to the younger woman's. "My son is being held by the Chinese and the hotel has our passports. I need to see the Ambassador now." The last words emphasized and drawn out seemed overloud, the desperate ravings of a deranged woman in the clean, calm building with its guards, its flags, its position in the world.

The receptionist's mascara lashes fluttered while her voice stayed diplomatically smooth. "You say the Chinese are holding your son?"

"He wasn't back to the hotel for dinner so I went to

Tiananmen Square looking for him, and a person I suppose was a student said the police took him."

"They took an American citizen?" Her eyebrows lifted, and she held up a hand and for a second looked past Christine to the people in line. "How extraordinary. Sorry, but I have to ask this: how do you know for sure? Did you see it? What caused it, if they did? Did the Chinese contact you?"

"No, but as I said, my son didn't return to the hotel, and this young man—he was wearing a red bandana—said he was being held. My son, I mean." Beyond the receptionist's desk, she glimpsed an office, a man at a large metal desk. Behind her feet shifted, murmurs rose, her words repeated.

The receptionist's face softened slightly. "The Ambassador's busy all day, but I can take the information, get back to you. We have some forms..." She swiveled around, pulled papers from a file cabinet.

Christine interrupted. "He's a boy, for god's sake!"

The girl paused to slip into a jacket matching her pencil slim skirt before saying, "Pardon me, but you're holding up the whole line. Now, if you take a seat I can see..."

Pushing by her, Christine headed toward the office she'd glimpsed earlier.

"You can't go in there!" High heels clicking, the receptionist hurried after her.

Christine burst through the door ahead of her. "I need to talk to you," she cried to the man behind the desk.

He looked up, annoyance adding years to his young face.

"Should I call security?" the receptionist asked, arms on the door's frame as if afraid Christine might bolt.

The man shook his head. "I'll handle this. Close the door,

please." As it clicked shut, he shot Christine a bored look.

His shiny, clean office, he wearing a suit and tie, his hair blow-dried and controlled with jell, said this couldn't be happening, these kind of things didn't happen in America. Christine imagined him pressing a button that would eject her into the street. "I assure you, I'm not crazy but a concerned American citizen." Talking fast, she tried to focus, tell a coherent story. "My son is missing. The thing is..."

He held up a hand. "I need your name and your passport number before we can proceed. "

"Christine Wainwright, and my son is Matt, short for Mathew." The mole on the man's chin seemed to grow as she stared at it. She shook her head, tried to stay focused. "As you know they're holding our passports at the hotel. It's a thing hotels do." She berated herself for allowing sarcasm to sneak in, her voice to rise. How could he relate, his skin looked baby-soft, not a sign of a wrinkle?

"Most countries do that. It's routine." He spread his hands in a gesture of futility. "Now tell me in sequence what's your problem."

She collected her thoughts, relayed details in a linear fashion.

He nodded and ticked items off on his fingers. "Your case is slight. You have only the word of a nameless student in a red bandana. You have not contacted the Chinese, and they have not contacted you. Unless they admit they have him, there isn't much we can do. In the past strict protocol told us how to act and react in any given circumstance, but today's political climate leaves little room for anything except diplomacy. And, let me suggest, as someone who was your son's age once, he might have found some friends, lost track of the time…" He smiled and shrugged.

She scowled. "He's not that type. He always came back on time."

He let several beats go by before saying, "We can inquire if they have seen a young man—did you say Mathew Wainwright? —who is separated from his American mother and she's worried."

"Worried?' she repeated, the word. It seemed slight, inconsequential, her concern the hysterical imaginings of a mother whose seventeen-year-old son would soon be leaving the roost.

The man's official smile stayed in place. "Believe me, I sympathize with your concern, but the American Embassy cannot act precipitately. In your case, we have so little to go on." He glanced at his watch.

"I think you have a lot to go on." She spit the words out. " We came as guests of the Chinese government."

He lifted his brow and thrust his lower lip forward. "Hmmm." He rocked back in his chair. "Really?

"Yes." She could hardly look at him; she was so irritated.

"That's a different proposition. I suggest you get in touch with the Chinese who have been hosting you. Surely someone's been escorting you from trains to hotels, that sort of thing. They're good at such things. Showed me around when I arrived." He smiled.

A sinking feeling invaded her, like waves bathing the Titanic as he glanced at his watch again. How to explain in a minute or two? The whole trip had fallen into an abyss, no one knowing anything. "You mean you can't do anything?"

"We can file a report saying your son is missing. Do you want us to do that?"

She glanced toward the ceiling, sighed and said, "Of course, I want you to." She bit out the words and glanced toward the chair facing the desk. "Do you mind if I sit down? I think I might fall otherwise." Seated, she dug through her pockets, found a card, handed it to him.

Reading her title, his round eyes got bigger. "Professor Wainwright, let me assure you we will do everything we can." He walked to the door, opened it. "Miss Manly, will you bring the appointment book, please." He stood in the door until the book was in his hands. Running his finger down page after page, he shook his head. "As you noted, things are rather hectic in the city."

Christine's voice went flat, her throat constricting. "I need help now." She turned her card over, wrote the name of the hotel. "That's where we're staying."

"Professor, I suggest you wait there. If we hear anything, we'll let you know immediately. I assure you, the Chinese will not harm an American." He did not look at her again.

She emerged into the dark with a fuzzy idea of where she was, and saw to her astonishment, the pedicab was still there. Obviously she'd given him enough money he felt it to his benefit to hang around. She climbed in, leaned back gratefully, only adrenaline driving her. She gave the man the name of her hotel.

The temperature had soared. Reeling from the heat, she pictured Matt, as she often saw him, his eyes soft and dreamy as he sang a ballad, hunched over his guitar, his hair falling over his forehead. His guitar! She had forgotten about it. The Chinese could surely identify him by that.

At the intersection with Nanheyan the pedicab edged by a bus with flat tires blocking the crossroads. At the hotel, she gave the man all the *yuan* she had left.

Inside the main door, she paused to catch her breath. All week guests had checked out. Now two people at the reception desk spoke in harried tones. In a grouping of chairs and sofas nearer the door, Dr. Norton-Smythe sat talking to someone about a coup he'd witnessed in a banana republic. He called, "Any luck?" And said no more when she shook her head.

In that brief time with Logan she'd been a girl again, the sun in place in the sky, and the lunatic world washed away. Daddy would take care of everything. She'd let her body sag, let him hold the weight of her, and it was as good as she'd always imagined. But almost as rapidly the dream world had disappeared.

As she reached her room, the phone rang. She stared at it, not believing it was really ringing. "Hello," she said taking it up as if it were an aberration.

"Christine Wainwright?" a male voice asked in English.

"Yes."

"This is Wu Gang-jo."

The room tipped, righted itself slowly. She supported herself on the edge of the nightstand next to her bed.

"Your son will be with you soon."

"Is he all right?" she whispered, almost afraid to mouth the words.

"Yes. We will be with you in a few hours."

Chapter 19

Christine

The People's Republic of China - 1989

Touching her face she found it wet with tears she hadn't known she'd shed. Matt was all right. Hanging up, she stood shaking her head, trying to make connections beyond the words she'd heard. Matt was safe, and Gang-jo had said so. Gang-jo was bringing him home, and she knew nothing else, had been too exhausted to push beyond what he told her. She should have asked him how Matt came to be with him. Should have asked about her father, about the links that had held for years. All her life she had pictured her father, remembered him, not as he was but as he'd been, a young man with dark hair wearing a military uniform. Now, she had seen the real man, the remnants of the younger man observable in the man he'd become. In his face she'd read the promise of all she'd always wanted. But now she had heard from Gang-jo, and in this upside down world, too much was happening at once. In two hours or so her son would be with her, and she'd see Gang-jo again, and she'd find out everything that had lingered unbidden in her mind. What did it all mean? Did she want to know? She wasn't sure. A note slipped under the door said she'd had a call from America. It had to be Jason, but she was too tired, too confused to talk to him now. She had to make sense of the feelings ripping through her. Was it possible to change the dreams of a lifetime overnight?

She lay down, but sleep would not come. The unanswered questions were racing through her mind, obscuring all that had happened, all that she knew. She took a shower, let the water wake her somewhat from the cloud surrounding her. Too hyped to sleep, a nerve jumping in her jaw, in clean underclothes and a white pants suit, she waited for Matt and Gang-jo to arrive. It was ridiculous to dwell on the past; it was over. But her mind couldn't stay away from the past, from suppositions, from worry.

When the phone rang she jumped as if shot. "Yes?"

"I am calling for Logan Wainwright's daughter," a woman's voice said in accented English.

"This is Logan Wainwright's daughter."

"I would not bother you, but Mr. Wainwright would want me to call. His happiness at seeing his American daughter no question," the voice said. "He like very much."

Christine's heart beat rapidly. "I don't understand," she replied in English, could hear the woman at the other end of the line drawing a quick, sharp breath.

"Logan Wainwright is no more."

Was this the Chinese way of saying he had no use for his American name or that he had nothing to do with America? Was he a pawn in some political play she couldn't fathom? "I understand he is Wai Liang,"

"Yes, Wai Liang, Logan Wainwright, same man."

"I still don't understand. Do you have a message from him?" The words sounded like a commercial repeated until acceptance came.

"Message yes. He would like his daughter to know."

Christine tapped a foot. Could this be someone from Wu

Huixia's office? "Know what? Please be explicit."

"Yes, excuse my poor English. I call about Logan Wainwright, Wai Liang. I explain his heart bad. He is with his ancestors."

With his ancestors. The letters for the word "dead" took shape in front of her eyes, the first d, the vowels, the final d. Clearing her throat she asked, "Do you mean Logan Wainwright is dead? Is that what you're saying?" Sharp pain pierced her, raced through her body. Her father, the man she'd just met, called Daddy and saw for a brief time, was dead. No, she couldn't believe that, didn't want to believe that. For too many years she'd held out for the promise of him, invested her life in him.

"Your father is no more." The Chinese voice became a tiny whisper. "I am sorry. I do not want to cause you worry. He would want me to call you. Telephone working again."

For a while Christine listened to the crackle of the telephone line and to the other woman's breathing. Oh, Daddy, she cried inwardly, a vision of him in his World War II uniform shimmering in the air around her, the feel of his chest beneath her head, her hand on his arm. Would the hurt never stop?

"There is more," the unfamiliar voice said.

What else could there be? For a short time her father had been with her, and she'd hardly acknowledged him. Now he was gone. The loss produced a hollow, empty feeling. She gasped.

"Your son, Mathew, is here. Wu Gang-jo take him to you. They arrive hotel soon."

Outside, the city was hurling its sounds against the abstract notion of death. She heard the murmur of voices, the hum and roar of life turned on its head. In the mirror over the three-drawer dresser she saw the blank look in her eyes, and belatedly said in Mandarin, "Thank you for calling me."

"I did not know you spoke Chinese. It was my privilege to call you. I met your father a long time ago in Shanghai. He was a very good man."

Christine heard a sudden catch in the caller's throat, and for a few seconds nothing sounded but the hum of the connections.

"I am Lin Sulin, wife to Wai Liang, Logan Wainwright's wife."

"Oh!" But a click was sounding in her ear. Had the other woman hung up or had the phone line gone out again? "Hello, hello," she cried, but the line was dead, like her father. But how could that be? He was American, spoke like an American, looked very much American. She could not dessert him, let him rot in some grave in a China that was rapidly blotting out her dreams. Did they bury or cremate? The thought jolted. She didn't know. Damn, it! Anger at herself, at all that had happened swept through her like a tornado. She paced from the window to the bed, from the bed to the window. She wanted to see him again. Hold his hand. Say the words she'd not had time for before.

She hurried downstairs and opened the front door where official cars and taxis had jockeyed for position only days ago. All was quiet, the immediate vicinity deserted, but a strong smell of dust and gunpowder hung in the air, and a mist obscured the trees beyond the hotel. She could see little. She had no idea where he'd lived, and the thought slammed into her like cold water in the face. "Oh, Daddy," she whispered, unshed tears clogging the words.

Shoulders slumping, she started back toward the elevator, a voice in her head saying, "Get hold of yourself." Behind her the outside door burst open and a whiff of cordite and warm air entered the modern air-conditioned lobby. She turned, and the words she'd only partially listened to came again. Gang-jo was bringing Matt back, and now her disheveled son stood framed in the doorway.

The hurt and anguish disappeared like water in a boiling teakettle. "Oh, Matt," she cried, "Matt, Matt, Matt, Matt, Matt." Laughter bubbled, tears threatened to spill over. Needing to feel him— know he was really there—she rushed to him, aware but not aware of a Chinese man standing behind him. Concentrating on her son, her sweet American son, she blurted, "You're sure you're all right?" She hugged him, kissed his cheeks, his forehead, held his face in her hands. His shirt was missing a button, his pants had a tear, weary lines stamped his face.

"Just tired. Really tired." He grinned sheepishly.

He was so young, so beautiful, so treasured, but apparently unhurt, and for this she was grateful. She brushed the hair from his forehead.

He tucked in his wrinkled shirt. "A lot happened. My grandfather got me out of jail, and," he looked over his shoulder, "my birth Dad brought me here."

My birth dad! Not long ago she had said the same words, but now Logan was gone, and Gang-jo was waiting for her to recognize him, say something. But what? Why did the past have ways of tripping one up? How could she deal with anything more? Stalling for time, she said to Matt, "Did they really put you in jail?"

"Oh, yes, I was there." He grinned. "Grandfather got me out and we went to his house." His face lost the joy it had shown momentarily. "He was okay and then he had a heart attack or something, and then *fuqin* came." He indicated Gang-jo. "He brought me back here, and now I'm so tired all I want to do is sleep."

"You look exhausted." *Fuqin*, the Chinese word for father, a word she'd never taught him, but in this instance right.

The muffled sounds from outside rose and fell, the air conditioner hummed. The Norton-Smythes waved on their way to the restaurant, and he, apparently noticing the tableau taking place at the door, held up two fingers in the sign of a V. Unable to delay the moment any longer, Christine allowed her gaze to drift beyond Matt, to settle on the man who was at once familiar and so much a stranger. Still a striking figure, a handsome man, his face had weathered, grown lines that hadn't been there before, but his hair remained midnight black, his figure slim.

"Hello Christine Wainwright," he said.

His voice had the same low soothing quality she had once admired. "Hello," she murmured, trying to pretend he was any ordinary Chinese who had brought her son home. "Thank you for bringing Matt back safely."

Matt said, "Mom, I'm going up. I need a shower. I think I stink." He laughed. Had the strangeness of everything he'd witnessed eased the shock of suddenly meeting a grandfather and a father he'd never seen before? Watching him go toward the elevators, she called, "I'll be right with you," the China of the past rapidly gaining ground, her gaze went from Matt to Gang-jo and back to Matt again,

Gang-jo said, "He's been through a lot and needs you."

His concern apparent, she brought her gaze back to him.

"You and I need to talk, too. Much water has gone over the dam, but the dam is still full." His smile was tentative.

She said nothing, the metaphor pulling her back in time.

"I'll wait for you in the restaurant." His voice became low, realistic. "Forgetting was never my *forte*."

It was a statement without flirtation. She could ignore it, or run with it. Looking into his face Christine tried to read what sort of a man he had become. His appearance, although different, had achingly familiar elements of the past, his mouth curving as if he were about to break into laughter, his hands moving delicately as he spoke, his eyes.... She looked away. "I'll be down later."

"I'll wait. Now, he needs you."

She turned away, almost ran to where Matt was holding the elevator.

"Mom, he's great," he said as they rode up. "I never thought he'd be so, well you know..." He gestured much like Gang-jo.

"I'm glad you got along." She hurried to their door, unlocked it and went in. The beds were unmade, the smell close. "Were you in a real jail?"

"Yeah, but it wasn't so bad. They didn't know what to do with me."

She sighed with relief. "And your grandfather came and got you out."

'Yes."

"And?"

"Mom, I'm too tired to go into it all now. I'll talk later. I promise."

“At least let me know, did you have any problems getting here? It’s terrible out there.”

“Mom, my Dad is some kind of big shot.” He sat down on the bed and began to untie his Reeboks. “We came across these soldiers, and after they saw his identification, we had no trouble. I thought he was some kinda communist, but he said something about being practical. I don’t remember exactly. I think he supports the students.” He grinned. “You know, a son is a big deal here.” Grinning even more, he took off his shoes and socks, wiggled his toes. “He says if I stick around for a while he’ll show me around.” He leaned back on the bed, smiled with satisfaction and closed his eyes. “He said they have some decent schools here, and he could get me in if I wanted to attend one. I mean if it’s okay. I could, couldn’t I? Not that I’d stay forever.“

She wanted to shout, he’s a Communist, capital C! But was he? At least Matt wasn’t talking about staying always. She busied herself straightening her bed. Staying longer could work. Hadn’t she been planning a proper finish to all that had happened? Trying to put a rational spin on what could spin out of control like the Democracy Salons, she said, “I think China is beginning to invest in capitalism while holding on to the past, too. Everything’s convoluted.” Including her own desires. She smoothed the sheet, reached for the spread. From far off she heard, “What did you say?”

Matt had fallen back and was snoring lightly. She pulled a cover over him, and went to the bathroom and stood looking in the mirror. What did she want to happen? She didn’t know, but she knew what she had to do. She combed her hair, put on fresh mascara and lipstick, and studied herself, looking for whatever Gang-jo had seen but seeing only the need to make herself right with the past. Matt was the key, and he was American, Gang-jo Chinese. Two countries, two ideologies. But such factors were not insurmountable. Jason would tease her, call her a teenage wanabe. Jason! She'd never called him back. The hollow feeling invaded her stomach again.

Downstairs, Gang-jo jumped up from his seat in the restaurant, and suddenly her legs refused to move. All that had happened hit her with the force of a tsunami. The tears that had threatened to flow earlier came in a flood. Leaning against the ornate doorway, she tried to contain her sobs.

He was with her in a moment, holding her, providing warmth and comfort, his words low, words she had heard seventeen years before telling her it was all right, saying things she had thought never to hear him say again. Were the words coming from her mind, his lips or both she wondered as he rocked her until her soft sobs subsided.

"Sorry," she said, dabbing at her eyes. "I didn't mean to get your shirt all wet." It sounded so inane, she had to smile. Throughout the sparsely populated room people were concentrating on their food. No one sat in the lobby; the manager was not at the desk. "Shall we go in? Matt's sleeping," she added irrelevantly, or was it?

"Are you sure you're all right?" His eyes showed concern.

For answer she preceded him in, let him seat her. White tablecloths, napkins resting in tall Waterford water glasses, silver bud vases gave the impression of business as usual. She unfolded a napkin, spread it over her lap. "Tell me what happened. Matt didn't say much." Her voice sounded impersonal even to her own ears.

He waved a hovering waiter away. They'd order later. "Wai Liang's wife, Lin Sulin, asked me to come over. When I was very young, Wai Liang was my teacher and mentor. He also helped me with idiomatic expressions before your visit in 1972."

"He was my father." The words sounded choked but combative. Tears invaded her eyes again.

"Lin Sulin loved him very much. She wanted to honor his wishes, but everything happened so fast, she didn't know what to do about Mathew."

She bit her lip to keep from shouting, this man she knew and didn't know speaking so calmly. It was all too soon.

"She contacted me when she couldn't contact my father."

Bitterness crept into her voice. "Wu Huixia," she muttered. He was behind her escalating frustration; he had helped fuel the tightening chains of China, had ruined all her preconceptions and was Gang-jo's father..

Gang-jo's head went up. "My father, your father and Sulin had a long relationship. Since Shanghai."

She wanted to curl up with self-pity, think through recent and past happenings, make sense of it all, but he piqued her interest with his straight-forward speech. "Sorry," she murmured and indicated he should continue.

"Mathew overheard Sulin say my name. Evidently you had told him about me, and for this I am grateful." His gaze came back to her. "He told me he was my son."

She looked away, Gang-jo's scrutiny unsettling. *He told me he was my son.* Spying the Norton-Smythes, she waved as if normalcy had to be respected, as if what courtesy thought was important, took precedence while inner thoughts prodded her, tore down crooked paths. She turned back to meet Gang-jo's searching gaze. "I need to meet Lin Sulin, talk to her. Will you help me?"

"Of course."

"You make everything sound so easy, but it's not."

He shook his head. "Nothing is ever easy, Christine. Long ago, after you and the other Americans left, I tried to contact you, but there was no way to get ordinary messages out. I wish I had known… about you, about my son. Mathew is a fine boy."

"At the time, I wish you had, too." She shrugged, looked away.

He rested his arms on the table, leaned toward her, his voice lowered. "I'm sorry for what happened. For years my heart was empty. Now tonight, Mathew fills it…and you." His smile didn't erase the permanent lines between his eyes. "You are still a beautiful woman and a professor. If you want to lecture in China, I can help. No matter how we would wish it, the problems in Tiananmen will be over, and our students will need to hear what you have to say."

With the trip to China eroding daily, control slipping from her grasp, the focus of her aspirations expiring, the future rode on winds she couldn't fathom. "You have that much power? As for Matt and me, you don't know anything about us."

"I know enough."

She frowned, swallowing words as the waiter approached. Beyond the Norton-Smythes a sprinkling of Europeans glanced away. So everyone was watching her.

"Good evening, Madame Wainwright. Sir. I fear our menu choices are eggs and rice. And tea. Sorry, but that is all."

"That will be fine," Christine said.

"You're angry with me," Gang-jo said after the waiter left. He leaned across the table, forcing her to face him directly.

She held her hands in her lap to keep them from shaking. "No, I'm not angry, I'm afraid. Afraid of what you'll want. Matt's only your birth son. An American boy."

"The world has changed, Christine. Even as my father and the others try to hold on to old ways, change is coming, just as certain things are inevitable. Mathew wants to go to school here."

"That's what he thinks now. Tomorrow he'll want – oh, I don't know, something else."

Gang-jo's voice softened. "You're afraid I'll fight you for custody. Isn't that what you do in America? Whatever happens, he's my son, and I'll honor his choice." His voice grew softer still. "Christine, I would never do anything to hurt you. I expected you to be married, even though I hoped you weren't." His gaze roved her face. "Your husband's a lucky man."

She glanced away from the warmth in his eyes. "You've been married a long time," she said, feeling anger, not only at him but also at herself, at what might happen. "Even when we met."

He shook his head. "Shortly after you were here, I got important enough to divorce her. She married a farmer. It was better for both of us."

For a while he looked into her eyes, and she felt the magnetism that had drawn her so long ago. He hadn't changed, just gotten older, the charm still present if subdued. "Do you have children?"

"Mathew is all."

"So you didn't re-marry?"

"No." He looked aside, and then shaking his head slowly, said, "No one could compete with my memories."

Although he'd spoken simply, the words were loaded. She looked away from the compelling warmth covering the distance between them. She'd felt safe when he held her. She wanted to blurt out, my husband became a father to Matt, did all you should have done. But it was obvious, didn't need saying, and she was close to crying again.

"I'm going to the United States of America. Probably New York. Your father suggested it. My father made it possible." He shrugged, his mouth momentarily tight. "I promised to come back, use my knowledge of international law for the People's Republic. I'm determined to bring China into the world community. You and our son could make the journey with me." His eyes glowing, he looked across the table to her. "What happened in 1972, happened, and I'll never regret it."

She wanted to say, don't go there, don't bring up what can never be, but she was remembering, too. She spoke flatly. "I think I saw you near the Square." Amazed, she realized most of the evening they'd spoken Chinese. Deliberately, she added in English, emphasizing the words, "With a military man who wore medals as if they were badges of honor."

Gang-jo made a dismissing motion, as the waiter, apologizing again for the lack of choice, set down bowls of rice, and hard-boiled eggs served on hand-made pottery with the characters for long life on the gold-trimmed plates.

"This is fine." Christine pushed the ivory chopsticks aside and deliberately picked up a fork. Did she want to stay with him, find out what it was that drew her still? For days she hadn't thought of Jason.

As the waiter walked away, Gang-jo said as flatly as she had, "You saw me at The Square? Why didn't you say something?"

"I thought you were carrying out your father's business."

"I'm his son. Just as Matt is my son." He set down his chopsticks, put the lid on his cup of tea. "You have had him for seventeen years. I have not."

She let the unspoken say what she would deny in words. How could she be drawn to Gang-jo? That was another time, another place. Not now. Was this because of her father, because of Matt? Because her son looked so much like his father, because the past was alive in her mind again, because so much had happened, and she was so tired? She wanted to curl up in Gang-jo's arms, be protected, but no matter how fatigued she was her mind worked better than that. "It will be Matt's decision." Matt had called Gang-jo *fuqin,* undoubtedly learning it from him.

Gang-jo's smile was wide, his words confident. "He will stay."

She felt as if she were floating in a sea that had suddenly gone wild. She plowed rice into her mouth. "I cannot leave him here alone."

"Are you saying you will stay, too?"

"I don't know what I'm saying."

Once again he exchanged a look with her. "Stay here now. Both of you. What difference can another week or so mean? I'll take you to Xian, to wherever you want to go. Show off my son," his voice dropped a few degrees, "and his mother."

She picked at the eggs, which had been peeled and presented in slices. "You make it sound so easy."

"You're happy?" he asked, ignoring the rising decibel level outside, it penetrating the quiet of the hotel.

Although it was obvious he meant her marriage, how could she describe Jason to him? Born on the cusp of a new age, he'd melded into her world, a world she'd created out of her fantasies of China. Yet, lately he'd made a world of his own. She launched into a description of her work at the University. As Gang-jo watched and listened, from the corner of her eye she saw people entering the kitchen, pushing in from outside, the rumbling, shouting, gunshot sounds outside following before the door closed and the rapid fire Chinese of the kitchen staff and the newcomers ceased.

Gang-jo shook his head slightly. "I've thought of you through the years, you and President Nixon and Chairman Mao, but mostly you." He paused a look of musing introspection passing over his face. "I dreamed impossible dreams. You symbolized freedom, modernity, America." His smile became self-deprecatory. "And now change is coming to China, and I'm going to America."

"And returning to China."

"Yes."

"Because you have to?" Just as she had to piece together the past, make sense of it.

He pushed his empty dishes aside, head thrown slightly back, eyes half-closed in contemplation and shook his head before meeting her eyes again. "Because I'm Chinese." He stood. "I believe you have a saying similar to one we have, stop beating a dead horse." He paused briefly. "May I see Mathew before I go?"

"If I said no, what would you do?"

He laughed. "I would see him anyway."

"That's what I thought." Smiling, because she'd known his answer before he'd spoken, she preceded him from the restaurant and to the bank of elevators. Going up, the enforced intimacy pushed at the barriers she'd tried to erect.

Matt turned from the window when they entered. "Come see; something's happened." He sounded older than his years, his voice loaded with newfound experience. "They've called out the big guns, the armored tanks!"

"I hoped this wouldn't happen." Gang-jo's words bounced off the walls.

Matt nodded vigorously. "It's not your fault. Like I told Mom, you support the students." He was clearly in alignment with Gang-jo.

Chapter 20

Christine

The People's Republic of China - 1989

While a line of tanks moved slowly down Chang'an Street, Christine glanced from Matt to Gang-jo, and the thought appeared in her mind: "We're sharing this horrendous moment as a family." The sentence brought concern she couldn't voice. Although tremendously aware of Matt and Gang-jo, son and father very much alike in appearance, the two agreeing in low voices about what was happening, she kept her gaze below. No other vehicles marred the gut-wrenching symmetry of the scene, each behemoth spaced an equal distance from the following one. Ponderous and lethal, they were as unreal as beings from another planet, and they would be pitted against the youth of the Square. No wonder ordinary citizens had sought refuge in the hotel kitchen. People were scurrying like ants ready to be ingested by praying mantises. People pressed against storefronts, hunkered in doorways or, or arms pumping furiously, were running ahead of the slow-moving tanks. As they ducked into alleyways, pushed through doors, the tanks rolled closer, bristling with guns. Soon nothing moved ahead of them, and for the first time since coming to China, she saw absolutely empty streets. A stitch struck Christine's chest. Thank god Matt wasn't outside.

Except the creak and groan of the column, preternatural quiet descended. And then, in the stark silence, the strange half-light, a young man ran into the street and came to an abrupt stop in front of the advancing column and stared up at the gun turret. Defiance and bravado shrieked form every line of his body.

"Holy shit," Matt cried. "Can't we do something?"

Gang-jo put a hand on Matt's shoulder. "Nothing now."

Time seemed to stand still as the boy faced down the tank.

Matt whispered, "What if they don't stop?"

"He will be a martyr for the cause." Gang-jo spoke matter-of-factly.

Feeling as if she stood with the boy in the street, as if life was tearing her apart, Christine eased back from the window. Awareness of Gang-jo and Matt was growing like a weed she couldn't eradicate.

"How would being a martyr help?" Matt murmured.

"I'm not condoning it, but martyrdom would provide a rallying cry, an incident to remember always, generations to repeat. Today it would be broadcast around the world." Gang-jo spoke confidentially, father to son.

Christine said, "Gain sympathy everywhere and pressure the Chinese government, I suppose?" She posed it as a question with barbed antenna, and directed the comment to Gang-jo.

Matt cried, "The tanks are slowing down. They've stopped! He faced them down!" He slapped a high five at Gang-jo, grinned at Christine. "Power to the people!"

"Ah, yes," Gang-jo added, responding to the high five a few seconds late as if he'd recently learned the American greeting.

Christine put a hand to her rapidly beating heart. "He can't stand there forever." Gang-jo pointed. "He's not. See those men running into the street? They're hurrying him away."

Matt smiled, the smile, so much like Gang-jo's, Christine's eyes grew moist.

"His friends are saving him!" Matt shouted. "Way to go!"

"Or he's being arrested," Christine speculated.

"What do you think...Dad?" The American word echoed like gunfire in the close confines of the room.

Christine steeled herself. How could she blame Matt when her own thoughts were muddled, strings tied together, the ends invisible? She heard Gang-jo say, "We'll never know unless they identify him, and I doubt that will happen." He turned to Christine. "If you're ready, I'll take you to Lin Sulin now."

Was she ready for this? She had to be. Picking up her purse, she nodded.

Gang-jo went to the door, looked back at Matt. "Son, wait here."

"Don't even think of going out," Christine added, needing to restore her authority.

Gang-jo's eyes widened before he ushered her through the door ahead of him.

In the car going to Sulin's, they sat in the back, together but alone. Lost in her thoughts, Christine glanced up when Gang-jo's driver stopped the car in a narrow alley in back of the house. The houses behind the walls had the look of low California bungalows, ubiquitous in the nineteen fifties. But the walled garden he led her through was well tended, slightly bigger and immeasurably prettier than the average back yard in an American city. "My father lived here?"

"He had privileges denied others," Gang-jo stated in the same voice he had used to talk about martyrs.

"This is lovely," she admitted as he guided her down stepping stones toward a sliding door at the back of the house. She tried to envision her father there…couldn't. She felt as if life was on hold, the meeting with Logan playing again and again in her mind with no time to think it through, get past the ache and guilt inside her.

"A little more private than most. Wai Liang was more fortunate than others."

She put her hand on Gang-jo's arm, stopped him. "I doubt anyone burns paper money today to assuage hungry ghosts after a death, but condolences are always acceptable, aren't they? Help me through this. Tell me, will I be intruding?"

He took her hands in his, and his look said he'd help her through anything. "Whatever you do will be all right, Christine. He was your father."

And you were my lover, she thought, and I'm so tired I can't sort right from wrong. Why do I like having you look at me like that?

"And no, they won't be burning paper money." His warm smile enfolded her.

"Thanks." She knocked on the slider, the interior hazily seen through the glass was pushed open from inside.

"You must be Christine?" a woman, who looked to be forty or so, stepped back so Christine could enter. "Wu Gang-jo said you were in the city. Please follow me. My mother awaits you."

She had not thought of other children. Always she had been the one. She glanced at the other woman, this half-sister she'd never known.

'I am Meiling, the elder daughter."

The eldest except for me, Christine thought, looking over her shoulder, seeing Gang-jo join people in what she assumed was the living room. A dozen men and women were arrayed around a western TV. She followed Meiling down a short hall to a bedroom where two upholstered chairs faced one another over a small corner table. The woman she assumed was Sulin sat in the chair farthest from the door.

Indicating the chair partially facing the bed and a high, black lacquered chest of drawers, the woman said, "Please sit down. Meiling will get us some tea. It is always a comfort."

Sulin's voice held a soothing quality not evident on the phone, perhaps because now she spoke Chinese, not broken English. She appeared fragile, lost among cushions, her wrists and ankles slim, delicate, but her arm seemed to flow as she pointed to the chair, and her eyes, though filmy, were expressive, her face like porcelain lined with age. "You wish to talk about Logan Wainwright?"

"Yes." Christine sank into the chair. "Thank you for seeing me."

"As you know, Logan Wainwright became Wai Liang, meaning good foreigner." Her head went up. "He was. Also a good Chinese. A good writer. A good husband. A good father."

"I have no doubt."

"But always Logan Wainwright wanted to go home." She shrugged. "He told me of the Changs. Of you. Many times he suggested we go. But I wouldn't. A citizen does not leave because her country has temporarily lost its way."

"You did not want to come to America?"

She shook her head. "Not until your son came home with him, and I saw: his family was not only here. I regret many things conspired to keep him from his ancestral home. For my part, I was young and patriotic, and those were good years. And there were the children and grandchildren, and I am not apologizing, but explaining." Again, she gestured delicately, a faint fragrance, like incense, coming from her.

"I'm sorry. Sorry for him, for you, for all of us."

"No, do not be sorry. Fate pointed the way. He belonged to China; and to me."

"I didn't come to take him from you. I merely wanted to know…." What? She glanced at the bed where he had lain, saw his brush and comb upon the chest of drawers, Sulin's sparse personal items trailing along the top of a smaller chest. "I wondered what the final arrangements would be."

"We will do what is proper for such an important man of China."

Meiling, returning with tea and a plate of almond cookies, added. "It is my mother's wish and mine. He will be where we can visit and where he can find eternal peace." Murmuring, "Excuse me, please," she left again.

Realizing both women meant Logan's burial, Christine blinked away tears.

Sulin said, "You did not know him, but you loved your father."

Christine nodded.

"Wai Liang was happy to be able to help his grandson. But now your son has found his father, and the cycle of life goes on." She poured the tea, proffered a cup. "Gang-jo will go to

America, but he will return. You will return, too?"

She took the cup. "I am married to an American."

Sulin shrugged. "Life is never easy or just. It just is. It is regrettable you had so little time with your father, but as you see, he had a life here, and sometimes it was good and sometimes not so good. But it was his life. And mine. If possible, I would have raised you as my own."

'Thank you for your honesty."

"I am too old not to speak the truth. Once your father told me I resembled your mother. I've never told that to anyone else. I deem it an honor to have worked with him these many years, been with him these many years." Her birdlike voice faltered. She dabbed at her eyes with a lace-trimmed handkerchief.

Christine murmured, "Thank you."

Straightening, Sulin stuffed the handkerchief into her pants pocket. "Now, you must meet our youngest daughter." She raised her voice. "Weiping, come please."

A woman, slightly younger than Meiling, entered the room, hand outstretched. "I am Weiping, and I must say I am outnumbered, two to one. We have little wood for coffins, little land for burial, but Mother and Meiling insist on tradition. Chairman Mao was the first to suggest cremation, and all officials second this today, but my mother and sister are as superstitious as the mandarins in the imperial days." She pointed a finger at Christine. "You speak Chinese like a native. It doesn't happen often with capitalists."

"I studied your language for many years." She shook hands with the younger woman.

"I guess you've been here long enough to witness that show

at Tiananmen." Weiping pushed her hair back from her face.

Christine said, "We were in Guilin and then here." Both Sulin and Meiling wore dark pants and tops, but Weiping's clothes resembled a Mao suit. Since her youngest daughter's entrance, Sulin seemed to have shrunk into the upholstery, her eyes making contact with no one. I'll leave soon, Christine thought.

Returning to the room, Meiling looked toward her mother and then Christine. "You must forgive Weiping her bad manners, speaking governmental affairs during your visit." She stood behind her mother's chair.

Christine shrugged. "It would be hard not to when soldiers fire artillery at the Square."

Weiping pulled a small footstool over and perched on it. "Unfortunate, but it is necessary to control actions that can turn into anarchy."

"I'm not sure the students would go that far," Meiling countered, frowning at her sister and glancing towards Christine. "My father spoke often of how students were free to speak in America. I think they were emulating that. But I may be mistaken. I am not learned."

"We all do our part in the People's Republic," Sulin said rousing herself. She pushed to the edge of the seat and faced Christine. "Meiling's work in a textile factory is as important as her sister's work in the courts. Both speak truth."

"As do you," Christine said, wanting to let the older woman know she appreciated this time in her father's house.

"It is an element your father admired. I told him often, I am Chinese, a part of this country, despite its mistakes."

"What is happening in Tiananmen is a mistake?" Weiping asked.

"A misfortune. The students spoke too soon, perhaps."

Weiping nodded. "Not only that, they pushed too far. They could not expect to push forever. We, too, are a country of laws, but we are not a clone of the west. "

Christine felt a great roaring in her ears. She got to her feet. "I cannot in good conscience intrude further. You have been most kind to share your time with me."

"Wai Liang's daughter is never an intrusion," Sulin said, but she did not try to delay Christine.

"Will we see you again?" Meiling asked. "You are my children's *yima*."

Their aunt. "I don't know." She took Sulin's hands in hers, said the proper words, the roaring in her ears lessening.

"Your son will return," Sulin said.

"I'll see you out." Weiping jerked a thumb in the direction of her mother and sister. "They have gone backward. Not mentioning death, not even the word. I'd have had father cremated, given you the ashes to take with you. When do you leave?"

"Soon," Christine said. Bile was rising in her mouth again, but she fought it down. She knew without thinking it through, she and Matt had to be on the next plane out of China.

"Are you all right?" Gang-jo asked as they walked through the garden to the car blocking the *hutang*. Big, blocky, the automobile shrieked importance.

"Yes."

He said nothing, but she could see he wasn't buying it. After a while she said, "Since the shooting started, people left the hotel like rats leaving a sinking ship. Matt and I should leave, too. Will you help us get to the airport?"

He shot her a look before saying, "Do you have to go now? I need to spend time with my son…and you. The troubles should be over soon."

Noticing the driver glancing in the rear view mirror, she said through clenched teeth, "All hell's breaking loose, and you act as if it's nothing. If you notice the driver is staying away from the Square."

"It's not nothing, Christine. But Matt would be safe with me. You would be safe." He glanced at her, the street ahead clear except for a few bicyclists.

The closed car kept out the battle raging at Tiananmen. Angrily, she opened the window, cried to Gang-jo, "Hear it! I can't have Matt getting caught up in that kind of thing."

"You think I'd let that happen?" Speaking in English, he reached for her hand.

Thwarting him, she pulled away, her hand closed tight in a fist. "I think you might not be able to prevent it."

He shook his head. "You don't understand, do you? When I tell him about his grandson, my father will do whatever is necessary to keep you both safe."

"His grandson," she echoed, realizing fully for the first time Wu Huixia would be her son's grandfather. A cold wave hit her, took away the sense of seclusion she'd felt with Gang-jo, the sense of family she'd felt momentarily when Matt was with them. Now, the wider world pressed in. She closed her mind to the hurt she read on Gang-jo's face as the car stopped in back of the hotel. In the depth of his eyes lay more than she wanted to see. She needed to get out of China as quickly as possible, and yet, she wanted to lean against Gang-jo, take the comfort he offered. Too tired to sort it out, she repeated,

"We'll be ready to leave in the morning." She entered the hotel through the kitchen.

Christine sat in the hotel lobby with Matt, their suitcases at their feet when Wu Huixia's big, black car came to a stop at the front door. Flags fluttered on the fenders and curtains obscured the rear windows. Gang-jo, wearing a western suit, shirt and tie, jumped out, came in and took a chair near them.

She frowned. "You're not taking your car."

"His carries more clout." He spoke English, and his gaze went to her, studying her as if knowing he might not see her again before he said, "Here's the plan." He handed Matt a pair of white gloves. "Son, you're going to drive. I'll ride up front next to you. Your mother will sit in the back. If we're stopped, I'll do the talking." He lowered his voice. "Conditions are not good. I talked to my father last night. He's leaving the city. I was lucky to catch him before he left. This morning I found his office empty, his papers gone. The janitor said he saw two men taking them off. I found him at home packing." He took a deep breath.

She didn't let him look away. "Our tickets?"

"They're still good, and my father apologizes for any inconvenience he caused you."

"I don't understand. Why is he leaving?"

He shrugged. "He saw the democracy movement wrong. Someone has to bear the blame." He picked up the largest piece of luggage. "Let's get your things loaded."

Matt hoisted his bag. "What's going on?"

"I'll explain later." Christine reached for her bag, but Gang-jo took it from her.

"I've never driven a foreign car," Matt said following Gang-jo out. "At home we call something that big a gunboat."

Gang-jo smiled. "A gunboat is it? No matter, you'll do fine."

Sun was pushing at the horizon, but the sky still held its pre-dawn look, the gunmetal gray symbolic of all that had happened. No cabs vied for parking places, no people milled around, and the acrid air caught at Christine's lungs. Thank goodness Gang-jo looked properly worldly and unflappably in charge. But he should drive, not Matt. She told him so, quietly, hoping not to alarm Matt.

Busy loading the bags in the trunk, Gang-jo paused. "I always have a driver. If I drove it would arouse suspicions." He glanced at her. "Trust me, please. Today everything is upside down. The military is anti-democracy. We must be careful."

She raised her voice, turned to Matt. "Think you can handle a stick shift?"

"He'll be all right," Gang-jo said, opening the back door and ushering Christine in. "We'll be fine if you both just do what I say."

She'd never seen his eyes so serious appearing, his voice so hard. She nodded.

Matt pulled on the gloves and eyed he car, his smile containing a touch of bravado. "Sounds like a movie."

Gang-jo accompanied Matt to the driver's side, saw Matt settle behind the wheel. "This hotel is practically in The Square, and the military are coming from all directions. We have to get through the lines and then take secondary roads until we get to Capitol Avenue." He added a few quick instructions to Matt, before he ran around and got in the passenger seat.

Matt started the car, Gang-jo repeated gearshift instructions, and with a minimum of trouble, the Mercedes moved regally and slowly forward. Matt grinned.

Christine leaned forward, "Matt, you sure you will be all right?"

He attempted a grin. "This is not your Honda, Mom, but I'm okay."

Gang-jo said. " I'll tell you ahead of time where to turn. Just don't let anything startle you. After we're away from the Square, it will be easier."

An uneasy silence prevailed, broken at times as Matt murmured, "Did you see that?" as they passed a still smoldering barricade, or "What do you think happened there?" when a street was closed off. Christine welcomed the concealing shadows of dawn. Soon the sun would illuminate everything. Finding herself pleating and unpleating her scarf, she stuffed it into her carry-on bag. Had she packed everything? Once again she checked the tickets, located passports. Through a gap in the curtains she glimpsed fire flaring, smoke billowing. As Matt entered East Chang'an Avenue, military appeared everywhere. Expecting to be stopped any minute, she had trouble sitting still. But their car was waved on, military men occasionally saluting, the avenue wide enough for them to pass trucks full of soldiers headed for the Square.

As Matt turned from Chang'an, he headed straight into a convoy of tanks.

Christine put a hand to her mouth to keep from screaming. Matt slammed on the brakes, and Gang-jo put a hand on Matt's shoulder.

The car rocked to a stop, and two soldiers with guns converged on Matt's window. An order was barked in Chinese.

"Open it," Gang-jo said softly.

One soldier stuck his head in the open window. "You're blocking the intersection. You must turn around. Where are you going?"

Gang-jo passed over his identification. "I am escorting a VIP, a very important foreigner to the airport." He jerked his hand toward the back seat.

The soldier perused Gang-jo's papers before handing them back. "Sorry, sir." He glanced at Matt.

Matt stared blankly ahead. Sweat beaded Christine's forehead.

Gang-jo glanced at his watch. "We will be late. The Chairman will not be happy." He gestured toward the tanks. "And now you're holding up a convoy of the People's Republic of China. I may have to report you."

"Go!" the man cried.

With much maneuvering, Matt turned the car around, this time fighting the clutch, the Mercedes jerking ahead incrementally before going smoothly forward.

Christine swallowed an exclamation.

Looking over his shoulder, Gang-jo said in a calm voice, "We have to work over to Capitol Avenue. From there it's a straight run to the airport. We will be okay."

Christine read caring in his eyes, his voice. "Thank you."

He turned to Matt. "Son, you're doing great. We'll take side streets, and you'll have to make several turns, but you can do it. I have faith in you."

Christine peered out the rear window. The Square was

choked with young people, and the tanks were closing in. Gunshots, screams and shouts were only partially muffled by the glass and steel surrounding her. Flames lit the sky, smoke billowed, and people were yelling and running in all directions. "Oh, my gosh," she cried, as Matt accelerated. At the Workers Exhibition Hall, he slowed down but barely avoided a roadblock. Grubby-looking men with tired faces stared at the car. She sank into the upholstery. A group of officers, standing together smoking, snapped to attention.

"Thank God, they know the car," Christine whispered, leaning forward again. Except for Gang-jo's directions and Matt's occasional question, no one spoke. How soon, she wondered, before the soldiers would learn Wu Huixia was no longer in favor? She alternated glancing back and looking forward.

At Capitol Avenue, Gang-jo said, "It won't be long now."

She relaxed visibly, the final lap to the airport almost over.

Then an overturned truck partially blocked the road. Soldiers with guns riding their shoulders, hand grenades hanging from their belts, clambered from the truck bed.

Matt slowed down. "What'll I do?" he whispered. His English sounded loud and harsh in the enclosed interior.

"Ease by. Stop if I tell you to," Gang-jo said.

Christine peeked out the side curtains. Shadowy figures gave way, were replaced by more shadowy figures, all staring at the car.

Christine's hands shook. She checked and rechecked their tickets. "We have exactly thirty-five minutes to catch our plane," she announced.

Matt's startled gaze met Christine's in the rear-view mirror.

Hers swept to Gang-jo. "Can we make it?"

"It will be close, but we can make it."

If no one is looking for the car, she thought. *If Gang-jo's not trying to put a positive spin on it.*

With the Mercedes in the open, Matt bore down on the gas, and the car shot ahead.

Christine met his gaze in the rear view mirror; he was smiling.

Stopping in front of the airport, he asked, "What about the car?"

"Leave it." Gang-jo jumped out and got their bags from the trunk.

Christine with Matt close by followed him into the terminal.

Both Westerners and Chinese were trying to leave Beijing. People and bags were everywhere, and thousands of voices echoed. Chinese barked orders, Westerners pleaded for directions. People pushed and shoved, anxiety showing in all faces. Gang-jo elbowed their way forward and jostled for position.

Christine shouted, "Matt, stay with me." She called to Gang-jo, "Where do we go? Which line should we be in? Here, give us our bags." In the chaos it would be easy to get separated. She could take care of her own luggage.

"Stay close," he said moving forward, past a pile of bags and boxes.

A woman cut Christine off. Hesitating, but keeping her gaze on Gang-jo, she pushed her way after him, called, "Matt, I said stay with me," but a babble of voices, shouting questions in a dozen languages, drowned her out. Did he hear? She saw him nowhere. People shoving carts with bags piled high rammed through the lines. Everyone wore the same harried, worried look she supposed stamped her face. Women inched suitcases and hand luggage forward. Men manhandled gargantuan loads. Everything and everyone was at a fever pitch, news and rumors circulating in shocked tones. Tanks had entered Tiananmen Square. They were mowing down tents and students alike. People were dying. The government was dissolving. The government was beefing up. Pulling her Samsonite luggage with its little wheels, Christine made slow progress, the suitcase tipping over, she having to right it before she could continue. She lost sight of Gang-jo.

When panic grew, he materialized at her side. "This way." He directed her to a shed where overseas travelers were checking their luggage. "I'll verify your departure gate."

Coming from the opposite direction, Matt hoisted Christine's bag up. "It's a zoo,"

The woman clerk muttered in English, "Why everyone want to leave Beijing?"

"Can you blame them?" Christine cried, all that had happened tying her into knots. Her words, like firecrackers in a war, fizzled in her ears. She had lost their place in the line she'd been following and now wasn't sure which line was the correct one. "Matt, do you know what line we're supposed to be in?'

He shook his head.

The knot of fear in her stomach spread. Now what? She glanced around, heard Gang-jo shout in English, "Christine, Matt, over here." Far ahead she glimpsed him waving, calling, "Let them through, they're with me."

Grabbing Matt's hand, Christine pulled him forward.

"Mom, you don't have to drag me," Matt protested as a few

people stepped aside. Others flowed into the spaces they'd vacated.

"Just stay with me." She let go his hand, excused herself alternately in Chinese and English as she pushed through a mob of people juggling for position, using luggage as battering rams.

At the front of an overseas line, Gang-jo pulled her in next to him.

"Thanks." Christine glanced back. Now, where was Matt?

"Passport?" an official looking man demanded, his hand out, a stamp at the ready.

She dug into her over-the-shoulder bag, found hers beneath a myriad of objects, looked around and saw Gang-jo retrieving Matt from the midst of a shouting group. As he pushed in by her, the clerks exchanged glances.

Pointing at Matt, the examiner shouted in Chinese, "Wrong line. Americans only."

"He is American. He's my son," Christine cried, pawing through her purse, trying to locate Matt's passport. She'd just had it. Damn!

"They are guests of the People's Republic," Gang-jo said in Chinese.

"This line is for Americans going home. Comrade, get out of way."

"I am assisting them," Gang-jo said.

The examiner motioned and two police grabbed Gang-jo, pulled him aside. Christine and Matt were shoved forward.

"Hurry, get seat. We already late," an attendant shouted.

"I want to say goodbye to my Dad," Matt cried, turning back, trying to get to Gang-jo, being hollered at by both Chinese and Americans. The crowd shoved him back in line.

Christine grabbed hold of his sleeve. No matter how much she wanted to bid Gang-jo a proper farewell, she could see it would not happen. She glanced back, spied him standing by himself, watching.

The woman attendant said in heavily accented English, "Get on plane, please."

"Stop holding us up, " several Americans cried. They shoved against Matt, against Christine.

Now Gang-jo was several lines away, waving, speaking, his words drowned in the racket. She lifted a hand, shouted, "Thank you, thank you very much." Again she was shoved forward.

"Hurry, please," the attendant said.

Christine looked back again, but once more Gang-jo had been swallowed by the crowd.

As he took his seat, Matt hit one fist into the other. "What a stupid damn government shooting its own kids, putting me in jail. And not letting me say goodbye to my own father."

"Quiet, please, we haven't gone yet," Christine whispered. Who knows what could happen?

He gave her a startled look.

"It's not safe," she whispered, the enormity of it all closing in on her.

Hours later, landing in Hong Kong, the once British colony seemed startlingly bright and Western after the People's Republic, and Christine wondered if she'd ever feel normal again. As she swept through Hong Kong's modern terminal, went out into the street, the past hung on. Hong Kong's ultra modern skyline helped bring into perspective all that had happened, the glittering lights of Kowloon and Nathan Road's Golden Mile reflecting jewel-like into the sky. She fought back tears. China was a small part of a world that moved on a grand scale only dreamed about in the People's Republic. All that had happened would become less important the closer she got to home. She realized this was true, but a part of her remained with her father, stayed with Gang-jo. Her world and Matt's was not the world of China, but would its hold remain a part of her forever? She was too tired, too emotionally distraught, to know.

In the hotel room she and Matt shared on Nathan Road, the city pulsed with activity, red double-decker busses going up and down, taxis darting in and out, tourists and locals mingling.

Matt blamed himself for not saying a real goodbye to Gang-jo. He had trouble settling down but paced the carpet of their hotel room.

"You can't blame yourself," Christine said over and over. Yet, long after he slept, she lay wide-awake thinking. The past often predicted the future, and no one could entirely escape either themselves or their cultures. Gang-jo had been so confident, his father so important. And in the blink of an eye....

In the morning she attempted to get an earlier flight home, but nothing was available. "Everyone wants to leave China," the voice from the airlines said.

She bought the New York and London papers and spread them out on her bed. Photos and stories captured details. Tiananmen Square had been a massacre.

Matt slammed his fist against the wall. "Mom those were my friends."

"I know. I know." She put her arms around him, held him as she had when he was younger.

The following days she tried to divert him with sightseeing and shopping trips, but he was unusually quiet. At night he watched Chinese language movies and news broadcasts from Taiwan. She called Jason, left a message on the recorder. "We're in Hong Kong," she said. "Too tired to talk. See you soon."

One day pictures from Mainland China showed Army men with bandages wrapping their heads. Others showed soldiers in a hospital. The text said they were military men wounded by rioting students. An older man was pushed in front of the camera. Stooped and hesitant, words of apology burst from his lips. "I am a traitor," he said beating his chest. "I helped those who worked against the government."

"No," Christine cried as his name flashed across the screen. "That can't be." It was Wu Huixia.

A frightened look lodged for a minute in Matt's eyes, replaced by increased anger. "He's my grandfather, isn't he? He brought us to China, was going to let my father come to America." He shook his head as if to shake away tears.

What would happen to Gang-jo now? Christine switched channels, watching the broadcast three times. That night she heard Matt sniffling; her own tears flowed.

Their third day in Kowloon, the shrill ringing of the telephone on the stand between the twin beds woke her. A pale light showed beneath the lined draperies. It was almost dawn. She snatched up the phone before it woke Matt. "Yes?"

“I called sixteen hotels before I found you,” a deep soothing voice said in her ear, a voice so familiar, she felt wrapped in its timbers, warmed by its coals. Jason! Hope rose like summer dazzling her with its splendors. “Oh, Jason, it was so horrible.” She’d been in a bubble, and now the bubble was broken, and she could only mumble, “I was so scared, and the phone was out, and they were killing people….”

“I know, honey. I watched it on TV. It’s over, Christine. Over, sweetheart.”

“I can’t get it out of my mind.”

“That’s why I’m here.”

“Here? What do you mean?”

“I arrived in Hong Kong a few hours ago. I’m in the lobby. It wasn’t easy tracking you down, but I finally connected. Lady, believe me, I wasn’t going to let you stay in China, no matter what.”

Relief rose like a Chinese box kite floating against a blue sky. “Wait right there. I’m coming down.” She hung up, grabbed the room key and rushed to the lobby.

For a few seconds she stood in the hall watching the people come and go, watching Jason. Gang-jo was wed to China, as firmly as Sulin and her daughters, and despite his intellectual curiosity, his ease with people from the West, he was a Communist. An ocean of ideology as well as years of differing experiences ran between him and her. But Jason! A smile replaced her look of introspection. At thirty-six he was in his prime, making his way in a deeply competitive society. Looking little different from any other American, his jeans faded, his pullover blue, and his shock of blonde hair and Rolex watch catching the sun, he was undeniably Western.

Tied to her in ways too complex for her to list fully, he waited with the sophistication and aplomb of an American. A cry of relief burst from her, and laughing joyously, she ran across the lobby and threw herself at him.

He wrapped her in his arms, and then looking deeply into her eyes murmured, "I'm glad you're over your love affair with…" He left the sentence dangle.

"China,"she finished.

His smile was broad. "Yes, China," he agreed

Arm in arm, they went up to the room where Matt waited.

Epilogue

People's Republic of China, 2009

Cultural Attaché for the American Embassy in Beijing, China, Mathew Wainwright leaned back in his chair and spoke to his mother in Seattle. That morning he'd finalized a tour by an American country music band, made arrangements to speak at the Chinese Foreigners Club, and left home before his wife and daughter were awake. After Tiananmen, Matt had received one cryptic, but loving, note from Gang-jo, and then nothing for ten years. His father had been imprisoned for Wu Huixia's actions as well as his own. Now, Matt heard surprise in his mother's voice.

"Matt, what are you saying? We have dinner guests, and I admit I've had a few glasses of wine. Wish you could have been here. Your Dad fixed salmon the way you like it. How are you, dear? And Judy and little Chrissie?"

"We're all fine, Mom. I don't have much time. It's almost noon, and I have to give a luncheon talk. But I need to know if you and Dad will host a guest for a few days? He's on his way to a conference on Cultural Differences And Similarities Between the US and China and wants to stop by."

"Of course. Is this a struggling artist or one of the new Chinese entrepreneurs? Do you need a home stay?"

He took a deep breath. "Mom, your guest would be my Chinese father."

"Oh," she said softly.

"Is that a problem?'

"Oh, my dear, no."

He could hear the emotion in her voice. He said, "Mom, you don't have to answer if you don't want to, but if you hadn't been in love with Dad, would you have stayed in China that time?" *Stayed with Gang-jo?*

"Oh, Matt, what a question. I don't know."

"But you loved him once."

He heard her sigh and almost interrupted, apologized for trespassing on her privacy, but she was saying, "I expect in some way I always will. But never the same way I love your American father. Never like that. You know...you're American, too."

"I know, Mom, I know."

CPSIA information can be obtained at www.ICGtesting.com
262765BV00001B/1/P

9 781432 768683